The Chimera Rebellion

Amara Holt

Published by Amara Holt, 2024.

Copyright © 2024 by Amara Holt

All rights reserved.

No part of this book may be reproduced, distributed, or transmitted in any form or by any means, including photocopying, recording, or other electronic or mechanical methods, without the prior written permission of the author, except in the case of brief quotations in book reviews.

This is a work of fiction. Names, characters, places, and incidents are the product of the author's imagination or are used fictitiously. Any resemblance to actual events, organizations, locales, or persons, living or dead is coincidental and is not intended by the authors.

PROLOGUE

Rio de Janeiro, 1972

The sky was hauntingly dark, heavy with gray rain clouds that seemed ready to collapse over the city. The thunder was threatening, as if the sky itself roared its fury and challenged anyone foolish enough to confront its power. It was impossible to tell for certain whether it was day or night due to the thick, gloomy fog.

Phelipe looked up only once. His jaw tightened as he saw a lightning bolt cross the darkness, illuminating everything around him for a split second. He gathered all the saliva in his mouth and spat it on the ground, close to his own foot. *You're not going to scare me*, he thought as he walked with slow, dragging steps.

People hurried around him, running back and forth, clutching their umbrellas tightly in their hands, desperately trying to escape the open space before the rain came crashing down on their heads. However, Phelipe was not afraid of the impending storm; he didn't even care about the strong, cold winds sweeping through the street, making the long hair of women sway and their dresses flutter. He continued calmly on his way, his hungry eyes scanning everything around him, his teeth clenched tightly in his mouth, and that fierce expression he always wore when someone bumped into him in a hurry to avoid the rain.

His face was petulantly beautiful, but his aggressive and fierce expression made everyone avoid looking at him for more than two seconds. There was hostility in his gaze, which caused others to steer clear of his strong, almost palpable dark aura, as if darkness emanated from him and he was some ally of Satan or even the Devil himself. Once, an elderly woman looked at him and made the sign of the cross, praying softly to her God, asking for protection against the incarnate evil she had just encountered. Phelipe merely offered a half-smile in response, unable to hide the pleasure he felt from the terror he caused.

It was like finding a black cat on Friday the 13th; a beautiful creature to behold, yet, for some credulous people, a bad omen.

He crossed a street with calculated steps, already knowing where it would lead him. Or rather, to *whom*.

Phelipe had never feared anyone. Not only due to his natural arrogance but also because he had been raised like a soldier, meticulously trained, with extremely sharp senses and honed battle reflexes. He had never lost a fight in his entire life, even entering many — most of the time, he was at a total disadvantage.

Still, when he stopped in front of the yellow, faded house, with a shabby and dying garden outside, his legs wobbled. He was armed, almost like a walking arsenal, though he thought he wouldn't need to use any of his weapons. Beneath his black leather jacket, strapped to his back, was a bronze blade, a short sword with a hilt encrusted with the face of a fearsome dragon, which he called Death. In his sleeves, he carried sharp silver darts, and in his inner pockets, a frightening collection of bronze and silver knives of various types. On the waistband of his dark pants were his daggers, as well as a curved knife, the complement to Death representing the creature's tail. He had named the knife Dolorosa.

It was not an enemy that made him feel breathless before turning the doorknob. It was a defenseless woman.

As soon as he crossed the threshold, the rain began to pour heavily on the roof of the house, which made Phelipe uneasy, yet also arrogant. As he silently closed the door behind him, his eyes scanned the entire space for signs of threat or someone lurking. His instincts kicked in within seconds, searching for possible strategic exits, hidden places, and even weapons. However, the only thing he felt, besides the perfume he already knew all too well, was a presence. Someone was there, waiting for him.

He didn't know why he felt so disturbed. He had wandered through that abandoned house in the city center, in a state of lamentable devastation, numerous times; he had looked at the strange shadows on the walls cast by the trees outside through the broken windows. He was so accustomed to the environment that he could mentally count how many stains of dirt and dust sullied the roof, how many tiles were broken, and how many leaves were scattered across the floor. He could also provide a complete inventory of the names scribbled on the walls, which young people wrote when they came there for their stupid betting games. Phelipe had walked for so long on the cracked wooden floor; he knew every detail, room, and object in the place, but he was always alone. And somehow, having company felt even more terrifying.

"You came." Her voice filled the room, laden with a mix of disbelief and excitement.

Phelipe swallowed hard, struggling. He was torn between crossing what had once been a luxurious living room toward the room where she was or turning his back and fleeing immediately. The second idea became more tempting with every passing second. But he didn't do it. He gathered all his willpower and walked toward the young woman, hearing the thunder outside echoing louder with every step he took.

She didn't turn when he entered the dark room, remaining motionless, shrouded in shadows. Standing in front of the cracked glass of one of the windows, she looked determinedly at the city landscape submerged in fog and rain, unfazed by the furious raindrops splattering on her face.

A lightning bolt sliced through the sky, momentarily illuminating the place in a ghostly light. Although the winds howled with their cold gusts, the environment felt too warm to Phelipe. He shifted his weight from one foot to the other, feeling uncomfortable.

"Tell me why I'm here." His voice sounded cold and sharp, obscuring the insecurity he felt.

At the sound of his tone, she turned. Even in the darkness, he could see her clearly; her face was still as beautiful as he remembered — small, heart-shaped, with slightly flushed cheeks. Her pink lips formed a perfect arch, making his fingers itch with the desire to trace them, harmonizing with the straight angle of her nose, which resembled a little button. Her eyes were black as the voids between the stars in the sky. Her long brown hair fell like a smooth curtain down her back, and she wore a pearl dress that acted as a point of light in the darkness, accentuating her waist attractively, highlighting her bust. So beautiful that she looked more like a painting than a real person.

"You know why you're here," she replied sweetly, fluttering her long black lashes.

Phelipe took a step toward her without even realizing it.

"No, I don't know," he growled in anger. He was furious with her, with everything she had done to him; he wouldn't let her beauty make him forget all he had suffered because of her. "Why now, *Sofia*?"

Even her name on his lips sounded like poetry. For hell's sake, what had this woman done to him?

Sofia had betrayed him. She had shattered his heart into so many pieces that it was hard to know if he even had one left. While he had been rotting in a cell, she was the face he clung to, the voice he loved to hear, the laughter that made him count the hours, minutes, and seconds to hear her again. The touch of her hand was comforting amidst all the horror he lived through; it made him dream and desperately wish for the day to dawn again so he could see her once more.

After years of being treated like an animal, tortured day after day, locked in an underground cell, exploited like a damned laboratory rat, the gentle presence of his beloved made everything bearable. It gave all that suffering a purpose, in the end. He longed for the moment when he would see her outside of his prison. In her daily stories, she had made it seem like the outside world was paradise, where they would live happily together forever. And when she finally confided how she would escape without getting caught, to meet him so they could finally have a life together, Phelipe could barely contain his ecstasy. He felt like he would burst at any moment, so great was his happiness; he would have a real life, where he could do what he wanted, go where he wanted, and no one would torture him or lock him away again — and he would still be with the woman he loved.

However, reality had slipped from the plan. On the day of his escape, Sofia had given him the address to find her, and even though he had never been in a city before, completely dazed by the people, streets, cars, and buildings, not to mention the brightness that hurt his eyes, he managed to reach the house. The house that was supposed to be their meeting point, the beginning of an extraordinary life, but all he found was emptiness. She was not there.

So he waited, since there was nowhere else to go, no one else to see; he simply did not know anything about the world. All he could do was wait for the exact moment she would walk through that door and ignite his heart with happiness.

That moment never came. Years passed, and she never showed up, no letters, no notes, no other place he could go to see her. Nothing. Phelipe was utterly alone.

But now, inexplicably, she had summoned him there. The shock he felt upon finding her note with that perfect handwriting, which he would recognize in any case, almost made him lose his mind.

At first, he thought it was a prank. If she knew where to find him, why would she reach out after all this time? But then he began to convince himself that it might be true, especially with the storm approaching the city. Either way, he needed to confront her.

"I need you to listen to me, I probably won't have much time," Sofia said, staring at him with her deep black eyes. "They are after me. They know I was the one who taught you how to escape and helped others escape too. They are going to kill me."

There was distress and despair on her face, which made Phelipe hesitate for a moment. But he couldn't let that happen.

"And why do you think I care?" he spat fiercely. "You left me here like an idiot, not caring if I was caught or killed. And don't come tell me it was for my sake that the others escaped, because I know very well that you taught them how to escape too!"

He practically hurled the words at her like venomous snakes. She shrugged and looked away.

For a long time, since the escape, he had only sat and waited, nearly starving and thirsting in a filthy corner of the abandoned house. He began to realize she wasn't coming. Even so, an impulse still dragged him back to that house every time he left.

At first, he hesitated to leave for even a second, afraid they would miss each other; then, as time passed, he began to just visit the house every day looking for signs that she had been there. While he tried to learn to live in society and go unnoticed among other people, his daily visits became weekly, then monthly, bi-monthly, and eventually, they stopped altogether. During that time, Phelipe had searched for clues indicating her whereabouts.

Maybe she was dead; they could have discovered that she was the one who provided confidential information to one of the prisoners and freed him, and they could have caught her before she could reach him. But it didn't take much investigation to discover that she was not only alive but still worked in the same place where he had spent years locked up and being tortured.

Phelipe had followed her routine from a distance, trying to come up with a plausible explanation for everything that had happened before confronting her directly. After all, he loved her and deep down believed she loved him too. He imagined that Sofia had changed her mind, realized how risky it all was, and given up trying to pursue a life with him. Maybe that really was the case, but either way, she should have warned him and not left him to fend for himself. In his investigation, he had also discovered that, apparently, the young woman had promised another man the same thing she had promised him. She was a master manipulator, cunning and treacherous.

Sofia was a blind spot in his vision, disorienting him and giving him headaches. The more he tried to understand her, the more confused he became.

"This house belonged to my parents a long time ago," she said, adjusting her posture. Her hand wandered freely over the wall, ignoring the chipped paint and accumulated dirt as if admiring it. She seemed lost in memories. "I spent my childhood here."

Impatient with the situation, Phelipe let out a furious growl, throwing his head back. Her gaze turned to him with curiosity.

"Answer the questions, Sofia."

"I already told you. They are after me." Her hand stopped gliding over the wall. She tilted her head to the side, assessing him from head to toe. "I know you were with Viviane."

Phelipe's hands trembled with rage. She had vanished for years, abandoned him to fend for himself, and instead of giving him answers to the questions that had tormented him all this time, she had the audacity to look at him with accusation, as if somehow he had betrayed her.

"I thought you were safe, considering you were warming the bed of Teodoro Warner!" Phelipe shouted.

Shame colored her porcelain face. Sofia hadn't expected that.

Phelipe had taken the time to search for clues about her whereabouts. He had learned that not only was she still working in the lab that had cursed him, but she was also secretly meeting with the owner, Teodoro Warner.

"I was protecting myself, Phelipe," she replied softly, her eyes brimming with tears. "When you escaped, it raised a lot of suspicions; it was only a matter of time before they turned against me, the rookie. So, if I stayed close to Teodoro, he would protect me. *Us*."

The emotion in her voice almost softened him. Almost.

"You want me to swallow that you did this for us? Where is the *us* if you abandoned me the moment I stepped out of that place?"

The rain poured harder on the roof, causing the only sound that interrupted the brief silence of the tense conversation. Sofia shrank back; whether from cold or shame, Phelipe didn't know.

"You don't understand," she whined, her bottom lip trembling.

"No, I don't understand." Phelipe clenched his fists tightly at his sides. "I don't understand why you taught me how to escape if you didn't intend to stay with me. I don't understand why you continued working at that place you claimed to despise for everything they did to me. Why crawl under Teodoro's sheets to divert attention from you when all you had to do from the beginning was leave with me? Why go after *my brother* with the same false promises you made to me and free him if you didn't want him around?"

Once again, she gasped in shock at how much Phelipe knew. Sofia thought she could approach him after all this time and seduce him with her treacherous beauty, just as she had before, to earn his forgiveness. But he wouldn't give in. He had lived alone, without her, and had done very well. He was no longer the vulnerable boy in a cell, or the kid huddled on the dirty floor of the abandoned house waiting for her. No matter how much seeing her so close twisted his insides, he wouldn't let her manipulate him again. Life in society had turned him into an adult man.

"I don't have much time to explain, but I love you, Phelipe. I always have. Only you," she sniffled. "I need you to help me. Help me get out of here; let's run away together, and I can explain everything you want, far from here. Teodoro and his men are after me right now. It's only a matter of time before they find me."

"Why didn't you ask my brother for help? Wasn't that why you freed him? He's around here, as you must have noticed with this storm. You know what he's capable of."

She turned for a moment, watching the torrential rain through the window. With a long sigh, she turned back to Phelipe.

"I love you. Only you."

"Then why do you need all these men at your feet, Sofia? Why seduce all of them with your false promises?" His entire body trembled with violent spasms of rage. He needed to control himself; he didn't know what could happen. He tried to calm his irregular breathing. "If you say you were with Teodoro to protect yourself after freeing me, why did you free my brother too? Didn't that get you discovered immediately?"

She shook her head, drying her tears with the back of her hand.

"You don't understand... Please, come with me, and I'll give you all the answers you need. We'll live the life we dreamed of, together."

"No," he murmured, unyielding.

With a choked sigh, Sofia stepped closer silently. Phelipe wanted to move; every cell in his body begged him to run away, but he simply couldn't. No, he couldn't. The blood turned to ice in his veins as her face hovered inches away, so close that the sweet, nostalgic scent she emanated filled his nostrils, her extremely black eyes locked onto his. In a calm, calculated motion, the woman closed her fingers around the silver necklace on her neck, with the pendant of a leaping feline, which she loved so much and had never stopped wearing. With a rough gesture, Sofia ripped it off, placing it carefully in Phelipe's hands.

"I don't have much left to do then," she whispered. "I love you, Phelipe."

She closed her eyes, leaning toward him. No matter how hard he tried, Phelipe was weak, foolish. He had no choice but to give in, and closing his eyelids, he anxiously awaited the kiss that was to come.

All he felt was a searing stab in his gut, where Sofia had buried her dagger.

CHAPTER ONE

Sophia

Araxá, 2018

The wind relentlessly lashes against the leaves, making them rustle and sway on the branches of the trees. It's night. Or maybe it's day. It's impossible to tell. The sky is a vast expanse of black, devoid of moonlight or stars.

I run. I run desperately through the damp grass, caring little about the mess that the mud and leaves make of my dress. The pearly hem drags against the ground as I push my way through the trees and the tall grass that I can barely see ahead of me.

I can feel his approach even when he isn't close enough to me yet. I can invade his mind easily, just as I can share all his feelings. As if we were the same person.

When his dark silhouette emerges among the trees, struggling to run toward the center of a clear glade, I feel deep within my core that something is terribly wrong. His body, covered by a pearly dress that acts as a point of light in the darkness, stands upright, realizing at the same time as I do the great X of the matter as our gazes meet for the first time.

His long brown hair sways in the wind, long and straight like mine, over a pearly dress like the one I wear. His small, heart-shaped face is frozen as our black eyes, dark as the vastness above our heads, stare wide-eyed at each other, telling us everything our mouths cannot pronounce. That is my face. My body.

That is me.

No noise. Just our hearts beating in the same rhythm.

Like a waking moment, our moment is interrupted. Figures move beside me, walking slowly. I look at them, but they ignore me. They continue to walk with a rigid and severe posture, fixed on a single target opposite where I am.

"Sophia, no!" I scream.

She does the same. Her mouth opens and closes, and the words pouring from her are the same as mine.

At first, I thought we were a reflection, that a mirror separated us. But now I know that isn't the case. I'm trapped in a glass box. I extend my palm, touching the transparent surface that separates us.

On the other side, the other Sophia drops to her knees in the grass, sinking into her own dress. Her despair fills my chest like a slap. I want to scream for her to run, but I can't. There's nothing to be done. Nowhere to run. The end has come.

I sink silently into my own despair as a woman with a wave of blood-red hair positions herself next to Sophia, curled up on the ground. Her green eyes, like two emeralds, give me a slight wink, as if we were old friends. I throw my body uselessly against the glass. I want to shatter it into pieces and escape far away, where no one would ever dare to find me. That way, I would save the other Sophia. *I* would save myself. As long as I'm trapped, she will never be able to hide. She is a part of me, or I am a part of her. And, like a magnet, one will always be drawn to wherever the other is. Together, we are one.

I realize this too late. They realized it before we did. They used me as bait. They knew that if they trapped me here, she would be drawn to me, because as we are part of the same being, a part of her would be trapped here with me and would be forced to join me. Only together could we finally be destroyed.

On the other side of the glass that confines me, the woman with green eyes and a radiant smile looks at me, grinning. Then I know that everything will cease when the woman raises her arm in the air, ready to attack the other Sophia.

My mouth screams, but not enough to make the woman stop. It is only enough to bring me back to reality.

I am going insane.

I am 99% sure of that.

A completely sane girl does not dream of a woman she has never seen in her life, especially not one trying to kill her!

I throw off the covers, sitting up in bed with my heart pounding in my chest. My breath is quickening, and I feel sweat trickling down my back. I run my hand through my sticky hair, pulling it away from my face.

What the hell is happening to me?

First, the strange dreams that make me afraid to sleep. Then, there's this strange sensation that I'm being constantly watched; a supernatural chill makes the hairs on my neck stand on end. Yesterday, while picking up my little sister from ballet class, I could swear someone was following me. It could just be paranoia from my fertile imagination; that's what I want to believe, but the shivers and discomfort don't cease.

I stretch until my bones crack and slowly slide out of bed. I grab the clothes I picked out last night, folded by the bedside, and head from my room toward the bathroom. As the hot water from the shower hits my bare skin, I feel rejuvenated. I let all my worries wash down the drain as I cheerfully sing along to an Ariana Grande song.

I step out of the bathroom, releasing the steam from the hot water, and head to my room, noticing that the house remains in deep silence.

The terrible dream is still on my mind when I notice, through the mirror, my six-year-old sister watching me through the small gap of the ajar door. I comb my hair with my eyes locked on hers. She remains motionless, showing no embarrassment at being caught peeking.

Isa is always sneaking around to see me with the fascination of a child. When I go out somewhere, staying away longer than necessary, I always find her in my bed when I return. She bombards me with random questions as she rummages through my things. Sometimes, she quietly slips in during the night and crawls under the covers with me, stroking my face and asking to sleep with me. Again. Because she had a nightmare. Because she wanted me to pray with her. Because she was cold. Or simply because she loves me. She asks me to sing songs that she chooses and then wants me to teach her to sing "as cutely as you, Sophia." It's almost a routine.

I continue to stare at her through the glass. Her blonde curls are messy and tousled, just like they look when she has just woken up. Her gray eyes are swollen from sleep. I know why she's here. She wants me to comb her hair, as I do every morning.

"Good morning, Isa," I say almost singing.

"Hi, Soph," Isa murmurs.

A long moment passes in which the only sound is the brush gliding through my brown hair.

"Have you eaten anything?"

"No."

I huff. My mom always leaves the house late for work, leaving a note on the door for me to take care of Isa. Me. Because if it depended on Lily, my older sister, the girl would starve.

"Come here, let me tame this lion!" I say, patting the stool at my vanity for her to sit.

My sister beams with a toothy grin as she practically dances across the room. I tidy her curls to make them look nice and well-defined while she chatters about her ballet class, school, and the new video from her favorite YouTuber.

I leave her in the room, admiring herself in the mirror, and head to the kitchen. The first thing I see upon entering is Lily's dirty feet on the counter. She's naked from the waist down, wearing only an oversized men's shirt, her legs stretched out. Her hair is a blonde rat's nest with the ends dyed blue, shocking me immediately since the last time I saw her, her hair was intact. Additionally, the black makeup is running down her eyes, just like the red lipstick, which is now just a smear around her mouth.

She grins at me when she sees me, wrapping the phone cord around her fingers while spewing obscenities to whoever is on the other end. Probably a man.

"There's a child in the house," I murmur, sourly pushing her legs aside to get through. "Phone sex can wait."

She flashes me her familiar cat-like smile, cleaning her teeth with her nail.

"Sabrina, you're in a bad mood; what's the big problem this time? Did your little boyfriend dump you, or did your hair wake up frizzy?"

"It's Sophia," I murmur, unconsciously running my hand through my hair to smooth down the nonexistent flyaways.

I try to remember the last time I saw Lily at home; I think it's been just over a week. Not that I mind not seeing her regularly, obviously. But my mom is much kinder when Lily is home, trying to please her in every way possible to keep her around.

It's not my mom's fault that Lily stays out of the house. It's my mom's fault that my sister *remains* out of the house. She never pressures us into anything, leaving us free to do whatever makes us happy. Lily just abuses that freedom. She doesn't work, spends whole afternoons locked in her room with loud music blasting. She goes out at night and returns days later completely drunk or with a massive hangover. She never tells where she's going, or who she's with, or what she's doing. Of course, not having her around sometimes is a relief. When she's home, she drives everyone crazy with her choice of words, her clothes, and her unpleasant, suggestive comments. However, having her out of the house automatically puts us on high alert — it's common to find my mom sound asleep with her phone clutched between her fingers, fearing calls from the police or some hospital informing her about Lily's whereabouts.

I rummage through the cupboard looking for Isa's cereal, grab a bowl and some milk, and start preparing. Lily is still talking promiscuously to someone on the phone, hardly caring that I'm listening. I take the food to the room so that Isa can eat as far away from our sister's bad influence as possible.

We finish having breakfast, and I tidy up my things while helping Isa get dressed, and we head to school — by bus... ugh! — not without listening to a bit more of Lily's lewd conversation.

"Why isn't Izec coming to pick us up anymore?" my sister asks minutes before the bus approaches her school.

Izec. His name makes me clench my teeth. How do I explain to my little sister, who idolizes him, that we broke up because he's a jerk?

The driver makes a turn, and I shake in my seat as I shrug my shoulders and try to stare at my own nails to avoid the embarrassment.

"He's not picking us up anymore," I reply too softly, my voice more emotional than I intended.

"Oh." It's all the little one says.

Her mouth curves into an involuntary pout, her eyes dimming slightly. I have to remember that I'm not the only one in this house who is attached to Izec. In the absence of a male figure in a house with four women, his presence was comforting, bringing a certain stability that we somehow needed. My mom always asked Izec for help with technical problems, whether it was a broken faucet, a burnt-out light bulb, or even a clogged toilet. Of course, my mom is an extraordinary woman, very capable of any kind of service, but she works too much and dedicates so much to Isa, doing everything possible to ensure she doesn't feel the absence of a father.

Izec always helped. Sometimes, he would do the grocery shopping since he spent so much time at my house that he knew exactly what we needed; he would take us where we wanted and almost always fixed my mom's car, helping with absolutely anything without us needing to ask. He and my mom got along very well; she even allowed us to sleep together — after a long time, of course. Izec charmed my mom with his mischievous smile; not only her but my sisters too. Lily behaved like a non-problematic person when he was around; she even laughed at the jokes he made about her hair, which always looks like a rat's nest. But the person most attached to him, by far, was Isa. He taught her her homework, helped her color, and chased her around the house just to tickle her. Once, he tried to teach her to play the guitar, but it didn't go very well since Isa is extremely impatient. And at night, when she had nightmares, she would always sneak into the room, lying down on my bed between me and Izec. When I woke up, I would see them sleeping together, her blonde curls falling over his face; that always brought a smile to my face.

Now, as I watch my little sister wave at me while getting off the bus at her school, still wearing a sad expression from the news, I realize that Izec hasn't just opened a wound in me. He's a great person, but as a boyfriend, he's terrible.

That's what I'm still thinking about as I walk through the school campus with my boots sinking into the grass, observing the euphoria of my classmates, happy with the reunion on the first day back to school after the July vacation.

I need to look back once. The supernatural chill on the nape of my neck, which has been bothering me since yesterday, making my hairs stand on end and my heart beat harder in my chest, is bothering me again. I feel as if I'm being watched; it's as if someone is close enough that their breath is blowing against my neck. But when I glance over my shoulder after jumping in fright, I see no one lurking. Still, I feel like I'm being followed and watched; I just don't know by whom.

I hurry to enter the building with the false hope that I'll be safer inside. Fortunately, I find my best friend, Ane Sampaio, who immediately makes me forget the strange feelings I've been having as she chatters endlessly about her vacation trip to the beach.

"I think you should talk to him, Sophia," Ane says, closing the locker more forcefully than necessary after finally asking me about Izec.

"Whose side are you on?" I ask, narrowing my eyes at my friend.

"My *side*," Ane replies, tossing her blonde hair back. "Honestly, Sophia, if I have to hear this story again, I might go crazy! — I cross my arms, staring at her with a false expression of hurt. — Now, let's go. We're almost late."

The blonde girl breaks into a smile, giving me a light tap on the shoulder. I adjust my skirt to make sure it doesn't show more than it should and follow Ane down the hallway with a pang of irritation. She practically struts in front of me in high heels that are definitely at least five centimeters taller than the school's dress code allows, greeting the students passing by us. It's no wonder the blonde girl attracts so much attention wherever she goes; in addition to her stunning beauty, which is almost like a blessing from Aphrodite, Ane has such a pure and charismatic aura around her that it's nearly impossible to keep one's eyes off her.

Naturally, we would both walk together and wave to the people who stopped to watch us pass through the hallway, but I'm still sulking over the whole thing with Izec, and although I would never admit it out loud, I'm afraid to run into him.

"Are you still on that?" Ane asks, glancing at me over her shoulder. I wonder if my expression is worse than I imagine. "I've already told you: you two need to talk! Whether it's to make up or not, it's a thing that needs to be resolved between the two of you. I can't do anything."

"Easy for you to say; it wasn't your boyfriend who slept with someone else," I retort, in a bad mood.

After a futile fight between me and Izec, Ane saw him take a girl home and immediately told me. That was the decisive factor in my decision not to seek him out to clarify things because I'm already tired of the boy's indiscretions. No matter how much I like him, it was becoming a vicious cycle: we would fight, Izec would seek comfort in another person's arms, I would find out, forgive him, and we would reconcile... only to fight again. This time, he wasn't even aware that I knew about his latest infidelity.

"If Jimmy had slept with someone else, I would do exactly what I told you: I would sit down and talk to him." Ane is about to say something more but falls silent when a group of boys approaches us, greeting us. We smile in response, although my smile doesn't reach my eyes. "Besides," she starts again in a lower tone so that no one in the hallway can hear us, "you two were broken up, so it's not *really* a betrayal. I'm not saying he's right; I'm just saying he's not entirely wrong either. And if I know him well, by now, he must have kicked the girl to the curb and will be crawling back to you."

Ane knows him as well as I do — if not better. In fact, the four of us are extremely connected: Ane, Jimmy, Izec, and me. We are best friends, and as proof of that, I have the friendship bracelet we exchanged when we were about twelve shoved in the junk drawer of my room. We met in sixth grade when we entered the school, except for Izec and Jimmy, who had known each other long before, since Izec's mom worked at Jimmy's dad's house, meaning they lived on the same property.

I'm not worried about the girl who is with my boyfriend; he sleeps with someone and disappears the next day, like the jerk he is. What bothers me is the whole story in general.

"We broke up three *days ago! I wouldn't even call it a breakup, just a silly argument. Frankly, my period lasts longer than Izec's depression."*

Ane laughs, moving closer to me, and I playfully push her shoulder.

"Look, I don't think—" The blonde girl stops abruptly, making a face. "What's that smell?"

"Smell of what?"

I turn my head from side to side, sniffing the air for something different. I smell nothing. She leans in toward my neck.

"Your perfume," she murmurs, pulling back immediately with a look of disgust. "It's awful."

I widen my eyes in disbelief. Ane covers her nose and mouth with her hand, her skin taking on a greenish hue.

"What are you talking about? It's Chanel No. 5!"

"Is it fake?" Her voice sounds strangled, and she closes her eyes.

"You gave it to me!"

"Soph, I'm so sorry..." she murmurs, her voice choked before she runs toward the bathrooms at the end of the hallway.

What the hell was that? I think, furrowing my brow as I try to understand what just happened. Did my perfume make her nauseous? Out of nowhere? We've been together all morning, and she just now noticed it? It doesn't make sense.

I shake my head, pushing away the mental confusion. I walk toward the girls' bathroom, unsure if my entering will help or hinder Ane, but willing to show support.

"Hey, Sophia. I love your skirt," Laila compliments as she passes by me.

Her hair, with colorful highlights, is tied up in a messy ponytail, and she looks at me over her glasses that keep sliding down her slender nose, with envy disguised as sympathy. I smile, trying to ignore the sudden pain in my toe after my new boots start to pinch my foot.

"Thanks, I love the hairstyle," I lie.

Her smile in response is as forced as mine. I leave Laila behind and continue on my way. I need to see if Ane is okay, if she managed to get to the bathroom on time, or, God forbid, threw up all over herself. I'm almost reaching the door when someone mutters a curse behind me; I immediately turn to see what's going on.

Oh crap! There he is: Izec Dias... walking through the main door of the school, causing the sunlight to stream through the crack and illuminate him as if he were surrounded by a pearly aura. He's wearing that smile I love so much, that damn flashy smile that makes my legs turn to jelly. His bronze-colored hair is perfectly styled with gel in the usual pompadour, framing his divine face like a teenage rock star.

It could be just another normal day at school, where Izec would arrive late wearing his usual black leather jacket and jeans, with drumsticks shoved in his back pocket. Another ordinary day where the other boys would cluster at the entrance to greet him, shaking his hands in various creative ways because Izec is the popular guy they want to be. Izec is the guy with a band, a long list of girls who like him, and a jeep. He's cool, handsome, and charismatic. That's the reason for all this commotion.

The door slams hard behind him, cutting off the sunlight that had just bathed his head, breaking the spell that had paralyzed me. My eyes can finally roll past his handsome face to his hand. His fingers are intertwined with another person's.

A girl.

Natália Campos.

My heart sinks in my chest and shatters into a million pieces. No, it can't be; my eyes are betraying me; it's just a mirage or a nightmare.

I refuse to believe that Izec has moved on; that, in less than a week after our breakup, he has entered into a relationship with another girl and is practically rubbing it in my face.

But that's exactly what's happening right in front of my eyes.

Izec has a wide smile plastered on his face and greets the boys crowding around him, never letting go of the girl's hand. Natália stands patiently beside him, equally smiling.

I only know her by sight. Well, I know all the students at this school, even if I'm not friends with almost any of them. Natália, as far as I know, is in her first year. I never paid much attention to her and had even forgotten how pretty she is. Damn. A thousand times damn!

She has long brown hair, a round face with big cheeks that somehow looks symmetrical. She's wearing a button-up denim skirt that, like mine, is at least a hand's width shorter than allowed by the dress code, and a really nice wool jacket. Damn!

For some reason, I can't move. I want to get out of here before they see me, before they notice how surprised and affected I am, but I feel like I'm under hypnosis. I have a vague awareness that the other students are staring at me and whispering. Someone is holding their phone up, filming or taking a picture of this embarrassing situation. And I know it's only a matter of time before Izec sees me paralyzed, like a horrified idiot, as I know I am. I regret that Ane didn't throw up on me, which would have made me run to the bathroom, oblivious to this scene.

"Damn!" Ane's voice surprises me from behind. "I'm not feeling well. I feel strange. I think I caught that virus that..." I don't need to turn around to know what interrupted her. "What the hell is this?" She verbalizes what's been running through my mind for minutes.

I don't know if Ane said it too loudly or if the commotion caught Izec's attention, but finally, his eyes find mine. His exuberant smile falters for a fraction of a second.

Ane, now would be the perfect time to vomit. Or faint. Please!

Unfortunately, none of that happens. I only see the newest couple at school parading right in front of me, with Izec looking completely at ease with it all.

It's a nightmare! It has to be.

"Hey, girls," he greets as he passes by us.

I still haven't turned to see Ane's expression, but it makes Izec shrug and run his free hand through his hair as he looks at her. Natália waves and gives a smile that, for some reason, doesn't seem mocking. I'm still staring at their backs when they turn at the end of the hallway, finally disappearing from my sight.

Ane puts her hand on my shoulder, forcing me to turn.

"Okay, that was totally... Hey, turn off the damn phone!" she yells at someone behind me using her serious voice. When Ane uses that voice, it intimidates anyone, forcing them to do what she wants. Her eyes meet mine, making me unconsciously shrug my shoulders. "Don't feel bad."

That's it. I won't give the lurking vultures the satisfaction of seeing me shaken. I take a deep breath, pushing away the tears I didn't even realize were coming, adjust my skirt and posture again. I stride confidently with my chin held high toward the bathroom. Ane silently follows me. Out of the corner of my eye, I see her scold another boy who was filming me. Great, the first day back at school, and I'm already considered an idiot.

A freshman is leaning over the sink, looking at herself in the mirror while applying cherry *gloss* to her lips.

"You." I point my finger at her, my voice three times higher than normal. "Get out now!" The girl looks at me, mouth agape, stopping the gloss brush in mid-air just inches from her lips, visibly confused. "Are you deaf or an idiot? Get out!" My tone of voice is enough to scare her into quickly gathering her things and running out.

Ane appears seconds later, locking the door behind her. After squatting down to check each stall and finally ensuring we're alone, I let out a strangled sigh and close my eyes. I lean against the sink.

"This can't be happening," I whisper with a tearful voice. "Everyone saw Izec with Natália, Ane. Everyone saw my idiotic face staring at the two of them. If no one knew about the betrayal before, they will be sure now."

"Calm down..."

I had taken such care to keep it a secret! I even emailed to volunteer, a day prior, to join the organizing committee for the talent fair to have an excuse not to be together at lunch. But now, a week after our fight, he's strutting down the hall with Natália.

"Was it Natália?" I ask, turning to Ane. "The girl you saw him take home, was it her?"

Ane told me she didn't recognize the person because she was too far away to see clearly. Now, she wrinkles her nose.

"I think so. The hair is identical; I just didn't remember her to make the connection."

Neither did I.

"Why would he start a relationship with her? Why? How are we going to get back if everyone has already seen them together? I'll look like an idiot if I forgive him," I sniffle. "Ane, you told me he was going to kick the girl to the curb. Why didn't he?"

Ane shrugs with an air of exhaustion.

"What do I know? I confused Chanel No. 5 with a fake perfume."

I would even smile if I weren't so devastated. My social life has been completely ruined in a matter of minutes. I'm sure that photos and videos of my idiot face are already being shared by all the idiots at this school at this very moment. I can imagine Ana Catarina relishing the moment, smiling, thrilled to witness my humiliation. Even Laila, adjusting her glasses to mock me at will.

My stomach churns. Maybe there really is a virus that, hopefully, I've already caught and will earn me a doctor's note so I won't have to go back to class so soon.

Ane comes closer to me with a sympathetic expression. I realize she's going to hug me, and I feel that's exactly what I need... to lean on someone while I think about how to fix the mess my life has become and how I'm going to leave this bathroom and face all those people out there.

But just a half-step away from reaching me, Ane's phone starts ringing loudly in her pocket. I groan quietly. She apologizes with her eyes and pulls out the device.

"Hey, babe," she says in a melodic voice as soon as she presses the phone to her ear. Jimmy. Ugh! Izec's best friend. Couldn't he have called at a more inconvenient time?! "Yeah, of course," she agrees after a moment. "I'll be right there!" She hangs up and shoves the device into her back pocket. "It's Jimmy. They're waiting for me in Drawing class; I need to go."

I shrug slightly. I look at myself in the mirror, happy to see that my makeup remains intact and my hair is still perfectly styled.

"Alright, I need to go to Music class too."

I pull out the *gloss* from my bag, leaning toward the mirror to touch it up.

"See you at lunch?" Ane asks hesitantly.

"Sure." I force a smile. I rub my lips together to spread the gloss before applying another layer. "Don't worry, I'll be fine."

"I know you will."

She smiles back supportively. I blow her a kiss in the air before she unlocks the door and steps out into the hallway.

I sigh, letting the smile fade from my face. I feel a chill run through my body, causing my back to stiffen automatically. The door of one of the stalls slams shut by itself with a bang, making me jump.

My heart races in my chest, the blood rushing quickly through my veins, leaving me deaf for a few seconds.

I swallow hard. I have reasons, unfortunately, to fear being followed. There is someone I won't allow myself to think about, but who, if given the opportunity, would like to hurt me. So every time my neck burns when I feel someone's watchful gaze on my back, I fear that *he* has somehow come after me.

My eyes scan the entire area, but I know I'm the only person here, as I've checked before. I shake my head to dispel the uncomfortable feeling. I take one last look in the mirror before stepping out to see what awaits me for the rest of the day.

It's then that I see a shadow in the mirror. It's quick, like a *flash*, but enough for my mind to associate that image with the woman with red hair who has been appearing in my dreams.

CHAPTER TWO

Sophia

Handing out flyers. That's what I'm doing after the horrible morning I had.

I'm still unsure if standing in the sun, walking down the streets, is better than being at school watching Izec strut around with Natália. Well, I definitely prefer the discomfort of my boots hurting with every step and the ugly faces of people when I extend the flyer towards them than having to see those two again. My stomach twists just thinking about it.

After doing a thorough inspection of the bathroom for the second time that morning, just to make sure I was really alone, so that the apparition I saw in the mirror was nothing but a figment of my imagination, I went to Music class. Damn hour! I went there only to be publicly humiliated upon discovering that I had been cut from the musical performance I was supposed to be a part of at the talent fair. Apparently, due to a suggestion from student Izec Dias, as Professor Camilo himself told me, there had been a music swap, and the new version sounded better in the voice of student Natália Campos.

I had to leave the room in a hurry or I would have strangled Izec with one of his guitar strings.

I found a greenish and dizzy Ane, still feeling nauseous, on her way to the office to ask for permission to go home. I considered using my friend's malaise as an excuse to get out of the rest of the classes, but I didn't expect to run into Helena from the talent fair organization. She dragged me to hand out flyers on the street for the rest of the afternoon. Damn hour when I lied, saying I wanted to participate in this stupid organization!

Helena walks ahead of me, glancing back over her shoulder to see if I'm keeping up. My stride is much slower; my smile is stiff and frozen on my face as I extend the flyer toward people.

I wipe the sweat from my forehead. There are still many flyers to go, and this must be the twentieth street we've crossed. Helena remains expressionless, showing no signs of fatigue. I'm melting from the heat, feeling my makeup turning greasy on my skin. My hair is sticky, clinging to the back of my neck, my lips are dry, and my feet are sore.

"What is that smell?" I ask as we cross the street.

"Looks like a sewage pipe burst," Helena replies, pointing to the middle of the street.

Two cones are signaling the huge hole in the asphalt, from which dark water is gushing. Helena doesn't seem bothered by the smell; she smiles affectionately and extends flyers to the people passing by us. I'm about to complain and ask to go somewhere else, but then I realize why we're here. This is one of the busiest streets in the city; if we stay here with this large flow of pedestrians, we'll quickly run out of flyers.

I adjust my posture, putting on the best smile I can. I make an effort to breathe only through my mouth in an attempt to forget the awful smell.

"So, this guy..." I murmur, looking at the flyer to read the name. "Tom Warner. He's going to give a speech on the day of the fair?"

Helena looks at me as if I just burped loudly. I feel so embarrassed by her stare that I turn my face away, feeling my cheeks flush.

"He's the leading presidential candidate in the polls," she says as if it's obvious, rolling her eyes in disdain.

Should I know this? I'm not that tuned in to what's happening around the world, especially when it comes to politics; it feels like I live in a bubble.

"I thought Antônia was the favorite candidate," I say, regretting it the moment I see Helena's face.

"Antônia got involved in a corruption scheme, her numbers dropped in the polls. Frankly, Sophia, what world are you living in?"

In Izec's world, I could respond, because that's the truth.

I keep the smile on my face, extending the flyer toward people. Then I look for the first time at the papers in my hand and am shocked by the photo of Tom Warner. He looks much younger than I imagined he would, appearing to be in his early thirties and quite handsome. In the picture, he's wearing a crisp suit that fits his body well, his brown hair perfectly styled, and he displays an attractive smile. If I were only looking at the photo, I would never think he was a politician.

"But why is he going to speak at our school?" I ask, knowing that with every second I seem more stupid in front of Helena.

"The new auditorium was named after him as a tribute."

"Really?" I'm taken aback. "Why... exactly?"

Helena turns to me, impatient, like an adult annoyed by a curious child's questions.

"He's from here; he studied at our school, you clueless girl."

"Oh!"

I should know these things; Ane probably knows and would make a chronological and alphabetical list of events if I asked her. But I've never been tuned into this kind of stuff; in fact, I don't understand anything about politics, and that's just fine with me. I don't care who's going to run or win the presidency, who won the Nobel Prize, or who's the ambassador of the UN. I care about the new Chanel collection, waterproof mascara, eyebrow micropigmentation, and Izec.

I take a deep breath, impatient to realize that there are still many flyers in my hand. All I want is to go home and forget the terrible day I had by lying on my bed watching some cliché romance movie. I can't wait to get rid of these cursed boots that are mutilating me, one toe at a time.

"That guy won't stop looking at you," Helena suddenly says, extending a flyer to an elderly man passing in front of us.

"Which guy?"

I turn to her with my eyebrows furrowed.

"The one on the motorcycle."

Then I see him across the street leaning against a shiny red motorcycle that would have made Jimmy jump for joy. He's wearing a leather jacket that's definitely making him sweat buckets. In fact, he dresses like a punk; everything is black and made of leather. The first thing I conclude is that he's handsome, despite the sunglasses covering his face. He has naturally tanned skin like an Indian, full, red lips, and a muscular, well-defined body.

Helena is right; he's gazing at me eagerly, fists clenched at his sides, his expression too serious. However, it seems like he's in a trance, unable to look away. I involuntarily break into a wide smile.

"How old do you think he is?" I ask Helena.

"About twenty-eight." She pauses, assessing him. "He can't take his eyes off you; it's kind of creepy. It's like he's about to punch you or something. Are you sure you don't know this guy?"

Indeed, his face isn't the friendliest, I note with a tinge of bitterness. I hadn't realized it at first while admiring his appearance, but he emanates a completely dark aura; my body prickles all over in contact with the heavy energy. The guy continues to stare at me intently, tightening his fists and grinding his teeth. Helena is right; it's as if he wants to punch me in the face.

I frown, confused. Still staring at him, I forget everything: the flyers, the unbearable pain in my feet, my goal to get home as soon as possible... until a very familiar noise fills my ears. A car is crossing the end of the street, coming toward me with the music turned up to the max. It's not just any car; it's Izec's jeep.

Damn! Can't I get one minute of peace? What the hell is he doing on this side of town, practically the opposite of where he lives? Unfortunately, I get the answer to my questions way too soon. As the car approaches, I can see that sitting beside him is Natália, sporting the amused smile of someone who has just heard a good joke. She must live around here, and he, pretending to be the gentleman, is taking her home.

The weight of an anchor sinks in my chest. The reason I agreed to hand out flyers in the scorching sun instead of enduring the end of class or going home was precisely to keep my mind as far away from Izec as possible. Now, his almond-colored eyes find mine through the windshield, and he runs his bronze-colored hair back, visibly uncomfortable. The relaxed expression he wore for Natália sours immediately. Damn!

In a stupid impulse, I force my feet to move, pulling Helena along with me. The girl protests, staring at me as if I've lost my mind. I'm not thinking about what I'm doing; I just move forward, crossing the street in slow strides, heading toward the surly guy on the red motorcycle. Helena yells something as we advance, but I'm not listening. Izec is forced to slam the brakes on the car in the middle of the street to avoid running me over; I don't need to turn around to know he's cursing me.

The other guy is staring at me in surprise.

"What are you doing?" Helena hisses at me. We cross the street to the sound of frequent honking. The people around us look at us curiously but continue on their way. "Seriously? All this to annoy your ex-boyfriend? He's already with another girl; you don't need to humiliate yourself."

"Who here is humiliating themselves?" I retort, feeling my hands grow cold with nervousness. "Give it a break, Helena. That idiot doesn't bother me anymore..."

"It's impressive." A rough voice in a tone of astonishment interrupts me.

Helena looks from me to the owner of the voice, the guy leaning against the motorcycle. I pivot on my heels to face him and feel heat just from seeing him dressed in that jacket, as if he walked straight out of the 1980s into the present day. Even through the dark lenses, I can see he's examining me with sharp eyes like a hawk, which makes me feel intimidated. At the same time, I'm aware that the jeep hasn't left yet, remaining still in the middle of the street.

"Excuse me, did you speak to me?"

The stranger straightens up and doesn't divert his attention from my face.

"Definitely not the same," he murmurs more to himself than to me.

"What the hell are you talking about?"

I feel a strange courage take hold of me, tingling my nerves. He, in turn, wears a half-smirk that's teasing.

"The audacity is the same."

I hear the jeep finally starting up, and I assume Izec has been watching me all this time. I sigh, relieved. I decide it's time to get out of here, away from this weirdo who's eyeing me curiously. Suddenly, his gaze drops from my face to... Oh, I can't believe it!

"Are you staring at my boobs, you perv?"

"Come on, don't be so full of yourself, miss," the stranger retorts without lifting his eyes; only then do I realize what holds his attention. "That necklace..."

To my astonishment, he leans in my direction in such a swift motion that I barely have time to pull back. His fingers brush against the pendant of my necklace, tracing the silver figure hanging from it with interest. I quickly yank it from his hand, giving him a warning glare not to come any closer.

"Sophia, don't you realize he's a druggie? Let's get out of here now!" Helena pleads, lightly touching my arm.

I can't explain what's holding me here, but I suspect it's the insane curiosity this stranger stirs in me.

"What do you want with my necklace?"

I touch my neck with the tips of my fingers and find the chain, aware that I have an obsessive love for the object. It's made of silver and has a pendant shaped like a leaping panther. Isa, my younger sister, says it's a very large dog because there's a collar around its neck, but I've never believed that. I received the piece as a gift from my paternal grandmother when I was born, the same one who also chose my name. My dad once told me she was obsessed with it too and never took it off. But my grandmother passed away before I turned one, so I never had the chance to know her or to ask what the pendant means.

"Sophia!" Helena insists in a reprimanding tone. "What are you doing? We need to get out of here now! You don't even know the guy."

"You don't even know the guy." Her words make me recoil, a deep pang in my stomach drawing my attention. I know what Helena is warning me about. Horrible things have happened to me, memories I struggle to forget but that occasionally surface. Unknown boys are not a good sign, at least not for me.

"You should listen to your friend, *Sophia*," the stranger says, emphasizing my name. "You really don't know me, miss."

His words sound like an explicit threat.

"You sound like an old man," I shoot back, frowning in disdain.

He widens his ironic smile even further.

"Then you should show more respect."

"Go f..."

"Sophia!"

Helena finally pulls me firmly by the arm, dragging me down the sidewalk. I allow myself to be led, but I still glare at him, burning with hatred.

"Nice necklace, Sophia. Unlike your boots," mocks the idiot who looks like a poorly made copy of the protagonist from *The Terminator*. Before I can protest, Helena yanks me away, and the time traveler turns his back to head toward the hotel doors in front of him. Suddenly, he stops and turns before entering. "By the way, I'm Phelipe."

CHAPTER THREE

Sophia

After a restless night, with the now-familiar nightmare waking me up sweaty and scared, I feel like a zombie dragging myself back to school. Besides that, I'm not used to taking the bus; the seat always chafes my thighs, and the open windows make my hair look like a rat's nest.

Lamenting this misfortune, I shuffle down the hallway where students are rushing to find their classrooms; some pass by me and greet me cheerfully. I need to hurry if I don't want to miss the first class. I head to my locker to grab some books and stash my backpack. As I turn around, desperate at the sound of the second bell, I feel a strong pressure on my shoulder, followed by a thud on the floor.

"Don't you watch where you're going?" a female voice asks. I try to bend down to help her pick up her things. I grab a notebook with a black leather cover and am about to grab another when she pushes me away with a hostile gesture, brutally yanking the notebook from between my fingers. "Just what I needed! It had to be you, right, Sophia?"

I look at her for the first time. Her voluminous, completely black, curly hair brushes her waist. She's thin, tall, and curvy, with large brown eyes, full lips, and a flat nose. I'm absolutely certain I've never seen her in my life.

"Do I know you?"

The girl bends down and quickly gathers the rest of her stuff, shoving it into the backpack hanging from her shoulder. I notice she's wearing tight leather pants and a matching black t-shirt, balancing on heeled boots with a flamboyant and formidable pose. When she turns back to me, the smile on her face is too wide, showcasing her white, straight teeth. It's diabolical.

"Unfortunately." Her voice is naturally mocking and ironic.

Inexplicably, there's something about her face that seems vaguely familiar, as if I've seen it before, but in someone else. I try to remember who she resembles, but it feels like my brain is suffering some sort of blockage. It's then that a silver glint catches my attention. Incredulously, I realize after a second that her necklace is identical to mine. I immediately recall that guy Phelipe and his visible interest in my accessory.

"Your necklace... Where did you get it?"

I've never seen a necklace like mine. For years, my mom searched online for one that was at least similar since Isa wanted one too, but she never found it.

"If you try to touch it, I'll rip your arm off."

She tosses her hair back and walks away, bumping into me again as she passes by. I find myself staring at her graceful walk, not knowing where I recognize her from. The way she struts down the hallway like a cat is sensual and elegant. Her bag remains open, and as I notice a paper under my feet, I judge that the shove she gave me was enough to make it fall out. Even from afar, I can recognize the face of Tom Warner smiling and his electoral number, but the girl has drawn horns and a mustache on it. Below, where the candidate's propaganda phrase previously read, she wrote: "Rot in hell."

I look around, but no one seems to have noticed the unusual encounter.

"Hey, Sophia." I jump in surprise at hearing my name so close, and I'm even more startled to see Natália running toward me, her cheeks flushed from the lack of breath. She stops when she gets close enough and smiles, pausing to recover from the run with her hands on her knees. "You okay? Izec told me the teacher cut you from the performance. Wow, I thought that was really unfair! But if you want, we can share the song. That way, the three of us can perform together. You know, your voice is so beautiful..."

I force a smile at her.

"It's fine; I'm not in the mood to participate. I'll just help organize."

"If you change your mind, let me know. I'd really like you to sing with us." The worst part is that she seems sincere.

I nod as I watch her walk away. I think about everything I know about her, but it's not much. I know she sings well and plays the violin; she goes to church every Sunday night to rehearse with the children's choir. My mom always praises her on the rare occasions she drags Isa and me to mass. At school, she's never gotten into any controversy; I've never seen her with another boy or having a friend. In fact, the strongest memory I have of her, which also made me know her name, was last year when she organized a food drive to help those in need. At that time, Ane told me that she had a very poor childhood with her dad before moving in with her mom, which is why she dedicates herself so much to charitable causes.

Damn! That only makes it harder to hate her. Especially when I look down the hallway and see Izec shamelessly flirting with another girl, his eyes glued to her ample chest. I almost sympathize with Natália. Almost.

Fortunately, Ane walks toward me happily and bouncing, holding hands with her boyfriend, Jimmy, and I can push thoughts like: Natália is a better version of me out of my mind.

"Hey, Soph," Ane sings as she approaches. "Did you see we have a new student?"

"New student? In the middle of the semester?"

I raise my eyebrows. Then I remember the girl who bumped into me in the hallway just minutes ago. As I follow Ane and Jimmy to the classroom, I reflect on how she knows my name if she's a newcomer.

CHAPTER FOUR

Sophia

I'm thinking about the reasons that brought me here as I push the bar door open with my shoulders. In fact, *the* reason is just one: Ane.

The absurdly loud sound invades my ears as I step into the establishment. Within seconds, it feels like my brain is syncing with the music; everything begins to pulse in the same rhythm.

I adjust my outfit, the loose dress accentuating my waist and brushing against my thighs. The knee-high boots go up past my skinny knees; unfortunately, they haven't been worn enough to soften, causing my toes to hurt. I'm simple but well-dressed.

I make my way through the crowd, noticing for the first time that Izec's band is already on the makeshift stage. I see him smiling, so absorbed in the movements on his guitar that he doesn't even pay attention to the girls screaming for him at the edge of the stage. He gets along well with all the instruments. Music has always been his passion. The only one.

When I met him, we had just joined the music class in elementary school, around eleven years old. We had exchanged glances in preparatory school, but we weren't close. Until I saw him play the violin one afternoon alone in the classroom.

I hid and watched him for as long as I could, utterly fascinated by his skill and the calm way his notes filled the room. I remember feeling it directly in my chest, as if each chord could touch me. And then he turned around and smiled, asking what I thought. From that day on, I always found a way to ensure we were partners in any class activity; I just wanted to see him play any instrument and feel the notes reach deep within me again. When we started dating around the age of thirteen, he told me that music had brought us together. I never doubted it.

I knew that watching him play with his band would make me even more nostalgic and sad. All I wanted was to leave school and go home to curl up under the covers while binge-watching *Gossip Girl* for the seventh time, but Ane spent the entire break begging me to come, promising that we would have fun.

The place is packed, and from where I'm standing, it's impossible to see more than a foot in front of my nose. I feel a *déjà-vu* as I stand on my tiptoes looking for Ane in the crowd. Why has she been arriving late lately? Some people elbow and shove me as I force my way through, but I don't care. The only emptier place is the bar counter, and that's where I head. However, I stop short before reaching it as I come face to face with Penélope — Jimmy told me her name — the new girl, standing near the only tables in the venue. The girl stares back at me, giving me a mischievous smile.

"I see I can't get rid of you," she says before snatching food from someone else's table. "Wherever I go, you're there."

"Where do we know each other from? You're new at school, but you act like I've done something to you. You even know my name!"

"Maybe you did something..."

"What?"

I cross my arms over my chest, glaring back into her large brown eyes.

"Well, let's say you kind of... were born."

"No one can hate someone for no reason." She gestures to steal more fries, but I grab her arm, causing her to recoil as if I have a contagious disease. "Especially someone you don't even know."

Her lips curl into an ironic smile.

"I don't like you. End of story! Now, if you'll excuse me..." Penélope spins on her heels, making her black curls bounce. "I have other things to do."

"And the necklace?" The girl halts, visibly bothered by the topic. "Why is your necklace the same as mine?"

She throws me another one of her sarcastic smiles, but I notice it barely reaches her eyes, which suddenly seem heavy with tension.

"Poor Sophia, thinking that department stores don't sell duplicate pieces." She lets out a deep sigh. "By the way, that dress makes you look at least three pounds heavier."

She leaves me and my irritation behind, advancing among the people with an upright posture, balanced on her heels. Huffing loudly, I walk back to the bar and sit on one of the high stools. I order a drink and settle in, aware of the man next to me shamelessly eyeing my legs. I'm facing all the commotion when an unexpected presence places itself between me and the creep.

But it can't be, I must be in my personal hell!

"Are you following me?" I confront the guy all dressed in black, just like the first time I saw him in front of that hotel. As if I were invisible, he ignores me, signaling with his finger to the *bartender*. "Don't play dumb."

Finally, the bad boy with the messy black hair looks at me with total indifference. Silently, he receives a glass from the *bartender* with what I imagine is whiskey; his first long and leisurely sip makes it clear that he's in no hurry.

Now I can see his eyes. Although the lighting doesn't help, I notice his narrow eyes with a yellowish tint that makes me think of melted caramel.

"Still wearing those boots," he comments casually, opening a cheeky smile.

I let out a growl, rolling my eyes.

"Your arrogance is unbelievable. I'd rather talk to any other weirdo here than you." At that moment, the opportunistic creep leans half his body back to face me, displaying such a goofy smile that makes me huff. "Eww! I was being sarcastic."

He shrugs and returns to his previous position. I give up! I'm leaving this place.

I turn around and take my first steps towards the crowd when… Izec! I assume that for the first time tonight, he's focusing on something other than his band: me. My optimism tells me he's been watching my conversation with the stranger, igniting a spark of excitement in my chest.

I know it's silly to feel this way about a jerk of an ex-boyfriend, but I can't control it. Just like I can't control the idea that just popped into my head, making me take steps back to the bar. I force my best and most fake smile and stare at the arrogant guy again.

"Phelipe, right?" Without turning his head, he glances at me from the corner of his eye and empties his glass in one gulp. Yeah, it's going to be a long night! "Bartender, get me something strong and sweet, please," I ask, completely giving up trying to talk to the guy. "I've had enough bitterness for one night."

He raises his eyebrows, staring at me in surprise.

"Aren't you underage?"

He shrugs, extending his empty glass toward the bartender for a refill.

I'm not in the habit of drinking; in fact, I only drink on very special occasions. With my dad's history and a sister like Lily, I never saw much fun in alcohol like most kids my age do. But with the exhausting week I've had, maybe a drink will do me good.

My drink is delivered right away. I take a quick gulp, but the taste filling my mouth is far from sweet.

"Ugh! This is bitter," I complain, making a disgusted face.

The bartender completely ignores me, serving other customers. Irritated, I lean over the bar to grab the can of condensed milk he uses to make drinks. I only have time to pour a little into my glass before the bartender appears and snatches the can from my hand with a furious look. I take another sip, once again disappointed. It's still not sweet enough.

"Want me to sweeten it for you, miss?" Phelipe asks in a sarcastic tone.

Before I can think of a curse, his fingers quickly take the glass from my hand, tipping the entire drink down his throat.

"You animal!" I protest, resisting the impulse to punch him in the face.

"There you go, sweetie." He opens a wide, smug smile. "By the way, that's a good nickname for you, since you're as sweet as this bitter drink."

"You're a pig!"

I turn my back, moving away from the bar with my face burning with rage. What was I thinking for even a second about trying to talk to him?

Without warning, my attention shifts to Penélope, who is next to the stage, seemingly engrossed in an exciting conversation with someone. It takes me a few seconds to realize that the person she's entertaining is Izec, who apparently has been replaced in the band's performance. My heart skips a beat as I see her toss her hair back, my ex-boyfriend wearing that familiar look full of fascination and desire. And here I am, acting like an idiot trying to make him jealous over a guy who isn't even looking at me.

When Penélope catches me watching the two, her eyes widen instinctively, and all color drains from her face. The reaction intrigues me immediately, and it seems to Izec as well, as curiosity takes over his expression.

Why is she so scared? Why does she act like she's seen a ghost?

I shift my gaze back to Penélope and... What? How is this possible? Literally in the blink of an eye, the girl disappears into thin air like smoke. I gasp, scared. In response to the fright, I take a few steps forward, searching for the exact spot where the girl vanished. How is this possible?

Izec turns his body without moving from his spot, looking around, as surprised and startled as I am. Besides me, only he has witnessed this, and it's behind him that I go, determined, practically shoving people out of my way. I'm about to reach him, but I'm stopped by a strong hand around my arm. At first, I think it's Phelipe, but my eyes almost pop out of their sockets when I realize it's Jimmy.

"Jimmy?" I ask incredulously. "What are you doing here? Where's Ane?"

"She stayed home; she's not feeling very well."

There's something strange about his expression; I don't know exactly what it is. He's so tall that I have to stretch my neck to look into his blue eyes.

"Still sick?"

"Yeah."

"Well, I'll call her later. I need to go, Jimmy."

I feel like he's about to say something, but I don't stay to hear him; there's still something bothering me: Penélope. I push through the crowd, regaining my full concentration on what had left me confused.

I finally reach the spot where Izec and the girl were talking just minutes ago, but all I see is her open backpack, filled with chains, tossed in the corner of the stage. I rise on my tiptoes to try to spot Penélope over the heads of people, furious at the fact that a crowd is pushing me back as I try to get to the edge of the stage. Frustrated, I look around once more and spot the men's bathroom.

Of all the possibilities, that's the only place she could have run to—very quickly, I might add. If she had darted in the opposite direction, the crowd would have slowed her down. The bathroom is the most logical and unusual solution.

I approach hesitantly. I can't see what's happening inside through the slightly ajar door, only a piece of the mirror and a sink. The walls are covered in visibly stained white tiles, and through the mirror, I can see the reflection of a window on the opposite wall. I'm tempted to shout for Penélope, but I'd feel pretty stupid doing that.

I glance back, uncomfortable. I shift my weight from one foot to the other, holding onto the doorframe. Thankfully, no one seems to be paying attention to me. I'm completely convinced that I should go in, however, as I take a step forward, I bump into someone exiting the bathroom.

"Oh my God! I'm so sorry," I say, completely embarrassed.

I feel my cheeks flush, but then I realize who it is and let out a heavy sigh. Phelipe is rubbing the top of his head where I bumped into him and looks me up and down.

"Are you following me?"

"I'd rather die," I retort without thinking. "I thought I saw a... classmate go in there."

"I can guarantee there's no other girl in here besides you."

I fiddle with my hair just to keep my hands busy.

"Um... I must be mistaken. Fine, I'm outta here."

"You don't want to..."

"If you're trying to hit on me, just know I'm not interested in going out with you."

"I was going to ask if you wanted to check if your classmate didn't go into the bathroom. Apparently, your ego always jumps to conclusions."

"Are you going to tell me you don't want to kiss me?" I dare to provoke him, keeping my head held high.

If it weren't for the loud music, we would be in an awkward silence right now. I wait for a sarcastic response, a laugh, or something of the sort, but his expression remains serene, with a camouflaged amusement as if he's laughing inside. His bright eyes quickly scan every feature of my face.

Suddenly, Phelipe steps closer, and I find myself unable to move. He stops so close to me that the tips of our shoes touch. With a calm movement, he gently holds my chin, forcing me to look into his eyes. I feel my heartbeat quicken. His head tilts toward mine, hovering inches from my face. The mocking expression has been replaced by such a profound disdain that it makes his eyes shine with fury. I instinctively recoil, still feeling the warmth of his hand.

"I'd rather die," he whispers in a hoarse voice with a seriousness that sends chills down my spine.

We stare at each other for a second before Phelipe turns his back and walks away calmly, leaving me here... scared and frozen. I need a moment to collect myself and process what just happened. My neck tingles with that uncomfortable feeling of being watched, and this time I'm too frightened to look over my shoulder. As I move, I swear I hear a feminine laugh.

I notice something strange in the air as I weave through people, looking for the exit. Many are swearing or complaining about something, and only then do I realize the absence of music. I catch a glimpse of the stage, which is now empty. It seems the show has been interrupted.

Out of the corner of my eye, I see Penélope's backpack tossed in a corner. She really left in a hurry, or she wouldn't have left her things like this. Driven by an impulse of curiosity, I approach and crouch down, frantically looking around. I unzip the backpack and rummage through its contents. There's only a black leather notebook, a packet of Doritos, a crumpled soda can, and another dozen pamphlets for Tom Warner, "the man of the people," with his face scribbled on them. I open the notebook, ready to snoop through her class notes, but what I see startles me. On the first page is a drawing of my face with perfectly clear features, and what shocks me even more is that Phelipe is also drawn there, right next to me, our faces close together, just like the day we argued in the street.

How does she know this? Was she there?

A chill runs through my body as I stare at that notebook in horror. A bad feeling settles in my stomach, making every hair on my body stand on end. Penélope is the one who's been watching me all this time; I feel that certainty burning in my mind.

Before I can think about what I'm doing, I abruptly tear the page from the notebook and hide it under my dress, securing it in the waistband of my underwear. I hurry to get out of here, eager to analyze the drawing in peace.

The night is pleasantly cool, but the cold, rainy wind is enough to give me chills. The sound of my boot against the pavement doesn't drown out the sound of giggles. I frown and immediately stop walking. As I turn my face to an alley opening beside the bar, I find Penélope and Izec leaning against the wall, kissing as if it were the last night of their lives.

And I truly wish it would be.

CHAPTER FIVE

Sophia

"Isadora Márcia, stop playing with your food!" Vanessa, my mother, shouts as she sees her youngest daughter mixing her food back and forth on her plate, creating different shapes.

Isa rolls her eyes, but Mrs. Vanessa raises an eyebrow in her direction, prompting the six-year-old to huff in frustration before reluctantly taking a bite.

We're in a restaurant in the city center. Our cunning mother thought it would be convenient for us to gather in the middle of the week for dinner. She even managed to take a break from the beauty salon where she works just so we could go out. It took endless chatter to convince Lily, my older sister, to come too.

From a distance, I see the resemblance between my mother and my sisters. It's like they're various stages of the same person: the child, the young woman, and the adult. The same smile, the same pale skin, the same large gray eyes, and the same platinum hair on all three heads. I look nothing like any of them. My brown hair, black eyes, and cream-colored skin create a strange contrast, like that shadow that sometimes spoils pictures, or when someone completely random appears in the background. I was unfortunate enough to take after my father.

The restaurant is cozy. The ambient music sounds soft and pleasant to my ears, and the food is well-prepared. It's not completely full, and most of the occupied tables are filled with families.

"So, Sophia, how has school been?" my mother asks, looking pleased.

Isa rolls her eyes again, returning to play with her food. Lily glares at us, bored, wiping her teeth with the tablecloth in a hostile manner.

I sink further into my chair, stuffing my mouth with food to buy time to think of an answer. Apparently, only my mother seems happy with our family gathering. The rest are so desperate to leave and go home that it's almost comical.

"School's going well..." I hope she hasn't noticed the false tone in my voice.

Lily has definitely picked up on it; she's always been very sensitive to lies. Somehow, she always knows when we're not being truthful. At first, when we were kids, I thought she knew when I lied because she knew me well, and something in my expression would give me away. But over time, I discovered that Lily can tell when anyone lies. I should have taken her seriously when she laughed at the letter from Izec saying I was the only girl in his life.

"This weekend is the talent show, right?" my mother asks excitedly. I nod. "I heard Tom Warner is going to give a speech that day."

"That idiot?" Lily scoffs.

"Magali, how dare you say that? He's likely to be our next president! An upstanding man, philanthropist, young, full of good ideas and..."

"Liar," Lily cuts in, looking directly at me.

Damn it; as I deduced, she knows I lied about school. Mrs. Vanessa sharpens her gaze at her.

"And what do you understand about this, Lily?" As soon as the girl makes a move to respond, their mother silences her with a hand gesture. "We're not going to discuss this. So, Sophia, you're going to sing at the presentation, right?" The food struggles to go down my throat as if I've been punched in the stomach. I shake my head, causing Vanessa to gasp in disbelief. "You're not participating in the music classes?"

"No," I respond, pretending to take an interest in my glass of Coke. "I won't participate in any activities this year."

It's the first time I'm not excited about the talent show; my family surely notices that. I spent the entire vacation talking non-stop about the event, about the presentation that Izec and I would perform, and now I'm announcing that I won't be participating anymore. Not to mention that it's the first time I'm not chattering endlessly about everything happening at school.

My mother threatens to ask more questions but is interrupted by Isa:

"I'm going to perform at the ballet at the end of the year."

She's been taking ballet lessons for two years now. My mother smiles at Isa, but gives me that look of "we'll talk later."

"Big deal! No one cares," Lily mutters.

"Mommy, look at Lily!"

"Magali! Don't talk to your sister like that."

Lily makes a face at the youngest, then lifts the loose shirt she's wearing as a dress to wipe her teeth, exposing her tiny black underwear. A lot of people are staring at us when Mrs. Vanessa leans over the table and smacks my sister's hand to make her pull down her shirt.

"There's a wonderful thing called a toothbrush, Lily," I say. "You should use it."

"Soraya, why don't you shove the toothbrush up your..."

"Enough!" my mother yells. "Let's keep it civil, please. We're a family. We're dining out so we can talk better, spend more time together. No fighting! And, Lily, please behave. Don't pretend you don't know your sister's name. Yours and hers were chosen with such care by your grandmothers..."

Lily rolls her eyes. She hates her name, says she doesn't know how they had the courage to give it to a baby. Our maternal grandmother chose this name in honor of her own grandmother; conversely, our paternal grandmother thankfully chose mine for personal taste.

The truth is that I wish I could have known my paternal grandmother, Márcia, whom my mother talks about all the time. During my pregnancy, Vanessa had some *complications*—which means my dad beat her until she almost aborted me—and ended up staying with my grandmother, who was a doctor. I would love to ask her the meaning of the necklace, which lately seems to be the object of interest for many people.

"Not all grandmothers have good taste," Lily mutters.

"Don't be silly." Mrs. Vanessa smiles. "Your grandmother was a wonderful person, even as my mother-in-law. Márcia was a very determined and intelligent doctor. She reminds me a lot of you, Sophia."

"Because of the necklace?" I ask, but I can't help feeling my ego swell from the comparison.

"For everything. I believe that when she was younger, she looked a lot like you." When my mother interrupts the cutting of her steak, I know she's about to deliver some unpleasant or, at least, curious news. "By the way, your father called."

She shifts her cautious gaze between me and Lily, as a form of warning.

I huff. This is why Mrs. Vanessa arranged this dinner out in the middle of the week at my favorite restaurant. All the flattery to talk about my father, who, as she well knows, is a very delicate subject.

"If you're referring to that man who donated sperm, he's not my father," Lily says, and then she takes a gulp of her Coke.

Her platinum curls, with blue-tipped ends, brush against her plate of food. My mother's face turns scarlet. I chuckle, exchanging a conspiratorial glance with my sister. Isa doesn't seem too happy either.

"He wanted to talk to you, Sophia." She directs her attention to me. "To see if you were okay."

"Good thing I didn't answer, then."

"He's your father, Sophia."

"I don't have a father!"

"I'm with Samira on this one," Lily admits.

"Exactly, Sophia!" Vanessa shouts, causing everyone in the restaurant to look at us. She regains her composure, adjusting the collar of her jacket with embarrassment. She takes a deep breath before speaking again in a much lower tone. "Don't pretend you don't know your sister's name, Lily. Both of yours were chosen with so much love by your grandmothers..."

Lily rolls her eyes. She hates her name, claiming she doesn't know how they had the courage to give it to a baby. Our maternal grandmother chose this name in honor of her own grandmother; conversely, our paternal grandmother thankfully chose mine for personal taste.

The truth is that I wish I could have known my paternal grandmother, Márcia, whom my mother talks about all the time. During my pregnancy, Vanessa had some *complications*—which means my dad beat her until she almost aborted me—and ended up staying with my grandmother, who was a doctor. I would love to ask her the meaning of the necklace, which lately seems to be the object of interest for many people.

"Not all grandmothers have good taste," Lily mutters.

"Don't be silly." Mrs. Vanessa smiles. "Your grandmother was a wonderful person, even as my mother-in-law. Márcia was a very determined and intelligent doctor. She reminds me a lot of you, Sophia."

"Because of the necklace?" I ask, but I can't help feeling my ego swell from the comparison.

"For everything. I believe that when she was younger, she looked a lot like you." When my mother interrupts the cutting of her steak, I know she's about to deliver some unpleasant or, at least, curious news. "By the way, your father called."

She shifts her cautious gaze between me and Lily, as a form of warning.

I huff. This is why Mrs. Vanessa arranged this dinner out in the middle of the week at my favorite restaurant. All the flattery to talk about my father, who, as she well knows, is a very delicate subject.

"If you're referring to that man who donated sperm, he's not my father," Lily says, and then she takes a gulp of her Coke.

Her platinum curls, with blue-tipped ends, brush against her plate of food. My mother's face turns scarlet. I chuckle, exchanging a conspiratorial glance with my sister. Isa doesn't seem too happy either.

"He wanted to talk to you, Sophia." She directs her attention to me. "To see if you were okay."

"Good thing I didn't answer, then."

"He's your father, Sophia."

"I don't have a father!"

"I'm with Samira on this one," Lily admits.

"Exactly, Sophia!" Vanessa shouts, causing everyone in the restaurant to look at us. She regains her composure, adjusting the collar of her jacket with embarrassment. She takes a deep breath before speaking again in a much lower tone. "Don't pretend you don't know your sister's name, Lily. Both of yours were chosen with so much love by your grandmothers..."

Lily rolls her eyes. She hates her name, claiming she doesn't know how they had the courage to give it to a baby. Our maternal grandmother chose this name in honor of her own grandmother;

conversely, our paternal grandmother thankfully chose mine for personal taste.

The truth is that I wish I could have known my paternal grandmother, Márcia, whom my mother talks about all the time. During my pregnancy, Vanessa had some *complications*—which means my dad beat her until she almost aborted me—and ended up staying with my grandmother, who was a doctor. I would love to ask her the meaning of the necklace, which lately seems to be the object of interest for many people.

"Did you draw this?" There's uncertainty in his voice.

"Of course not! I'm being followed, and I'm almost sure you have something to do with it."

"Who's following you?"

"Don't play dumb; I know very well that you're involved. Wherever I go, you're there. Have you noticed that coincidence? Someone was watching us that day on the street; what is that? Some bitter ex-girlfriend? Or are you two teaming up to..."

The door swings open loudly, making me jump and my heart nearly leap out of my chest. My mother and sisters step out of the restaurant right after.

"There you are, sweetheart. Let's go," Vanessa says affectionately.

I look back to where Phelipe was, questioning why my mother hasn't asked who the boy talking to me is, but all I find is emptiness. Where on earth did he go? And he took the drawing with him!

"Oh my God, it's freezing!" Isa complains.

The strong wind is whistling in my ears and shaking the tree branches violently. I take a few moments to move, still searching for an explanation for Phelipe's sudden disappearance. I'm struck by that sense of *déjà-vu*; he vanished into thin air just like Penélope.

A noise catches my attention. I automatically glance toward the dark shadow behind the tree, where he just stepped out minutes ago. I could swear I see a figure lurking.

"Phelipe?" I call softly, feeling foolish.

The shadow doesn't move and remains silent, but something about its shape suggests it's a person, not just a tree branch. I swallow hard.

"Come on, Sophia!" Mrs. Vanessa shouts after unlocking the car doors.

"I'm coming. Damn it!" I mumble, turning my back on the dark, strange figure, willing to believe it's really just a tree.

CHAPTER SIX

Sophia

I run.

I know it's futile, but I run.

It's only a matter of time until *she* finds me, but I need to run, even if my steps are slow and I stumble over my own feet most of the time.

I bump into a few trees along the way, the leaves on the ground rustling under my feet. I fall again, sinking my hands into the mud as I try to support myself. I hear her laughter *echoing* around me. Quickly, I get up and start running again, taking a different route.

But no matter which path I take, I know she's on my tail without even needing to run. She laughs and delights in my falls as I desperately try to escape. The woman simply follows me, walking solemnly and whistling, like a child in an amusement park.

I stop when I bump my head against a hard surface. I step back, desperate, blinking hard. I run my fingers over the top of my forehead and realize I've hit a tree. Before I can even remember to run again, *she* is already by my side. I jump, seeing her right in front of me. A triumphant smile crosses her face.

"When are you going to learn that running is useless?" she mocks, smiling and tapping her fingers on her hips.

I stand still, perplexed, letting the wind sweep my hair over my shoulders. It's inevitable to admire such beauty. She is tall, with a slim and graceful body. Her ample bust stands out in the plunging neckline of her tight black dress. Her hair is a blood-red hue, completely straight, just like mine. A fringe covers half her forehead, swept to the left.

My eyes meet hers. Hers are green like two emeralds, sparkling, hungry, and they are everything my dark, opaque eyes are not. I can even see my pale, frightened reflection in her iris. I look incredibly fragile and small, an easy target to be taken down. My appearance is so sad, ridiculous, and depressing compared to hers that my stomach churns.

A feeling that doesn't seem to be mine sweeps through my chest like a bomb—a feeling I don't know, that I've never felt before, but that I quickly identify as envy. Envy for everything I am not, for everything I should be, or even for everything I want to be. Above all, envy for having such a tragic, painful, pathetic, and futile end. She will have a long and happy life ahead. I will not. The arrival of death—my own death—awakens a clock inside me without my consent. I feel each second pass with excessive calm, dragging the hands and almost freezing time around me. My heart falls into rhythm, gradually slowing, beating slowly just to avoid stopping. The sudden envy has been replaced by fear and panic, which is becoming real, like a dive back to the surface.

I close my eyes and wait for time to finally run out. However, I am knocked to the ground with a burning force. I don't dare open my eyes, squeezing them tightly. Just by the wind shifting direction, I know she's going to attack.

With a loud, suffocating gasp, I return to reality, blinking repeatedly to make sure I'm in Art class, and not fleeing from a maniac who wants to kill me.

Soon I realize I'm in a terrible mood. I can't stand reliving the nightmare with the terrifying red-haired woman, which has now become constant in my unconscious. I crack my knuckles and neck, trying to focus on my tasks, even though I know that the restless night will make it difficult for me to do anything.

I try not to think about the dreams anymore. I concluded this morning, while brushing my teeth, that they are actually products of my troubled and scared mind; I shouldn't worry about it. The chase, that familiar feeling of being watched, the drawing... all the strange things that have happened lately are messing with my subconscious, which reacts by creating disturbing nightmares with a woman I've never seen in my life.

I huff, frustrated. I'm in the middle of Art class, staring at my easel with dismay. I should have painted something conceptual or at least abstract, but all I managed was a blue blot with green and yellow splatters. I dip the brush in red paint, hoping to at least draw something acceptable. I mentally curse, pulling the brush away from the canvas. Now it's even worse.

I stretch my neck, trying to see the paintings of my classmates. They're not much better than mine, so I relax instantly. I might even get a six with this.

Penélope is absorbed, making a beautiful sketch of her face while devouring a sandwich with the other hand. She looks so serene admiring her work that she even stops eating a bit to evaluate it better. So much narcissism. Just like the drawing she made of me, this one is very well drawn, highlighting her skills.

Since yesterday, after Phelipe vanished into thin air before my incredulous eyes with the drawing in his hands, I've been wondering what Penélope's role in all this is. Is she after me or him? The more I think about it, the more I conclude that he is the target. The girl drew me beside him, acted as if she had seen a ghost when she saw us together at the bar, inexplicably disappearing shortly afterward. Perhaps she is indeed Phelipe's ex-girlfriend, which explains her aversion to me.

When Penélope notices she's being watched, she rolls her eyes and shows me the middle finger. I return the gesture without thinking twice.

My eyes instinctively drop to the easel beside me, which I was trying with all my might not to look at. Ane takes a step back to admire her work. She's the only one in the room with a clean white coat, free of paint stains creating new patterns. Her blonde hair is tied up in a high ponytail, perfectly arranged on her head. I regret not having that idea, as my loose hair is tipped with paint. I envy her discipline in keeping her materials organized, her brushes so clean they hardly look used, and the floor without a trace of paint. My paint pots are scattered in complete disorder; some fell to the ground with their lids open and stained everything around me, including my white sneakers. Great.

When she realizes I'm looking at her, my friend opens a radiant smile, which I return immediately. Jimmy signals for me to be quiet as he enters my line of sight, approaching Ane stealthily. Observing his girlfriend's work, he breaks into a wide smile, then their gazes meet before he pulls her into a hug.

I allow myself to look at Ane's painting for the first time and regret it in the same second. As always, her drawing is so meticulously perfect that it makes me want to eat all the crap I've created. It's a realistic piece where the strokes of a child form a robust, fruit-laden tree. That's why I consciously avoid looking at the drawings Ane makes.

The teacher approaches my friend's easel with a clearly amazed expression and pats her on the back.

"Magnificent!" she praises with enchantment in her voice. "You're going to display it at the talent fair, right?"

"Oh, yes, I'm creating original works for the event. I'm following this trend."

"You are very talented, Ane. It would be a waste if you abandoned your gifts when you graduate." The teacher adjusts her glasses and her eyes observe Jimmy's presence as if it were the first time. She furrows her lips. "I see your easel remains empty, Mr. Jimmy."

"Is it? Maybe it's part of the concept of my work," he jokes, displaying an amused smile. Ane rolls her eyes, and the teacher looks at him with irritation. "I'm off to my game, love. I'll see you later," Jimmy says goodbye, leaning down to kiss Ane on the forehead.

My phone vibrates in my back pocket, making me jump. As soon as I take the phone out, I see on the display that it's a new message from an unknown number.

"We need to meet. See you later. Phelipe."

My mouth drops open in astonishment, and I quickly type a response, being careful not to get caught by the teacher:

"How did you get my number?"

The phone vibrates again almost immediately.

"I would be surprised by the number of things people share for money. I'll meet you at 7 PM. Before you ask, I also have your address."

Did he pay someone to get my number? Who would do that? Probably some idiot from school.

"I didn't say I would meet you!"

The response comes so fast I barely have time to close the screen:

"I wasn't asking!"

I'm typing a curse when the teacher shoots me a look that feels like a bucket of cold water, so I hit the send button before I even finish:

"Shove your orders up your..."

He must be a psychopath to have gotten my number without asking me, not to mention the fact that he keeps appearing in the places I am. There's no way I'm meeting him tonight or ever. I don't care about the drawing anymore or trying to find an explanation for all the strange things that have been happening.

My painting is so horrible that I feel like crying. With a long sigh, I grab my pen, ready to sign my name and just get out of here.

"I see someone who was strongly influenced by Monet." I jump at Izec's voice, closer than expected. I roll my eyes, pretending my heart isn't pounding frantically in my chest. "Let me guess... um..." He taps his fingers on his chin, furrowing his brow as if he's really thinking. *"The Japanese bridge?"*

"I won't deny it; I'm more impressed that you know any work by Monet than by comparing this disaster to something professional."

Izec opens a splendid smile, showing all his white teeth. I hope he doesn't notice how weak his presence makes me feel, like a pathetic little girl.

"I'm a complete artist," he replies, diverting his gaze to some point behind me, making his smile falter for a brief moment.

I turn and see Ane looking at us cautiously. She shrinks back, having been caught, and goes back to painting.

"So... um... artist, show me your work," I ask as I bend down to grotesquely sign my name in the bottom corner of the canvas.

"Let's say yours is more professional," he replies dismissively.

"You paint that badly?"

"Yes." His almond-shaped eyes narrow, and he opens his famous roguish smile at the corner of his mouth. "I'm much better at doing other things."

"Oh!" That's all I can say.

He casually leans against my easel, tilting his head in my direction. His rough, calloused fingers from so much contact with musical instruments play with a paint stain stuck to my lab coat.

"I was thinking..." Izec sighs, letting the fabric of my lab coat slide in his hand. "What are you doing tonight? I thought we could go out."

"Why don't you invite Penélope? Since you were shoving your tongue down her throat."

"Oh! That?" His smile loses some of its enchanting effect. "Her mouth came onto mine." Liar, false, cynical. "Actually, the hangout is an excuse for us to talk. Don't you think we should?"

I ponder the request because, well, we do need to talk. Moreover, it's the perfect pretext to be out of the house in case Phelipe shows up. I nod, pretending to be indifferent, and he smiles.

"Are you going to call someone else?" I whisper; what I really want to know is if Natália will be there.

"No, just the two of us. Like the old days." I swallow hard. I don't trust my voice, so I just nod. "I'll pick you up at seven. Bring blankets."

"What?"

He smiles, unperturbed. Then he pulls me close and kisses my forehead, lingering there a little too long. I take the chance to feel as much as I can of his shaving lotion scent.

"I'll see you later."

The bell rings as Izec steps away, heading for the door without giving me an explanation as to why we need blankets. I shudder just trying to imagine.

I gather my materials, tossing my dirty lab coat to the back of my backpack. I wash my hands and try to wipe the paint stains from my hair with the moisture of my fingers. After I think it's satisfactory, I leave the room heading towards the cafeteria.

"What was that?" Ane asks, breathless, as she catches up with me in the hallway.

"I have no idea. He said he wants to talk."

"I told you this would happen. Izec is so predictable! So, where are you two going?"

"He didn't tell me."

I draw on all my self-control not to jump for joy. My stomach is growling with hunger, but maybe I won't be able to eat anything out of pure anxiety.

"No break for you!" Helena says in a tone that makes it clear it's an order, stopping between me and the cafeteria door with her hands on her hips. "Hi, Ane."

Ane nods, looking back and forth between us.

"And can I know why?" I grumble.

"We have a lot to sort out about the talent fair organization," she replies, shaking a folder full of papers in front of me.

I curse quietly; damn the time I volunteered to be part of this stupid committee. Izec's fault. I don't even want to go to this talent fair, but unfortunately, attendance is mandatory.

I say goodbye to Ane, asking her to save a sandwich for me; my stomach growls in protest as I turn my back on the cafeteria, following Helena to the auditorium. When we arrive, she talks non-stop, pointing to the seats, each with a nameplate indicating who will sit there. I'm nodding along, pretending to agree with everything Helena is saying about the decoration and the placement of the red carpet at the entrance, but my mind is miles away.

"And Tom Warner will sit here," she announces as if it's the best thing in the world, showing the chair with the nameplate right in front of the stage. "So he has easy access to the stage when it's time for the speech."

"And here I will give the best performance of all, making them fall to their knees," Ana Catarina chimes in, appearing God knows where. She theatrically throws herself on the floor with a big smile on her lips. I roll my eyes, aware that I completely forgot she'll be doing a dance performance. "Hey, Sophia, you're dirty here," she teases with a giggle, pointing to my ear.

I try to clean the area and feel my fingers get sticky from the paint I didn't clean properly.

"Oh, Sophia, I forgot to mention: Ana Catarina is also on the organizing committee. Isn't that great?" says Helena, flashing an enthusiastic smile at me.

I can think of several words to describe what it means to spend more time with Ana Catarina, and "great" is not one of them. So I just nod. We simply detest each other since elementary school; I can't even remember why.

"But I think Tom Warner should make a grand entrance from above," Ana Catarina says, lifting her legs in the air while still lying face down in the center of the stage, resting her head in her hands. "What do you think, Sophia?"

"I don't care." I try to keep politeness in my tone, which is difficult due to the girl's unbearable smile and my overwhelming hunger.

"That's a good idea, Ana," Helena praises, resting her chin on her hand while thinking, looking from the auditorium steps to the chair. I close my eyes, wishing I could teleport to another galaxy. "Sophia, do you mind going up there? I want to see how it would look."

Sighing, I drag my feet up the stairs to the top. I place my hands on my hips, assessing the view.

"See? Everyone will see him; it's going to be amazing," Ana Catarina reinforces her argument.

"I don't know..." Helena drums her fingers on her chin frantically, analyzing. "But where will he sit? The principal said Tom Warner insists on seeing all the performances."

The two continue a heated discussion about where the presidential candidate should sit, and I'm grateful they don't need my opinion. When the bell rings to signal the end of the break, neither of them has come to a conclusion about Tom Warner's seat. As I leave, Helena tells me something about a badge, which I naturally ignore but smile in response as if I'm paying attention. Ana Catarina quickens her pace and insists on passing through the door at the same time as me, pressing me against the doorframe with a smile on her lips.

※

THE FIRST THING I SEE when I enter my house after class is my older sister's red underwear. Lily is lying face down on the living room sofa wearing nothing more than a miniskirt that could easily be mistaken for a belt, her legs spread wide apart, exposing her underwear to anyone who walks in. Her blonde curls fall over her face, her mouth slightly open. Isa is sitting on the floor, resting her head near Lily's knees, watching SpongeBob SquarePants.

I head to the kitchen and grab an apple. The pile of dirty dishes is enormous, so I make a mental note to take care of it later. I hear an abrupt change in the TV programming and a loud protest from Isa. I lean against the doorframe, watching my two sisters fighting for control of the remote.

I walk to my room, leaving the two of them to battle it out without any remorse. I unpack my backpack and get dressed after a long shower. Izec sends me a message saying he's already left home, which means he won't be long. I instantly feel nervous.

My nails are already chewed down from anxiety when I finally hear the sound of a car parking outside. Butterflies drop in my stomach. *Don't be a coward, Sophia,* I think, because I'm actually willing to run away and hide like a ball under my bed.

Is there time for me to make up an excuse that I'm sick? A sudden flu? A virus?

A nervous honk sounds loudly. My sisters watch me out of the corner of their eyes. I rub my hands on my jeans to dry the moisture. I let out a long sigh and calm myself.

"I guess that's my cue," I say, passing by them.

I stretch to try to look more relaxed, but inside I'm having a panic attack. My phone vibrates; I see Izec's persistent message:

Hey? I'm already outside waiting for you.

As soon as I step out the door, I'm hit by a cold draft. I wouldn't give in to Izec's whims to take a blanket, but after much thought, I stuffed a throw into my backpack. Just as a precaution, since I didn't know what he had in mind.

I walk as casually as possible to the gray jeep. It's been a long time since I last approached the familiar vehicle. But, one way or another, it feels like I'm doing the right thing.

Izec opens the passenger door for me, extending his hand to help me in. I hope he doesn't notice how clammy and sticky my fingers are. Inside the car, I savor the smell of aftershave and cologne coming from him. His hair is wet and tousled as usual.

"Where are we going?" I ask to break the silence after a few minutes.

Izec smiles, making my heart race again.

"You'll see. I hope you brought a blanket. It's pretty cold today." My attention turns to his strong arm, then to his smirk when he realizes he's being watched. "You look beautiful, Soph," he compliments, letting his eyes roam over my body before turning back to the road.

Very gently, he releases the hand that's on the gear shift, brushing my knee.

"So, the piano for your performance on Saturday is already in the auditorium."

His smile falters.

"Yeah."

"Natália is really nice." I have no idea why I say this.

Izec clenches his jaw and removes his fingers from my knee, suddenly needing both hands to drive. His expression hardens. I know I'm touching on a topic that makes him uncomfortable.

"Yeah," he says again through clenched teeth.

Then why are you taking me out? is what I want to ask; it's what my mind screams, begging me to verbalize every word. However, I swallow hard, making the question on the tip of my tongue dissolve in my saliva and go down my throat.

We spend the rest of the ride in silence.

"Wow..." That's all I can say when Izec parks the jeep.

I open the door and quickly slide out, eager to feel the place he's brought me to. I hear Izec shut the car door, letting out an amused chuckle at my expression. I make sure not to look in his direction.

We're at Christ Park. Few people wander around the green, damp grass, completely oblivious to the two new visitors. The trees sway in the wind, causing my hair to stand on end and filling my nostrils with the familiar scent of leaves. My heart is exploding in my chest with excitement for being here. I can hardly contain the urge to skip while admiring everything around me, awestruck.

"Why did you bring me here?" I ask when I feel his approach behind me.

"We used to come here all the time when we were kids. Why not? It's a special place," he admits, his affectionate eyes searching mine.

I swallow hard. I feel his fingers brush lightly against mine as he stops beside me.

"Izec, this is..."

"Wonderful?" he asks with humor as he realizes I'm unable to finish the sentence.

"Splendid."

"Wow! What an honor." He smiles widely, displaying the dimples carved into his face. "Shall we?"

Izec takes my hand and nods toward the park. I let him guide me, walking carefree. I still can't grasp everything that's happening. He was very considerate in his choice, and my heart races in my chest with gratitude. Izec is right; there is no other place in the world that is more special.

I look around, completely enchanted. I'm astonished with myself for not even having considered the idea of coming here before. After all, this is where I spent the best days of my life, my childhood, puberty, the beginning of my adolescence. Why did we stop coming?

We're approaching a tree that I would recognize from a distance. It's the tree under which I always sat with Ane by my side so we could talk freely. Every time we needed to discuss something important, she would drive calmly here so we could sit under "our tree," as she called it.

It was here that she told me about her first kiss with Jimmy when she realized she was in love with him. It was here that she cried for hours on end after her parents' accident and all her relatives refused to take her and her brothers in.

"Jimmy's dad wants to adopt me," she told me while we were sitting under the tree. "It's either that or me and my brothers are going to end up in foster care."

Tears streamed freely down her cheek. Ane was fifteen when her parents had a mysteriously tragic car accident, since according to the firefighters' reports, it seemed that the brakes had been cut. They were following leads on the whereabouts of Ane's twin sister, who had been kidnapped when she was seven. The rest of her family, blinded by a fanatical belief, viewed this as a curse, refusing to take custody of Ane and her younger twin brothers, who were six at the time, fearing that those responsible for the accident that killed their parents would come after them.

"But isn't that a good thing, Ane?" I tried to see the positive side of the situation, if there was one. "You know Jimmy's dad. You love Jimmy. They'll be close; your brothers will be with you!"

"That's great for my brothers, Sophia. I know. I don't want them to end up separated in an orphanage, far from me." She tossed pebbles away, her face turning redder. "But... what about me and Jimmy? We've been dating for two years. How is it going to be for us to be raised together, like siblings?" I fell silent, unsure of what to say. I couldn't see the positive side regarding their romance at that moment. "Jimmy..." She wiped her tears with the back of her hand, trying to sound calmer. "He proposed that we make a chastity pact. No more intimate involvement until... we get married."

"Ane, that's..."

"Horrible, I know." She sniffled. "But... I don't want to risk losing Jimmy, or for his dad to go back on his decision to adopt us. I... I don't even know what I'm feeling, Soph."

With nothing else to say, I did the only thing I could do at that moment: I hugged her tightly and let her cry until the pain was numbed by exhaustion.

Now, the memory of that conversation hurts deep within me.

"You're very quiet," Izec observes, bringing me back to reality.

He stops when we reach the familiar tree. I lean against it.

"I'm just..." My fingers trace the surface of the trunk where Ane and I had crudely carved our initials and a heart with a pocket knife, which seemed to have been done centuries ago. "Taking it all in."

Izec studies the carving with interest. His brow furrows. I wonder if he told Ane where he was taking me when he got home. Izec's mother works for Jimmy's family, something he hates to reveal. His family wasn't financially well off, and moving to the Belmonte family's huge estate, with all its luxuries and extravagances, was a big leap. Besides, Jimmy's dad always treated Izec like a son since he saw him practically grow up, which made the already inflated ego of the boy swell even more. Jimmy has a sister named Helen, who's about twelve, but lives with their mom in another city. Izec has a fourteen-year-old brother, Lucas. The family got bigger with the arrival of Ane and her two siblings.

"Did you bring the blanket?"

He raises an eyebrow, a mischievous glint in his expression. I slide my backpack off my shoulders, unzip it, and pull out the blanket. Izec chuckles softly but quickly spreads the pink blanket on the ground. He sits down, patting the spot beside him. As soon as I sit, he pulls a blanket from his own backpack and drapes it over our shoulders. That was the intention then: to keep us warm.

"We used to skip school here," Izec reminisces. "This place brings me good memories. If I remember correctly, we kissed right here."

"We kissed in a lot of places," I say, trying to sound casual.

He gives his seductive side smile, leaning in closer to me.

"But that kiss was special; it was the first."

We both laugh. His fingers glide across the blanket until they touch mine. His hand is warm and cozy over mine, pressing lightly.

"That was my first kiss," I say, the vivid memory flashing in my mind.

I remember that we were playing hide and seek with Ane and Jimmy, who were already a couple at the time. I was thirteen. Jimmy was finishing the countdown, and I needed a place to hide. I saw Ane's blonde hair flame pass by me, entering among the trees. I hid behind the sturdy tree, knowing I wouldn't have time to look for a safer place. That's when I heard Izec calling me from a higher branch of the tree, reaching out his hand to help me climb. As I sat beside him, with our knees touching, we stared at each other for a long time. I completely ignored Jimmy's shout saying he was coming and the sound of his footsteps approaching. At that moment, it was just Izec and me, getting closer and closer, a breath away from our lips touching.

"That was my first kiss too," he admits, tightening his grip on my hand.

"Oh!" I'm not actually shocked since the kiss itself was a total disaster. But I didn't expect him to admit it. "I remember your braces hitting my tooth."

We both laugh again. Izec lightly touches my cheek, brushing the hair away. His warm touch makes me curl my toes inside my sneakers. Our gazes remain locked.

"Why did you ask me out?" I ask before I can control myself.

He lets out a long sigh.

"Because I like you, Sophia." His voice sounds tired, as if he's struggling against his own words. "I really wanted to free myself from this feeling, wanted to move on, but every time I see you, I can still feel this energy. I still feel like you're my Sophia. And I'm still me."

"Izec..."

I gasp. His fingers move from my face and snake to my neck, tangling in my hair, pulling it gently back. My limbs turn to jelly; thank God I'm sitting, or my knees would have buckled. I freeze in his penetrating gaze, watching him take control of the situation as he leans in my direction, stopping two centimeters from my lips to take a deep breath.

"Tell me you feel this too and that I'm not going crazy," he whispers, brushing the tip of his nose against my neck, leaving a warm trail as he explores my skin.

"B-but... you're with Natália now," I stutter, trembling.

I don't know why I said those words, as I really wanted to give myself completely to the moment, which is all I've wanted since our stupid fight. However, I'm feeling condescending toward Natália. And I feel horrible for having any mere thought of compassion for my ex's current girlfriend. It would be easier if she were detestable. But I also don't want to be dragged back into the emotional rollercoaster that is dating Izec.

He pulls back to look at me. Bringing up the topic of "girlfriend" is a pretty stupid thing to do when you're about to kiss a guy.

Suddenly, his cell phone starts ringing inside his backpack, and he grabs it without thinking twice. I see him make an effort to try to hide it from me, but I can see "Carol" flashing on the screen. He declines the call and opens the messaging app; there are several from this Carol asking where he is with multiple question marks. Further down, several names of different girls, including one named Amanda, to whom he replies:

"I'll talk to you later."

My phone is also vibrating insistently in the back pocket of my pants. I'm sure it's Phelipe, probably very pissed to find out that I'm not home; I feel more than happy to ignore it.

"You're right," he agrees, turning back to me. But there's no trace of regret in his expression or his hardened gaze. The chemistry in the air dissipates like smoke. After seeing his phone, my compassion for Natália rises uncontrollably. "I got carried away by the familiarity of the place."

"Izec, I..."

"Shhh." He silences me by pressing his index finger against my lips. "It's okay, Soph. I saw you with that guy."

"Oh! He's just a... friend."

In fact, he's a psycho, sick, strange. But it's good to know that the plan to make him jealous worked.

"Seeing you with another guy isn't cool."

"Seeing you with another girl isn't cool." I take a deep breath. "By the way, why did you do it, Izec? Why did you start dating another girl just a few days after breaking up with me? You didn't even tell me... It was awful to find out in front of everyone."

"Because I'm an idiot."

Fearing he might hurt me with his answers, I don't press any further. I sigh as I feel a cold breeze sweep across the area, tossing my hair in every direction and threatening to lift the blanket off the ground. I huddle closer, wrapping the soft blanket around myself, and slide nearer to Izec, resting my head on his shoulder.

"Thank you," I whisper.

"You're welcome." He wraps his arm around my back, pulling me closer into a hug. "By the way, I have something for you."

He fumbles in the pocket of his jeans until he pulls out a harmonica, making my breath lose its rhythm. Izec begins to play a sweet tune; I remember having heard him play it several times before. My eyes involuntarily well up with tears, and I feel overwhelmed with nostalgia.

Izec has always been everything I wanted since I first laid eyes on him in music class. I used to sneak away from Ane when I went to Jimmy's house to see her and watched Izec through the crack of the door. Before that, I would hide in the music room to listen to him practice, and I always tried to find a way to partner up with him in all our classes together.

And even now, wrapped up in him, us against the cold, listening to him play his harmonica, which is by far my favorite instrument, I still feel like I did the first time in that music room.

"I love you, Izec," I whisper, my eyes burning, tears about to spill.

"I love you, Sophia," he whispers back, pausing the music. He pulls me tighter against him. "I will always love you."

With that, he resumes playing the harmonica, making my heart soar out of my chest.

CHAPTER SEVEN

Sophia

"I promise, Soph," my mom keeps saying, and I continue to shrug as I get out of the car. "As soon as Isa's ballet performance is over, we'll come running."

"Alright, Mom."

I force a smile, but I know frustration is etched on my face. I've lost count of how many times she's said this in the last forty minutes as she drove me to the talent show at school. I think she's apologizing more to Tom Warner for not attending his speech than to me.

I close the car door and wave one last time to my mom and Isa, who is dressed as a ballerina in the backseat. They both smile back, and then the car drives off, leaving me alone in the school parking lot. I walk casually among the other students and guests arriving for the ceremony. The night is partially warm, with the full moon shining high in the sky, illuminating the entire courtyard.

My reflection in the glass doors catches my attention. I'm glad I chose the long red dress with a v-neck, because it really looks fabulous on me, even if it makes me feel overdressed for the event. It hugs my body so tightly it feels like a second skin, tailor-made. Through the side slit, you can see my black high-heeled sandals. My hair is tossed to one side, and the waves I tried to create have already started to fall apart, reverting to their natural state.

"There you are," Helena says, appearing behind me. I can see her perfectly in the reflection of the glass door before I turn around: she's wearing a suit that looks too big for her, completely hiding all her curves; she looks like an efficient secretary, which must be the main goal. "You forgot to get your badge."

"What?"

I turn just as she sticks something onto the neckline of my dress. A white sticker with my name and "organizing committee" written underneath.

"This makes it easy to find you if someone needs something."

"How great!" My voice reveals irony, but Helena seems to notice none of it.

As soon as she turns her back, I rip the sticker from my chest, crumpling it several times between my fingers before tossing it away. If she asks me, I'll say I lost it. No way I'm helping with anything at this stupid ceremony.

"Sophia, hey," Izec calls out cheerfully. I stop in my tracks, watching him stride towards me with a crooked smile on his lips. His eyes wander over my body. "Wow, you look beautiful."

"You too."

He looks so handsome in his white dress shirt and gray blazer that it's almost disturbing. His bronze-colored hair is messy as always, and his face is freshly shaved.

"What are you still doing here? Aren't you going in?"

"I'm waiting for Ane, do you know where she is?"

"Oh!" His confident smile wavers. "When I left home, she wasn't ready yet."

"What? But she's running out of time!"

Ane has been late to absolutely everything lately, which isn't like her. She leaves class every five minutes to go to the bathroom and hasn't been eating properly either. When I ask her about it, she says she's fine, that I shouldn't worry, but I'm ready to confront her.

"You should go inside and wait for Ane in there; otherwise, you'll end up standing."

"That's a good idea."

I follow him in silence, my eyes fixed on the back of his neck. This is the first time we've spoken since our trip to the park. In yesterday's class, he acted as if we'd never been out and just waved when he saw me. I was tempted to say something to him but thought it was better to let things remain as they were. After all, he's still dating.

As soon as I enter the anteroom of the auditorium, I'm shocked: it's all decorated with students' paintings on display. The art teacher bounces from side to side in her elegant long black dress, her smile so wide it looks like her face might split in half at any moment as she shows the works to the parents, who listen attentively.

I veer away from the crowd that follows her closely, walking to the other side to admire the paintings. I pass by Izec, who seems to have finally found Natália and is chatting animatedly with some guys from his band in a corner.

"Um... a tension vibe," Penélope mocks, appearing in my line of sight with her familiar devilish smile on her lips. "I wonder if Natália already knows about your adventures with her boyfriend?"

"How do you know about that?"

Considering the temperature of my face, it must be bright red, betraying my anger. So she is really spying on me!

"Oh, come on! You weren't in some ultra-secret place, were you?"

"Great talking to you, but if you'll excuse me, there are other things I'd rather do. Like gnaw on my own eyes, for example."

"Go ahead, it must be wonderful not having to see that face in the mirror ever again."

I glare at her, noticing for the first time how beautiful she looks, which isn't really a surprise. Her black curls are neat and shiny, cascading majestically to her waist. She's wearing a canary yellow dress, which is at least strange considering that until now, I've only seen her in black leather clothes. It's fitted at the waist and falls in layers below the hip. The neckline reaches her navel, and I wonder how she managed to get past the principal with such a severe violation of the dress code.

"How many snakes had to die for you to have that dress?" I point a finger, raising an eyebrow. "Is it python skin? Be careful, cannibalism is a crime."

"Funny you mention that; I was just going to say I'd never seen a chicken in red before."

Her smirk is so annoying I feel like punching her in the face.
"Weird bitch!"
"Whore!"

I turn my back, determined to ignore her; Penelope is not going to ruin my night. I take a deep breath, trying to calm myself as I distance myself from her horrifying presence. I shift my attention to the exhibition. My eyes fall on a very specific painting in the center of the anteroom. It's a realistic drawing, half of the face of a blonde child with gray eyes. But it's no ordinary child, it's my sister. Isa.

I move closer to the image almost automatically. The precise and detailed strokes depict my sister's smile with clarity, even capturing the dimples in her cheeks and the little wrinkles around her eyes. I feel as if I could touch her curls if I stretched out my hand. I don't need to read the signature to know that this is a work by Ane.

"She's beautiful, isn't she?" A sweet and familiar voice surprises me. "Forgive me for being late. I couldn't find my shoes, and Jimmy kept insisting we take his car."

"When did you paint this?" I ask.

She opens a bright smile and tosses her blonde hair back. She looks so beautiful in her long cream dress that it's like I'm in the presence of a legitimate daughter of Aphrodite. Her makeup is light and well done, highlighting her lovely pair of green eyes. Her wavy blonde hair is partially pinned back.

"It was yesterday. I found a photo of her at home and thought it fit perfectly with the theme of my exhibition, which is about children."

Some people greet Ane and compliment her. She thanks them and smiles broadly. As soon as we are alone again, she gestures with her chin toward another painting hanging on the wall. It's a protruding belly, a pregnant woman, and it's possible to see the baby inside her.

"It's beautiful, Ane," I say, admiring it.

"Thank you."

The art teacher approaches with some guests to showcase Ane's work, showering her with compliments. My friend blushes as she eloquently explains the concept of her painting.

"Sophia!"

I close my eyes. It can only be a nightmare. I turn to find Phelipe staring at me from a few meters away. He looks so absurdly handsome in a gray shirt, black blazer, and jeans that my mouth involuntarily drops open. Then my eyes fall on the person next to him, and I nearly collapse from shock. He is arm in arm with Ana Catarina, who has a wicked smile as she sees me in a state of embarrassing shock.

"What are you doing here?" I hiss as I approach the two.

"Always so welcoming," he mocks. "As you can see, I came as the escort of this lovely lady."

"I don't see the lady, let alone the lovely one."

My eyes size up Ana Catarina from head to toe; I reluctantly admit to myself that she looks beautiful in a long black dress.

"So delightful..." Phelipe laughs sarcastically. "I would give you the benefit of cursing my date if you hadn't left me hanging yesterday."

I put on my best smile.

"I told you where you should shove your order."

I can see out of the corner of my eye Ane approaching us three, alternating her attention between me, Phelipe, and Ana Catarina, her forehead slightly furrowed. Phelipe's expression upon seeing my best friend is one of absolute astonishment; he can't even disguise it before composing himself, assuming his usual smug smile, but still with surprise in his eyes.

"Sorry. Are we bothering you?" he asks, analyzing the blonde girl with interest.

Ane quickly shakes her head and opens a sweet smile.

"Oh, no. I just came to tell Sophia that the ceremony is about to start so we can sit down. By the way, I'm Ane."

She extends her hand in greeting. Phelipe takes it between his fingers and places a soft kiss there. I glance quickly behind to see if Jimmy caught the scene, but I don't find him. Instead, I see Izec's very serious gaze, watching us. He doesn't seem even a little pleased.

"Phelipe."

"Ane and Sophia are best friends, aren't they, *sweetheart*?" Ana Catarina jibes.

Phelipe raises his eyebrows, looking at her as if she has revealed a big secret. Her cheeks turn a reddish hue.

"Where do you know each other from?" Ane asks curiously before I can say anything, looking from me to Phelipe.

"From many places," he replies, smiling. "I'm new in town."

"New, huh?"

Ane looks at me with concern; I know exactly what she is thinking.

"Can we go in already?" I turn to Ane with pleading eyes. "It must be starting."

Indeed, the anteroom has emptied quite quickly. A disorganized line begins to form in front of the auditorium, under a sign nailed above the doors that reads the name Tom Warner, in honor of his donation for the school's renovation. The auditorium has truly been named after him.

"Let's go," she says, wrapping her arm around my shoulder. "Hey, get in line! No cutting in!" Ane says loudly, using her furious voice.

Automatically, people turn to her and start organizing themselves into neat lines. A smug smile escapes my lips; I love when my friend can intimidate everyone.

But just as we are about to take a step forward, we are stopped by the Art teacher:

"Ane, there are still people wanting to know more about your artwork, dear."

My friend nods, giving me an apologetic look before heading over to where her paintings are. I join the line to enter the auditorium, expecting to see Penélope sneak up on me any minute to get on my nerves, but fortunately, I don't see the flash of the canary-yellow dress anywhere. Mysteriously, every time Phelipe is around, the girl disappears.

I hear my name being called with enthusiasm and turn toward the voice. A boy runs happily in my direction, skillfully dodging people.

"Lucas!" I exclaim, startled.

It's Izec's younger brother. As usual, I'm impressed by the physical resemblance between them: equally tousled bronze-colored hair and brown eyes. I'm surprised to notice how much he has grown.

"You disappeared during the holidays. I missed you," the boy says as he approaches me, a little out of breath from running.

"Oh, it was the rush with organizing the fair," I lie.

Does he still not know that his brother and I broke up?

I spend a lot of time at Jimmy's house with Ane and Izec, and consequently with Lucas. He loves to follow us around and try to chat with us. Izec hates his little brother's meddling, but I kind of like knowing that we attract his interest.

"So, how are you?" he asks.

"I'm great," I reply without thinking much. "So, big night for your brother, huh?"

"He's a bundle of nerves; you should see. He's already cursed everyone out."

"Hmm... better not." I smile. "We should go in or we'll run out of seats."

"I'm waiting for my mom. You can go if you want; I'll see you later."

I nod. Lucas smiles, extending his arm toward me to hug me. When his hand touches my shoulder, the expression on the boy's face changes drastically.

"Lucas, are you okay?" I ask, worried. His skin takes on a strange, greenish hue. "You look like you're going to vomit or something."

"*Sophia...*" He turns to me with a voice that doesn't belong to his body; it's guttural, spine-chilling.

"Lucas, you're scaring me." He grips my arm tightly, digging his nails into my skin. I let out a scream of pain and fear. I try to pull back, take a step back, but the boy seems to possess superhuman strength. Without warning, Phelipe appears at my side, trying to free me from Lucas's grip, but any effort only makes his nails dig deeper into my skin. "You're hurting me."

"*He carries your death, Sophia.*" Again, the supernatural voice escapes from Lucas's lips.

"What?" I stop struggling, concentrating on his words. Phelipe watches him, confused. "What are you talking about?"

"*Your death, Sophia. He is your death..*"

The boy's glassy eyes stare at Phelipe without showing any emotion. I am terrified; I feel that my legs can no longer keep me standing.

"That's enough!" Phelipe growls.

With a swift gesture, he pushes Lucas's hand away from me and positions his body protectively in front of mine. As soon as the contact with my skin is broken, Lucas blinks several times, coming to his senses. He looks confused. The normal color returns to his face.

"What happened? I feel weird," he mumbles. His eyes land on my red arm from the squeeze. "I'm sorry."

He gestures to stroke the injured skin, but Phelipe steps forward and growls, making him retreat immediately. The boy looks as disturbed as I am. He shakes his head before running away from us with teary eyes.

"What was that?" I ask, my voice trembling.

"I have no idea. Are you okay?" Phelipe asks, examining my arm carefully.

"I think so; it'll fade." I point to the red mark. "I'm just scared. Why do things get weird whenever you're around?"

"It's a gift I have."

"Did you hear what he said? About you carrying my death?"

"I heard."

His expression is inscrutable. I feel a chill run through my body, like a bad omen. I've never been superstitious, but I start to consider the idea of demonic possession; I can't find many other options.

My instinct is to run and tell Izec and his family what happened; maybe Lucas needs help, but I hold back. This is not the moment. I try to control my shaking by taking deep breaths.

A few people glance at me sideways. I force a smile so they won't think I'm unwell. It takes me a few seconds to compose myself before returning to the line with Phelipe by my side. Ana Catarina has disappeared.

The auditorium is packed. It's quite spacious, with boxes forming a *u* above our heads and a majestically decorated stage. The principal is still making his speech in front of everyone, and I regret not missing this. We walk down the red carpet, looking for empty seats.

By now, everyone has completely ignored the name plaques, which must be driving Helena crazy. Occasionally, someone greets me, and I respond without really seeing who it is.

I find two empty seats in a row further back and pull Phelipe down. We push past some people before finally managing to sit down. He is staring intently at everything around him, trying to absorb the place.

"So, where's your date?" I ask.

The woman sitting in front of us abruptly turns around and puts her index finger against her lips. Phelipe smiles and leans closer to me.

"She had to warm up for the performance," he whispers.

"I only let you sit with me because I want some answers."

"What makes you think I have any?"

"You know way more than you're letting on. I mean, you're not really saying anything. But you disappeared with the drawing that day, then showed up wanting to talk, and now this death thing. And someone is following me; I already told you. I think you have all the answers to these gaps."

His lips curl with mischief. I frown as I notice something familiar in his face, from the oval shape to the black hair, the narrow eyes, and the smug smile. The smile is so familiar that I feel like my brain has frozen with the obviousness. I have that sensation of missing something that's right in front of me. But I'm sure I've never seen Phelipe before, and I have no idea who he resembles.

"Have you thought that maybe you're just paranoid?"

People stand up and begin to clap enthusiastically. Phelipe and I join them without even knowing what we are applauding. I see Ane gracefully descending the stairs hand in hand with Jimmy, disappearing behind a crowd of people. She has a light and happy expression on her face.

The principal's speech finally ends, kicking off the performances. The dance troupe begins to present a well-synchronized choreography. Ana Catarina and some of her students are right at the front. I have to admit, she's good.

Stealthily, during the performances, I glance sideways and catch Phelipe staring at me with curiosity, but we both remain silent. I have so many questions to ask that I'm trying to formulate them as best I can; something tells me that at this moment, he will dodge all of them. However, I can't ignore the ominous feeling in my chest, the bad omen I feel, the chills that make me shiver from head to toe.

And I can't forget the episode with the out-of-control Lucas. Something very bad is going to happen; even the air seems to whisper that in my ears.

When it's time for Izec and Natália to perform, I stiffen in my seat. If Phelipe notices, he says nothing about it. The bile is hard to swallow.

"You're red," he observes.

"It's hot in here."

I gasp, breathless. It's a blatant lie, given that the air conditioning is set to an arctic temperature. Not understanding why, I nod my head, nervous. My face is burning, my foot shaking frantically.

A piano begins to rise from a platform on stage, slowly revealing its shape. Izec is seated at a bench, his hands resting in his lap, his tuxedo perfectly aligned on his body, and his expression serious and focused. The background lights turn on, and Natália's figure appears just as Izec's agile fingers touch the keys. She looks so beautiful that I feel like crying. Her white dress flows, fluttering over the stage like a cape. And when she parts her lips and her voice escapes, it's so pitch-perfect, high-pitched, and sweet that it seems magical.

My eyes are misty. I don't know if the performance is truly as perfect for everyone as it is for me or if seeing the two of them in sync is too powerful, but I'm holding back firmly to keep from breaking into tears. Every note, every perfectly right tone feels like a slap, and I feel my body shrink, diminishing in the seat while Izec and Natália grow more and more. The voice, louder by the second, fills everything around me, trapping me, suffocating me.

"Are you crying?" Phelipe asks.

I'm so grateful that he said something and brought me back to reality that I involuntarily smile through my tears.

"The music... it's perfect. I always get emotional with music." With my free hand, I gently dry my face so I don't smudge my makeup. I turn to face him and see that he looks amazed while watching me. "Why are you looking at me like that?"

"For no reason," he replies, shrugging. "You look like someone I know."

Suddenly, a loud noise reverberates from somewhere nearby, causing me to jump in my seat and pull away from Phelipe completely.

The music stops immediately.

In a blink, everything turns into chaos.

Everyone is screaming, hastily getting up and starting to run. Phelipe looks alarmed and grips my arm tightly, anchoring me to him. It's then that I see the reason everyone is screaming, crying, and fleeing in a panic. Right at the center of the stage, Natália's white dress turns red; it takes me a moment to realize it's stained with blood. She clutches her neck with her hand before collapsing with a dull thud. Izec jumps to her side, completely terrified, and remains there, petrified.

Someone just shot Natália Campos.

CHAPTER EIGHT

Sophia

I cover my mouth to stifle the scream.
They killed Natália right in front of us. She is still clutching her neck, her body convulsing as blood stains her entire white dress. Izec is kneeling beside her, distraught, his hands completely covered in blood.

Phelipe grabs me by the arm, yanking me to my feet. People are crowding together, desperately trying to flee, but the emergency exit is absurdly small for this chaos.

More gunshots. More screams.

Phelipe pulls me by the arm, heading in the opposite direction of the sea of fleeing people. Exactly toward where the gunshots came from.

"Ane!" I scream, alarmed, remembering that I saw her sitting up front.

Is she hurt? And Izec?

I stop, willing to turn back to try to find my friends. Phelipe gives me such a hard tug on my arm to keep moving that I fall brutally to the ground.

"We have to get out of here!" he growls furiously, dragging me along the floor without giving me a chance to get back up. "They're here! They'll find us."

"What are you talking about?"

I try to free myself from his strong grip, with little success, but he stops long enough for me to get back up. We are approaching the bathrooms. He pushes me into the men's room, and I clutch his arm tightly, desperate to break free. Phelipe doesn't give an inch; he's determined.

With his free hand, he punches the window, shattering it into a thousand pieces. He lifts me off the ground, holding me by the waist as if I were a child. I'm kicking and screaming for him to let me go, but he seems made of stone. None of my movements can stop him. I end up going through the window, trying my best not to cut myself on the broken glass, and I brace myself to avoid falling. It's not high, and luckily my feet hit the ground with a thud. I run off immediately, unsure of what I'm doing, but determined to create a large distance between myself and Phelipe. I'm trembling, completely scared. My head is racing, about to explode. I'm breathing hard. My heart feels like it's going to leap out of my chest at any moment. Everything around me is just a blur.

I look back, expecting to see Phelipe coming through the broken window after me, but he doesn't come. When I look forward again, I collide with someone, nearly losing my balance.

A man grips my elbow tightly, almost breaking my arm in half. He looks at me incredulously. His mouth is a rigid, thin line before he grits his teeth hard and bellows:

"Who are you?!"

CHAPTER NINE

Artur

Something is very wrong. I know this simply by feeling a different weight in the air, a climate of tension in the atmosphere. Something is definitely out of place.

I remain lying on my bed, not moving a muscle as I let my instincts alert me to whatever may be lurking. There is danger; I know it. I can feel something evil, like a spirit of darkness, hovering around me. It's stealing my breath, suffocating me, and clouding my senses. Icy blood flows through my veins.

I hear footsteps coming down the stairs. Three pairs of legs stomping on the hard floor. Three steady breaths. Three hearts beating, one faster than the others.

I sit up in bed, straightening my back. The corridor lights turn on as the rhythmic footsteps reach it. Through the glass of my cell, I can see that, like me, many of my neighbors are awake, looking around in confusion, not understanding what is happening. A break in routine is not common around here.

Their thoughts are confused; I can't understand clearly. I know there are two caregivers carrying a third semi-conscious body. A female body. One of the caregivers is anxiously thinking about when to leave. He is exhausted; he didn't expect an urgency to happen today, after being on duty for almost two days. The other caregiver is lamenting his sore muscles from having to bear the girl's weight. Although she isn't heavy, there was a struggle, and it took several men to subdue her; and he had to drag her for a long time. *But tomorrow she will get what she deserves,* he thinks.

I slide down the mattress, moving closer to the glass of the cell so I can see them as they pass in front of me. I can't show too much curiosity; I have to be as neutral as my neighboring cellmates, who seem merely bothered by the disturbance. But I'm curious; I want to know everything that is happening. I want them to think about what occurred so I can understand. However, the caregivers seem too tired to relive the memories of the incident, and the woman isn't necessarily thinking, although she is conscious.

When they finally approach my cell, I can see the two caregivers in their usual white outfits: a white jumpsuit with a silver stripe at the waist and the omega symbol embroidered on the chest, holster on the belt, properly armed, struggling to drag a body between them. I am dumbfounded.

I thought I would never see that blood-red hair again.

They stop. The cell in front of mine is empty, but they choose to leave it that way. Next to it, there's another cell, where the caregiver with very short black hair, who is exhausted from his shift and can only think about finally lying down next to his wife, presses his thumb on the small monitor. With a familiar clatter, the glass door begins to slide to the right. They shove the woman's body inside the cell without any gentleness, and the other caregiver, with thinning white hair and a large bulge in his belly, presses his thumb on the monitor, causing the door to close quickly. He presses another button, initiating a call.

"Listening," a female voice answers.

The chubby caregiver leans over the intercom.

"Test subject 141 in her cell. Wing B."

There's a second of silence before the woman on the other end responds:

"Okay."

Suddenly, the redhead begins to move, then lunges at the glass with a quick motion. She shows her teeth to the caregivers, groping the glass for an escape. Wild growls erupt from her throat.

The caregivers simply stare at her, bored. They cautiously back away, marching down the corridor. I take a good look at the newcomer, still unable to believe she is back. Her very penetrating green eyes focus on me. I try to find a crack in her mind to discover what brought her back. It's been a long time since her cell was empty. A very long time.

"Viviane," I whisper.

Viviane smiles, enjoying my interest. She looks nothing like the savage who just growled and bared her fangs at her caregivers. That was an act. She is here because she wants to be.

Her smile widens, and she sits on the bed, softly whistling, playing with a strand of her red hair. She is happy; I can feel it. Apparently, things are going just as her cruel mind planned.

The corridor lights go out, and the sound of footsteps going up the stairs fades. A dull thud of a door closing, followed by silence.

I focus my attention on Viviane, and soon I realize she is trying very hard not to think of anything. Covered thoughts.

This is definitely not good.

CHAPTER TEN

Artur

Viviane hasn't slept all day.

And neither have I.

Although she was sedated with a heavy dose to quiet her down and be taken back to her cell by just two caregivers, she fought bravely against the sleep that clouded her mind. Every now and then, she would succumb to the fog in her brain, on the brink of a dream that was about to take her into unconsciousness. But suddenly, with a jolt, she would snap back to reality and stare at me with a mocking smile.

You're not going to steal my secrets today, Artur, she thought at one point during the night. I shrugged; it was only a matter of time. Sooner or later, her mind would give in. But I had to admit, her self-control was enviable.

The siren blares shrill in the early afternoon, waking everyone up. Many groans of complaint echo from the cells near mine. I don't need to use my abilities to know what's going through everyone's minds: anger at the sound of waking and even more anger at it being time to start working.

Viviane gives me one of her best smiles and stretches, lying back on the bed, relaxed. She seems quite confident.

The second siren sounds loudly, echoing through the corridors, and I know I'm late to start getting ready.

All the lined-up cells are made of glass, as if we were trapped in a box. The glass is impenetrable, coated with a layer so protective that none of the efforts we've made in our lives to break it have come close. And believe me, we've tried far too much.

All the cells are the same. A small, suffocating square, with nothing more than a bed in the center. There's a compartment in the lower corner of one wall, where the cleaners place our clothes and food. I lift the metal lid, already expecting to find my usual freshly washed uniform there. There's no privacy in the glass cells, so seeing each other change clothes is already a common occurrence. Although I always feel uncomfortable having to show my intimacies in front of everyone, no one seems to care or actually look at anything beyond themselves. I put on the gray pants and the long-sleeved shirt, followed by the silver vest that protects my chest. It is well-padded and therefore heavy. The black knee-high boots are equally heavy and uncomfortable.

I finish getting dressed just in time for the third siren. The sliding doors make an almost deafening noise, vibrating at the base, and slide open to free us. This is reassuring.

I walk down the corridor in deep silence, closely accompanied by the other test subjects, who also leave their cells wearing uniforms identical to mine. I notice that Viviane hasn't moved from her bed. I can't break the rules and remain still in the face of the warning sirens. No one can. Unless under a specific order, and of course, she has one, as she has been on the run for so long. She can't just return to activities as if nothing has happened. She would be punished, tortured, and interrogated. And I am the only one showing interest in that.

The test subjects don't speak. They communicate with words only in front of the testers or caregivers when necessary. Their thoughts, which I can hear all the time, are mostly wild. They are primitive, raised in cages, and never developed any emotions beyond hunger, anger, and desire. A lot of desire.

However, there are exceptions to the rule, like me and Viviane; long ago, there were others. We managed to think rationally and develop feelings, like any other human being. That's why they all escaped. I am the only one left, although, thanks to my psychic abilities, I know exactly what to do to get out of here.

We are the test subjects. The successful scientific experiments. We are test-tube babies, genetically modified, placed in the world for study. Our biological parents are not nurturing; after all, we are generated by surrogate mothers or altered without the consent of "our mothers," who always die in the process. We are children of science. If we want to survive, we have to obey the laboratory blindly and be useful.

We live caged, without seeing the sunlight or the night or the stars; I have caught the word "subterranean" in the mind of a careless caregiver. We never go out. We have no access to technology, books, calendars, nothing that could give us information about the outside world. We are only released to practice fighting and be tested. This prison makes us creatures of explosive genius. We can't socialize when we are free. The more we destroy our own kind, the more trapped we become.

The only people we see are the caregivers, the testers, and the cleaners. All very "kind." They invade our cages, sedate us forcibly, and conduct tests and examinations without our consent. When we behave differently than they want, we are eliminated without the slightest compassion. We are stronger than they are, but no one dares to threaten them, as they walk armed with a device that, upon penetrating our skin, causes excruciating pain. I speak from experience.

We are deadly machines. We were created to kill. Genetic aberrations generated with only one purpose: to serve them and stay alive, or to challenge them and die. We have no feelings, no desires, except for sexual ones, or dreams. We are professional killers; we learned to kill with our own hands and to hate our superiors' enemies. Any slip-up, any mission unfulfilled is the end. There's no other world for us. Not a single thought passes through our minds of a world where our hands don't end up stained with blood.

I know a lot because I listen too much. Always eager for knowledge, for any detail of the outside world. I know the warmth of the sun only in the memories of other people, just like the light of the stars, smells, tastes, and so many other things. Most of the time, I'm hoping one of our superiors is lost in memories that they might share with me. But those moments are rare, precisely because they know about my abilities. They don't want their test subjects to be capable of feeling anything or knowing an emotion, even if it's through a memory.

I could have escaped. I could have experienced all the sensations I longed to feel for myself. But I've always been afraid of the outside world. I didn't know how to go unnoticed, how not to be easily detected as a genetic aberration. More importantly: I didn't know how not to be killed out there. That's why I want to know so much about Viviane's experiences out there. What did she really find when she escaped to her freedom? I shouldn't call it freedom, since she went after someone else: Phelipe.

I remember all her possessive thoughts regarding him. All her desire, all the resentment and hurt at being left behind when Phelipe didn't hesitate to leave, never thinking of her. Or waiting for her. Viviane wouldn't rest until she had him. And being back means she not only found him but did something extremely bad. She probably took revenge. I'm convinced that she would never have been caught and brought back to her cage unless she really wanted to.

When I arrive at the training room, I notice that something is different: there are many testers scattered around the place, clipboards in hand, sharp analytical gazes. This is abnormal. Usually, they aren't this numerous.

The room is large, completely covered with iron and glass, as seems to be the entire laboratory. There's a door at the back, which I know leads to a corridor filled with other smaller rooms than this one, but serving the same purpose. On the other end, there's another door leading to an infinite number of other rooms, but these are used for psychic testing.

The training room is stocked with many pieces of equipment for us to train our physical skills: strength, agility, and fighting. There are weights, dummies, hanging ropes, a twisting climbing wall, obstacles, and an array of other things. The testers give us separate orders on what they want us to do, then evaluate us closely, prowling around. We cannot stop until ordered to, and usually, we spend the entire day doing the same thing without rest.

The separate rooms are used for us to fight each other while being assessed by a tester. With whom and when I will fight is something I have no control over.

A caregiver orders us to remain lined up. The other test subjects also find the break in routine strange. Why are they acting differently? They are trying to clear their minds to prevent mind readers like me from hearing their thoughts. This is becoming very annoying.

As the line moves forward, I see what they are doing. A caregiver presses a metal object against the surface of a test subject's neck. She flinches as something sharp pierces her skin. I shudder. A tester carefully analyzes her and sticks a label on her uniform. The test subject looks scared, still not understanding, and moves to the other side of the room, where the other subjects who have already been punctured are.

Someone opposes the needle. He growls fiercely and crouches down, about to attack. I can read in his mind that he won't submit to anything else; he is tired. His fangs protrude prominently from his mouth, and his long claws grow wildly. But before he can make any move to tear the testers' throats, as he wishes, he gets shot in the skull. Quick, precise.

A regular bullet would never have taken any of us down. But this is not a regular bullet; it has been modified in the laboratory and contains unknown properties. It is not capable of killing us, but it causes unimaginable pain. The bullet that can kill us is yellow; this one is blue.

As the testers drag the inert body of the test subject, two others start a fight. Something routine. They are fighting fiercely, throwing punches, displaying fangs and claws, while the testers alternate the aim of their weapons, waiting for the perfect moment to shoot with the blue bullet. That's when, unexpectedly, one test subject sinks his teeth into the other. The one being bitten screams in pain, dropping to her knees on the ground. Suddenly, there's an explosion of yellow bullets.

We can kill each other. And since this has become common knowledge, biting has become constant. Just she, of course, isn't capable of killing, but she immobilizes the other immediately due to the pain.

Caregivers drag the bodies. The line begins to move again. When it's my turn, I look fearfully at the metal object in the caregiver's hands. I know what the pain will be like; I've managed to pick it up from the minds of others, but I also know it will be quick. I probe the caregiver's murky thoughts as he pierces my skin, feeling something hard lodged in my neck, and I catch a single word: "tracker." I have no idea what that means. I've never heard that before.

A tester approaches me with a smug smile on her lips. She thinks "very useful" as she looks at me, sticking a green sticker on my chest. I'm led to the line of green stickers. I notice that there are only twelve of us; the others, with red stickers, number over a hundred.

As soon as the line ends, all the test subjects are properly stickered and have the tracker in their necks; we're still twelve. The tester approaches us and gestures for us to follow her. The last thing I see before following her through the door is the test subjects with red stickers biting each other, trying to escape and keep up with us, before another explosion of blue bullets immobilizes them.

The tester smiles harshly, pretending that nothing happened. She should be afraid to lead a pack of crazed, uncontrollable test subjects with explosive tempers, but she seems quite at ease with it. The testers and caregivers try not to show the fear they feel towards us, but it doesn't work with me. Our subspecies is much stronger; we could destroy them without much effort, with just a quick movement of our hands. And they know this. We do too. But we were created to fear them, because the consequences of going against orders are disastrous... and deadly. Not that I take pleasure in living, but something in me fears nonexistence.

I can catch a glimpse of Viviane's face in the tester's memories. She seems pleased with the capture of the woman and looks over her shoulder to evaluate us again. She is anxious. Whatever Viviane has done is related to the green and red stickers today, and the *tracker* in my neck.

In other words, it's not good.

Especially when the testers are in such a good mood.

CHAPTER ELEVEN

Artur

All I want is a shower.

But, although I'm holding a fluffy towel and waiting for my turn in the large showers, I wish I were in a completely normal, human bathroom, where I would be the only naked person, and the water would run warm over my skin, making the steam rise and filling the space with haze. I also wouldn't hear any alarms telling me that my shower time is up or see anyone else using my soap.

I know how human bathrooms work because I've seen them in the memories of the caregivers. Here, the reality is different.

We are many test subjects lined up, waiting our turn to use the various showers hanging side by side. Naked men and women everywhere, not seeming to mind that everyone can see their intimacies. But in truth, no one really looks at each other, except when they're ill-intentioned, like a group of test subjects at the end of the line engaging in sexual acts in front of all of us and the caregivers without caring about the noise.

The truth is that we are free to engage with whoever we want, since we have physical needs stronger than any ordinary human. And that's practically the only interaction we have with each other when we're not fighting or trying to kill each other. I myself have had sex with several people in simpler times. However, since I started thinking rationally and found myself as Artur, not as test subject 138, just being naked in front of everyone, waiting for my turn in the showers, makes me embarrassed. However, I can't make the slightest movement to cover myself since there are caregivers scattered throughout the area — any hint that I'm in control of my mind, thinking like a human, not like a genetically modified chimera created to have no feelings, will lead them to shoot me without hesitation.

The alarm blares sharply, indicating that it's time to switch showers. It's my turn, which makes me happy. The cold water falls on my body, giving me a sense of relief. I'm eager to clean myself.

The tester took us earlier, the twelve green sticker test subjects, to a training room where we were put to duel. I beat all of them. Several times.

Not that I'm an *expert* in fighting; I'm far from being the strongest, but I have the advantage of being able to hear minds. I can foresee their movements in advance, which allows me to rarely get hit. Besides me, there are others with the same ability. Many of them. But I'm much better.

The tester was quite pleased with my performance. I remember her thinking that I would be the best test subject to help them. I couldn't figure out what I would be useful for, nor what happened since Viviane's strange return.

The chimera bathing next to me looks at me strangely. I like the word "embarrass"; it sounds pretty and explanatory. And I think that's exactly what I'm doing; I'm embarrassing myself by feeling her gaze on my genitals. I know what she wants, and although I squirm with the urge to physically satisfy myself, I pretend not to have noticed. Even with her touching me, I need to use all my self-control to close my eyes and appear completely focused on washing myself.

I won't deny it; there was a simpler time. When I was just a chimera acting on impulse, with almost no awareness of anything. I trained, ate, and satisfied myself. As I said, simple. Even though my gift was well-developed back then, I didn't use it much, as I didn't see much importance in another person's thoughts. I wasn't concerned with what the testers, caregivers, and cleaners planned for us or with the outside world and its unknown wonders. I just acted like the animal I was created to be.

And then she appeared.

I didn't give her much credit at the time; I remember thinking she was just another caregiver. My mistake.

She was more than that. Much more.

When I saw her walking down the corridor towards the cells, I should have noticed that there was something different about that caregiver. She seemed happy to be working there, unlike the others, with her mind full of memories, colors, scents, flavors... She made no effort to cover her thoughts.

She was radiant, polite, and good-humored. She didn't treat us like pathetic animals. She always smiled beautifully, lighting up everything around her and tried to talk to us. She told us what she was going to do, why she would do it, if it would hurt or not. Usually, the caregivers invade our cells without showing any reaction or mentioning a word about what they are going to do. They simply jab us to conduct tests, draw blood, cut us, or pierce our skin. If we don't cooperate, we are tied up or drugged mercilessly. But the new caregiver wasn't like that. She was attentive to the smallest details, doing everything carefully and in the most comfortable way possible. She looked into our eyes and smiled. Always.

I had never had contact with any other human being. I knew nothing of the outside world, of what existed beyond the walls surrounding me, of why we were different. I was born and raised in the laboratory, like any of the chimeras. My childhood wasn't much different from the life I lead now. I trained day after day, was cut, pierced, and drugged without my consent, plus I had lessons until I was sixteen. That's how I learned to read, write, and calculate. But today I know it was only the basics, nothing that could instruct us too much. They don't want us to be stupid, so they taught us the minimum. The only thing they don't want us to know is how to develop emotions. And locking us up is the most wrong way to achieve that.

They probably have no idea that, just like physical needs, a test subject's emotions are much stronger and more uncontrolled than human ones.

At that time when the new caregiver had just arrived, there were no empty cells around me. In front of me was 139, who would later become Phelipe. Right next to him was Viviane, in the same cell to which she has now returned.

I don't know why Phelipe sparked such interest in the caregiver. I rummaged through his mind for a long time and never got a concrete answer. It was like magic: as soon as her eyes landed on him, there was an instant connection. It wasn't much different from what I felt when I saw her. There's no denying it; she was irreparably beautiful with her long brown hair that looked like silk, very dark eyes, and slightly tanned skin. I had never seen a skin tone like that, since down here in the underground, without the slightest contact with the sun, we are very pale.

I remember perfectly when it all started. The fear that Phelipe initially had with the strange friendliness of the woman. He looked at her suspiciously, huddled in a corner, never bothering to respond to any of her questions. And she talked to everyone. She told us things about the outside world, about the experiments they were conducting on us, made observations about our appearances, and occasionally offered a gentle touch. The other test subjects didn't seem very interested in the gentle caregiver. They ignored her as if she were just another one; however, they showed more trust when she calmly handled the needle against their skin.

I don't know when Phelipe began to trust her enough for his shoulders to relax every time he saw her enter his cell. It was as sudden as the woman's interest in him. I just know that, one day, he began to nod in response to everything he was asked, and then I could hear his voice and his laughter.

I think the laughter was the spark that ignited Viviane's curiosity, since we had never heard laughter before. I heard in the thoughts of the red-haired girl that she wanted to laugh like that. Not just that; she wanted to be looked at with the same devotion that Phelipe had for the caregiver, she envied that sparkle in his pupils, the goofy smile, and the expression of reverence on his face. But she didn't want that from just anyone. In fact, Viviane *needed* Phelipe, and only him, to want her that way.

There were other test subjects paying attention as well, but they remained silent, like Viviane and me. The caregiver also seemed to know this, considering how she treated us.

One day, the new caregiver noticed me. I remember the exact moment her eyes landed on me and recognized my interest in everything she said to Phelipe. And it was when she flashed the biggest smile that I knew I wanted to see her smile just for me.

"How do you feel?" she asked as soon as the glass door of my cell slid open and her slender body entered the room.

It was the first time she addressed me directly. She always talked to everyone, but she was really just babbling to the four corners, not expecting any replies. This time was different; there was eye contact, and she actually waited for me to say something.

"Good." My voice sounded strange to my ears due to disuse.

"Great, because today we're going to do some tough tests. Oh, come on, no long faces. It's going to be fun, 138."

I took a deep breath, calming myself. Her presence stirred strange sensations in my body, ones I had no control over. Once, I heard in her thoughts that she referred to these emotions as butterflies in the stomach, which I found quite absurd but terribly fitting.

"Hmm..." She seemed to hesitate. "You know what? I hate having to refer to you by numbers. I think it's time you all had names, like regular people. What do you say?"

"I don't know many," I replied, uncertain.

"Lucky for you, I do." She placed her hands on her hips. "How about I tell you the names I think suit you, and if you like one, just let me know." I nodded, completely fascinated by her smile. "You are so sweet!" She moved closer to me, squatting down to bring her face close to mine. I felt her sweet breath, her equally intoxicating scent, and eagerly heard the beats of her heart. I didn't flinch when she reached out and gently stroked my hair. "I like your hair like this. Curly. Like a little angel."

From the confusion on my face, she immediately knew that I didn't know what a little angel was. When she closed her eyes, smiling, I could see in her focused mind the image of a child with curly blonde hair and white wings sprouting from her back.

Her very black eyes opened to me, playfully blinking several times before she parted her pink lips and said:

"Artur." I liked the name right away; it was simple, short, and sounded just as good to me as hers did in my mouth. There was a growl of protest coming from another cell. She turned, stepping back immediately. "Don't be so possessive, Phelipe," the new caregiver said. The man on the other side of the glass looked shocked at being called something other than a number. "And you... Viviane." Although the red-haired girl had never said a word, she knew she was being addressed. Viviane shrank back, frightened, averting her green eyes that were usually fixed on Phelipe. "Because you're strong, empowered, and it fits your personality."

Even in different cells, I read in the girl's mind that she liked the name; she repeated it several times to savor it. A hint of a smile crossed her lips for the first time.

That's when I realized that a smile was contagious.

The siren sounds sharply, waking me from my daydreams. With a soft sigh, I step out of the shower, making way for another. As I grab my towel, I see that the woman who showed interest in me during the bath has already found what she wanted. I dry myself quickly and put on the light gray clothes they set aside for me.

When everyone is clean, we are led back to our respective cells, but as I approach my corridor, I know something is happening.

It's Viviane.

Whatever she did has left her in a precarious situation. She was probably interrogated for a long time by the caregivers and, for that reason, didn't attend training. She must not have cooperated much, as she was punished. The oxygen in her cell was cut off; not just sealed, but sucked away to another place. A huge sucker, located on the floor, sucks all the air out of the chamber, causing the girl to writhe in agony, her lungs struggling to breathe. Her skin is red, veins prominent, and her eyes bulging from their sockets. This won't kill her; I know. I've seen it happen to many others, and I've felt the excruciating pain through their memories. As soon as her chimera heart begins to fail, which can take a long time, they will stop the sucker long enough for her to catch her breath before passing out.

It's the first time, since she arrived, that she can't fight to hide her thoughts. When I catch an image in her mind, I hesitate at the door to my cell. The caregiver behind me automatically puts his hand on the gun at his holster, imagining that I will rebel. But I don't, obviously. I wait for the glass door to slide open and enter as always, obedient.

But I'm scared. It can't be.

Why is the face of our former caregiver in Viviane's mind? Is she still alive? It can't be.

Images explode in my head like the shots of blue bullets. I see Viviane watching her from afar. The other girl is standing on the street with a bunch of papers in hand. I don't know what it means. Viewed from this angle, the woman doesn't look like our caregiver. They are identical, but there's a different sparkle in her black eyes, a few more freckles splattered across her nose, a scent, and a voice that shouldn't belong to that body. I notice it, and so does Viviane. If they are the same person, why are they different? Can there be two physically identical human beings with years of difference?

The image blurs, and then I see Phelipe and her talking somewhere in the outside world. He looks extremely nervous, with his heart racing, as he receives a paper from her. I can feel the anger that Viviane felt watching them, crouched behind a tree.

There's no more doubt that they are different people. Viviane has been spying on her for a long time, watching her wake up, sleep, talk, leave home... live. Phelipe also seems to know, but he is too interested in this mystery and displays the same unhealthy fascination for that face. He doesn't even feel Viviane's presence spying on him closely. Even so, Viviane doesn't care that she's not the same woman; she wants her dead, can't stand Phelipe's fanatical eyes on her. She hates that face so much it hurts. And that's why she runs, fleeing far away, planting dreams in the girl's head, nightmares in which Viviane kills her in disturbing ways to let her know there will be no escape. No one will take Phelipe away from her. Never.

She has already killed so many people who got too close to him, all who dared to come too near. Why hasn't she killed this stupid girl whose face is the same as the only first woman he ever loved?

That's why she willingly surrendered to the laboratory, pretending to have been cornered when in reality she came of her own accord. To provide all the necessary information: exactly where

Phelipe is and with whom. Thus, he will be dragged back to his cell, where they will live locked up, but with the full certainty that no one else will be there but her. And the girl will be murdered. The laboratory will not seek differences; they hate that face as much as Viviane does.

After some time, following the day the caregiver gave us names, she vanished. Inexplicably. On an ordinary day, she didn't show up, and in the days that followed, it was the same. Phelipe became furious, completely beside himself, not knowing what had happened. Viviane tried to calm him down, but it didn't work. I tried to listen to the thoughts of the other caregivers, but, as always, they were well hidden. Until, weeks later, she returned one night in an unconventional manner, outside her working hours and without her uniform. She looked thinner, worn out, and terribly frightened as she headed towards Phelipe's cell.

"It's not safe." Those were her first words. "They're after me."

I heard her mind more than her voice because it was there that she addressed me directly, showing me in memories that they had discovered how she had been treating us and how we had been behaving in front of the security cameras. Because before we had merely been caged animals, then we started to talk, display reactions, and show emotions. They were furious and, above all, fearful that we might rebel due to everything she had taught us. There are no methods to fire someone who works in the laboratory. Everyone knows too much, so they can't just piece things together and leave, pretending they will never tell anyone what they saw there. When she entered, she knew that. They repeated many times that any slip-up would be enough for her to pay with her life. She hadn't cared about that at the time, as she never imagined she would love a creature like us. But she loved very much; the chimeras were the most important thing in her life. She had delved so deeply into the subject that she ended up knowing more than any other caregiver. They knew that. Therefore, they planned her execution.

She had escaped and was safe. To enter, she had to turn off the security cameras and break thousands of rules. She knew every inch of this place; she knew exactly how everything worked. It took days of preparation to manage to get in. After succeeding, she wanted us to know how to escape.

I remember being so shocked at the time that I had an unexpected reaction of opening my mouth and just standing there. A caregiver teaching us how to escape captivity. There was so much she wanted to tell, so much information she had discovered. Especially regarding Phelipe. She hadn't chosen that name by chance; it was his real name. He had a family, two brothers who were also test subjects and were trapped here. They were the only ones, unlike us, who hadn't been born from surrogate mothers; they had biological parents, had records with a first and last name. But she didn't have time to explain; she needed to escape soon. She pleaded in tears that Phelipe run away and meet her at the designated place. She wanted me to go too.

And that's when, for the first time, Viviane displayed a true reaction. She didn't just stay in the corner, huddled, watching. She howled too loudly, making the glass of the cells tremble with her rage at realizing that the woman would take Phelipe away from her. Her hatred was so strong it flooded me in a way I never imagined possible. I had never felt such an overwhelming emotion.

Then the caregiver fled without saying another word, avoiding being caught by the others after the scandal that Viviane had deliberately caused. Days later, Phelipe was gone, followed by Viviane and two other test subjects.

I never left; I stayed here all this time thinking about what had happened to them outside. From Viviane's hatred, I deduced that

Phelipe hadn't stayed with the caregiver: she was certainly dead, murdered by the chimera.

Reading Viviane's mind now, as I see her writhing in her agonizing lack of air, I see that's exactly what she did. She killed the woman I fell in love with after learning her memories. It was she who showed me, through her mind, the brightness of the outside light, the warmth of the sun touching her face, the hot water from the shower running over her naked body, or the rain washing through her silky hair. I loved her memories; I was fascinated by her mind, by the way she saw the world. She had been my eyes, my ears, and my touch. I still clearly remember how I felt when I witnessed her memory of a kiss; for many nights, I secretly wished I could touch her lips like that man had.

Viviane killed her. I believe Phelipe never found her outside. But, some time later, he found the other girl, the copy. And Viviane will kill her too.

I lie down in deep mourning, feeling for the first time in my life my eyes burn; it's the same feeling the girl had when she appeared here in the middle of the night asking us to escape. The same excruciating pain in my chest.

All I have left is to think of her name, the sweet taste of the pleasant sensation it brings to my lips.

Sofia.

CHAPTER TWELVE

Artur

"Point to which image is correct," the tester orders, holding three different figures in her hands.

I'm lying in one of the training rooms with my wrists and ankles bound by thick iron shackles fixed to the gurney. I could easily break them and free myself. They know this, but the intention isn't to immobilize us, but rather to ensure a few seconds of advantage to grab a weapon if one of us tries to attack.

There are many cables attached to the top of my forehead, directly linked to a monitor. This device picks up brain waves when I listen to someone's thoughts. Only reverberations are displayed, like a cardiac exam, but this is due to the fact that they haven't yet managed to create a machine capable of decoding thoughts.

I point to the yellow square drawn on the sheet that the tester is holding because that's the image she is thinking about. She smiles, proud. I control the impulse to roll my eyes, a human habit that I admire.

I see her place the figures on the metal table in the corner of the room and pick up a red ball that was there. She extends it in my direction.

"Move this."

Now I need to concentrate. My forehead furrows with the effort. All I have to do is feel the object within my mind, just as I feel the thoughts of others, but for me, it's very difficult.

After twenty minutes, my head is starting to ache, and all I've managed is to push the red ball back three centimeters.

When we undergo the mutation process, our minds expand, allowing us to develop any psychic abilities. However, each seems to have more aptitude in one specific ability; the better one excels in it, the worse they perform in others. For example: I am by far the greatest mind reader among the test subjects. The testers also know this. While my cellmates hear only a few scattered words and see blurry images, I not only hear everything clearly but can also allow anyone — genetically modified or not — access to my mind.

I discovered this when Sofia was still working here. At that time, I was so eager to have a private conversation with her that my brain provided me with an unexpected solution. I will never forget how her eyes welled up when she realized I could hear her mind. The smile that crossed her face was more beautiful than any memory of the starry sky I have ever seen.

The tester looks at me with curiosity. She is thinking of a better way to communicate with me, choosing each word with her usual condescension towards my rationality.

"Can you understand me when I speak verbally, 138?"

I control the impulse to exhale all at once. I nod once with my head. It's the first time she has referred to me with the word "you."

"You are one of the best *organisms* we have." Much friendlier than calling me a test subject. "Your psychic and intellectual capacity is superior. We consider you fit to become a guardian."

I watch all the effort she makes to choose her words. I know what a guardian means: it's the new class they want to create, a superior caste that sparks the interest of test subjects to strive for such merit.

"A guardian will be able to use all of your abilities on specified missions in the outside world. Do you understand?"

I nod again.

"You will be able to go on a sanctioned expedition with other similarly trained organisms on behalf of the laboratory, to carry out a task. And you will be quite rewarded for it."

The many tubes connected to me are bothering me. My wrists and ankles are sweating in the restraints. There's a face lingering in her thoughts, one she struggles to keep hidden. It's a handsome man, not too young, radiating power. I'm sure I've never seen him, but I dare say he's one of our superiors; quite close to how I imagine they are.

"There are some *lost ones* that need to be *rescued*." She leans over my gurney, her eyes locked onto mine deeply, almost as if she wants to hypnotize me. As she says this, a flash of Phelipe's face and the other runaway chimeras spark in her mind, as does Viviane. I hold my breath. "And some traitors that need to be annihilated."

I can swear my heart stops beating. Seeing Sofia's face, even if it's her copy, associated with death makes my chest ache in a way I've never known. My body begins to tremble involuntarily. The tester notices and goes on high alert. I take a deep breath to calm myself.

"Do you think you can do this? You will be tested closely and watched more intensely. No slip-ups will be forgiven."

Again, the face of the powerful man lingers in her thoughts. He is synonymous with "being tested closely and watched more intensely." She also has reasons to fear, as none of the testers will be forgiven for any failures.

I look deep into her eyes and do the thing that is probably the most foolish I have ever done: I agree. Her smile in response is one of contentment, but to me, it represents something else: death. I know I will make many mistakes, going against everything they want me to do. However, I can't miss the chance to see Sofia one more time.

CHAPTER THIRTEEN

Artur

I feel more trapped than ever.

I once learned, when I was younger and receiving lessons, that people in the outside world kept wild animals like us in cages so they could admire them without being attacked. I thought it was something they invented to make us fear escape, but through Sofia's memories, I discovered that this place is very real and has a strange name: zoo.

That's exactly how I feel: caged. My arms are glued behind my back, causing the chains to pull at my ankles. My genetically modified animal half wants to break the chains that bind me and link my feet to my wrists. The other test subjects also seem uncomfortable.

There are twelve of us in total. The twelve who received green stickers in the test. We jolt together in two vans; one of the goals of the trip is certainly not comfort.

Before we entered the van, we took a trip on a vehicle called a private jet with the caregivers and testers. It was extremely unpleasant; I trembled in fear just thinking that I wasn't on solid ground. I had never known what a private jet was until I picked it up from the thoughts of my superiors. Seconds before getting on, when I discovered it flew, I nearly cried for real for the first time. The other test subjects felt equally terrified.

As soon as we returned to solid ground, the vehicles were already waiting for us. It was the first time I had seen one in person, and I wanted to have time to admire it. But before any of us could get in, the man I saw in the tester's mind and assumed was one of our superiors appeared, causing our caregivers and testers to bow. I was right about him. He is by far the most powerful and influential of all.

I remember his boastful thoughts as he saw his test subjects for the first time in the flesh. He was supposed to have seen us before, but our many mutation failures, like aggressive temperaments, excessive hunger, and the ability to kill, had prevented him from getting close.

He is a prestigious politician and, as soon as he takes office, which will be soon, he will use his laboratory experiences to create an unprecedented dictatorship. I don't know what a dictatorship truly is, but the word sends a strange chill down my spine. I presume it's not good from the cruel thoughts that pass through the minds of the creators.

Today, he will see up close what we are capable of doing.

"Good, very good," he said after appraising us with eyes shining with some kind of sick excitement.

His name is Tom Warner.

The van jolts again, pulling me from my thoughts. I nearly fall to the floor. Damn chain! Finally, it gives one last jolt before parking. The caregivers seated in front get out first. The other *organisms* and I wait in silence. They are all apprehensive.

The door swings open with a bang, and the first thing I see is a weak beam of light, although the brightness is strong enough to make me squint my eyes. I don't care about the tester's facial expression when she starts to pull me by the chain or the panic in the eyes of my companions or the nervousness of the caregivers. The only thing I focus on is the sight of the starry sky. The moon is full in the sky, with a clear, pearlescent light. How many times have I imagined seeing it with my own eyes?

It's the first time I see the outside world. The journey from my cell to the jet and then to the van was made inside a completely sealed wooden box. And I was a bit groggy from the injections administered to me; there was no chance for me to even look for a crack to try to snoop.

I'm in ecstasy with everything I see, the bright colors of the sky, the streetlights, the loud noises coming from the other vehicles and from other people. And the thousands of smells swirling around me. All of it makes me dizzy.

The testers are giving us new instructions, but I don't hear them. I look around, marveling at all the bright, noisy chaos that is the city. There's a smell I can't exactly pinpoint; it seems to come from everywhere at once; it makes my insides churn with hunger. A different hunger, one I have never experienced before.

A school, the tester is saying, is where we need to go. I would have been excited about the idea of visiting a real school. But I'm *dumbfounded*. I almost smile at the thought of that word, which had never made much sense to me. Until now.

That's also why no *organism* has tried to escape yet. First, because they fear the yellow bullets located in the guns of our caregivers. Second, because they are scared of the world around us.

I can't contain my curious gaze, darting in every direction. I don't need to pretend I'm not interested or act cautiously. The other test subjects are a mix of fear and confusion as they admire the place they are in. There are many vehicles parked around us, of various models and colors. My urge is to approach each one of them and try to catalog them in my memory to differentiate them later. The space is open; it seems designed to accommodate cars. I wonder why we are in the farthest part, away from the large building that seems to be the epicenter of some event. People are moving about, getting out of vehicles in long, strange clothes, shoes that seem balanced on spikes; I can't understand how the women wearing them don't bleed from their feet, but everyone rushes into the building.

Why aren't we going in there too?

Instead, we are at the edge of the *courtyard*. I discover this word in the mind of a hurried girl, who thinks about how late she is and curses her boyfriend for parking so far from the entrance. Her boyfriend has a date with another girl and doesn't want to be seen getting out of the car with her, as he lied about having broken up.

The jargon is hard to understand; after all, what does *breaking up* mean?

Trees sway beside me, and a branch even pokes me. Is this path between the trees a forest?

It's horrible not to know anything.

The caregivers pull my arm, forcing me to focus on them. Someone grabs me by the shoulders. I'm at a loss as something metallic and cold closes around my neck. What is this?

I touch the object, feeling its circular shape around my neck. I try to tear it off, but I can't. I see that the other test subjects are also wearing them. A tester mocks my confusion in his mind. *Finally, they're on a leash,* he thinks.

But what is a leash?

The testers are showing us pictures of the people we need to capture: a female test subject, whom I've seen before; Phelipe, which is obviously no surprise to me; and the copy of Sofia.

In fact, the photo is of the original Sofia, but since they are naturally identical, they will know how to identify her. My heart tightens. I feel stupid for getting attached to someone I don't even know simply because she resembles a girl I shouldn't have liked in the first place.

As I weigh the extent of my idiocy for agreeing to this assassination mission, a song begins to play in the distance. It's so beautiful and sweet that even the caregivers pay attention. A feminine voice sounds hypnotically around me. It's the first time I've heard someone sing like this, accompanied by an instrument. The other test subjects, I notice in shock, seem equally captivated by the sound. I want to close my eyes and follow the voice. I have never felt so calm and light in my entire life.

But suddenly, just like the beginning of the beautiful melody, a gunshot rings out.

I've lived with that sound my whole life, so I recognize it and feel scared. I look at the test subjects beside me, waiting to see which one is down and possibly dead. Only when I see the pale, startled faces of our superiors do I realize that the shot didn't come from them. It came from inside the building, causing the woman to stop singing.

Up to this point, I smell that familiar scent. I don't know if it comes from my nostrils or from the thoughts of the other test subjects, who also feel it.

Blood. Flesh. Food.

Before I realize it, my fangs are already bared, and I'm running. My cellmates are too. The caregivers and testers are screaming desperately among themselves, trying to follow us, but I can barely hear them now. They will never catch us; they are foolish, weak humans compared to the mutant beasts they created.

This is the smell I had sensed from the start: flesh.

Our superiors were clever enough to appear near us fully covered in their jumpsuits and often wearing helmets to mask the smell. But the humans of the outside world don't have that concern. They walk around with much exposed skin, and from what I sense, some different perfumes. But the blood is unmistakable; it enhances the fragrance of the flesh.

Hunger blinds me. My animal instinct possesses me so thoroughly that I can't even hear thoughts.

People are screaming and shoving at the building doors, wanting to get out. They are surprised by animalistic beasts leaping with magnificent precision, sinking their fangs into any exposed piece of skin. More screams echo as, with sudden movements, the test subjects dismember and gut the humans before they can react. Blood everywhere.

I need to feed, so I leap into the midst of the chaos of dismembered bodies. Someone tries to hit me, but it's so ridiculously weak that I smile. The man who punched me lets out a shrill scream at the sight of my smile, with my long canines exposed. He will be my victim.

"It's the son of the devil!" he screams, stepping back a few paces.

"Of science, actually."

I crouch in an attack position, balancing on the tips of my toes before leaping onto the man's throat. He falls to the ground still screaming and thrashing uselessly beneath me. His body stops fighting as soon as I sever his head with my teeth. His flesh completely separates from the bones. I discover it's much more delicious to eat directly from the kill, unlike the pieces of dead meat given to me in my cell. The blood that splatters in my mouth enhances the flavor and makes everything better. And there's no denying the pleasure of immobilizing the victim by pouncing on them as they try to fight back. I even have an erection.

After licking the bones clean, I'm still not satisfied. I doubt I can keep this banquet of bloodied people writhing to escape our reach. Is that why they don't let us leave the laboratory? Do they know we will never be satisfied?

I'm already holding a woman by her wrists when I hear a buzzing near my ear. Yellow bullets. I flinch. They're shooting at us. Instinctively, I go on high alert, to the point of forgetting to hold my prey, who runs as far away from me as possible. I dodge a bullet.

The other test subjects also notice the attack and gradually take up defensive positions.

Suddenly, one test subject starts to tremble and collapses to the ground. Her claws scrape around her neck, trying to tear off the collar. I see her eyes rolling back in her head, thin foam dripping from her bloodied mouth. Electric shock. That's what the collar is.

When another one falls to the ground, clutching their throat and having a spasm, I automatically run behind the building, away from the bullets and the electronic device that, when activated, releases shocks through the collars.

I notice for the first time that my gray shirt is completely destroyed, covered in blood and scratches. I am slowly coming back to myself. My dilated pupils are returning to normal, my fangs retracting, as do my claws. The overwhelming hunger seems to have taken a pause; the instinct now is survival. How long will it take for the collar to activate and for me to collapse to the ground? The testers will come to collect my body and kill me.

The mission was a failure.

Some people are fleeing through the back. Everything is a chaotic mess of screams and pushing. The thoughts of many people echo in my head at the same time, making it throb. I can't hear anything. All these voices weaken me and leave me almost blind. I feel like my temples are about to explode.

How do I disconnect from all this?! I want to roar.

That's when I see her. My eyes are almost closing, my knees buckling under the pressure in my skull. But that face awakens me. It makes me bury those voices deep in the recesses of my subconscious and take control of my body.

She runs desperately, looking back. She's afraid someone will follow her. Only her thoughts are inside me now.

I advance towards her, grabbing her by the elbow. She startles.

"Who are you?" That's really the question I want to ask since the moment I saw her in Viviane's mind.

"Get your hands off me!" she screams. I can read the panic in her black eyes as she looks at my bloodied features and clothes. It's so easy to hold her under my grip that it doesn't even feel like she's struggling with all her might to break free from me. "I'm warning you, you better let me go, or I..."

"Or what? What do you think you can do against me if you can't even free yourself from my hand?" In an impulse I didn't foresee in her mind, the girl leans over me and gathers all the saliva in her mouth before spitting it in my face. Right in my eye. "Very well, then. It's going to be the hard way."

I wipe my face with the back of my free hand. Then I throw her over my shoulder against her will and start running. I feel her punches and kicks and wonder if this is a joke. How can they be so weak? It feels like tickling.

I search for a place to hide us, which is difficult since there's chaos everywhere and we are in an open courtyard. Many people are hiding behind cars, which is out of the question, the most ridiculous hiding place I've ever seen. I decide to try my luck in the woods. Or whatever that pile of trees and tall bushes is.

The girl is curled up with her eyes closed in the face of my speed. Her stomach contracts, and she wonders how out of her mind she must be to imagine such rapid movement. I venture into the brush until I find a satisfactory and clear place to stop. I believe I'm far enough away not to be captured by the caregivers and testers.

I put her on the ground. She's ready to scream at me and hurl the offensive words I've spent all these years reading in the caregivers' minds. But as soon as she steadies herself, her head spins, forcing her to lean against a tree. Her stomach gives a spasm before expelling a jet of questionable odor from her mouth.

I watch her, cursing myself inwardly for thinking about what the hell I'm doing. I've just tied the last knot in my noose.

When she recovers and her stomach gives her a reprieve, she looks in my direction with her deeply black eyes. I'm sure I've never seen anything so beautiful. It resembles the night sky. Her hair is loose, a bit messy in a wild and even sensual way. The dress fits her body perfectly. The blood from my victim is on her shoulders and clothes due to contact with my body. It's impossible not to find her attractive.

"You're beautiful," I say without thinking.

She rolls her eyes, and I feel strange... almost offended.

"So why did you bring me here? To kill me? You should have spared the trouble of going this far."

"I won't hurt you," I reply too quickly. The truth is I don't know how close I can get to her without wanting to dismember her. My animal instinct seems under control in the face of my curiosity and fascination. But for how long? Her scent is absurdly good. "I just want to know who you are." I manage to catch a name in her head. *Sophia*. I smile before reining myself in. "Sophia. It's a beautiful name; I should have guessed."

"How do you know my name?"

She takes a step back, looking at me in horror.

"I just heard it in your mind."

"What?!" The incredulous scream echoes among the trees, making me look around, alarmed. "Are you sick?"

"I can't explain it to you."

I step closer to her. My fingers are restless, wanting to feel the softness of her hair or the velvety feel of her skin. But Sophia steps back another pace, pressing her back against a tree. She's trembling, her hands extended toward me in a gesture that asks me to stay where I am. I freeze in place.

Why is she so afraid of me? I don't want to hurt her. But then I see myself through her eyes, covered in blood, with tears in my shirt. My superhuman strength and speed aren't admirable... they are feared. I'm a monster.

I lower my guard, feeling my cheeks heat up. I didn't want her to feel that way.

"Why did you bring me here? What are you?" she asks in a faltering voice.

I can hear the restless thoughts in her mind as she plans how to escape, considering the possibility that I would lose her in the trees. We stare at each other for a long second before I reply:

"You can't escape. I would find you even with my eyes closed." She swallows hard. "I could smell you even if we were on opposite sides of this forest."

"This isn't a forest; it's the vacant lot behind the school," she says quickly, as if the explanation spares her from an evil. I am that evil. I have no idea what a vacant lot is. "Is it really in my head? Ho-how is that possible?"

"Yes, and I can't explain it to you. I know few things, actually," I finish softly.

"Go away!" she suddenly shouts. She needs all her courage to step away from the tree and confront me. "What do you want?"

"I don't know exactly. I shouldn't be here," I admit. Sophia nods. "They came after you. They will kill you."

She stops crying, her face filled with shock.

"Who wants to kill me? Why?" she whispers, her voice weak.

I feel when chills run through her body.

"You look like *her*. — I see another memory in her mind: Phelipe. He told her she looked like someone he knew. — Phelipe." Her face turns incredibly pale. She's scared of my ability to hear her thoughts. "Where is he? Do they want to kill him too."

"Do-do you know him? Who are you?" she stutters. Her black eyes are so wide they almost pop out of their sockets. I can hear the irregular pounding of her heart. It's a fascinating sound. "Why are you all covered in blood?"

"I was hungry. I had to feed." I've never seen, in all my life, a more terrified expression than Sophia's. Her skin takes on a greenish hue, and she's about to throw up again. "But don't worry, I'm in control."

"My God, what kind of sadistic monster are you? What are you?"

Not able to bear another second, I move closer to her. She protests, but there's no escaping me. With my arms, I corner her against the tree.

"Artur. My name is Artur."

"Get away from me, *Artur*," she growls, trembling all over.

My name sounds like something poisonous on her lips. I barely feel her pushes. From where I'm standing, I can feel her warm breath. The sweet aroma of her skin is practically intoxicating.

I weave my fingers into her hair, bringing it to my nose. The scent is good. Sweet. I close my eyes, completely dominated, and smile. Then I feel the impact. I immediately open my eyes. Sophia just slapped me across the face.

"Don't get hurt, Artur. It's not the first time you don't get the girl." A voice echoes behind me.

I should have noticed her presence earlier, but I was so engrossed with Sophia that I abandoned my state of alert. She gasps in front of me, I don't know if relieved or terrified. Then I turn around.

"Phelipe," I snarl through clenched teeth.

He smiles. He leans casually against a tree with his arms crossed. The last time I saw him, he was locked in the cell in front of me before he ran off after the woman I *liked*. Now, she's dead.

"I should say it's a pleasure, but you know me well. I'm not lying." Calmly, he brushes off a leaf that fell on his coat before walking towards me. "I think no one explained to you the basic human rules. Never steal a companion from an old friend."

"She's not your *companion*," I growl.

Sophia remains still, alternating her gaze between us. Phelipe stands at a safe distance.

"Sorry, is she yours then?" He raises his eyebrows. "Seems you were making quite the advance. Far be it from me to interrupt; continue. That slap represents the lady's high level of interest." I crouch in an attack position. I won't tolerate Phelipe's arrogance this time. Because of him, Sophia is dead, and now he thinks he has some ownership over the copy too? "Don't be pathetic, Artur. My jacket is new, and I don't want to ruin it by having to kill you. Just get out of my way and go."

But before I can leap and immobilize him, I feel a searing pain in my neck. Damn collar. My knees give way, and I collapse to the ground, with no control over my body.

Sophia screams somewhere; I can't see.

The pain tints my vision red. I feel like my organs are dissolving. I bite my tongue so hard I could rip it out at any moment.

"Don't touch him," Phelipe says. "He's getting an electric shock."

"Phelipe..." I don't know if my voice comes out right. I clench my teeth in my mouth, preventing them from chattering. I can't see him. "They...." The pain intensifies. "They are... here. They will...." I let out a howl of agony. "They will kill you!"

"How did they find you?" he asks in a serious tone.

I don't know how long I'll remain conscious before I pass out. I scratch at the collar fiercely, trying to pull it off, but I can't even locate my neck. My nails dig into the dry earth.

"Viviane..." I gasp for breath. "She was... caught."

"She let herself get caught to rat me out? Just nod your head."

I nod, or I think I do. It feels like my flesh is pulling away from my body.

"I-I have... a... tracke..."

"Tracker?" he asks urgently. I shake my head. "Shit! I need to get her out of here. They will come for you."

"Help..."

"No!" he growls. "You're a dead man, Artur. I'll see you in hell."

"Take it off!" I gather strength to scream. I don't know if they're still around. "Please!"

I imagine I'm pointing at the collar. There's no response. I start shouting again, begging for them to help me, but I think Phelipe is already gone.

What a beautiful way to die. For so long, I avoided escaping the laboratory for fear I wouldn't survive in the outside world... And here I am, drooling in agony, with my face buried in the dirt, waiting for the merciful yellow bullet.

Alone while Phelipe runs off again with the girl.

It's a beautiful way to die. It's all I think about before everything goes dark.

CHAPTER FOURTEEN

Sophia

It's quick. Fast as lightning.

My last memories are of watching Artur's body convulsing before I am brutally thrown against a tree.

In an atomically fast moment, my feet stop touching the ground, and I find myself being hurled. I feel the palms of my hands scrape against the trunk, trying to absorb the impact of the fall. My body hits the tree, and I roll to the side, coming to a stop when I collide with the ground.

I open my eyes as soon as I feel my body become still. My head rests, dizzy, on the scraped palms of my hands. In front of me, I can't see anything clearly. There are flickering black gaps that leave my vision dark and blurry. The dirt on my face prevents my eyes from staying open due to the stinging.

I try to get up, propping myself on my elbows. But as soon as I sit up, trying to rise slowly, I'm hurled away again.

This time, I feel it. Something sharp enters my skin, piercing the flesh of my neck, and lifts me into the air. Then, I'm thrown away again.

I don't have the same luck. My head hits a tree with such force that I become blind and deaf for a few seconds. I feel something sticky running down my forehead. Blood.

I open my eyes, reluctant. What actually happened? Who threw me away?

In the clearing where we are, I hear roars. Animal sounds that make the hair on my body stand on end. I sit up, ignoring the dizziness and the darkness that clouds my vision. I'm expecting to see a wild feline approaching me, but all I see is Phelipe fighting against two other men, whom I swear I have never seen in my life.

One of them suddenly turns and looks at my forehead. Mechanically, he abandons the blow he's about to land on Phelipe and advances toward me, baring his enormous canines. I panic and recoil, not really having anywhere to retreat. His eyes are just two vertical slits, like the pupils of a cat. I can only cover my face with my hands, fearing what's to come. This horrendous creature is about to gut me alive with its fangs, its corpse-like breath puffing in my face, but Phelipe miraculously appears and, with a quick and decisive swipe at the monster's neck, decapitates it. Its skull hits the tree next to me before rolling to the ground and coming to rest near my feet. Its eyes are still open and frightened, its fangs still bared, and its pupils dilated.

I never thought I could let out such a piercing scream in my life. My throat feels like it's been ripped apart.

Phelipe gives me an inscrutable look before turning his back and kicking the chest of the other creature that was planning an attack from behind him. He brings the creature down to the ground and climbs on top of it. I hear an awful shriek of pain, deafening enough to burst eardrums, before another head is sent flying away from the body.

My body begins to tremble in fear. What are they? Why are they after me?

Phelipe kneels beside Artur's lifeless body. I brace myself to hear that unforgettable sound of decapitation when I see him with his hands around Artur's neck, but all he does is tear off that metal collar. Something in Phelipe's hard expression tells me that the contact with the electric shock hurt much more than he can bear.

Artur sits up immediately, looking around, disoriented.

"I hope you still want to help. We have a lot of guinea pig asses to kick," Phelipe says.

"Is there a better way to spend my last minutes of life?" Artur tries to sound firm but seems sad. "It looks like you've already gotten rid of a few."

"How many are there in total?"

"Eleven."

Artur runs a hand through his curly hair, then turns to me. Just like with the first beast, his eyes widen at the sight of my bloodied forehead. I automatically cover it with my hand, feeling the flow coming from there is intense. My eyes are loaded with pleading; if Artur can really hear my thoughts, he knows the panic I'm feeling.

Blood runs freely down my neck and collarbone. I remember something piercing my skin, perhaps a knife or blade, although no one there seems to have a blade.

"Phelipe..." Artur growls through clenched teeth.

He digs his nails into the ground; the pain is visible on his face due to the effort he makes to remain still, with his brown eyes fixed on my head, the pupils beginning to dilate.

"Better behave, Count Dracula, or you'll say hello to your headless friends."

Phelipe's expression is calm but focused.

My injury has little effect on him, to say none. Whether they are the same creature or not, I don't know. Although Phelipe is equally strong and fast, like the other *guinea pigs*, as he said, he still doesn't seem like a cannibal like Artur and the others.

"I can't..."

Artur's nails dig deeper into the ground, his jaw so clenched it seems ready to snap in half.

"Breathe through your mouth," Phelipe growls impatiently, punctuating each word.

Then he calmly walks over to me, taking off his leather jacket and extending it in my direction.

"Cover yourself," he commands in a cold, distant voice, like his eyes; he seems like an absent stepfather dealing with his bratty stepdaughter.

Only then do I notice that my dress is torn. My heel is also broken. I rip off the sandals while keeping my eyes fixed on Artur and his internal battle, and I finish tearing the red fabric.

Phelipe squats down next to Artur again, yanking his shirt over his head. He doesn't protest, not taking his eyes off my forehead for an instant. I lean against the base of the tree to stand up. Phelipe moves closer, but this time he doesn't extend the shirt to me. Without my consent, he brushes my hair aside and examines the wound on my neck. Deep, grotesque. Whatever cut me has penetrated deeply into my skin.

His fingers touch my forehead, pushing the sticky, wet hair away. He wipes the blood from my face with Artur's shirt before pressing it against my neck to staunch the wound.

When our eyes meet, all I can think about is one thing: death.

The words Lucas said to me minutes before the world exploded into chaos come back to my mind: "he carries your death."

It would be ironic at the very least if it weren't tragic that Phelipe just saved my life.

"They're coming!" Artur roars desperately. My heart skips a beat, and I grip the bandage around my neck tightly, ready to run at any moment. "Get her out of here now."

"How many?" Phelipe asks.

"Does it matter? Just get out of here. I'll hold them off." The two exchange a tense look before Artur's attention shifts completely back to me. Suddenly, he offers me a weak smile. "The kid was wrong, Sophia. He doesn't carry your death; he is your death. Now go, I have some asses to kick. I'll see you in hell."

CHAPTER FIFTEEN

Sophia

I'm throwing up again.

I don't know if it's because Phelipe ran too fast or if I was already nauseous beforehand. Maybe witnessing decapitations isn't good for my digestive system.

I vomit once more. There's nothing left to come out but saliva and bile. I wipe my mouth with the back of my hand and try to focus on my breathing, containing the nausea. Inhale. Exhale. Inhale. Exhale.

Sweat and blood stain my face. I let my back slide down the wall of some random house, forcing my knees down until I sit on the sidewalk. We're in a deserted street, a completely residential area of the city. By my calculations, far enough from the school not to be detected, yet close enough to leave Phelipe restless, kicking the curb. We only stopped because I asked. If we hadn't taken this break, I would have vomited all over him — not that the idea completely displease me.

"Now that the *milady* has finished politely disposing of everything she ingested, including the fries from lunch, can we leave? If it's not too much trouble, of course," he mocks, impatient.

"What the hell just happened? Who are we running from, and what the hell kind of grotesque creature are you?" My voice sounds more irritated than apprehensive, and I'm surprised that I'm able to ask anything.

"It's a beautiful story, truly moving, that I'll dedicate myself to sharing with you later. Now, if you don't mind..."

He extends his hand toward me. I give him a disdainful look, ignoring his outstretched arm, and push against the wall to get up. Suddenly, I realize a possibility and freeze, scared.

"Can you get into my mind too?"

The idea that someone has accessed my deepest thoughts bothers me. My head should be a safe place, where I can stew over all kinds of subjects and relive my intimate memories without anyone knowing. Or so I thought until Artur said all my unspoken words to my face.

"No, I can't." Phelipe seems ready to say something disdainful but holds back at the last second. "Can we go already, or do I have to throw you over my shoulder against your will again?" No, we're not going anywhere until I know who or what we're running from. My day has turned into a mess since the moment Lucas bizarrely prophesied my death. "Come on, Sophia, we don't have time for this."

I dodge his quick hand that is about to grab me forcefully at the last second.

"What are you?"

I stumble out, trying to keep a significant distance between us, but not far enough that he can't answer me. Phelipe stares at me, annoyed. Before he can say a single word, his head lifts as if he has been summoned, and he looks down the street. I can't see anything but darkness, but whatever is hiding there triggers the boy's alert mode.

He crosses the distance between us with a speed my eyes can't follow. My heart races with fright.

"Sophia, pay attention. Run away now," he whispers in my ear. Why is he whispering? "Don't say anything; they can hear us. I need you to get out of here and hide, or I won't be able to protect you. I'll find you as soon as it's over."

I'm about to question what he intends to do, but Phelipe raises an eyebrow suggestively, and I gasp silently in understanding. He's going to rip off more heads of cannibal beasts.

I stumble out, gathering the rest of my strength to run as fast as I can. I turn the first corner, cursing myself for never having practiced a sport and not learning how to run properly. Just a few meters and I'm already gasping, feeling cramps in my stomach.

"What the hell!" I curse softly and cover my mouth.

"They can hear us," Phelipe warned.

I'm about to stop to catch my breath when I hear loud growls echoing around me. My spine chills. I stumble out, running the best I can. The important thing is not to stop and increase the distance between me and these *creatures*. I still can't think of an appropriate word to describe them.

I can hear the sounds of the busy part of the city not far from here. A few more streets and I'll be in a well-lit area, full of shops, bars, and nightclubs that are still operating because it's a Saturday. I hope to find a police patrol on the street to ask for help. I feel a slight relief beginning to grow in my chest.

But this lasts only a moment, as I soon realize that I am being followed. I can hear footsteps on the sidewalk, following me. My stomach drops inside me and the pounding of my heart closes my throat. I don't know if it's just in my mind, but the temperature seems to drop. I hug my body tighter, forcing myself not to look back. The blood runs so fast in my veins that it produces a deafening sound. My eyes are so glazed over that I can't see.

I curse, hating myself for being so weak; who can't even run properly?! My pursuer is just walking; the distance between us isn't increasing.

I gather all my courage to look over my shoulder. Somewhere deep in my mind, I believe I'll see a familiar face, a safe one, even Phelipe. Or Artur, even if reluctantly. But I see a figure just a few meters away; it's a man I've never seen before, his jaw clenched. There's something deadly in his face that sends a wave of chills through my body. A silver collar shines around his neck.

I keep running, determined to reach the busy area before he catches me. I can feel his eyes burning into my back.

I know he'll follow me, but still, I hope he doesn't get close. I cross the street, turning right at the first corner that appears. Quickly, I notice — with a pang of relief, like someone who has been trapped underwater and can finally return to the surface — that the man didn't follow me. Maybe he was just a citizen or a local resident, and my fear-damaged brain idealized him as a potential serial killer.

But my relief turns to shock again in less than half a second. As soon as I turn my head forward, I come face to face with the man. Panic rises in my throat and a supernatural cold liquefies all my organs. He smiles crookedly upon noticing my despair.

If he's as much faster than me as I think he is, if he's yet another one of the creatures Phelipe is trying to decapitate, why isn't he attacking me right away? Why play with his prey, like cat and mouse? Maybe the psychological terror of the victim is the most interesting part of the game. Can he also hear my thoughts?

I think about retreating, going back to the previous street, or just continuing to run. But I can't move; I'm frozen in place. Waiting for someone to attack you is never the best option. However, I don't have that much courage to take the first step.

A car suddenly appears behind me, honking frantically for me to get out of the way. This seems to have piqued the interest of the man, who watches the vehicle as if he has never seen one before. I notice that the driver keeps honking and cursing. He begins to flash his headlights wildly, and finally, I take a deep breath, determined to move. This is not the time to be paralyzed by fear. I must take advantage of my pursuer's distraction and use it to my advantage.

Before I can move, the lights go out, and everything goes dark faster than my eyes can keep up. I look around, confirming the lack of light. I squint to try to see something close to me, but there's nothing to see. Everything is pitch black, a terrible darkness.

The persistent driver, still distant, stops honking like a madman. I hope he gets out of the car and personally comes to tell me all the curse words, but nothing happens. I stand in silence, waiting for some noise from the car or the bizarre man in front of me. Nothing.

The voices of the city have completely silenced. There's no indication that there's a living soul around me. The bars, shops, restaurants, all the commercial establishments in the city are dead. The buildings and houses are in absolute silence.

Something is terribly wrong.

I start to walk, stumbling over my own feet. I hesitate, afraid of bumping into my pursuer as I weakly walk down the street. But there are no signs of cars. They're all paralyzed, barely parked, as if the drivers had fainted at the wheel.

I trip on the curb and barely manage to keep from falling to the ground. My mind spins in the darkness. The emptiness and dark send shivers down my spine. My body trembles with panic and cold. I feel my toes freezing against the icy ground.

It's then that I hear the low growl of my pursuer by my ear, almost like a muffled laugh, enjoying the game he has created. I am the target. I blindly shove him, feeling as if I just tried to push a rock.

I run toward the grumpy driver; I would kick him out of the car if I had to. All I want is to drive as far away as I can. For a moment, I feel satisfied for the first time that my father was crazy enough to teach me how to drive when I was just twelve years old.

I fumble for the door, trying to open it. Just before I can, something happens.

CHAPTER SIXTEEN

Sophia

Nothing is so bad that it can't get worse. I should have considered the possibility.

There isn't just one pursuer lurking in the shadows. There are three.

I can count the number of legs when I'm thrown forcefully to the ground. My cheek slams hard against the asphalt, and I taste blood in my mouth as my face is crushed by the impact.

Apparently, they got tired of playing with their prey. The game must have become boring.

I try to dig my nails into the ground, but they only scrape, and some even break from the friction. I'm dragged by my hair and forced to stand against my will. Many strands are ripped out with the brutality of the motion, and my scalp protests. I try to punch someone in the face, but all I manage is to hurt my knuckles, as if I had punched a brick.

"Let me go!" I manage to say, but my voice is a barely audible whisper, faltering and dying in the silence that fills the air.

I'm thrown against the side of a car. I raise my palms to defend myself in a completely foolish act. Three figures advance on me. They are close enough for me to see them in the dark. They move like robots, preparing to attack me now that they've cornered me.

The only woman among them stares at me with paralyzed eyes, as if she were hypnotized. The other sniffs the air like an animal, revealing his teeth to me in an attempt at a smile, moistening his lips as he gazes at the blood on my arm. They smell of sewage and rotting flesh. Their teeth are large, sharp, and protruding against their lips, which are stained with blood and exude a putrid odor.

I try not to look at them. I try not to smell them. It's almost impossible. My stomach churns, my body succumbs to fatigue, and I'm nearly surrendering, almost giving my weak and feeble body over to these bloodthirsty creatures that seem intent on devouring my soul.

I force myself to close my eyes. I don't need to see this.

It takes the time of one breath and two irregular beats of my heart until I hear an unusual sound. I open my eyes wide just in time to see a headless body fall onto me. I scream and push it away.

"You're welcome," Phelipe growls sarcastically.

There's a ferocity in his gaze as he turns to the other two creatures, who roar at him furiously. It's admirable how he fights; his body spins and jumps as if he were dancing, his expression focused, dangerous, and deadly. It seems as though he has received a blessing from Ares. But no, Phelipe is far from being a demigod. He is a demon.

Without the slightest ceremony, he drives his hand into the woman's chest and rips out her heart. The organ still pulses in his bloodied fingers after the body hits the ground. My eyes nearly pop out of their sockets.

Phelipe is about to attack the other beast, but suddenly it lunges forward, spitting blood on his face. Its lifeless body falls to the ground. I'm wondering what just happened, how this *thing* could have died without anyone touching it.

Phelipe turns to me and curses under his breath. I don't see the fierce, murderous expression that always overwhelms his face when the test subjects approach; I only see irritation that makes him huff.

There's someone else here.

Then she approaches, entering my line of sight.

Penelope. Still in her canary-yellow dress, with her curls perfectly styled and wearing Louboutin heels, the usual ironic smile on her lips.

But that smile is familiar. They are the same lips, the same white teeth, the same irony, the same face shape, the rounded chin... My God, it can't be!

I'm still paralyzed with the horror of the sudden realization.

"Did you miss me, little brother?" She confirms my suspicion.

CHAPTER SEVENTEEN

Sophia

I am in shock. My jaw drops from my face, my eyes are so wide open that they begin to burn.

Siblings? Damn! That's what I've been trying to process all this time. The familiarity I felt in Phelipe's face, which I didn't understand where it came from. How did I not notice before? That damn devilish smile! They have the same face shape, the same black hair color, although Penélope's is voluminous and full of curls, and her brother's is completely straight. Her skin, although tanned, is lighter than his naturally indigenous color. There are similarities, but there are also obvious differences, which made it hard for me to grasp the relationship right away. But now, with them side by side, it's impossible not to be certain.

Penélope directs her cat-like smile at me, licking her lips.

"Sophia, I would say you look awful, but... let's be honest, I think you already know that," she mocks, giving me a wink.

Even the sarcasm in her voice is the same.

"What the hell are you doing here?" Phelipe hisses, asking exactly what I want to know.

"Oh, little brother!" she dramatizes, tossing her head back. She lets out a long sigh before smiling at him. "I've always been here. I've been very busy. You know how it is; school consumed a lot of my time. I had a really tough Physics exam. By the way, Sophia, you got a 3.5. I'm really upset that you didn't notice me before, Phelipe. I guess you were too busy playing cat and mouse with Sophia to notice my presence. As always."

Then I remember the day at the bar, which now seems like it was years ago. Penélope looked at me as if she had seen a ghost, or so I thought. In fact, it wasn't me who scared her and made her disappear into thin air. It was her brother talking to me and too distracted to notice her in the crowd.

That explains her disappearance hours earlier, in the auditorium's waiting room. She vanished minutes before Phelipe appeared.

"That's a lie," the boy growls. There's an evident irritation in his eyes, a frustrated anger more than a fierce one. "I would have smelled you."

"Would you really?" She raises an eyebrow. "You get so obsessed when you're near her. You didn't even notice my approach while you two were grappling like rabbits. And what bad taste, I must point out, little brother! I preferred that chatty blonde from Copacabana. Potentially problematic, maybe. But she was pretty."

"You're bluffing!" Phelipe roars, not caring if anyone can hear us. "You can't have been following me all this time."

"Oh, please!" She rolls her eyes, sneering. "I have more important things to do than follow you in your pathetic, monotonous life. Sometimes, I would take a peek, yes, I won't deny it. And I wasn't the only one. Do you know what happened to the chatty blonde? She wasn't avoiding you. Viviane killed her."

Phelipe lunges at his sister, gripping her neck with his strong hand. His teeth are bared. He's so angry that growls come from his throat. Penélope, in turn, remains with her mask of irony and fullness. Her brother's attack should have taken her down, but apparently, she's as strong as he is.

"Argh! You and your explosive temper. Do you really think you're subtle? That you erase all traces so you aren't followed? Wake up. Viviane and I have been laughing at your face for years, and you didn't even notice." In a swift motion, she twists his arm and kicks his leg hard, knocking him face down on the ground. Calmly, she drives her black Louboutin heel into his neck. She steps down so hard that blood runs down Phelipe's neck. "If you lay your hands on me again, I'll rip your balls off."

I'm staring at her, mouth agape, unable to move, still pressed against the post. I knew she was crazy. But a freak? When I saw those bloodthirsty creatures strong enough to crush my bones with a light grip and fast enough that my eyes couldn't follow their movements, it never crossed my mind that Penélope, in all her designer splendor, could be like them. To me, she's just a spoiled, mean girl from school. Like Ana Catarina. God, and to think I considered her a heartbroken ex-girlfriend of Phelipe...

I had just thought there wouldn't be anyone more lethal than Phelipe and his blows. He seemed almost a god of fighting. But, considering how easily his sister took him down, I was terribly mistaken.

She removes her shoe and wipes the bloodied heel on his shirt. The boy crawls away from her before getting up from the ground. There are no words to describe the furious expression on his face.

"How pleasant, I should have guessed that you and Viviane had joined your evil forces," he sneers in a guttural voice full of hate. "So, what's the plan? Torture and kill Sophia? Then hand me over to the lab?"

"Frankly, little brother. Do you think I would team up with a jerk like Viviane?" Penélope seems offended. "As I said, it's boring wandering through this world without much to do. Every now and then, I would stop to peek at you, to see if you were doing something interesting that was worth my time. But all you did was crawl into the bed of some pathetic girl before Viviane killed her. And many times, you didn't even notice."

Penélope smiles devilishly. Phelipe growls low, closing his eyes and throwing his head back. Is there really a lunatic psychopath who kills all the women Phelipe gets involved with? Does that make me a target? My God! Things are starting to make some sense.

"What do you want, Penélope?" Phelipe asks, opening his eyes to stare at her. "Kill her?"

I hate how they refer to me as if I'm not here, but I'm so paralyzed that it really feels like I don't exist.

"If I wanted her dead, she'd already be dead." The attention of both falls on me. I'm so static that I seem to have merged with the post. I hold my breath as the girl tosses her hair back and walks elegantly toward me. The brother frowns when he sees her wrap an arm around my shoulders casually. "I've been watching Sophia in the only place you never thought of: at school. You should have seen it, little brother. We were in the same class and everything. We even shared a boyfriend."

The boy's eyes roll from his sister's ironic face to mine, pale.

"Shouldn't we be running?" My voice comes out weak, almost a whisper.

Phelipe crosses his arms and squints.

"You wouldn't be here if there were the slightest possibility of any risk. And since no hungry lab rats have shown up so far, I suppose I've taken care of the situation," he deduces, raising an eyebrow with visible suspicion.

Penélope hops, cheerful, gliding away from me. I brace myself defensively under my jacket.

"Thanks for reminding me, little brother." She looks at the black watch on her wrist. "Just a little longer now. Five, four, three, two, one and..."*kaboom*!

Before the devilish smile can fully form on her wicked face, there's an explosion. Or several, I can't tell. In the darkness, flames flicker in the distance, licking the black sky. Piercing screams are heard. People are burning in the place where Phelipe and I were just minutes before I ran off and was attacked.

"Y-you blew them up? All of them?" Her brother looks as dumbfounded as I feel as he stares at her.

"Didn't you hear the *kaboom*?"

Suddenly, brightness blinds my vision. The city lights turn on. The post I'm leaning against crackles a bit before illuminating my head. Voices echo around me again, as if there hadn't been an interruption. The music playing in a distant bar resumes from where the song had stopped.

What the hell is happening?

"Well, it seems I killed someone important," Penélope says, staring at the lit surroundings.

"What did you do?!" Phelipe thunders, gripping her firmly by the arm. "At what cost did you save us?"

She pulls away from him and shoots him a look of pure warning.

"Can we get back to this? It's not the first time *today* that I've saved your asses. Who do you think alerted you to leave the auditorium?"

Alerted? I'm replaying the scene again. Phelipe and I sitting, watching the presentations. Izec and Natália on stage... There wasn't an alert. In fact, we left because...

"You!" I scream, finally moving toward her, incredulous. I point my index finger at her face. I'm so nauseated by the understanding that I have to clench my jaw tightly to avoid throwing up. "You shot Natália! She's dead because of you!"

I want so badly to rip the damn contemptuous smile off her face that I'm about to leap at her. And she just looks me up and down, assessing my stance of hatred.

"Oh, frankly. Don't come acting like a good Samaritan now, Sophia. You didn't even like her."

"That doesn't mean I wanted her dead! An innocent person died, and you, you despicable bitch..."

"Two will die if you keep pointing that finger at me."

I clench my fist with all the strength I have, gathering momentum to hit her nose, but Phelipe immobilizes me, holding my arms behind me. It's so quick that it takes me seconds to comprehend. I try to break free and scream at the top of my lungs for him to let me go, but he remains unyielding. I can feel his rigid body pressed against my back.

"Don't be dramatic. Look: outside the school, the lab rats and their superiors were planning to kill you two. I needed to create a distraction that would make the lab rats abandon their plan altogether. In other words, I needed something bloody. And, of course, I had to get my little brother's attention, who was too busy dealing with his teenage hormones to sniff a hand's breadth in front of his nose. The plan was for you to flee far away while I blew everything up. I didn't imagine that Artur would rob you in the process. I should have foreseen that."

"That's the stupidest plan I've ever heard. You killed Natália to create a distraction? That's..."

"Who did you want to die? Izec?" she interrupts, narrowing her eyes at me. Phelipe continues to hold me tightly. The mention of my ex-boyfriend's name makes me squirm desperately, trying to free myself to hit her. "There were only two people on stage to serve as easy and notable targets. I chose by affinity. And also, Miss Perfect had been getting on my nerves for a long time."

"How did you blow them all up? It wasn't just the lab rats, it seems," Phelipe questions, huffing over my hair.

His body is tense, pressed against my spine. I can feel the movements of his chest rising and falling as he breathes. I don't need to look at him to know how angry he is.

"Explosives in the cars. I love human technological evolution." She claps, bouncing. "They were so disoriented by the lab rats' massacre that they didn't notice me rolling under their cars and placing the bombs. The other lab rats I had to hunt and kill myself. Manual and boring work."

"You killed all those lab rats by yourself?" he asks, incredulous.

"And without showing my panties." She winks at me, running her fingers over her immaculate canary-yellow dress. Mine is in tatters. "But I have to admit, against that group of three lab rats you cowardly fled from, little brother, I had help. I was busy activating the bombs. In fact, my help should have been back by now."

"Who would be stupid enough to help you?" I ask with disgust.

She looks at me provocatively, tousling her black curls. Phelipe's hands grip my wrists even tighter. He growls low.

"Artur," he murmurs through clenched teeth.

"I recognize a pretty ass when I see one." Penélope smiles wickedly. "Who would've thought, after all this time, and he still hates you, little brother. But he wanted to help me. For old times' sake." I don't need much effort to understand all the implications. Artur and her? My stomach churns at just the thought. By the noise her brother makes, he's as disgusted as I am. "Speaking of good sex..." she practically croons. "What took you so long, Artur?"

Artur enters my line of sight, looking a bit breathless. His arms and bare chest are bloody, and his pants are in a sorry state. He skids to a halt before getting too close. His brown eyes sweep everything around us before landing on me. I see him wrinkle his nose and exhale through his mouth. Penélope rolls her eyes in disdain. Phelipe's shoulders relax a little.

"We have a problem, folks."

CHAPTER EIGHTEEN

Sophia

"Well, I knew I shouldn't have left the pigs in charge of important things," Penélope grumbles, irritated. "What did you let slip, stupid thing?"

Artur remains with his eyes glued to my forehead. His fists are clenched at his sides, his jaw tight. I'm staring back at him, frightened. I thought he'd be dead by now. Knowing that he hears my thoughts bothers me.

"You didn't blow them all up." Penélope opens her mouth to argue, but Phelipe silences her with a hand gesture. She looks at him in irritation. "Besides the vans, there were cars with caretakers who kept their distance from all the commotion, just watching. But now they're going to counterattack. I saw them while I was killing the other chimeras."

The three exchange tense glances, a mutual understanding settling in. I'm the only one who doesn't seem to grasp what's happening. Phelipe releases me completely, positioning himself between me and Artur. I clear my throat.

"Who did you see?" I ask so quietly that I fear I wasn't heard.

Of course, he heard, not just through my mouth but through my mind as well.

"Tom Warner," he replies with more difficulty, and I believe it's because of my proximity.

Phelipe's shoulders tense up. Penélope rolls her eyes.

"The presidential candidate? What?" I'm incredulous.

He was supposed to give a speech during the ceremony, but since I didn't see him sitting anywhere, I thought he would make a grand entrance at the end of the presentations, as Ana Catarina suggested. But what the hell does he have to do with all these bizarre things that have happened?

"Now isn't the time for answers," the girl scoffs. I can barely look at her. All I want is to crush her with my own hands. "We better get out of here before... Shit!"

I don't know what's happening; everyone moves so quickly that I can't keep up. I'm pushed back behind Phelipe again, trapped in the center of a circle, between the backs of the three. Artur looks the most tense.

I'm confused, looking in all directions when I finally hear the sound of cars coming from both sides of the street, surrounding us. I gasp, panicking. Artur looks at me over his shoulder.

Before the black vehicles park, the doors swing open abruptly. Armed people jump out of the cars, dressed in a kind of uniform and white helmets.

A dance begins, and I clearly am not ready to dance. The men in white start shooting from all directions, forcing everyone to move away from me. They move like blurs in front of me, dodging bullets. They are *literally* dodging bullets.

I'm an obvious target, standing in the middle of the street, still processing what's happening.

The cars don't stop after emptying out. The drivers accelerate, coming straight at me. I run blindly, jumping at the last second before being run over.

Phelipe and Penélope are trying to get closer to the shooters, probably to kill them. Artur is the one closest to me, dodging the shots but keeping an eye on my movements.

But something feels wrong. Why aren't they shooting at me? I could never dodge; I'm as easy to hit as an inanimate object. But no one seems to want to hit me. Surround, yes. Kill, no.

The cars finally stop, and more people jump out of them. Penélope and Phelipe have already managed to kill a few of them. Artur too. He jumps, rolls, dodges, and lands a hit. Given how easily they fall, and the blood that spills onto the street, I know they are human. They are massacring humans.

The certainty only solidifies after I see Artur sink his teeth into one of their arms and rip it off with extreme ease. I let out a scream.

Phelipe and Penélope have grabbed the weapons that fell to the ground and are returning fire. It should be easier for them, but it isn't. It's hard to shoot and dodge bullets at the same time. The humans are outnumbering us.

They try to surround me. From their stances, I deduce that they are men. Three. I've never learned to fight, and that hasn't mattered until now. I'm cornered. Shit!

I dodge an arm that tries to pull me in. Perhaps I have the advantage of being quick due to my smaller size. However, I don't have much time to think as they keep trying to grab me. I weave and dodge as fast as I can. The other three seem to be having trouble, unable to come to my aid.

I act on impulse. In the movies I've seen, the weakest girl manages to defeat the opponent with a surprise element. They don't expect her to attack until she has already done so. I'm relatively thin, so my bony elbows and knees can be used to hurt.

I move closer, ready to knee the one closest to me. Before I make any move, he punches me in the face. The impact makes me stumble backward. My face throbs where I was hit. Another one takes advantage of my weakness and grabs my arms behind me, immobilizing me.

My first attempt at a fight is completely thwarted. I didn't even get the chance to land a single blow. They drag me toward a car. I kick, squirm, and try to bite... all in vain.

I should be able to trust the humans. Flee the murderous beasts and join them, since they have weapons and are trying to kill them. But if these two cars escaped Penélope's bombs, it's a sign that they were involved with the other lab rats that came with Artur. They aren't trustworthy.

Someone steps out of the black minivan. I was so stunned that I didn't even notice the vehicle's size. That explains the number of humans that jumped out. There are two minivans.

The man waiting for me is the only one not wearing a white uniform and helmet. On the contrary, he's dressed in an elegant suit, perfectly tailored to his body. The two uniformed men next to him seem tense, weapons at the ready, prepared to attack. But he doesn't. He looks at me, fascinated, with a smug smile forming on his lips.

My blood runs cold in my veins. I recognize his face from the pamphlets I handed out with Helena and from the ones I saw Penélope scribbling on. "The man of the people," my mother said.

Well, that's not exactly what he looks like.

"Tom Warner," I whisper, incredulous.

There's something in his expression that frightens me more than Artur's fangs. Something sickly, sadistic, and terribly proud. Even more so when he seems to devour every inch of my body with his thirsty eyes, as if I were a canary being dragged into the mouth of a cat.

The reason they spared my life isn't good. I scratch and struggle, trying to escape. Before I can get any closer, Artur and Phelipe appear to my total relief. They push away the men holding me, forcing them to let go, and engage in battle. The uniformed men guarding Tom Warner leap into the fray, ready to shoot.

Tom doesn't seem scared by the attack nor does he fear for his safety. On the contrary, he continues to look at me disturbingly, his smile tripling in size.

"Sophia..." he says melodically. His eyes roam over every inch of my body, as if they could devour me. I instinctively shrink back. "What do you have that attracts so many men?"

What is he talking about?

Whatever it is, I won't stay to listen. I run, seeing the image of Penélope in front of me practically dancing against the bullets. Before I can get closer, I feel a strong tug at my scalp. Tears of pain spring to my eyes. Someone is dragging me by my hair, pulling me back to Tom Warner.

Hell! I can't even react to the pain I feel. I try to scratch the hand that holds me, but the protective glove of the uniform prevents me from getting anywhere.

I see Artur kick at the air, striking the man's head and sending him flying. My hair is released, and I fall to the ground along with the uniformed man's pistol. My knees slam against the asphalt. Artur extends his hand to me.

Tom is furious. His nostrils flare, and he pulls a gun from his waistband. I struggle to get up, ignoring Artur's outstretched arm. The politician takes firm steps toward us, ready to shoot. And this time at me.

Phelipe is still fighting against the other uniformed men who surrounded me, and so is Penélope. It's just Tom, Artur, and me now. The difference is that I don't know how to dodge bullets.

When Tom's lips purse into a thin line, his dark eyes narrowed, aiming, I know he's about to shoot. Instinctively, I close my eyes when I hear the shot. I feel something burning on my arm. I've been hit.

My back hits the ground, and there's a weight on top of me. I open my eyes. Artur has pushed me down and is lying on top of me, using his body as a shield. He groans and curls up with each shot he takes in the back.

"How lovely!" Tom laughs, stopping his fire. "The monster using his life to protect the damsel. So poetic."

Artur's forehead is resting on mine, and he keeps his eyes closed, his jaw clenched, his body covering every inch of me. My breath blows on his face. His expression is pained. I feel something sticky and warm running down my belly, and I know it's his blood.

Of all things, what scares me the most is that Artur has given his body to protect mine.

"You'd give your worthless life to save hers, freak?" Tom asks, this time closer.

I can see his feet in my limited field of vision. He shoots again, and Artur curls up, his face twisted in a grimace. More shots. How long will he hold on?

I look around desperately, searching for a way to get us out of this situation. Phelipe is still engaged in his own battles, and Penélope doesn't seem to be anywhere in sight.

Then I see the gun still lying beside me. I stretch my arm to try to reach it, and the movement causes Artur to open his eyes, astonished. He knows what I'm thinking.

I feel the cold metal against my fingers and pull it close to me. I've never shot a gun before; my aim certainly isn't the best, but I don't have time to formulate a plan. I just grip the gun and aim in the direction where I see the politician's feet. A second of pure hesitation and nervousness. I pull the trigger.

The gun jolts in my hand, causing even more pain in my wounded arm. The sound of the shot is clear in my ears. So is Tom's scream.

Artur rolls off me, falling backward onto the ground with a low whimper. I can see the damage I've caused: Tom Warner bent over himself, clutching his bloody thigh. He howls in pain, tears streaming down his face, his skin a scarlet hue. The bullet that hit him isn't ordinary.

He looks at me with rising hatred before trying to lift his gun in my direction. I shoot again purely on instinct, hitting his hand that's holding his leg. The gun jolts, hitting my face. I see Tom fall back, still howling in pain.

His men stop fighting and shooting at Phelipe, rushing to his aid. They are desperate, hurriedly carrying him into the minivan, but not before our eyes meet. Mine are filled with panic, fear, and hesitation. His are filled with fury. He spits on the ground without breaking eye contact, as if marking the spot. I know what it means.

Revenge.

CHAPTER NINETEEN

Sophia

Phelipe was shot. Just when he crouched down beside Artur to try to help, I think. There was a buzzing of a bullet in my ears and a growl of pain. His hands grip the injured rib.

The minivans start up, and we roll out of their reach. Except for Artur, who can barely open his eyes. They stop close to where he is lying, quickly jumping in to drag him inside. Phelipe howls, but he's still in pain. My hands tremble as I grip the gun, causing the shots I fire frantically to miss them entirely. The door slams shut and they accelerate away, taking Artur with them.

"I need your help," Phelipe says, writhing in agony, fallen on the ground.

It's just him and me again. The attacks have ceased; the cannibal beasts are dead, Artur has been taken, and Tom Warner must be on his way to a hospital now. Penélope doesn't seem to be anywhere in sight either.

I hesitate. I really don't know how I feel about Phelipe now that we're no longer fighting for our lives.

"Please," he pleads through clenched teeth in agony.

Okay, maybe I owe him some favor for saving me thousands of times in the last few minutes. I move closer with the gun in hand, ready to shoot if he makes any wrong move. His shirt is soaked in blood, and there's a hole the size of a tennis ball in it. Apparently, it wasn't a regular bullet that hit him.

"What do I have to do?" I ask in a weak voice.
"Stick your hand in and take the bullet out."
"What?!"
I widen my eyes.
"Don't be such a wuss." He lets out a groan of pain. "This is a blue bullet. As long as it's inside me, I won't be able to move. Stick your hand in and take it out."

Blue bullet?

I look at the ground littered with bullets and only now realize they are colored. Blue and yellow. Shit! This is probably the grossest thing I've ever done.

I rip the remainder of his shirt. The hole in his chest is much larger than it should be. I touch the open, bloodied wound with the tips of my fingers. I hold my breath, feeling my weak stomach twist with nausea. I never imagined I would stick my hand inside someone. I try not to think about it as I search for the bullet. He writhes in agony and murmurs laments. I'm sure he's on the verge of tears when I touch something. Praying it's not an organ or a bone, I pull.

The bullet I hold between my fingers is much larger than a regular one and is far from being silver or any other material I know. Through the blood, I see a bluish shine on it. Phelipe sighs in relief.

"Big, isn't it?" He looks at me gratefully. He lets out a weak cough. "It was designed to increase in size when in contact with skin. The longer it stayed inside, the bigger it would get."

"Why?" I ask, still analyzing the bullet between my fingers.

"I'll explain later. For now, it's better to take you home."

Home... That idea sounds like paradise.

Phelipe steals a car; I don't have the strength to complain. I'm so tired that I don't care about anything else. All I want is to go home. I sink into the car seat, as far away from the driver as I can, resting my head against the glass. The pain is so much that, in a way, I feel numb.

I think seconds have passed when, suddenly, we are parked in front of my house.

I'm so pathetic and weak that I need Phelipe's help to stay upright. I've lost my keys, my phone, and my shoes. I stagger to the door and ring the bell.

My mother opens almost immediately. She's wrapped in a white robe. Her gray eyes are teary and wide. Her hands tremble on the doorknob. She lets out a relieved exclamation, throwing herself onto me, squeezing me and crying into my hair. She mumbles incomprehensible words as she hugs me for long minutes.

Phelipe is nowhere in my line of sight.

"Sophia! Oh my God. I was just about to call the police," she whimpers, trembling, pulling back to see my face.

It's the last thing I hear before the world goes out of focus, and I give in to exhaustion, completely blacking out.

CHAPTER TWENTY

Sophia

The light caresses my face tenderly. I don't open my eyes right away. I breathe slowly, as if purifying my lungs. I don't move for a moment. I'm afraid that if I do, I'll ruin the peace radiating from the sunlight that bathes my face.

A sound of a page turning alerts me to the presence of someone else in the room. I instinctively open my eyes. The light blinds me for a brief moment. I blink several times, trying to adjust. My first thought is that I'm lying in my room, the familiar yellow walls surrounding me. My second thought is that someone is watching me, sitting in a chair at the foot of my bed. I know who it is before I even bring my eyes to his face.

I try to get up from the bed but have little success. A strong dizziness envelops me, causing black gaps to appear around me. A piercing pain strikes my body.

"I wouldn't try to get up so fast if I were you," Phelipe says calmly, a relaxed expression on his face while he flips through an old photo album he found in my room.

I must have died and gone straight to hell since the first face I see upon waking is his.

"Why are you here? What are you doing with that album? And where is my mother?"

"Wow, so many questions!" he mocks, closing the album. "I thought you'd want me here to answer all your questions about what happened yesterday."

I feel my body tremble. The memories flood back to my mind like color reaching a black-and-white drawing. Slowly, I color in the details that pass through my head, remembering everything up to the moment I fainted in my mother's arms.

"Shit!" I grunt, feeling nauseous.

Carefully, I sit up in bed, my head spinning and my body entirely sore. I stretch to catch a glimpse of myself in the vanity mirror. I look better than I imagined I would. My eye is swollen and purple; I quickly remember the punch I took, which is also why my head is throbbing so much at this point. A band-aid covers the top of my forehead. My arm is bandaged where I received a grazing gunshot, but my neck is bare, revealing four deep gashes where the sharp claws of the cannibal beasts cut me.

"This looks horrible," I say, stretching my neck to see the damage better. "It needs stitches. Why didn't my mother take me to the hospital?"

"She tried to call an ambulance as soon as you passed out, but due to yesterday's events, there was an overload in medical responses. All the ambulances are at the school, the hospitals are packed. And there's another thing..."

"What thing?"

I panic automatically, immediately ignoring my neck.

"Your sister, Lily, was missing. Then they found her drunk in a stolen car that she and her friends crashed. Your mother had to go to the police station to deal with that, she took the little one with her... Isa, right? And left you here. We're alone."

I exhale with a puff of boredom. Well, it's better to have a thieving, drunk sister than a dead one.

"What the hell happened yesterday?" I ask, uncertain if I want to know more about it. "What was all... that?"

Phelipe sighs, straightening up in his chair.

"There's a woman..." His honey-colored eyes settle on me, impassive. "A woman who has your face. Someone I loved in the past."

Every hair on my body stands on end. My eyebrows knit together in a straight line.

"I have the face of the woman you loved?" I repeat, not understanding how this relates to the nightmare my life has become.

My breath hitches.

"No." His jaw tightens. "You have the face of the woman I want to kill."

I gasp. The terror of this revelation makes my blood flow faster in my veins and my heart hammer irregularly in my chest.

"How can someone have the same face as me?" The desperation in my question is clearly audible; I feel as if someone has poisoned me.

"I'm not very sure."

"That's not physically possible."

My whole body wants to abhor the idea of having someone else's face. But then I remember a conversation I had with Artur when I asked why they wanted to kill me. "You look like her," was what he said. Phelipe himself told me when we met that I resembled someone from his past.

"But how..."

"Have you heard of the Omega laboratory?" I nod. I was born in one of its maternity wards. "For years they've been developing a technique. It's cruel, actually. The goal is to create an army of genetically modified creatures that are invincible." His eyes stare at the wall. I hold my breath. "For years, scientists from around the world have been experimenting on humans illegally, trying to create a subspecies that goes beyond human limitations. Deadly machines." He pauses, as if waiting for the impact of his words to hit me. "We are the government's secret weapon. The final blow. Many lab rats don't even know the purpose of the lives they lead. They don't know, for example, that we are genetically approved mutations by the government secretly to be used by them in the near future; the democratic system will fall, and we will be there to ensure that no one opposes the New Order. We will be unleashed, defending our superiors, ensuring that nothing bad happens to them, but for that, they still have a lot of work to do to gain complete control over us. Just imagine the shock and horror of the human population when they realize they will have to fight against genetic abominations that possess extraordinary strength and psychic abilities capable of making the earth tremble. Literally. You won't stand a chance."

"The human chimeras," I whisper.

I had heard about them in one of our Biology classes in school. They are animal embryos that contain human cells. They should be discarded after fourteen days and never inserted into a human or animal uterus. Apparently, that's not what they've been doing.

He turns to me in surprise that I know about it.

"Yes. The human chimeras. The problem with the Omega laboratory is that the chimeras they created are uncontrollable. They cannot die by mortal hands or weapons, but they kill each other. Now, they've created genetically modified bullets to kill them as well. A failed attempt at control. Well, they are nearly successful genetic experiments, and still illegal. They are confidential while still being studied and educated. They are hidden in thousands of laboratories across the country, but the main one is in Rio de Janeiro."

"Let me guess: Tom Warner runs these secret experiments," I sneer in horror.

"And as soon as he wins the election—and believe me, he will win—he'll unleash his beasts and create his empire of blood and destruction against anyone who opposes him."

Phelipe studies me as if he can hear my thoughts. My mouth is open, and my eyes are wide with perplexity. I imagine the sound of my heart can be heard from the other side of the world.

"You're a lab boy," I assert.

"Yes."

Strange lights dance in his eyes.

"A human chimera."

"Yes."

"Created to kill." He doesn't agree with the last statement, and honestly, it's not even necessary. "Why aren't you attracted to my blood?"

"Because I'm not a vampire," he mocks. I'm tempted to punch him in the face. "What attracts us is the flesh; the blood merely enhances the smell and flavor, like a special sauce. But unlike my lab rat friends who live in cages, I've been among humans for a long time and can control myself. Moreover, I can eat regular food too. As long as my hunger is satisfied, I'm under control."

"That doesn't sound very smart for someone with the reasoning of a machine," I observe.

"It's not that kind of intelligence. Our reasoning is more related to proportion, probability, and physical space. Everything that helps in a fight."

"And what is your psychic ability? You said you can't hear my thoughts like Artur does."

Phelipe pouts, pondering.

"I don't have one." I raise my eyebrows, doubting. "Well, technically we have the capacity to develop any psychic ability. We can all do things with our minds and know that this is a general capacity, just as we are all strong, fast, and have sharp senses. But we still don't know how to handle it." I continue to stare at him, encouraging him to proceed. He sighs. "Artur can hear people's thoughts. There are many of us who can do that too, but I'd dare say he is the best." I still feel shame at the thought of someone accessing my mind. "It's not that easy for some, like me. There are some with grand abilities that no one can develop, like a boy who can alter our perception of time with the force of thought, and, well, that's exactly what he did yesterday. With the help of another lab rat who cut the electricity."

So that's why it still seemed early when I got home.

"Wait, he literally froze time? And left us immune? Why? Wouldn't it have been easier to kill us if we were paralyzed?"

"It doesn't work that way; he didn't really freeze time, but changed our perception of it. You can't move in a frozen scene. People enter a trance state, as if someone pressed the *pause* button on the remote. If you hit *play*, everything goes back to flowing, as if nothing had been interrupted. That's why he left free those who needed to be captured and those who would help in the capture. Time only resumed after he was killed and his mind stopped controlling us." I surely demonstrate the confusion in my mind through my expression, as Phelipe smiles and continues the explanation: "We all have a sort of internal clock controlled by the brain. And without specific receptors to measure time, it's all subjective. Emotional. That's why there are moments that feel endless or too fast for us, depending on the emotion we're feeling. For someone to control time this way, it's necessary to interrupt the activity of the brain's cortex responsible for emotions and amplify the visual cortex, which is responsible for temporal control. Our internal clock."

I remember that when the lights came on and life returned to the city, Penélope's exact words were: "It seems I killed someone important." It was right after the explosions caused by her and Artur. Now, things at least make some sense.

"What's your sister's gift? Wait... What do you mean sister? You don't have family. You're a lab embryo."

He doesn't seem to like my statement. However, it's the truth.

"It's complicated. Usually, lab rats are born from surrogate mothers or are fertilized in women without them knowing they're going to give birth to mutant creatures. The gestation is painful, and most women die in the process. Those who survive are left with aftereffects. But there's this rumor that Penélope and I were the result of a planned pregnancy. We're not twins; therefore, our mother survived my birth first and then hers. And with consent. It seems our biological parents always knew about our condition."

"So you and Penélope supposedly came from the same woman? Who volunteered to bear mutant children and give them to a laboratory?"

"It's a supposition. We're not sure of anything. When I researched it, the only thing I could find was the name Kyle. Phelipe and Penélope Kyle."

"That's a strange name... You look physically alike."

He sighs.

"I think the gifts are more related to the abilities that already exist in our DNA. For example, you humans also have capabilities, even if weak. Like your friend Ane."

"Ane? What about her?" I ask, a bit too hysterically. "Is she okay? And Izec? I need to know about my friends."

I threaten to get up, but he stops me by simply raising a finger.

"They're fine," he assures me calmly. My body relaxes immediately. "As I was saying... Ane's compulsion is very strong. I felt it yesterday. She makes people obey her will without her even realizing it. It's like an invisible bubble around her that attracts people. Everyone likes her; everyone feels good around her because that's exactly what she wants to happen. You would throw yourself in front of a moving train to save her."

"Because she's my friend," I retort, sulking.

I don't want anyone to think Ane psychologically influences me to be her friend.

"That too. I felt her power in the auditorium when she ordered everyone to line up. It radiates an aura around her in such a strong way... I didn't know this was possible for a human."

No, I can't believe that.

"Ane *is* good. She's a wonderful person, and don't come telling me this is due to some stupid supernatural manipulation because..."

"I'm not saying she isn't, okay? I'm just talking about her gift. That boy who approached us in the auditorium is powerful too."

Lucas? I had almost forgotten our unfortunate episode, which already feels like it happened years ago, when he grabbed my arm and told me that Phelipe carried my death. Well, I should have believed him.

"Was that a kind of premonition?"

He shakes his head.

"Basically," he replies indifferently.

"But you didn't kill me; on the contrary!"

"I haven't killed you *yet*," he says emphatically. "But it doesn't have to be me. With the number of enemies your copy has managed to accumulate, it could be anyone."

"This copy business is wearing me out. It's a curse to look like someone. What did she do to make them want to kill us?"

Phelipe's dark aura is almost palpable now.

"The thing is, we shouldn't have feelings, but we were bombarded with a surge of strong emotions. So, they trained us to learn to control them. They wanted us not to have discernment about right and wrong, just to act. Our physical needs are much stronger than normal, so we can relate to each other. But those relationships are strictly sexual, nothing more than that. We were created to fear humans, not to see them as equals. It seems they didn't calculate properly what a bunch of mutants is capable of feeling." All these explanations are making me feel nauseous, but I do my best to keep listening. "There was this caregiver. Very different from the others." He hesitates, and I notice the discomfort in his expression. "It's the part of the story I don't like to remember..."

"My entire past is hazy, but when she appeared, I saw colors. Colors she didn't care to turn gray later on. She talked about the outside world, about her life, about everything she liked. She gave us names so she would stop treating us like lab rats and began to get too attached, which is obviously against the rules. Caregivers are trained not to think too much, not to speak to us unless necessary... the idea is for them to stay as far away as possible. She was giving us information about the laboratory regarding what we were, what they expected from us, and what we would do for them. She was a nearly declared traitor."

"It wasn't just me who fell in love. Others did too, like Artur. And recently I found out she was involved with Tom Warner's family as well. When the laboratory discovered what she was doing, she told me about my family and taught us how to escape."

"When I fled, I was followed by others. Penélope, who was also curious about this family business, and Viviane, the sick one who developed some kind of obsession for me and has been making my life a hell ever since. And I haven't reunited with the caregiver. She wasn't where she said she would be."

I notice that Phelipe's hands tremble as he holds my closed photo album in his lap. His breathing is slow and deep, and I can feel how much he is controlling himself.

"And... did she die?"

"Yes." His expression is fierce. "Viviane probably killed her."

Viviane. Why do I have the feeling that I know her? I feel like I'm missing something important... I remember Penélope mentioning that name more than once, saying that Viviane had killed all the women Phelipe got involved with, that she had been following him for quite some time; a furious, out-of-control ex-girlfriend.

At first, I thought Penélope was his ex-girlfriend, which is why she was spying on us, which made me have that feeling of being watched. But the Kyle girl is Phelipe's sister and was following him for reasons still unknown, but not out of a desire for revenge. She hates me, of course, but as she herself said, if she wanted me dead, she would have already killed me; she had many chances to do so.

So there's someone else lurking, watching me, wanting to kill me. A cold chill takes over my body, making me shiver and gasp. I know Viviane.

"Is Viviane by any chance a redhead?"

"How do you know?" Phelipe asks, his eyes wide.

His fists are clenched so tightly at his sides that the knuckles are starting to turn white.

"That would explain the dreams..."

Phelipe punches the air brutally, letting out fierce growls.

"Sophia, this is very serious," he warns with the voice of someone trying to explain something to a child. "Have you dreamed about Viviane?"

"Yes." He curses under his breath. "She kills me in all my dreams. Phelipe... I think it was her who was chasing me. For a long time, I've had this feeling of being watched; I thought it was Penélope, but it was probably her."

"She must be... She must have arrived first; like me, she must have come here deducing that Tom Warner was hiding something in this city. That's the only thing that explains her risking exposure in a stupid school debate. She probably saw you, realized you weren't her, and stayed close to find out who you were before killing you. Don't blame me for thinking at first that you were her. They look so much alike. And I was filled with so much hatred for that face for lying to me, for leading me to flee in the hope that we would be together and just disappearing afterward... I spent a long time searching for her. A very long time. If Viviane found her, she only found her later too."

We fall silent. It's a story too complex for me to absorb. At another time, I would completely doubt the possibility of being someone's copy. Or that there's an army of entirely uncontrollable human chimeras, with society oblivious to it. But I have witnessed horrific beings that exude rot. I was attacked by them. People were killed.

I look at Phelipe and feel that aura of power and darkness emanating from his skin. This force extends to his sister as well. There's no denying the obvious.

"When I saw you on the street, I knew you weren't the same person. I wanted to get closer to you and try to get to know you better because I want to understand why you look so much alike. But Penélope followed me. And, from what Artur said, so did Viviane. She saw us together, and that must have made her furious. She reported us to the laboratory, which is why they sent the chimeras after you. Now everyone knows of your existence and will come looking for you."

My eyes widen in shock.

"So why didn't Viviane just kill me, like she did with the others?"

"Because when you weren't with me, you were under Penélope's protection. She wouldn't stand a chance against either of us, and she wouldn't risk exposing herself."

"So, technically, there's an army of genetically modified beings wanting to kill me? A legion of *you*?" My voice takes on a dead tone. "They don't know she's dead?"

"They know, but they don't care. They want to know why you look so alike, and I think that's why they didn't try to kill you. Tom

Warner must have wanted to get closer first with some sick plan in mind. The chimeras were only there to be tested and to capture us, the fugitive lab rats."

"Oh, they tried to kill me," I whisper.

"I'm sure that wasn't the goal. They wanted you alive. It's just that the chimeras are uncontrollable, as you must have seen. When Penélope shot that girl and they smelled blood, they went berserk."

Shit! Did Penélope have to do that?

"Why did your sister help me? What's her interest?"

He shrugs.

"Penélope always has her own interests; it's hard to say. And I wouldn't call that help since she shot at me."

Was it her? I was so stunned that I didn't realize where the shot came from. I didn't even know where the girl was at that moment.

"Why would she do that?" I raise my eyebrows. He shrugs. "Do you trust her?"

"No."

"How did Tom Warner find me?"

"I still don't know. But you need to know one thing: if before he didn't want to kill you, after he was shot by you, he will definitely want to decorate his living room with your head."

"Why did you save me? Why risk your life when it would conveniently be better for you to kill me? And I know you want to do that. I have the face of the woman you hate."

And I really know, almost as if his breath whispers the words to me with every exhale.

Suddenly, Phelipe stands up, leaving the album on the chair, sits on the edge of my bed, and leans toward me. All my nerves freeze in surprise. I'm left speechless when his hand touches my cheek gently; an incoherent act for a killer's hands. His warm fingers trace my lips softly, moving down to the pendant of my necklace.

"You're identical." His fists clench tightly. "And I want to find out why."

CHAPTER TWENTY-ONE

Sophia

Around me, the tall grass sways and spins in a frenzy. The green foliage brushes against my legs, causing my body to shiver and itch where it is touched. My entire body trembles, but at this moment it's not from being caught off guard by the wet grass. The wind lashes mercilessly against my thin sweater, leaving a trail of raised hairs all along the way. I stand rigidly, fingers curled against the hem of the black dress that barely covers my thighs. My lips are purple, completely stiff and numb, just like the toes of my feet inside the wet sneakers.

I'm in front of my school. Actually, in the unused part of it, where the gardener hasn't stepped in years. Several security tape barriers surround the crime scene. This is the only place we have permission from the police to be. People of all kinds are here; surviving students, parents of the deceased, teachers, onlookers, and the press, which circles like vultures over carrion. It's complete chaos.

The city is horrified by the barbarity that occurred. It's been a long time since there's been a major crime here.

The crowd leans over the security tape surrounding the courtyard, crying and yelling at the police and firefighters, who are still working tirelessly in the building. Occasionally, when someone emerges from inside, everyone falls silent, waiting for news. There are still people missing, and there are many mutilated bodies that are too damaged to be identified. The police are looking for clues about who could be responsible for this atrocity. The firefighters are searching for bodies and, perhaps, survivors. The families are seeking answers.

So far, there are thirty-two confirmed dead. But there are still at least twenty-five missing. Among the thirty-two are students, teachers, parents, and companions who attended the event last night. And, of course, Natália. The first victim. There's a television on, probably belonging to the police, on which a crew constantly huddles, watching the news that repeatedly airs photos of the confirmed victims.

My mother didn't want me to be here, but I needed to come; I need to know how my friends are, since I haven't been able to contact any of them so far.

This morning, when I turned on the TV to watch the news, I saw the gathering forming at the school's entrance. I wanted to know a little more about the investigations, if there were any suspects or even testimonies from the victims. More than anything, I want to see my friends.

Phelipe didn't take long to leave after telling me everything. He said he needed to get rid of the stolen car, but that he would stay close in case I needed him. I swear I saw his shadow in my window when I tried to go back to sleep. However, that paranoia was replaced by terrifying dreams about the red-haired woman. So, I took advantage of my mother's distraction with Lily, who threw up all over the room, to sneak away here. She's not going to be happy about this; I can already predict the sermon she's going to give me as soon as I get back home. That is, if she doesn't come here to scold me in front of everyone and drag me by my hair.

My heart leaps when I spot the faces I'm looking for, further away in the crowd. From a distance, I can see Jimmy, probably the tallest person here. I stretch my neck, catching sight of Izec's bronze-colored hair; he is leaning over the police tape, shouting at the top of his lungs, his face red—whether from anger or crying, I don't know.

Ane's blue eyes turn in my direction, her expression softening on her face. She waves for me to come closer to them; I know she has a lot to say just from the anxious way she looks at me. My mother told me Ane had called my house several times after I fainted to make sure I was okay.

But suddenly, there's a change in the air that is almost palpable. People start whispering, restless. Reluctantly, I try to approach my friends, but it's impossible due to the throng of people. It takes me a while to understand, and then I look around. Why are they looking at me? From afar, I see Ane's distressed expression directed at me, her eyes shining with anguish. The news broadcast is live. The reporter is speaking, but I can barely hear him. The caption makes my hands sweat and my body tremble with panic: "Tom Warner was attacked during the Araxá massacre."

Shit! This can't be good.

They're talking about his coming to the city to attend the school event, where he would be a speaker. Tom Warner was attacked by the possible perpetrator of the deaths, who was heavily armed. The amputation of the right hand and left leg of the candidate was necessary.

Amputation?! Holy shit.

They are detailing the surgical procedure he underwent, and all I can wonder is: why? Why are they only talking about this now?

And then the answer comes in the blink of an eye. The video from a security camera on the street reveals the exact moment I shot him. At first, I can't be seen. Just the tiny gun in my hand, with Artur's body sprawled over mine. Then, when Artur rolls away, I appear clearly holding the gun and shooting at the candidate's hand. They zoom in on my face just as my name and a photo of me appear on the screen; I'm being pointed out as the main suspect in the massacre and the attempted homicide. I cover my mouth, stifling a scream.

It feels like time has frozen again as everyone stares at me. Izec rolls his eyes at me, accusation and even betrayal shimmering in his expression. It hurts as if a spear has pierced my chest. I instinctively recoil.

Ane looks at me, terrified. Jimmy appears confused. The rest of the crowd isn't so comprehensible. They've lost people, been hurt, and are faced with the main suspect. I feel like they are going to pounce on me and strangle me with their own hands at any moment.

"I-I... d-don't..." I stammer, trying to defend myself, but my mouth feels like it's made of sand.

"Murderer!" someone yells.

More people join in, soon forming a chorus. They're going to attack me, I know that.

I look around, searching for a way out to try to run and escape all of this. Predicting my movements, they close in a circle, blocking my path. In the distance, I can hear the sounds of police sirens. They already know I'm here.

"Murderer!"

I feel something hard collide against my skin. Someone threw a stone at me. My already scraped knee hurts from the impact of the stone, and I grit my teeth, trying not to cry.

Ane is shouting something to the people; I imagine she's telling them to back off or to stop insulting me, but even her serious, authoritative voice isn't enough to quell the hatred the people are feeling. I see a man charging toward me with a huge rock in his hands, and I only have seconds to conclude that I'm going to be killed. Out of the corner of my eye, I catch a glimpse of Ane's terror and her futile attempt to stop the attack under Jimmy's protests.

Then a loud sound echoes around us. The man halts halfway through his throw, startled. I stretch my neck trying to decipher the source of that noise. I see a blood-red blur cross the parking lot at a surprising speed, coming toward me. The circle of people moves away, jumping back. I don't even have time to run when a shiny motorcycle comes to a stop in front of me.

It's not just any motorcycle. It's *the* motorcycle. Red, huge, and gleaming. Phelipe is riding it.

I open my mouth to ask what's happening, but he pulls me onto the back so quickly that I can barely understand. I just hug his waist tightly as he revs the engine and we zoom away from all the chaos.

Today is one of the rare cold days in this part of the country, and even with the sun shining brightly in a sky with few clouds, the cold wind cuts against my face, forcing me to close my eyes. My hair whips around in a mess as he accelerates faster and faster. I huddle, using Phelipe's body as a shield to protect myself. I notice he's taking side streets toward the city exit.

"The police were at your house looking for you," he shouts over the noise of the wind, his voice muffled by the helmet. Shit! "They waited until the last second to give the news, because then they would have the evidence in hand and there would be no way for you to escape. But I'm cautious. I anticipated that Tom wouldn't forgive something like this and I planned an unexpected escape," he comments with a hint of arrogance. We fall silent. "Aren't you going to say anything?"

"I'm running low on curses," I reply, sourly.

Even with my eyes closed, I know Phelipe is smiling.

"I broke into your house after the police left and grabbed some things for you. There was no one there," he shouts, turning his head quickly to look at me.

What do you mean, no one was there? Where did my family go?

I'm about to ask, but then there's a loud bang. A gunshot. I recognize that sound easily now. Phelipe is hit and loses control of the motorcycle. With a sudden jerk, it tips to the side, sparking along the way, and we crash to the ground. I fall backward onto the hot asphalt of the road. Luckily, I don't hit my head, but my spine hurts immediately. I touch my bandaged shoulder, which throbs and burns, as if someone has reopened the wound from the graze I took. Damn!

Phelipe is on his feet before he even hits the ground. He looks around in shock, trying to locate where the shot came from. Probably from the police. I try to get up just as a figure appears in my line of sight.

"Trying to go somewhere without me, little brother?" Penélope walks gracefully on her heels with a mocking smile on her face. Oh, what a huge mess! I sink back to the ground, wishing a lightning bolt would strike my head. Phelipe curses in nervous whispers. "Did you miss me?"

"Penélope! I should have guessed!" Phelipe grunts. His mood swings so abruptly that I startle. The anger is palpable in the air. "Always shooting at things. And at *people*."

With a weary sigh, I push myself off the ground. My back aches from the fall. Wincing in pain, I watch the girl approach calmly, carrying three backpacks between her fingers. Phelipe rips the bullet from his back with a growl. Luckily, we are on a road in the middle of nowhere, surrounded by dense foliage, with no witnesses to this catastrophe.

"Don't be so dramatic, little brother. I was trying to save your life. What were you thinking trying to drag Artur's body? They would have killed you too just for trying."

"Artur?" I ask. It hadn't crossed my mind what fate he might have met. He became a declared traitor by throwing himself in front of the bullets to save my life. "He's..."

"Dead," Penélope replies indifferently. "Yeah, I know, it's a shame. He had a nice backside. And did nice things with his tongue."

I roll my eyes. My grimace shifts from pain to disgust.

"Before I vomit with that kind of comment," Phelipe begins with trembling hands from rage, "could you tell me what you're doing here after shooting me and just disappearing?"

"I was planning everything to get us out of here. I got fake identities for the three of us, money, things we'll need for the trip, some weapons..."

"Trip? Us three?" I roar, looking from one to the other. "There is no *us three*. There's just me. Running away from all of this, including you two."

"Really, there is no us three," Phelipe agrees, crossing his arms. "It's just her and me. I had everything ready before you showed up. Or do you think I'm going to trust someone who shot me and left me to die?"

She bares her teeth, irritated.

"What's your brilliant plan? To escape in that stupid car where you left these shabby backpacks?" She throws the backpacks on the ground at our feet. Mine bounces with a strange clatter. The gun I stashed yesterday is apparently still inside. Great. Penélope's backpack still hangs on her back, with chains dangling, and is twice as big and fuller than mine and Phelipe's. "Are you just stupid or have you spent too much time with Sophia? She's wanted by the *police*. Obviously, they've blocked all the city exits; there's no way to escape in a car. Unless you're considering several stops to kill all the officers and expose your mutation. They'll love it!"

"I don't need your stupid advice and..."

"We don't have time for this! We need to get out of here now; we can talk during the journey," Penélope says coldly. "And you will carry my backpack," she adds to me.

"Why?" I ask, incredulously.

She snatches my backpack off the ground and throws it over my back, tossing her own in my direction. Hers is absurdly heavy, as if she were carrying rocks. Well, I doubt she isn't.

"Because I'm saving your life, and it's the only useful thing you can do for me. And also because it messes up my hair."

Cursing mentally all the swear words I know, I adjust the backpacks on my back. I know that if I refuse to carry it, she'll find a way to force me. Penélope takes the lead, practically skipping. Phelipe pushes the motorcycle off the road and simply leaves it there, discarded. We exchange a silent glance that says a lot. We don't trust her.

This must be the worst nightmare of my life. A fugitive from the police, with everyone I know hating me and thinking I'm a sadistic murderer, with an army of mutants hunting me down, and on top of that, stuck with the two most detestable siblings in the world. Phelipe is still reasonably better, even if he's sick. Looking at Penélope fills me with repulsion. There wouldn't have been mass murders if she hadn't shot Natália, to begin with.

"I presume you have a route in mind, little sister."

I follow between the two, wishing they would die with every step they take. We are on the side of the road, about to head into the brush. Fantastic! If we can't take the highway, since there will be police lurking, we'll go on foot through the thicket. My day couldn't get any worse.

"We have a long way to go, so I'm wearing my hiking boots," she comments proudly.

She's wearing long, stiletto-heeled boots from Chanel! Not to mention the short leather dress that barely covers a hand's width above her hips. I regret not opting for jeans and a sweatshirt before leaving the house. The day is cold, and the night is bound to get worse, especially considering I'll be sleeping on the ground under some tree.

"And where exactly are we going?" I ask.

The weight of the two backpacks is increasingly painful on my already sore back from the motorcycle fall and the massacre yesterday. Phelipe grunts softly. Penélope's plans don't please him at all. It's somewhere he hasn't even considered we should go, and for some reason, it was her first option. In other words, something diabolical.

"Oh, you're going to love it, Sophia." She beams a radiant smile, which means we're probably heading toward the worst nightmare of my existence. "We're going straight into the storm."

CHAPTER TWENTY-TWO

Sophia

With my back resting against a tree branch, I finally sit down, much to the relief of my tired legs. My spine and shoulders are burning from the heavy load I've had to carry the entire long way. Phelipe and Penélope have gone ahead, arguing too quietly for me to hear. The topic is putting him in a bad mood and making the girl huff and roll her eyes. Occasionally, they glance over their shoulders at me, just to ensure I'm still there. As if I could escape without them hearing.

My knees are shaking, whether from cold or exhaustion, I can't tell. The chilly night wind raises all the hairs on my body and makes me curl up like a ball. My arms and legs are bare due to the dress I'm wearing, and the ground I'm sitting on is cold and damp. I grit my teeth together to prevent them from clattering against each other.

Phelipe is visibly sulking. He sharpens the blade of his knife on a stone, casting furtive glances at his sister. He doesn't trust her. He's also not happy to see her take control of the situation.

Penélope kneels in front of her backpack, searching for something inside. Her smile widens as she pulls out a large rock. She raises it like a trophy, showing it to me. My spine throbs in protest. All the extra weight I carried during the long walk was unnecessary, just so she could humiliate me.

Happy with my expression of hatred, the girl throws a thin blanket that was among her things over me. I wish I had the strength to act difficult and refuse the blanket, maybe throw it back, but I'm so cold that my fingers are stiff and somewhat difficult to move. I wrap myself up as much as I can, trying to cover every exposed piece of skin from the cold night air. The sounds of nocturnal animals frighten me, but I disguise the fear.

Phelipe grumbles to himself, seeming bothered. He stops sharpening his blade, examining it between his fingers for a moment before sticking it in the side of his boot. The lab boy walks over to where I am, gently kicking the backpack in my direction. When I don't move to grab it, he sighs and opens it, pulling out my hoodie and cotton pants.

"Stop pampering her," Penélope murmurs as she spreads a blanket on the ground.

This is the second time she's said that today. The first was when, after three uninterrupted hours of walking, I asked for a break. My asthmatic lungs were already failing, and I could barely stay on my feet. She looked at me with pure disdain, ready to say "no" and comment on how weak and pathetic I am, but Phelipe leaned against a tree and waited. Penélope practically spat fire. To get back at that moment, hours later, she denied me water. Under the scorching sun, my tongue felt like sandpaper dry. She downed the whole bottle in one go and then threw the rest on the ground right in front of me. Minutes later, her brother gave me his water bottle and forced another stop so I could rest from hours of walking with the weight of stones on my back.

I accept the clothes Phelipe hands me. I'm so cold that when I stand up, I feel like a doll with stiff limbs that are hard to move. Feeling like I'm on a *reality show*, I hold the blanket tightly around me and begin to undress.

Penélope rolls her eyes and sits on the blanket she spread on the ground.

"No one here wants to see that, sweetheart," she mocks as she removes her high-heeled boots.

Phelipe has become curiously silent since we started our escape down the roads. At least with me. He's been arguing with his sister the whole time, appearing angry. He has barely spoken to me. However, I find his silence comforting. Better than Penélope's chatter, with all her sarcastic and malicious comments, especially when directed at me.

I finish changing, grateful to better cover my body from the cold, and I bring the backpack closer to me. Phelipe said he grabbed some things for me at my house, and it's convenient to know what they are. I rummage through the inside, finding some changes of clothes, a pair of boots, and a flashlight. I mentally thank him for the clean boots and socks, instantly shedding my worn-out sneakers and sweaty socks. I'll put on the boots as soon as we need to leave. There's also an empty water bottle, a lighter, insect repellent, and a hair comb. I feel around in the secret pocket at the bottom of the backpack, invisible to the naked eye, feeling the barrel of the gun still there. Either Phelipe didn't see it, or he didn't think having a gun in my hand posed any risk.

He gathers some twigs in the center of the clearing. With a flick of the lighter, he creates a small fire, but it's strong enough to warm me a bit. I wrap myself completely in the blanket, finally lying down. My back hurts, and the blisters on my feet throb, but I'm so tired that lying down is comforting.

I hear rustling of clothes and blankets and imagine that Penélope and Phelipe have changed and lain down as well. I keep facing the other way, not wanting to see them. My stomach lets out a low growl of hunger, which I ignore. Throughout the day, all I ate were two chicken sandwiches that Phelipe made for me. The two siblings each ate eight sandwiches. Then they stopped again to eat more, but I refused. Either they hadn't eaten in a long time, or the dna mutation increases appetite.

I close my eyes to rest. I try hard to think of anything that will take me away from the depressing reality I find myself in, and all I see are Izec's almond-colored eyes staring at me, accusatory. I involuntarily gasp, feeling the knot in my throat and tears welling in the corners of my eyes. I try to push the last images of my friends away from me, and my mother's face invades my mind. I didn't even have a chance to say goodbye or try to explain that I didn't commit any of those atrocities. She's probably disappointed. I shot twice and mutilated the man she had praised just days ago, pointing him out as worthy and upright.

What kind of person does she think I am? And what lies will she tell Isa to mask the horror that her sister is a murderer? Even Lily must be aware of this by now.

With tears in my eyes and a sob caught in my throat, I cry myself into a deep sleep.

⚡

"WAKE UP!" IT FEELS like I just fell asleep when someone screams desperately in my ears, shaking me by the shoulders. "Come on, Sophia!"

My eyes slowly open. It's still dark around me, the little light coming from the fire, which is dying out. Phelipe is leaning over me, gripping my shoulders, his face just a few inches from mine. My mind finally understands what's happening, and I recoil, scared, pushing him away from me.

"What the hell..."

I'm interrupted by the noise of helicopter blades. I look up with my heart racing. Helicopters are hovering over the area, casting beams of light on the trees.

"Quick," Penélope grunts, kicking dirt over the fire to extinguish it.

We plunge into darkness. Phelipe bends down to grab my blanket and throws it over my shoulders. He picks up our backpacks from the ground and throws them onto his back. His hand touches my elbow, encouraging me to move forward. I can't tell if Penélope has already gone ahead of us.

Awkwardly, still sluggish from sleep and frozen with fear, I start moving through the night. I stretch a hand in front of me to shield myself in case I bump into a tree. My clean socks slip on the damp ground, becoming an obstacle to my agility. I didn't have time to put on my boots. Phelipe keeps tugging at my elbow impatiently.

I glance back, seeing the helicopters hovering over the exact spot where we were. By a matter of seconds, we weren't caught.

The chimeras can run much faster than my human legs. Phelipe has carried me before in his arms and ran with me like a blur through the city, making me feel nauseous. So why are we moving so slowly, taking pitiful steps, if we're on the run?

I feel a strong tug on my other arm and barely have time to think when my back is brutally pressed against the trunk of a tree. I'm about to scream in fear, unable to see in the darkness who is holding me, but a hand covers my mouth. My eyes widen.

"Shh... Be quiet," Penélope orders.

I relax my shoulder tension a little upon recognizing her voice. We sink into a deep silence, except for the helicopter blades and the pounding of my heart. With the darkness surrounding us, I can't see where Phelipe is. In this section where we are, the vegetation is denser, and the tree branches are longer, almost completely blocking the view of the sky. So I assume we don't need to run; we won't be seen from above.

After a few minutes, the noises of the helicopter gradually fade, probably going to search in another more visible area. Penélope sighs, relaxing her shoulders. Her hand releases my mouth.

"How long do you think they've been looking for us?" she asks into the darkness.

"I imagine all day," Phelipe responds from somewhere in the shadows.

"Why?" I shoot back, unable to contain myself. "If they can run so fast, why not throw me on their backs and disappear? Why risk being seen, moving at my pace?"

"Things aren't that simple, sweetheart," Penélope scoffs. Even without seeing her clearly, I know she's rolling her eyes. "We can't expose ourselves to humans like that without starting an unimaginable war, and vehicles are still the best escape strategy. But while we can't escape in one, we'll go through here instead. Also, we have normal human needs, like sleeping and eating."

Phelipe approaches where we are. I can distinguish his silhouette more easily now. He extends my backpack to me, waiting for me to take it. I grab it and throw it over my shoulders. Luckily, Penélope doesn't hand me hers, but, in any case, with the exhaustion I feel, I wouldn't be able to take two steps with the extra weight without collapsing on the ground.

We start walking. Phelipe wraps his hand around my elbow to guide me more easily. I wonder why he has been so quiet since his sister found us.

"If you expose yourselves, humans will believe the government created this diabolical plan, believe in my innocence, and fight on our side. They won't do anything against you unless you present risks and..."

"Oh, I have no doubt they won't kill us," Penélope interrupts me. Her voice echoes from somewhere in front of me in the dark. Phelipe holds a tree branch so I won't hit my face when I pass by it. Before I can thank him, my foot slips on something damp, almost sending me crashing to the ground if it weren't for the quick hand of the lab boy. His sister lets out a giggle. "Humans are unpredictable and divided. Half will think it's absurd and revolt against the lab, and the other half will be fascinated by us. They'll want to study us and turn us into house pets."

"What makes you think anyone would find your kind fascinating?" I ask, horrified at the possibility.

"Oh, you'd be surprised at the amount," he replies with a hint of pride in his voice. "Like Sofia, the original, of whom you are a copy."

Sofia. I realize I never got to ask what her name was; I was so focused on understanding how it was possible that we both had the same face that it didn't cross my mind that this might not be the only thing we had in common. But now it all makes sense. It explains why everyone seems to know my name.

"Did you hear that?" Phelipe asks, stopping in place.

With his hand still holding my elbow, he pulls me, forcing me to stop as well. I don't hear anything besides the sound of cicadas in the trees around us and some other buzzing from insects and birds. Occasionally, I can hear a car on the road, not too far from where we are.

"Dogs," Penélope whispers. "Why are they coming in our direction?"

I don't initially understand how dogs can scare them. I tilt my head, trying hard to hear any other noise. Nothing.

"Shouldn't we climb a tree, then?" I whisper, starting to feel scared by the reaction of the two siblings; I don't want to stand in the dark with the threat of animals coming toward us.

The forest suddenly plunges into total silence. My blood runs cold in my veins. I have a *déjà vu* of the night of the attack when a chimera froze time, making the city dark and silent. The current situation isn't much different. The sounds of the night fall completely silent. There are no more noisy insects or cicadas singing in the branches of the trees.

In an uncontrollable frenzy, the birds take flight, seeming scared. They fly past me in all directions, completely startled. I cover my face with my hands, shielding myself from their sharp beaks as I feel their wings brush against my skin.

"What the hell is that?" Phelipe sounds perplexed.

"Whatever it is, it's not normal," Penélope responds, alert. "Flashlights, quickly. We need to see."

Finally, I hear what I imagine are paws slamming against the ground. Wild growls echo, followed by more grotesque snarls. The zipper of my backpack, which is on my back, is opened roughly. Phelipe fumbles inside, searching for the flashlight. Penélope lights hers first.

It's good to have some light, but I'm not sure I really want to see these dogs. If they can scare the chimeras, what will they do to me? Ice seeps into my stomach, caused by panic. The two flashlights are now on, illuminating the spot from where the growls are coming.

My heart is beating so fast that it leaves me deaf. I dig my nails into Phelipe's arm, instinctively shrinking behind him. He seems aware of my terror and covers my body with his, like a shield. I feel a poke in my ribs that makes me jump, startled, my legs turning to jelly. It's just Penélope handing me an extra flashlight. Still trembling from fright, I take it and turn it on. The beam of light is smaller than the brothers', but it doesn't matter. I aim it in the direction of the scratching paws just as a dog appears. It's so frightening that it paralyzes me instantly.

The huge and visibly unusual dog bares its sharp teeth at us. It rears back on its hind legs, gathering momentum to leap. It's the last thing I see before I regain control of my paralyzed body. I let out an uncontrollable scream that scratches at my throat. The flashlight drops from my hand, and I take off running, plunging into the deep darkness.

CHAPTER TWENTY-THREE

Sophia

Filled with terror, I only realize the stupidity of my decision to run without seeing a foot in front of me when I crash to the ground. I trip over a tree root, my socks providing little balance on the damp earth.

Penélope is screaming somewhere in the darkness. I can still see the beams of the flashlights zigzagging around them. Roars and growls sound in my ears. But I can't tell if they're coming from the dogs or the chimeras.

I struggle to get up, using the trunk of the tree for support. From the roar Penélope lets out, which makes the hairs on the back of my neck stand up, followed by a curse from Phelipe, I assume she's hurt. If a mutant as strong as she is has been injured by one of those *dogs*, what would they do to me? It wouldn't do me any good to run blindly, slow and weak as I am. My best alternative is to try climbing. If I can reach a high branch, I'll be safe, assuming that this beast can't climb a tree.

I'm not quite sure if *dog* is the right word to describe that thing. From a distance, it looks like a pit bull, judging by the shape of its ears, mouth, and build. However, it's the size of a wolf, with claws as long as an eagle's and teeth that look like silver blades.

I rip off my socks, which slow my movement and impair my balance, tossing them into the bushes. I feel around the tree trunk, searching for a handhold to give me stability to start climbing. When

I find one, I begin to climb. It's not so difficult. During my childhood, Izec, Jimmy, Ane, and I spent most of our time climbing trees. That's how I ended up giving my first kiss, sitting on a branch while Jimmy was looking for us. The biggest hindrance now is my weight and elasticity. Plus, my injured arm doesn't seem capable of exerting much force without causing a stabbing pain.

I hear a low growl and freeze automatically. Gathering all my courage, I look down, praying to the heavens not to find a dog. At that moment, a beam of light illuminates us for a brief second, enough for me to see two fierce dogs at the roots of the tree. One of them jumps. Its leap is so high that its mouth passes inches from my foot. And by my calculations, I'm more than two meters high.

I scream. If its teeth had touched me, they would have mutilated me.

Horrified, feeling my palms sweat and my body begin to slide down the trunk, I struggle to climb higher. Without the flashlight nearby, I can't see them anymore. But I can hear their furious roars. My hands reach a high branch sturdy enough to support my weight. When I finally sit, my pulse is racing.

The dogs continue jumping, trying to reach me. I see their metallic teeth like knives shining in the dark. I curl my legs as much as I can, taking them out of the animals' line of sight.

A little ahead, the fight between the brothers continues. I can't see them in the darkness of the night, but by the sounds they're making, I know it isn't easy.

A noise surprises me from below. There's a tremor; the whole tree shakes. I need to hold onto the branch more firmly. Another noise, now of wood being broken. New tremors.

What the hell is this?

I squint my eyes in the dark, trying to see what's happening. With great effort, I see the silhouettes of the dogs advancing against the tree. What are they doing? Only when one of them spits something on the ground do I finally understand. They're tearing pieces off the trunk to destabilize the tree. It will fall.

I enter a panic. What am I going to do? If I fall, I'll be torn to pieces by the dogs before I can even scream. Penélope and Phelipe are too busy with their own battle to come to my aid. I'm completely screwed. If only I had a knife or...

The gun. I had completely forgotten! In a hurry, I pull the backpack off my shoulders, holding tightly to the branch to avoid falling. I rummage through it until I find the gun at the bottom. I grab it with my free hand, squinting to aim into the dark. I hope my aim is as good as it was with Tom Warner. But before I can shoot, a flash explodes in front of my eyes, right where Penélope and Phelipe were.

Fire.

Flames grow wildly, licking the trees around us, spreading rapidly. It's so fast that I can barely keep up. My eyes burn as I watch the flames flicker.

"Sophia?" Phelipe shouts; he's looking for me.

I was so shocked by the fire that I didn't even notice it had driven the dogs away. It was intentional.

"I'm here," I reply.

A strong taste of smoke fills my mouth. My throat itches, and I cough.

"It was clever to climb up there," Phelipe praises from beneath me. "You can jump; I'll catch you."

"Damn dog," Penélope curses from somewhere. "Did you see what he did? He ripped my dress! Do you know how much it cost? That's why we, felines, are much smarter. Well, at least the glass of gasoline I saved was useful. I knew it would come in handy."

"Damn dogs. The lab always surprises me with the creation of new beings."

"I still can't believe they created a race of animals to kill us."

I'm still paralyzed, gripping the branch with the gun in hand. For some reason, I can't move, even though Phelipe is calling me. I know it's only a matter of minutes before we're engulfed by the fire. The smoke is already making my eyes burn and preventing me from breathing properly. My cough only gets worse.

"Get down now!" Phelipe insists.

But the truth is I feel cornered. I don't want to have to come down and blindly follow Penélope and Phelipe like a trained puppy. I hate what they are. I hate Penélope and everything she has done. Even though Phelipe is a little better, easier to deal with, and has saved my life more times than I can count on my fingers, he is still a chimera. And I don't want to spend the rest of my life following him. I feel like I'm tied to him for the rest of my days, and for a debt I never wanted to incur in the first place.

Everything that has happened in the last few days is because of the chimeras: Natália's murder, the massacre at school. The attack. The shots I fired at Tom Warner, even though he deserved far worse, since the lab experiments are his creation. I'm tired of being caught in this crossfire just for having this damn face.

Before I can think clearly, I point the gun at the voice of Phelipe urging me to come down, ignoring the dry cough in my throat and my tear-filled eyes from the smoke. My trembling fingers brush against the trigger, and then... the shot echoes into the woods.

CHAPTER TWENTY-FOUR

Sophia

The scream that cuts through the air doesn't come from Phelipe. It's Penélope.

It's practically impossible to breathe now. I pull the collar of my sweatshirt over my face. I tuck the gun into my waistband and hold tightly against the tree crown, gradually sliding to the tree beside it. I know I have only a few seconds before one of them attacks me.

Taking a deep breath to gather all my courage, I stretch out my leg, feeling blindly until I find the branch of the other tree. When my feet touch the surface, I throw my body toward it. My pulse quickens as I jump, having nothing else to support me. I land on the branch I aimed for, feeling immediate relief. I allow myself to look down just once, finding Phelipe's fallen body and Penélope kneeling beside him, trying to pull the bullet from him. The shot apparently hit his head.

Before I can jump to the next tree and continue my escape, I think it's only a matter of seconds before she pulls out the bullet and they both come at me spewing fire. With trembling hands, still driven by adrenaline, I draw the gun from my waistband and shoot again. This time, I hit Penélope squarely in the back, and she falls to the side.

Now, yes, I'm at an advantage.

Without further delay, I continue jumping from tree to tree, focusing on trying to breathe and squinting against the smoke. I try not to think about the fear I feel with each new jump or about all the times my sweaty hands slip on the branches, nearly sending me crashing to the ground.

I reach a point where there are no more nearby trees. I stretch as far as I can and jump, landing on the soft earth. As soon as I stand, I feel my entire body ache from exhaustion. I can breathe better now, far from all the smoke. Looking back, I see the flames consuming half of the underbrush. I conclude that if Phelipe and Penélope didn't manage to pull out the bullets, they've likely been devoured by the fire by now.

I shudder at the thought. But still, I feel free in some way. I run away from the flames, using the light of the new moon in the sky to guide me. My feet are tired and blistered, my back throbs, and my legs feel like they might give out. I grit my teeth, determined to ignore all the pain.

When I reach the edge of the highway, I can hardly believe it. I take a deep breath, stopping my run for a moment to catch my breath. I'm coughing so much that my throat is sore. My chest fills with hope when I spot some lights not too far away. A police barrier.

As ecstatic as I am, I don't wait another second before running toward them. I want to get out of here, even if it's to a police station. I want to explain all the horror I've been through; to tell them everything I've discovered about the country we live in, the government, and its sadistic lies. I'm going to expose Tom Warner to the world. And finally, return home to have the peace I deserve.

However, I am not welcomed so warmly by the three police officers. This is something I obviously did not foresee. Upon seeing me stumbling toward them, covered in dirt from head to toe, they instantly point their guns at me.

"Raise your hands! Stay where you are!" shouts a blond officer near the patrol car.

I freeze in place, raising my hands high with my palms visible. I'm at least seven meters away from them. The other officer, with black hair, grabs the radio communicator and starts talking rapidly. I can't understand what he's saying. The other two slowly walk in my direction, their guns still drawn.

"What are you doing here?" asks the blond one hostilely.

His blue eyes pierce mine, filled with acidity.

"I'm running from the fire," I shoot back.

My throat is scratched from all the coughing. It's better not to immediately explain who I am since they're being so cautious. In the dark of the highway, with a swollen purple eye and a forehead covered in bandages... I must look unrecognizable.

"Are you hurt? Are you alone?" asks the other officer.

"I'm alone."

The two seem satisfied with my answer and advance more quickly. However, before crossing the remaining four meters, the tanned officer suddenly stops, as if he's seen a ghost. His skin pales, his dark eyes nearly popping out of their sockets, recognition flashing across his expression.

"It's her! Sophia!" he screams in horror. The other blond officer also stops, frowning as he evaluates me. "Oh, and she's armed!"

Crap. I completely forgot about the gun still strapped to my waistband. How criminal must I look now in their eyes? I try not to think about it.

In a split second, during which I can't think clearly about what to do next, before I can say anything in my defense, the blond officer tightly grips the trigger. I throw myself to the ground just as he fires.

I can't believe they're shooting at me! I feel fear and fury.

I shouldn't be testifying, being taken to the station, handcuffed, judged, or anything like that? They're trying to kill me seconds after recognizing me!

Phelipe's words from the day he told me about the chimeras come back to my mind: "You need to know one thing: if he didn't want to kill you before, after shooting him, he'll definitely want to decorate his living room with your head."

He couldn't have been more right. Tom Warner gave direct orders to kill me.

I remain fallen, with my face pressed against the cold asphalt, eyes closed, knowing it's useless to try to crawl or run away. They will hit me. It's three armed police officers against me. By the time I manage to draw my weapon and at least intimidate them into backing off, I'll already be full of holes like Swiss cheese.

I hunch over as much as I can, my whole body shaking in violent spasms, waiting for the fateful shot that will kill me. My teeth are chattering so hard that they involuntarily bite my tongue. I'm forced to close my mouth, tasting blood. Ice runs through my veins. Waiting for death is harder than I imagined.

But when I hear no noise at all, I turn my neck in the direction of the officers, finally opening my eyes with fear. I'm so startled by what I see that I instinctively recoil, scraping the skin of my cheek against the asphalt.

Phelipe.

He looks like a demon coming from the darkest depths of hell, his eyes bloodshot with hatred. In a swift motion, he grabs the officer who was talking on the radio by the collar of his uniform, causing the device to fall to the ground and shatter into pieces. The man's feet dangle about fifteen centimeters above the ground, flailing frantically. Then, Phelipe throws him away like a rag doll. The officer falls unconscious on the shoulder of the road, motionless.

The other two are as stunned as I am, unable to move. The blond finally seems to snap out of his stupor, cocking his gun and firing continuously. The smile that Phelipe opens is so diabolical it paralyzes my breath for seconds. He walks slowly, absorbing all the bullets that pop against his body as if they were merely unwanted flies. The three of us stare at him, horrified.

My eyes widen in panic as I see him slap the tanned officer so hard that he spins like a top and falls several meters later. The blond tries to run when his bullets run out, completely disoriented by the fact that the entire magazine wasn't enough to even injure his enemy. Only the lab's weapons could do that, but they don't know this.

Phelipe pulls him by the ankle, making him fall to the ground. From the sound of the man's jaw hitting the asphalt, I'm sure it's broken. Spinning him in the air to gain momentum, the lab rat throws him against the patrol car. The officer crashes through the windshield with brutality, shattering it into a million shards of glass. A deadly silence ensues, except for the crackling fire destroying everything to my left.

Phelipe calmly turns to me. The flames cast strange shadows on his demonic face. I freeze.

With wide, quick steps, I watch him approach. I can't move; all my limbs have turned to jelly under his murderous gaze. His lips are pressed into an extremely thin line. His expression carries much more than just the wrath of the devil; there's betrayal in his face.

I shot him and left him to die in the fire. I shot the person who tried to help him: his sister. I *betrayed* him.

When Phelipe crouches near me, I curl up, feeling sobs form in my throat. The lab rat simply looks at me for a long time, saying nothing. His caramel-colored eyes study my face, furious. I'm not sure what he's looking for. Regret? Forgiveness?

"I hope you finally understand that the police are not on your side," he growls through clenched teeth after some time; his voice is three times raspier than usual.

"I-I-I..."

"Spare me your explanation," he interrupts with acidity. It's so hostile it hurts more than a slap. "Did they shoot before you could get close?" I nod. "Looks like you really pissed off Tom Warner."

I curl up even more, hugging my knees in a fetal position. His deadly gaze hurts me in a way I never thought possible.

"Where is she? I swear I'll tear every last hair from that vague..."

"We're here, sister," Phelipe impatiently interrupts the colossal roar coming from Penélope; even the hairs on the back of my neck stand on end at the sound of her furious voice.

I tremble, looking around, frightened. Penélope is the living portrait of chaos. She emerges from the burning underbrush with her tight dress ripped up the side of her thigh, dragging what's left of her scorched backpack. Her curls are completely full of leaves and dirt. One of her heels is broken, and she holds it in her hand like it's a weapon. Probably is.

There's nothing more lethal than her expression. While Phelipe is a warrior demon, she is a goddess of darkness, threatening. The ground seems to shake beneath her fury.

"I'm going to kill you." It's not a threat; it's a warning. I try to seek protection from the boy beside me, but to no avail. This time, he doesn't seem willing to defend me from the explosion that is his sister. However, when she approaches with determination, Phelipe stands up, placing himself between us. "If I have to take you down to strangle the neck of that skinny girl, I will," he growls at his brother, baring his teeth.

I don't know if she's angrier with me or with him for daring to defend me.

"There are ropes in your backpack. Tie her up," she replies curtly.

"What?!" we both ask in unison, incredulous.

Phelipe huffs, getting annoyed.

"Tie... her up," he growls the two words separately, as a threat.

Penélope opens a glorious smile. I'm looking at him as if he's gone mad, which apparently has happened.

Tie me up? Why? What will they do to me?

"I'd prefer a quick and painless death, if you want to hear my opinion," I say, finally sitting up.

I'm still trembling from the horror to come. Penélope raises an eyebrow at me in total disdain. Phelipe glares at me for half a second before turning his face away. His gaze is like a whip of ice.

"You won't have," he warns coldly.

His sister is practically skipping, about to hum to the wind. The broken heel has been forgotten and thrown away. She bends down to rummage through the partially burned backpack, trying to find the ropes.

"What happened to the guy who said, 'let's not be so hard on her'?" Penélope asks with a conspiratorial smile on her face.

Phelipe looks back at me with disgust.

"They shot him, and he's pissed."

CHAPTER TWENTY-FIVE

Sophia

Being tied up at the wrists and ankles is not pleasant, I must say. Phelipe stole a car. He believes it's safe to travel in a vehicle now. Whether Penélope agrees, I don't know, but his mood is so bitter that I believe she won't bother him anytime soon.

The two of them took my gun and stashed it God knows where. They tied my arms so I could walk being pulled by the end of the rope, like a prisoner from the last century. Still, this is better than I thought they would do to me.

At first, I had to carry the backpacks, including Phelipe's, for a long way. They didn't let me say a word. However, I was so exhausted that my legs gave out. I thought they would drag me along the asphalt until my skin was completely scraped off, as if I were being subjected to a cheese grater, but the boy let out an impatient sigh and carried me in his arms, provoking furious growls from his sister.

"Just give me a moment to rest. Then I'll be able to walk again," I said in a voice that barely passed as a whisper.

I was completely exhausted. My eyelids struggled to stay open as he carried me like a baby in his arms. My legs swung in the wind, burning with pain.

"Sleep," he ordered.

His jaw was clenched tightly, accentuating the rigid line that his lips formed. Phelipe looked straight ahead with enviable determination. Not once during our journey did he dare to look at me.

Penélope began to complain in the background, but my mind switched off before I could understand what she was saying. I woke up sweating and panting in the back seat of the stolen car.

At this moment, the discomfort of having stayed in the same position for too long starts to hit me. My leg is numb, and my arms are tingling. I lift my eyes, finding Phelipe's rigid back as he drives. Penélope has her feet up on the passenger seat; her face buried in a newspaper, which she reads intently. Neither of them seems to care about the struggle I'm having to try to free myself from the ropes, although they obviously know I'm awake and squirming in the back seat.

"I wouldn't do that if I were you," Penélope warns without looking at me, her voice oddly calm.

"You don't need to keep me tied up; I won't run away again. I swear," I plead.

My tongue is so dry it feels like sandpaper.

"You should have thought about that before you shot me. You're lucky I haven't broken your windpipe yet," she replies coolly, turning the page of the newspaper.

I huff, irritated. I roll onto my side, staring at the ceiling of the car.

I wish I were home with my family. I wish I could wake up in my bed, listening to Isa's laughter and my mother scolding Lily for being pantsless again, wanting to trip over her drunken body lying on the living room floor as I try to make my way to the kitchen. I miss when my only problems were having to dodge Ana Catarina's pink Channel bag, always strategically left in the hallway for me to trip over, and Izec flirting with some girl.

"We bought your breakfast," Penélope says after a while; I'm still lost in my memories.

With her face still buried in her reading, she doesn't look at me as she hands me a paper-wrapped bundle. I wish I had the energy to pout, stomp my feet, and go on a hunger strike until they untie me. But the smell filling my nostrils is so good that it makes my stomach growl instantly.

"I can't eat with my hands tied," I complain.

Penélope stretches her arm, turning the volume knob of the radio up to an unpleasant level. Fine, I got the message.

I unwrap the bundle with difficulty, relieved to find a huge hamburger loaded with sauce, along with a large cup of orange juice. I drink almost all of it in one gulp.

As the ketchup runs freely down my chin, dripping onto my already dirty clothes, Penélope sits up straight in the passenger seat, as if she's just received a shock. She whispers something to her brother. I can see in the rearview mirror that he furrows his brow in response. The music playing on the radio keeps me from hearing them. The girl points to something in the newspaper, and he nods.

"What is it? What happened?" I ask, unable to contain myself, wiping my face with the back of my hand; I end up smearing more sauce over my bandages.

Neither of them answers me, returning to the positions they were in as if they hadn't heard me. Damn it! Shit! A thousand times shit!

I look out the windows, seeing nothing but the roadside around me, with no idea where we are. I don't know how long I slept or where they are taking me. The only thing I was told is that we are heading into the storm. Whatever that means.

*

I WAS ABRUPTLY AWAKENED from my rest by Penélope's unkind hands. We had to abandon the stolen car on the road and set it on fire; now we will walk a distance before getting another vehicle. I imagine there are more police barriers ahead.

Phelipe is pulling the end of my rope. I feel like a horse being led by a halter. The sun is already setting as we walk through the brush at the roadside. Again.

My legs burn so much that they can barely support my own weight. My arms feel like they've been crushed by an anvil; they hurt so much that I can't even lift them. The heavy backpacks slow my progress, making me think of a thousand different ways to kill Penélope with the stones she makes me carry. At least it distracts me a bit from the torture of staying on my feet.

Penélope walks ahead with a newspaper open in front of her nose, seeming absorbed in it. Her hair is styled and perfectly arranged. She wears tight leather pants and a corset that narrows her waist too much, along with stiletto sandals with straps; all black. I have no idea how she manages to balance on the sloped terrain. But it seems to require no effort at all. I imagine she must have gotten ready while I was sleeping. She even put on makeup!

Phelipe is the mask of toughness and hostility. Occasionally, he glances back at me over his shoulder with impatience, probably lamenting my slowness. I instinctively shrink back and try to quicken my pace, without much success. His clothes have been changed to dark jeans, a black shirt, and a jacket, with typical leather boots on his feet.

I must look like a zombie with my tangled and knotted hair, my face covered in dirty bandages, clothes loose and filthy, and worn-out high boots. I don't even want to imagine how my breath must smell after all this time without brushing my teeth, or how I must smell without having bathed. I feel itchy just thinking about it.

The most embarrassing moment of my day was having to pee behind a bush, with Penélope holding my rope and murmuring something about cow urine being good for fertilization. My face heats up just remembering.

I feel like we are more paranoid, alert to any little noise, ever since those hellhounds came after us. I heard Penélope telling her brother that the dogs' knife-like teeth are bizarre. So my suspicions are indeed true; the dogs have razor-like fangs. Great! From what I understand, most animals are afraid of chimeras. Dogs are less friendly, since the test subjects are half felines. That's why the lab created these hellish offspring to chase after the runaway chimeras. I don't know if they can kill them, but I wouldn't bet against those teeth.

"They could at least tell me where we are going," I complain, tired.

"I already told you," Penélope mutters, irritated.

"Following the storm. Wow, that makes everything so clear," I retort.

"Great."

"Or at least what they're going to do to me when we get there." I'm addressing Phelipe directly, who is purposefully ignoring me.

Penélope gives my rope an unexpected strong tug, making me fall face-first to the ground. My weakened knees buckle easily under the weight of my body. Penélope lets out a giggle. With hate in my eyes, I rise from the ground, spitting out the dirt that got in my mouth. We glare at each other for a long time.

I start walking again, thinking of a thousand ways to kill Penélope with a stone. It comforts me. For now.

CHAPTER TWENTY-SIX

Sophia

I am sitting under a tree, trying to warm myself by the fire as I watch Phelipe clean his daggers. My hands remain tied with tight knots that hurt every time I try to move. Occasionally, I receive a scowling glance from the lab boy, as if he is checking to see if I am still here. As if I could easily escape like this.

Fortunately, Penélope is running around the perimeter, doing the first watch. The day is almost dawn, which means Phelipe is ready to go to sleep. Apparently, so am I. Damn the mutant time zone.

"Sleep," he grunts at me as he gets up.

With the tip of his foot, he kicks dirt onto the makeshift fire, which is already weak. I shrink back as much as possible, shivering from the cold from head to toe. The sweatshirt that Phelipe stole from my house is no longer enough against the chilly night air. My teeth are chattering in my mouth so hard that it makes my jaw shake. The little light coming from the fire goes out all at once, plunging us into darkness.

I hear rustling clothes and deduce that Phelipe is changing. I lie on the damp ground, curling up like a ball, trying to get as comfortable as possible. Apparently, I lost the right to have a blanket or a sleeping bag since I shot the Kyle siblings. My nights are reduced to shivering from the cold, on the brink of hypothermia, while I cry until I lose consciousness.

"Phelipe..." I whisper after a few minutes, breaking the silence of the night, which is filled only by the sounds of the insects biting me; I can't even scratch properly.

He lets out an irritated sigh.

"I'm not giving you my blanket, Sophia. No use begging."

I squirm, restless.

"I don't want your blanket. I want to talk about the copy."

The copy, Sofia, that's what bothers me the most from the beginning. And it's the issue with the least answers so far. How can I resemble someone so much that my life is completely destroyed because of it? I want to understand the situation better, what exactly she did to be so hated, to put Tom Warner on my tail and leave all the test subjects in a frenzy.

"We're not talking about her," he replies tersely.

"That's not fair! It's my life, and no one tells me anything!" I practically whine. "Why can't you tell me about her?"

"Because I don't want to talk about her!" he spits the words at me.

Even without being able to see him in the dark of night, I know his jaw is clenched with rage.

"You still love her..." I whisper with conviction, so softly that I wonder if he really heard me.

I instantly regret my words when I hear an abrupt noise and realize he has sat down on his sleeping bag.

"I don't love anyone." His dry lips spit out each syllable separately at me, making the predominant anger in each of them explicit. "As you like to say: I'm a lab boy. I was raised not to have feelings. If you're looking for something good in me to try to soften me with your sweet talk, or to give you a blanket, or to untie you, or whatever your plan is, it won't work."

"I don't have any plan! I just want to know about her."

I sit up too, squinting in the dark; it's starting to brighten with the first rays of sunlight appearing, and soon I'll be able to distinguish his silhouette. With a heavy sigh, which sounds more like a growl, he throws himself back onto the sleeping bag, gazing at the sky.

"What do you want to know?" he asks, his voice more controlled.

"Why do we look alike?"

"I don't know."

"But you have a theory," I deduce.

"Yes, but I'm not sure."

"Why don't you tell me?"

"I don't know if you noticed, but I said I *don't have certainty*," he growls, impatient.

"But damn it!" I exclaim, returning to lie on the cold ground. The muscles in my arms ache from being stretched for so long because of the ties. I try to move until I can find a comfortable position, without success. I huff in frustration. "How is it possible that I resemble someone so much physically? Are we twins or something?"

The idea has crossed my mind a few times, based on the fact that I don't resemble my sisters and mother at all; they are all blonde with gray eyes, while I have dark hair and no features that resemble my mother. Unfortunately, I look quite a bit like my father. I considered the possibility that I was the result of his extramarital affair, which could have led to the birth of twins; my mother, with her big soft heart, would have been willing to raise one of the children as her own.

"You're not twins." And my whole theory just went down the drain. "Twins, no matter how similar identical twins may be, still have some differences. It's as if you were the same person," he says, looking thoughtful. "Besides, she's older than you."

"She got attached to the test subjects, taught them how to escape, but for you, she promised something more than just getting you out of that place, right?" I'm trying to piece together the facts I have so far to truly understand what happened. Maybe this way, I can get a more complete sense of what I'm living through. When he doesn't answer me, I take his silence as a yes. "So, after you both escaped, she just disappeared?"

A deep sigh. A restless fidget. I know he's thinking about his words.

"On the night she came to free us, she showed up desperate. It had been a while since she had seen us, and I was quite worried. She came in crying, saying they had discovered how she treated us, that they had seen it on the security cameras, caught her red-handed snooping through important documents, asking questions that shouldn't have been asked... Anyway, she dropped the bomb on me that I had a family, that I had two siblings, who were also trapped there, and gave me an address to find her once I got out of there because they wanted to kill her."

"But she never showed up."

"No."

"Have you ever thought that something might have gone horribly wrong for her not to have shown up?"

"Yes," he confesses. "So I did everything I could to find her, afraid that the lab had found her before I did, or that she had never managed to get out of there on the night she freed us. But it was only a matter of time before I found her still working in the same place where they tortured me for years on end, while she warmed the bed of Teodoro Warner."

"Teodoro?" My voice rises two octaves in shock. "Tom's father? Wasn't he too old for her?"

"Not too much," he murmurs. "I think they just kept her away from the test subjects, but they kept her close because she was an excellent professional. I mean, I'm not sure if the story she told me about them discovering her relationship with me was true. Maybe it's just another one of her lies."

"And why does Tom Warner hate her then? If his father kept her around, even too much."

"Shortly after that, she freed another test subject, stole important documents from the lab, and fled."

With every second, I understand less. Why would she free so many test subjects if she had no intention of staying with them? Why get involved with Teodoro Warner, the sick mind behind the experiments she despised? What the hell was she doing?

"We have the same name. What does that mean?"

"I don't know."

"But my grandmother chose my name." When he says nothing about it, I fidget restlessly. My necklace gets caught on a piece of the tree root I'm lying on, and I have to struggle with my tied hands to free it. I roll onto my side until I see Phelipe's figure illuminated by the morning light, lying on his sleeping bag, looking at the blue sky, so still that it makes me believe he has already fallen asleep, but I know he hasn't. "My necklace... my grandmother gave it to me too. And Penélope has an identical one."

I remember what seems to have happened years ago, when Phelipe and I met, his interest in my necklace, just as I was intrigued to discover that Penélope has an identical one. What does this necklace mean? Does the pendant represent the animal part of the chimeras?

"What you're wearing is mine," Phelipe reveals. "Penélope's is just an imitation."

"What do you mean, yours?"

He lets out a deep sigh, making condensed smoke from the cold escape his lips.

"Sofía gave me that necklace."

"But my grandmother gave it to me. Didn't you hear? How could she have access to something that *Sofia* gave you? Besides, I never met my grandmother; she died when I was born. My father told me she wore this necklace all the time. It can't be yours; it's physically impossible. It must be a copy, just like Penélope's. The question is: why would my grandmother have this?"

There's something I don't say. My grandmother was a doctor, and as far as I know, she worked at one of Omega Laboratory's clinics. My mother always told me this story about how my paternal grandmother, Márcia, helped her during the pregnancy, which was risky since my father had beaten her until she almost lost the baby. I've thought about it before, that my grandmother might have somehow known the copy since they worked at the same place, but the ages don't add up. That's why I don't say anything to him.

"You really don't think I know what your *grandmother* did, do you?" he ridicules. "Now shut up and go to sleep. The day will be long."

I take that as a sign that he won't reveal anything beyond what he has already said, and I let out a sigh, adjusting myself on the ground. My mind takes a little while to switch off before I enter the dream world with the red-haired woman.

CHAPTER TWENTY-SEVEN

Sophia

"Is this the best you can do? Seriously?" Penélope Kyle's nasal voice sounds sarcastic in my ears.

I huff in frustration. With a triumphant laugh, the slender girl with curly black hair releases my hand, which she had effortlessly suspended in the air just inches from her face.

This must be the hundredth blow I've tried to land on Penélope's face, all without success. She has already taught me exactly how to do it: how to articulate my arm, the position of my hand, the impact my fingers should have on the target... I know it all. Theoretically. In practice, I haven't even come close to hitting my target. My instructor has unnatural reflexes.

The sun is setting on the horizon, casting orange hues across the sky. Every muscle in my body aches from walking and now having to fight against Penélope. The girl insisted that we train a bit so I can learn to defend myself in case we are attacked. I think it's completely stupid since the hellhounds, or the chimeras, would shred me before I even have a chance to get close. Maybe it's just another attempt to humiliate me. Besides, I had no choice. Penélope knocked me down onto the ground before I could protest. At least they untied my hands.

I tuck a greasy strand of hair behind my ear.

"If you let me hit your face just once..." I ask, cordial.

"Do you really think that in a real fight your opponent is going to let you hit them on purpose?"

Penélope raises an eyebrow at me. I grimace in displeasure.

"Do you really think I have any chance of winning a fight against anyone?"

"Don't forget," she says as she trips me with her long leg, making me fall backward into the dirt; my whole body protests in pain, "our enemies are not just genetically modified creatures from the lab. Humans aren't on our side either." She steps closer to me, extending a hand to help me up. As soon as I touch her fingers, she skillfully twists my body, making me lie face down before she drives her stiletto heel into my neck and buries my face in the ground. "If we are attacked and you run away, leaving us to fight alone, I swear I'll use you as a shield."

She releases me with a triumphant smile on her lips. I stretch my arms and legs as I get up, making all my joints crack. I stretch my neck and take a deep breath, positioning myself for another beating.

Phelipe looks back over his shoulder at me with a hint of amusement and compassion on his face. He leans against something, carefully polishing his silver dagger. The branches of the tree shake above his head, leaving a trail of tiny leaves in his hair.

"You're weak," his hoarse voice whispers to me.

"Thank you very much," I murmur, sourly, wiping the dirt from my clothes.

Which isn't much help since I'm completely filthy, having gone days without a shower or brushing my teeth.

"Come here," he orders, extending the rope in my direction.

I walk toward him, huffing with anger with each step. I extend my bruised wrists in the air, feeling them burn even before Phelipe can wrap the rope around them. His eyes stare hard at the cuts that stretch across my skin, the deep wounds from my attempts to free myself, which left me raw. His expression is inscrutable as he ties the final knot, but I could swear the rope is looser than last time. He yanks the end of the rope, causing me to stumble. I shoot him a frantic look.

Penélope moves ahead with a newspaper open in front of her face. I'll never know what she reads in those papers. But every day she buys one, spends half the time reading each word, occasionally circling something with a marker. And, of course, every time I ask to read it, I'm ignored.

Deep down, I sometimes think it's for the best. I couldn't bear to read the distorted news about me, portraying me as a horrible villain, a murderer, or having to read anything that glorifies Tom Warner's benevolence.

We walk for a long time with the sun still setting on the horizon. It's nice to enjoy the last hours of the day, considering I've practically been living on bat time. The weather has gradually cooled, making me shiver all over, feeling the hairs on my body stand on end. My body aches with every step; all my muscles feel like they've been through a meat grinder.

"Are you hearing that?" Penélope asks, stopping and abruptly turning to Phelipe.

Phelipe furrows his brow, concentrating. He nods, which makes his sister smile. No matter how hard I try, I can't hear anything beyond the sounds of the brush, the birds in the trees, the unbearable insects, and the sound of the cold wind whistling in my ears.

The two of them quicken their pace, and I have to practically run or I'll be dragged along the ground thanks to this stupid rope.

"What is it? What did you hear?" I ask, anxious, already imagining new hellhounds or any other damn creature that that devil's lab might have created.

I am completely ignored. As we walk, I manage to hear a faint familiar sound before finally identifying it: water. A waterfall. I perk up, feeling my body relieve a bit of tension at the thought that I might be able to wash myself.

When we arrive, my heart fills with a good emotion. I see the clear water flowing over the stones, reflecting the end of the afternoon. My toes curl in my boots, practically begging to be washed.

I hear voices and laughter coming from afar; I need to stretch my neck to see. A group of friends is sitting by the waterfall with an unplugged electric grill, some coolers scattered around, and swimwear. They seem to have already organized things to leave after enjoying a pleasant day but are still chatting, prolonging their stay.

Penélope breaks into a big smile upon seeing the group; four boys and two girls.

"Looks like we'll have company."

With enviable skill, she rips off the black leather dress she's wearing in an absurdly elegant way.

She stands in front of us in nothing but *black lingerie*, not caring at all that her brother can see her, before gracefully walking toward the group.

"What is she doing?" I ask, frightened, moving closer to Phelipe, who watches her with amusement.

"Satisfying her sexual appetite," he replies casually.

"What?" I choke on my own breath. "Is she going to hook up with one of those boys?"

I see her approaching, tossing her long curly hair from side to side, catching the attention of everyone present. She smiles, as if she's just a pretty and friendly girl, not the psychotic crazy I know she is.

"Or one of the girls," Phelipe murmurs, starting to take off his own boots.

"Is Penélope bi?" I ask, astonished.

Phelipe turns to me, looking irritated.

"You humans and your obsession with labeling everything." He sighs. "When I escaped the lab, I was shocked to learn that you labeled this. You know, we lived caged like animals, but we always had the freedom to engage with whomever we wanted, be it a man or a woman; there was never any distinction. Just like in nature, sexuality is a natural thing, but you complicate it. So imagine how surprised I was to step out and discover that you humans kill each other for not accepting who others sleep with. That's sick."

"So you guys will sleep with anyone, no matter the gender or sexual orientation?"

I raise an eyebrow.

"Sex is sex, Sophia," he replies simply. "So, are you going to get in?" I nod eagerly, excited at the thought of being able to dive in. Phelipe approaches me, roughly pulling my arms to start untying me. "If you try anything, I'll cut your throat," he threatens.

"Thanks for the subtlety," I retort bitterly.

He smiles. After untying me, he turns his back and pulls off his shirt without ceremony. I've never seen him without clothes before, and I jump at the sight of his well-defined abs. I quickly avert my gaze as he begins unbuttoning his pants.

I move my wrists, smoothing them out to try to relieve the pain from the rope marks. I consider the possibility of entering the water with my clothes on due to the cold, but then I won't have anything else to wear and will freeze to death under a tree overnight. I look around, realizing that Penélope and the group have apparently vanished.

Phelipe is only in white boxer shorts, staring at me. I involuntarily gasp, quickly averting my gaze, feeling my cheeks burn.

"Are you going to get in or not?" he asks, raising an eyebrow.

"I thought felines didn't like water," I tease, walking toward him.

"Most don't," he retorts.

He turns his back to me, stretching his body before taking a leap and diving into the water. I watch until I see his head surface.

With night beginning to fall around me, I have no more excuses to delay taking off my clothes, so I start to undress. My body is shivering from the cold and embarrassment because, even without looking in his direction, I feel his eyes burning into my exposed skin. When I'm left in only my black bra and panties, trembling so much that my knees knock together, I approach the edge, assessing the depth. I close my eyes, taking a deep breath to gather my courage. The cold water hits me like a spear as soon as I dive in.

I surface, gasping for air. Phelipe is on the far side, watching me curiously. I need to keep moving my feet and arms constantly to avoid freezing completely.

"I thought you were going to get in with your clothes on," he comments sarcastically.

"I considered the option," I murmur, panting. "But I remembered that you've probably seen every curve of this duplicated body."

He laughs, amused, throwing his head back.

"That could be the case, but I've never been with Sofia like this."

"What?" I furrow my brow, surprised. "You guys have never slept together?"

"I never had the opportunity," he says, swimming away from me.

I pull away, diving farther. With my fingertips, I try to untangle the knots in my hair, rubbing my entire scalp.

We remain silent while cleaning ourselves as much as possible. Unfortunately, my clothes are filthy, and putting them back on won't be pleasant. The stench will still be there. I regret not having soap or toothpaste to use.

Night falls in the blink of an eye, bringing with it the frigid cold and the sounds of animals in the brush. My chin is trembling so hard that I bite my tongue several times; still, I can't bring myself to leave the water, which, even cold, I'm sure is warmer than the surface.

I can't see Phelipe in the dark, but every now and then I hear the sound of the water and know he's swimming somewhere nearby. I'm quiet, leaning my back against a rock, hugging myself as tightly as I can.

"Did you have fun, little sister?" Phelipe's voice startles me.

"A bit," the girl responds from some point in the darkness. "Shall we go?"

Penélope turns on a flashlight, and I mentally thank her for providing a beam of light to guide me through the darkness. I start to move, knowing that it's inevitable to have to step out into the cold. Phelipe's hand grips my elbow tightly, practically dragging me toward the shore.

"You don't need to hold me; I know the way, thanks," I growl, trying to break free from his grip; it's like trying to push one of the rocks from the waterfall.

Freezing cold and feeling like I'm about to get hypothermia, I walk toward where Penélope and my clothes are, feeling my legs stiffen with each step. The girl throws a towel in my direction, which she probably stole from someone; I, without a shred of pride, am forced to accept it. Phelipe appears while I huddle against the warm cloth, surprisingly already dressed, with the rope in hand to tie me up again; the wounds on my wrists begin to burn in protest.

But before he can tie the first knot, a sepulchral silence falls around us. All the sounds of insects and frogs die suddenly. A chill runs through my body. Phelipe stands still, still holding the rope wrapped around my arm, probably trying to hear ahead what's wrong. But I already know, without needing superhuman hearing. It's just like last time; I almost have a *déjà-vu*.

The hellhounds are here.

CHAPTER TWENTY-EIGHT

Sophia

Things happen so fast that I can't even keep up.

The sounds of paws against the ground start to reach my ears along with animalistic growls that make me swallow hard with fear. Before I can realize it, Penélope whispers something practically unintelligible to Phelipe, and he throws me onto his back with impressive speed.

We take off running like a blur, and I constantly feel like we're going to crash into a tree. I shut my eyes tightly as soon as I feel my stomach churn in response to the speed.

I feel the leaves brush against my face as we move faster through the dense forest. Vomit is stuck in my throat. The cold seems to slice through my wet skin with the precision of a thousand blades. My legs are wrapped around Phelipe's waist, my arms around his neck, holding on to him with all my strength. I know he wouldn't let me fall, but still, I grip tightly.

"Phelipe," I whine when I realize we're being followed. "They're catching up to us."

Three animal heads enter my field of vision as I open my eyes. We're practically flying from how fast he runs, but the dogs are closing in without much difficulty. Their razor-sharp teeth glint in the dark.

"We'll lose them," he says over the biting wind.

We continue to dart into the woods like a blur, somehow managing to go even faster. Phelipe is taking a winding path, weaving between the trees with impressive agility. But just when I think we've finally lost them, I open my eyes only to see them inches from snapping at his heel.

"Phelipe! They're right on our tail. If they jump, they'll be able to bite me."

He glances over his shoulder just as one of the dogs makes a move to sink its teeth into his calf; luckily, he dodges by a fraction of a second.

"Shit," he curses.

I press my body harder against his, making every effort not to move and get into the line of sight of the beasts, which seem to have yet to look up, or they would have torn me apart. If only I still had my weapon...

"Give me your dagger!"

I flinch at the idea, but I feel a rush of hope at the possibility of throwing something at those dogs.

"For you to use on me? No way."

"Don't be ridiculous! It's our only chance before we become mutant dog food." He seems to think for a moment. The animals attack his leg again, but he manages to dodge once more. "Phelipe, we're running out of time..." My plea comes out louder than I expected, finally catching the creatures' attention toward me.

I can see their eyes gleaming in the dark, staring at me, measuring the distance needed to sink their teeth into my leg. I'm the easiest target; I won't be able to dodge like Phelipe.

"Promise you won't use it on me."

"I promise. Now give it to me, quick!" I shout when I see the animal pull back a little to gain momentum and leap.

His fingers clasp something cold in my hand. A silver dagger. The dog jumps with its mouth open for a certain bite. I let out a scream and drive the dagger into its mouth. The blade pierces the roof of its mouth and exits above its head. The razor-sharp teeth slice my arm slightly upon contact, but I don't care at this moment. I pull the dagger back out, releasing the animal, and its body falls to the ground.

The other dog prepares to leap, furious at what I did to its lab brother. Before it can jump, I throw the dagger with all the strength and precision I have, hitting it in the eye. The dog whines, collapsing immediately. The third doesn't try to charge at us, staying behind with its injured siblings.

"Nice shot," Phelipe praises, slowing down a bit.

"Sorry about the dagger," I say, but I'm secretly proud of myself for managing to save our skin.

"No problem. You saved us."

"Do you think they're..."

"Dead? Hardly." Phelipe seems to ponder. "We need to find Penélope and get the hell out of here."

CHAPTER TWENTY-NINE

Sophia

We are far from the waterfall when Penélope catches up with us. And she is not alone. In her arms, she drags the body of a hellhound, the same one I hit, still with Phelipe's dagger lodged in its eye. The creature seems unconscious, but it's hard to tell if it's alive or not.

"Are you trying to kill us?" Phelipe hisses at his sister, completely beside himself with the situation.

Penélope throws the dog on the ground, kneeling beside it. I hold my breath, trying to stay as far away from the two as possible.

"I want to know what these things are," she murmurs, more to herself than to us.

Gently, perhaps out of fear, she pulls the dagger from the animal. I'm acutely aware of every muscle in my body, the blood buzzing in my ears, preparing to run as far as possible at the first sign of any movement. Phelipe is tense beside me too, his shoulders too rigid, his eyes nearly popping out of their sockets.

Penélope examines the dagger with curiosity. There's no blood. Not a drop. But how is that possible? After all, what are they?

Phelipe takes a confident step toward the dog and pulls out another dagger from inside his jacket before kneeling down beside his sister. The two begin to tear apart the animal's skin.

I'm ready to run at any moment, my hands sweating even though I'm trembling from the cold from head to toe, my skin still wet, wearing only my underwear and bra. My clothes were left behind near the waterfall; I didn't get the chance to put them on before the attack.

Phelipe holds a piece of the hellhound's skin in his hands, evaluating it carefully. My stomach churns, and I'm forced to look away.

"It's synthetic skin," he announces. "They're not real animals."

"What?"

I turn in shock. What do you mean, not real? Then I gather all the courage left in me and approach with bated breath. Penélope is tearing more and more at the carcass of the creature, opening a large hole in the side of its body. Its skin, as real as it appears to the naked eye, is synthetic, ripping slowly against the blade. I can see the mechanisms inside the animal, the metal prosthetics that serve as its limbs, providing flexibility for movement, connected to various cables leading directly to what must be the brain.

"It's a skin-like fiber mesh embedded in a silicone elastomer that coats the structure," Phelipe comments.

I have no idea what he's talking about, but Penélope does, as she nods and soon opens a huge hole in the robot dog's skull. As I suspected, what should be the animal's brain looks like a computer motherboard.

"Sophia hit it in just the right spot." Phelipe points with his thumb to a small hole in the middle of the robot dog's brain plate. "It probably wouldn't have stopped if it was hit anywhere else."

"Why would they create robots?" I ask, nervous.

Penélope rolls her eyes at me impatiently.

"Why do they create chimeras? Why is the sky blue? Sweetheart, we're talking about Omega Lab here. They create anything."

"It's not that; it's just that..." I pause, trying to organize my thoughts. I'm trembling from the cold, my chin shaking all my teeth. "I thought the chimeras were their main experiment, a failed one, but still the *masterpiece*. Phelipe told me that the main flaw of the chimeras is that they are uncontrollable, so why didn't they just make you robots that could be controlled, with a human appearance?"

The two siblings are staring at me intently now, my words still rattling in both their minds. They know my points make sense.

Penélope jumps up, standing away from the carcass of the robot dog as if she suddenly remembers she's contaminated by a superbug. Her eyes are incredulous and glazed over.

"Oh my God! I had thought about this, about why these hellhounds don't attack humans. If they were chimeras, they should have already slaughtered half the population. However, I imagined they were made just to hunt the chimeras, that they had heightened senses for that. But they also hunt Sophia, who is human..." Penélope rambles, trying to organize her line of reasoning. I think about this too, as the hellhounds not only chased me but also nearly ripped pieces off me. "The chimera test at school was a total disaster... The collars, like a failed attempt to control them... The hellhounds chasing the fleeing chimeras, a weapon created to kill us... Oh my God! They're going to do it, aren't they?"

Phelipe's eyes widen as he steps back quickly from the dog, just like his sister. Understanding shines in his eyes as he grasps what Penélope is implying. He utters a string of curses.

"What?" I ask, still not grasping the reasoning. My breath comes out like smoke from my mouth. "What are they going to do?"

It's Phelipe who answers without even looking at me:

"They're going to turn the chimeras into robots. It's the only way to control them."

CHAPTER THIRTY

Sophia

I lean against the car window to admire the view. It's so beautiful that my eyes start to well up. The beach is practically deserted, with only a few people that can be counted on one hand walking along the sand. The chilling cold is likely keeping everyone away. Above the sea is the most stunning sunset I have ever seen, with a purple hue in a brilliant gradient of pink. I'm awestruck, admiring it, a smile burning on my face amidst the tears that sting my eyes. I realize it has been a long time since I smiled. My fingers and nose are pressed against the car window, my breath condensing on the glass. I can smell the salt and fish so deeply embedded on my tongue that I can almost taste it. It's almost like I'm diving right in.

Phelipe glances at me through the rearview mirror while driving. I know he's curious since I rarely sit up in the back seat, even when he stops the car. I never want to look outside and know where we are or do anything other than sleep and stare at the ceiling of the vehicle. But when I caught a whiff of the salty water, I had to sit up.

Lately, everything reminds me of my mother and sisters. Even the crumpled McDonald's wrapper at the bottom of the car made me think of Isa and how I wanted to bring her a toy. The beach reminds me of our end-of-year trips, the three of us with hair turning green from the seawater; Lily complaining about everything all the time; Isa crying with a red face bordering on sunburn; my mother going into every shop looking for a bikini that would make her look slimmer, simply perfect.

I keep wondering how they are. What is it like for them to deal with all these stories about me; do they believe I'm a murderer or innocent? I wish I could at least call and hear my mother's voice.

I no longer know how long we've been on the road. Two weeks? Three? The days are a mental blur, in which I wake and sleep in the back seat of a car or on the floor of a forest, waking every five minutes in fear of being attacked. Especially after the Kyle siblings discovered what the lab plans to do with the test subjects; they are on higher alert than before, afraid of being caught.

I also have no idea where we are. Yesterday, when Penélope stopped the car to refuel, the gas station attendant had a very different accent than the one I'm used to, but I couldn't recognize where it's from. We are definitely far from Minas Gerais, especially since we have passed several beaches. The landscape is changing drastically; we're surrounded by hills, steep descents and climbs, the weather absurdly cold, a humid climate that makes the green even greener.

When Penélope said we were heading into the storm, she was being literal.

⚡

EVERYTHING AROUND ME is dark.

My heart pounds in my chest, drowning out all other sounds as I run. The adrenaline rushes through my veins so quickly that it momentarily leaves me deaf. The dress is heavy, hindering my progress, with a corset too tight around my waist. But I have no choice; I need to keep moving as fast as I can so that *she* doesn't catch me.

I can hear her laughter echoing in the dark forest, seeming to come from everywhere and nowhere at the same time, as if she were omnipresent.

"You can't escape me," she hums.

I glance over my shoulder, feeling her breath on my neck, but there's no one there. Her laughter grows louder, shriller, coming from all sides, forcing me to turn my neck in every direction. Yet I can never see her, even though I can feel her.

I feel her presence suffocating me, cornering me in the dark, which forces me to stop running. I don't know which direction to go, which way to take because no matter where I go, she will find me and kill me. I'm out of breath, struggling to breathe, my legs trembling and exhausted.

Then comes that spine-chilling second, that moment when I know she's preparing to attack me somewhere in the shadows. But something different happens.

Like a trance breaking, the dream shatters into pieces in my mind, splintering the entire scenery around me. I huddle up, closing my eyes, imagining this is some kind of new attack that makes my brain throb and my head feel like it's cracking in half.

My eyes open, but they don't seem like my eyes, and it doesn't feel like my body. I feel strange, with confused thoughts swirling in my mind; my vision is blurry, the colors seem to have different shades, and I don't recognize anything around me. Above me is a person completely clad in white, with the Omega Lab symbol emblazoned on their chest. They're the ones responsible for the chimeras; I've met them on the night of the attacks at school, along with Tom Warner. But why are they here? Did they catch us? Where are Phelipe and Penélope? And why is this man holding a huge syringe trying to inject me?

I feel a painful tug at the back of my head, as if my brain wants to expel me from my body. I try to roll to the side to avoid the needle piercing my arm, but my body simply won't obey me. As soon as I feel the sharp sting, I manage to move my eyes to the other side, trying to see where I am.

Through the glass, across the corridor, I see a pair of brown eyes staring back at me; eyes I never expected to see again.

"Artur?" I whisper.

The tug at the back of my head grows stronger, leaving me momentarily dizzy as I plunge into the darkness of my subconscious.

I wake up startled, gasping for air. The sun is high in the sky, burning my skin. I'm lying in a fetal position, with my arms and ankles tied, beneath a tree in the woods. It's exactly where I remember being before I fell asleep. But where is the lab? That suffocating place with the glass door? Artur?

Artur! Shit!

I sit up quickly, looking at the spot on my arm where I supposedly got pricked. There's nothing there.

Penélope is asleep a few meters away. Phelipe is approaching after running all over the area during the first shift; he will wake his sister so she can sleep a little while he keeps watch. His eyes narrow at the sight of my expression.

"Artur," I say with a dry throat. Penélope sits up, stretching her whole body. "He's alive."

CHAPTER THIRTY-ONE

Sophia

Once again, I'm jostling in the back seat of a car. This is the only time I can sleep, so I shouldn't complain, but my muscles ache from walking and carrying extra weight on my back. My feet are raw, bleeding with every step I take. My arm is cut and burning where the dog's teeth found my skin. Even though this is one of the only hours I lie down, I still can't stretch my body the way I need to, especially in this cramped truck. I questioned the choice, but they laughed at my face.

Penélope is driving. She drums her fingers on the steering wheel, absentmindedly singing along to the song playing on the radio. Surprisingly, I prefer her driving to her brother's. He drives too fast.

Phelipe is lost in a deep sleep in the passenger seat. The sunlight on his face doesn't seem to bother him. His mouth is slightly open, and his neck jerks from side to side with each curve taken.

I'm starting to adapt to this bat schedule since every time I try to sleep outdoors, I remember the hellhounds attacking us.

I told them about the hazy dream in which I saw Artur. We think something went wrong with the dream Viviane planted in my head, probably because she was abruptly woken up by the caretakers for routine exams, and I accidentally slipped into her mind. Just thinking about it gives me chills. I was inside a lab cell, several meters below ground, in the body of a human test subject. I don't know if

Viviane realized I was in her mind, but I haven't dreamed about her since, which is a relief.

Still, Penélope warned me to avoid that as much as possible since it's unclear what happened and, as far as she imagines, if something went wrong, I could end up trapped in Viviane's mind. That's horrifying!

But the Kyles didn't like knowing that Artur is alive. He is an open enemy of the lab, standing in front of bullets to protect me. The fact that they have locked him up again only further confirms the theory that they are planning to control the chimeras in a robotic way.

I still don't have a formed opinion about this. I just know that I desperately need a shower and dental hygiene. I can't even stand my own smell. The last time I washed was at the waterfall, days ago, and that didn't even come close to penetrating the layer of dirt. I don't even want to imagine how I look.

Even Phelipe and Penélope, who are always the picture of perfection, are starting to look scruffy. Her hair looks like a nest of dry, greasy straw; her clean clothes are running out, and her heels are wearing down. Her brother isn't much different. I, obviously, look three times worse than both of them.

I sink into the seat, trying to sleep more. The bindings on my wrists and ankles have hurt me so much that the skin seems to have lost sensitivity. I try to find a comfortable position, but I can't.

The sun is high in the sky. The road is clear, almost devoid of other vehicles. Every now and then, I see gas stations or restaurants through the glass. Soon I will feel hungry. Of course, Phelipe and I would be easily detected in any of those places, even with the false identities Penélope got us and the blue cap and sunglasses she insists I wear. My face has been plastered on the front page of every newspaper for days. The lab boy too, as my accomplice, even if not in the spotlight, after all, the government wouldn't reveal the identity of a test subject. I never want to read anything about it; I just glance at the front page of the newspaper Penélope buys every day, hoping there's another shocking story besides me, but it never changes. In any case, everything that needs to be bought or stolen is always the task of the Kyle girl, who for now is the only one of us not being hunted.

When sleep doesn't come, I try to focus on the music filling the car. I know it, although I can't remember its name or the band. I hum softly to distract myself from my thoughts.

Penélope suddenly turns to me as if I had punched her in the back. I frown, not understanding what's happening. Biting her lips, she firmly presses the button on the radio, changing the song until it reaches track one again. It's *Angra dos Reis* by Renato Russo. We've already heard this song at least ten times just today. Great, apparently, it's forbidden for me to like anything.

The girl turns the volume up to the max, making the speakers vibrate violently, annoying me. Her brother jumps in his seat, looking around, bewildered. He complains about something I can't hear due to the deafening noise, which makes my head throb. I can't even cover my ears with my tied hands.

The two start a battle for control of the radio. Phelipe lowers the volume, she insistently turns it back up. He changes the song; his sister goes back to the same one. We continue like this for long minutes; all I hear from them are grunts and growls. Until the lab boy sighs, leaning back in his seat. Penélope opens a triumphant smile, singing at the top of her lungs.

I want to bang my head against the glass until I die, or at least shove the shards in my ears and pierce my eardrums. When the song finally ends, she restarts it, and I'm about to chew on my own wrists.

"Let's stop," Phelipe announces, turning off the radio.

I imagine Penélope will get angry and turn the damn music back on, but she just nods and signals to pull over. I lift my head to see the reason for the stop, finding a small gas station and a convenience store. It's far enough and isolated enough that maybe no one will recognize us.

"One peep and we'll break your neck," Penélope threatens, turning to me.

"You promise?" I retort, without humor.

The girl rolls her eyes, advancing on me to untie the ropes. I take a deep breath. It's nice to feel my wrists and ankles free. I move them, finally able to stretch.

"Put on the cap," Phelipe murmurs.

"As if I needed to! She looks like a beggar; no one will recognize her."

His lips curl into a near smile at his sister.

Ignoring both, I choose to actually put on the cap since my hair looks terrible. Phelipe opens the door and holds the front seat so I can pass. Just having to bend to get out of the car makes my whole body protest in pain. My knee cracks loudly, causing the lab boy to raise an eyebrow at me.

Penélope joins us with a serious face. She nods toward the glass door of the store.

"Better stay here."

There's a photo of me plastered right at the entrance of the store, prominently displayed, along with others of missing people. But I'm not one of them. I'm a wanted fugitive. I involuntarily shrink at the poster with my face, feeling the weight of the last few days crash down on me. My new reality.

Phelipe tells her everything that needs to be bought. I barely pay attention. All I can think about is how much this image must have hurt my family and friends. How horrible I must look in their eyes now.

Penélope walks gracefully toward the store, distancing herself from us. Even disheveled, she still manages to look flashy. Her brother is fueling the truck, casting furtive glances at me, evaluating any movement I might make. Great!

"I'm not going to run away, okay?" I shoot back, impatient. "You should trust me more after I saved our asses."

"I know you're not," he replies casually, subliminally suggesting that I can't take a step without him catching up to me.

"Then stop looking at me like that, lab boy."

"Looking how?"

He gives a crooked smile. His eyes light up with a hint of amusement.

"You know." My voice falters. I swallow hard. "You're looking at me differently. Like you're about to grab me the minute I move too quickly."

A door at the back of the store opens suddenly. A woman walks out wearing what I believe is a gas station uniform, carrying a backpack with a towel hanging off it. It's a bathroom!

"Shower! Phelipe, there's a bathroom with a shower right there." The boy circles the car, standing right next to me. I stare at him, hoping he's as excited as I am at the prospect of a bath, but he seems tense. "Do you know how long it's been since I had a shower?"

I cross my arms defiantly over my chest. There's no way they're going to deny me the use of the bathroom.

"My nostrils are more sensitive than yours. Believe me, I more than anyone know how badly you need a shower. Urgently," he mocks, making my face turn a deep shade of purple in embarrassment. Is he really complaining about my smell? "But I don't think it's safe for you to be alone."

"You don't think it's safe or are you afraid I'll run away?" When he doesn't answer, I roll my eyes in impatience. "Oh, come on! You'd drag me by the hair, completely naked, if you thought I might escape." Phelipe raises an eyebrow at the idea. "Don't be disgusting!

Besides, you can hear me from here. All I want is to wash up. I'm not going to run. You can block the window if you think it's better."

"Or we can find a lake or river where you can bathe. It doesn't have to be here."

I blink hard, incredulous.

"Maybe I want to use a bathroom like a lady."

The lab boy seems to think for a moment. I'm tapping my foot forcefully on the ground, letting out all the anger I feel. I can't believe I'm having to ask for permission to take a shower!

Phelipe lets out a sigh, giving in. Great! Because I wasn't going to give up so easily.

"I'll give you a vote of confidence." I open my mouth to complain that this isn't exactly a vote but my legal right, but he silences me with just a look. "However, promise me that at the first sign of trouble, you will scream. And if the problem is you, remember I'll take great pleasure in carrying you naked." I make a disgusted face at him, receiving a smug smile back. "Good. So don't take too long."

"Get me clothes, a towel, and a toothbrush," I order, turning my back on him.

I walk calmly, almost skipping at the thought of the warm water that will pour over me when he calls me back.

"Have you seen where we are? There aren't any of those things around here."

I don't turn to face him.

"Do what you do best then: steal from someone. I don't care how you do it, but you have until I'm done to get it!" I shout over my shoulder.

I head toward the bathroom. There's no way I'm using these filthy rags again. They smell so bad that it wouldn't even seem like I cleaned myself. Plus, I urgently need to brush my teeth. My breath could kill a bird in mid-flight. I shudder at the thought.

I imagine the bathroom must be for staff use only. Outsiders like me aren't welcome. Fortunately, it seems to be lunchtime. The only employee I see is the one who just came out, and she's too distracted with her phone to notice my approach. There are no customers at the gas station. The only car parked is ours, which has already been properly fueled. There might only be one person working here.

As I pass by the store window, I can see Penélope leaning over chocolate bars with a generously full basket under her arm. A bell fills the place as the front door opens, and I see Phelipe entering. I hope he can hear me scream from inside if a hellhound follows me or a stealthy, murderous chimera tries to kill me.

I notice a customer in the store watching me through the glass. Did he recognize me? I turn my head the other way, picking up my pace toward the bathroom. I can't afford to be caught.

To my dismay, the door doesn't lock. So I just close it, praying no one opens it while I'm showering. That includes Phelipe.

The bathroom is small and relatively dirty; someone hasn't scrubbed the floor in months. There's a toilet, a small divider with the shower area, and a sink. The mirror is a bit too high and partially broken. Determined to ignore the grimy stains on the white tiles, I shrug it off and start to hurriedly take off my clothes.

I throw them on the floor in the corner of the wall, hoping I won't have to wear them again. I turn on the shower with excitement. My heart is pounding hard in my chest. I wet my fingers, feeling the warm water. Good, it's better than cold.

Fortunately, there's a small, worn-out bar of soap in the soap dish. I try not to think about who must have used it. I'll have to use it as shampoo, unfortunately.

I finally free myself from the bindings. The cut on my forehead has a disgusting scab. The scratch on my cheek is almost healed. Maybe it will look better after I wash. Where I was grazed by a bullet on my shoulder, there's just a thin red line left. Only my neck remains bad. It looks like a tiger clawed at my skin. I should have gotten stitches. I notice in the mirror that my face looks less horrible than I imagined.

I take off one of my small earrings, which I hadn't even remembered was still in my ear. I'm about to take the back off the other when I catch a movement behind me. There's someone here.

I turn around with my blood running cold in my veins, almost wishing it's just Phelipe being inconvenient, but it's not him. It's the guy from the store who was staring at me through the window. Before I can scream for help, he closes the distance between us, covering my mouth with the palm of his hand. With his other arm, he hugs me tightly against him, making it hard for me to attempt to run. I scream, but the sound comes out completely muffled. I try to break free from his grip, struggling violently, kicking and clawing, but to no avail. The man is too strong.

"Stay quiet, sweetheart," he whispers against my ear. "Did you know they're offering a pretty good reward for your lovely head?"

I'm crying, completely out of control. My legs give way under the weight of my body, my knees knocking against each other, trembling uncontrollably. I try to push him away in every possible way, but he doesn't budge even a step.

Out of the corner of my eye, I see our reflection in the cracked mirror. His nose is crooked, looking like it's been broken multiple times. His hair is thin and blond, and he dresses like a cowboy. He must be nearing fifty. He looks ecstatic as he admires my naked body. My stomach contracts in repulsion.

"Maybe we can have a little fun before I hand you over to them, sweetheart," he whispers, licking my neck.

One of his hands begins to caress my breast. I'm trembling, in deep despair and terror. Tears blur my vision, rendering me blind. My sobs feel like spasms, contorting my entire body. A strong taste of vomit rises in my throat.

When he pinches my nipple hard, causing me to let out a muffled cry of pain, he gives the most terrible smile I have ever seen in my life. I feel his erection against my back and know that my fear only excites him further.

I look frantically around, searching for something I can use to hit him. My gaze falls on the soap dish where I placed my earring. The other one is still swinging in my ear.

I quickly turn my neck, shaking my head, causing the dangling earring to slip and fall onto my shoulder. I snatch it quickly between my fingers, making it seem like I'm trying to hit him in the face. With my other hand, I fumble around the soap dish until I grab the other earring. The man is so engrossed in licking and touching me that he barely notices my movements. With all the strength I have, I drive both earrings into the back of the hand covering my mouth.

Surprised by the blow, the man lets out a roar and jumps back, reflexively pulling his arm away. This is my chance.

"Help!" I scream as loud as I can, ensuring Phelipe and Penélope can hear me.

I assess my chances of getting past him to reach the door. There aren't many.

"You filthy bitch..." he growls, recovering from the shock.

But before he can leap at me again, as I know he plans to, the door bursts open. Phelipe.

I think I've never been so happy in my life to see him.

His expression could make Lucifer seem harmless. I see the seconds it takes him to understand the situation. Me, naked and trembling in one corner, the other man with a bleeding hand and an angry expression. I've never seen him so furious.

However, Phelipe is paralyzed, completely shocked by the scene, unable to show any reaction. Silently, I practically plead for him to move, to intervene, to get me out of there, but he doesn't budge.

"What the hell is going on here?" Penélope asks, barging into the bathroom, pushing her paralyzed brother aside. It takes her half a second to understand the scene. Her irritated expression turns to pure disgust. "It's amazing how all the things that make my stomach turn have to do with men."

The cowboy assesses his opponents, trying to find a gap. He must have concluded that Phelipe isn't going to move, as he stands completely frozen, like a statue, and that taking down Penélope is his best chance, so he lunges at her, trying to catch her off guard. Bad idea.

She waits for his attack without hesitation. There's something strange on her face, a heavy shadow over her eyes that I can't decipher, but it makes the guy's eyes widen. The man tries to take her down with a rough gesture, which only makes her roll her eyes and huff, bored, as she twists the man's arm behind his back and pushes him to his knees on the floor.

"Why do men underestimate a woman's strength? Frankly, between me and my brother, you thought *I* was the weakest? Well, I have some bad news for you. Even though I'm wearing fifteen-inch heels and a leather dress that limits my movements a bit but still makes me look fabulous, I never lose a fight. Especially not to worms like you."

The man whimpers in a thousand different tongues as she twists his arm even more. When I hear a crack, I know for sure she broke it.

"Bitch!" he yells with a scarlet face.

Penélope shrugs, unfazed.

"It's one of the many words that filthy men like you use to describe me and all other women. If being a bitch means hurting rapists, misogynists, and any other male human trash until they wet their pants, then that's exactly what I am."

She shoves him to the ground. I notice that his pants are wet with urine, probably caused by the pain and fear. Still, the cowboy continues to hurl obscenities at the girl, swearing that he'll kill her.

"Oh, spare me your little speech!" She rolls her eyes. Lifting her leg until her heel is lodged in the man's groin. "This is what you should feel every time you think about touching a woman without her consent. Whether she's naked or not."

Without hesitating, she crushes his testicles, making him scream. Phelipe shows a brief, smug smile.

"This is the feeling that all men like you should know: having your balls crushed in an elegantly feminine way." She kicks him, spinning his body with her foot so that he ends up face down. Using her signature move, she drives her heel into the back of his neck. "And you won't do anything but piss yourself. I want the last thing you remember to be that you were defeated by a Louboutin heel. And that you'll never touch a girl again, with or without her consent."

With firmness, she drives her shoe with all her might into the man's neck until it penetrates his skull and his desperate screams silence.

I'm still trembling when it's over. I'm still trembling when Penélope yanks the stiletto from the man's skull. I'm still trembling when Phelipe snaps out of his trance, finally turning to me; his eyes soften immediately.

"Are you hurt?" he asks cautiously.

I shake my head, hugging my body to try to cover myself. I'm still paralyzed by fear. His eyes don't leave my face for a second.

"Frankly, and we are the animals here," Penélope grumbles, wiping the blood from her shoe on the man's shirt. "Are you okay?"

I shake my head again. Phelipe lets out a puff of air through his nose, controlling himself, visibly irritated. Without saying a word, he turns his back and runs out the door. Penélope is pushing the corpse, which just minutes ago was bothering me, to a corner of the wall when he returns with a coat that's too big and a tiny pair of panties that I believe belongs to Penélope.

He holds both out toward me, waiting for me to take them and put them on, but I'm too in shock to move. I know I need to. I want to get out of here, but my body simply won't obey me.

"It's okay," he says, uncertain about how to act. "Do you mind if I help you get dressed? I won't hurt you, I promise." *I know,* I want to say. I know he wouldn't hurt me, not like that at least. But my mouth feels glued shut; no sound escapes me. *Help me, please.* It's the first time I regret that he can't hear my thoughts. — Okay, I'm going to come closer to you, alright? If you want me to leave, just blink twice in a row, and I'm out of here." I don't blink. "Penélope, help me out here."

He cautiously moves closer. His eyes never leave my face, not wavering for a second, even when he kneels in front of me with a pair of panties stretched out so I can just slip my legs through. Struggling against my stone-like muscles, I force my feet to move. Phelipe dresses me as if I were a child.

Penélope leaves the body she was searching and calmly approaches. She throws the oversized coat over my shoulders and helps me slip my arms through the holes. It's too big and looks like a dress on me, covering almost halfway down my thighs. I have no idea where he could have gotten it.

Both of their eyes are careful not to look beyond what's necessary to help me get dressed. When I can't walk, Phelipe patiently lifts me into his arms, cradling my head against his chest. He closes the bathroom door with his foot as he passes through, leaving the now blood-soaked body in the deep darkness of the room. Penélope follows us, silent.

The commotion seems to have caught the attention of no one except the chimeras; my scream wasn't heard by the other mortals present. The gas station attendant is busy filling the tank of another vehicle that just arrived. The store continues operating, with soft background music playing. No one notices a trembling girl curled up in the lap of a man.

I'm laid down like a baby in the back seat of the car. No one bothers to tie my hands this time.

The girl looks at me for the first time as if she doesn't hate me, with an expression that says she understands me and is on my side. I silently feel grateful.

"Just another day where my shoes and I destroy the patriarchy," Penélope says softly as she sits in the passenger seat.

Phelipe just nods, throwing a forced smile at his sister. Then, he glances at me in the rearview mirror with eyes filled with an emotion I can't decipher.

CHAPTER THIRTY-TWO

Sophia

Finally, I'm under a roof.

Phelipe and Penélope thought it was safe to break into an empty house. I wasn't in a position to say no, especially after we encountered three more hellhounds and had to set fire to a stretch of the road to get rid of them. The environmental protection people can't be very happy with us.

I don't know what city we're in, what state, or any direction. The weather is particularly much colder. That's why I'm glad to be under a roof. The cold wind outside whistles against the windows.

The house belongs to a family of four. I saw their photos on a piece of furniture in the living room. Phelipe said their scent is quite faint here, that they've probably been traveling for at least three days. From the amount of food they left for their pet cat, it seems they don't plan to return anytime soon.

I thought the animal would be hostile to the presence of intruders in its home, but it just ignores me and follows Penélope every inch she moves, rubbing against her legs. Damn that cat DNA.

At least I can take a relaxing shower. Finally. The water that runs down the drain is black. I'm so dirty that my skin is irritated from the number of times I have to scrub myself. I use all the available shampoo to clean my hair.

Penélope went to a market to shop while Phelipe bought new clothes. We won't be using anything from the homeowners, except, of course, the shelter, although I saw both siblings trying the cat's food.

When I step out of the shower, I grab the bag of clothes that have been bought for me. Jeans and a T-shirt. It seems great. I get dressed, comb my wet hair, and march out of the bathroom.

Phelipe is sprawled out on the couch, watching TV. Upon seeing me, he gives a weak smile, an attempt to be friendly. I walk over and sit next to him. A long silence ensues as we simply stare at the movie playing on the television.

"So, where's Penélope?" I ask, trying to break the mood.

"She hasn't come back from shopping yet," he replies without looking at me.

"With the amount you two eat, she's probably going to have to buy out the whole supermarket."

The cat, furry and fat, with a brush-like tail, walks over to us gracefully. Its silent and elegant steps remind me of how Phelipe and Penélope move. Even when the girl is in her highest heels, she manages to make no noise. The furry creature jumps into the boy's lap, snuggling into his belly. He strokes it, tracing circles in its fur with his fingers absentmindedly.

I clear my throat.

"So, why do you seem so... different after Penélope killed that worm?"

His eyes shift from the television to meet mine.

"I didn't want that to be her concern."

He quickly averts his gaze, his jaw clenched. His mood turns dark again.

"What do you mean? You don't trust her?"

"It's not that."

"Then..."

He takes a deep breath, returning his gaze to me.

"I know this kind of thing happens in the human world. But it never seemed real to me, you know? Like those horror stories you have to scare children into eating their vegetables." He pauses, studying my expression. I still don't quite understand where he's going with this. "I thought we, lab subjects, beings who shouldn't exist, were the monsters of your society. But when I saw you in those conditions, in a tiny bathroom with that... *man* trying to... I don't know what came over me. That's not something any of us would do. I'm sorry I didn't react faster." I instinctively shrug. My throat tightens, making it hard to breathe just at the memory. The hairs on my arm stand on end. "What I'm saying is that we *are* the animals. Or we should be. But even with our physical needs much stronger than yours, all this daily explosion of hormones consuming us, no chimera *ever* did something like that. Never. When a partner doesn't want it, we simply leave. It's hard to believe that something like this really happens. It may sound stupid, but I wanted to spare Penélope from that kind of violence. I mean, I would have spared you too if you weren't involved. It must be more horrible for you women than it is for me. And believe me, it's already pretty bad."

I'm caught off guard. I never thought about the possibility that he would want to spare his sister from something like this, especially since Penélope isn't a defenseless girl. Yet, I saw how he reacted to everything. How furious he became, haunted and sympathetic at the same time.

"It's not stupid." My voice trembles. "Thank you for... you know."
Phelipe forces a smile at me. Another attempt to be friendly.
"You're welcome, sweetheart."
"Could you stop calling me that?"
"Like what, sweetheart?"
I roll my eyes.
"I wish someone had spared me from this before," I admit, my voice shaky.

He straightens up, becoming completely rigid on the couch.

"What are you talking about?" he asks in an accusatory tone.

I'm bombarded by memories I've fought long to forget.

The end-of-year school party. The tragic ending. The sound of police sirens approaching, louder and more unbearable each second. My choked scream that never really came out.

Phelipe's posture is unnaturally rigid, chin raised, eyes narrowed and focused on me. Strictly cautious. I have to swallow hard to chase away the lump in my throat.

"We were at the eighth-grade graduation party," I start, defeated. Somehow, I feel compelled to share this. "Izec had just broken up with me again and was dancing with Ana Catarina right in front of me. I saw a guy standing there, staring at me, and I called him to dance with me. Then, he pulled me into a private room so we could talk and..."

I let out a loud, painful sigh. The memories are knives piercing my flesh. My breath is ragged. I taste the tears burning in my throat.

"He... hurt you?" Phelipe's voice sounds forced.

I close my eyes for a second, wrapping my arms around my frail body.

"Yes," I whisper weakly.

Phelipe's perfectly upright and rigid body begins to shake violently. I can hear the animalistic growls escaping his lips, and judging by his clenched fists, he's controlling himself. His eyes are closed.

"How old were you?" he separates each syllable with severity.

"Fifteen." My voice is lifeless. "I managed to fight him off; I shoved a bottle into him. That was enough for me to run away and ask for help. He was arrested; he still is." I let out a strangled sigh. "That's why I was so shaken by what happened."

"How do you feel now?" he asks, opening his eyes to look at me, once again filled with an emotion I still can't define.

I don't know how I feel, it's true. I was in complete shock, unable to move or say anything for hours, reliving all the horror I went through years before. But somehow, speaking relieves me. Yes, it relieves me.

"Better," I admit. "I liked the way Penélope defended me."

A flicker of a smile appears on his lips. I smile back.

"She can put on quite a show sometimes." I nod. "So..." He clears his throat, looking uncomfortable. "There's something I want to give you. To... you know, maybe cheer you up a bit..."

I shift on the couch, curious.

"What is it?"

He seems a bit embarrassed as he fumbles inside his jacket. He pulls out something I don't recognize at first; I have to strain to remember what the rectangular object in his hand is.

"Your mom's photo album? Seriously?" I ask, incredulous.

I have a *déjà-vu* of the day after the night of the attacks when I woke up in my room after fainting and saw him flipping through that same album.

"I grabbed it at your house. I was snooping around looking for clues as to why you're a copy of Sofia. I thought knowing more about your childhood and family could help."

He shrugs.

"Did you find anything?" I ask, flipping through the album.

"No. We had to flee that day, so I didn't have a chance to return it." I pause to analyze a photo of me with my mom and sisters at Christmas three years ago. Isa was still using a pacifier. Lily had smeared lipstick and her usual drunk face. My mom was holding her breath to look thinner. I smile. "I'm glad I didn't return it. I know you miss your family; maybe this will cheer you up a bit."

"Thank you," I whisper with a choked voice.

⚡

HOURS LATER, PENÉLOPE crosses the living room pushing a fully loaded shopping cart. I wake up, startled, after dozing on the couch with the photo album firmly tucked under my arm. At some point, Phelipe must have laid down on the rug with the cat to give me more space.

"You know you weren't supposed to bring the cart with you, right?" I mumble sleepily, rubbing my eyes.

"You'd be surprised at how many things I'm allowed to do thanks to my spectacular ass."

I smile sarcastically. Just thinking about it makes me feel nauseous.

"What did you bring? I'm starving," Phelipe asks, getting up from the floor.

Penélope extends a liter of Coca-Cola toward him. His eyes shine as if he's seeing an oasis in the desert. He uncaps the bottle and drinks straight from the neck.

"I had an idea," Penélope confesses, looking at me with curiosity. I sigh. It can't be good. "Now that we're finally under a roof, with more utensils than we usually have and electric light, I thought we should change your look. You know, we can't keep traveling through deserted roads so you won't be seen; that would only slow us down even more. We should have arrived by now. So I thought we could cut your hair or dye it so you don't look like the copy."

All I want since discovering I'm a copy is not to look like her. It's such a simple thing that I don't know how I didn't think of it before: a haircut or a different color. We'll still have the same face, but this small difference might ensure I'm not identified right away.

"Let's do it," I say confidently.

Her smile widens.

"Great. I bought a few things," she sings. She rummages through the pile in the shopping cart with agile hands. Then she places a bottle of hydrogen peroxide, bleaching powder, and scissors on the side table next to the couch. "Luckily, I'm really good at cutting hair. Can we start?"

The idea of bleaching my hair makes my muscles tense up. It would look terrible.

"You can't be serious, right?" Phelipe suddenly interrupts.

Penélope crosses her arms at him, arching her eyebrows in challenge.

"Is there a problem?" she asks, almost growling.

"Sophia..." He looks at me apprehensively. "You really don't want to do this, do you?"

He seems terrified at the idea of me changing anything about my appearance.

"Let's just get on with it, Penélope."

The girl smiles at her brother and grabs the scissors. Phelipe is looking at me, stunned. I sit on the arm of the couch, lowering my head a bit to avoid seeing him. Even with my back turned, I know she's shining with happiness as she holds my hair between her fingers.

"So, how's it going to be? I'm sure a pixie cut would look great on you." I feel like Penélope is about to bounce with delight. "Or we could shave it all off. Don't worry; it'll grow back... in a few years."

"No!" Phelipe yells, practically frightened.

"What's the problem, lab boy? Are you afraid I won't look like the copy anymore?" My voice sounds accusatory.

He looks deeply into my eyes with seriousness. That glimmer of emotion I can't identify shines in his pupils.

"No," he asserts with some confidence. "I'm afraid you won't look like yourself anymore."

"Ignore my brother," Penélope says with an irritated tone; Phelipe is cutting into her fun. "What do you think he understands about this? Have you seen how he dresses? Like a pathetic metalhead from the 1980s!"

"You dress like a gothic hooker. No judgments, little sister."

"You son of a..."

Penélope abruptly interrupts the discussion. Phelipe sits up too straight, his shoulders tense, quickly turning to the television. I glance at the screen only to find my photo plastered on the news again. The same photo from the "wanted" poster I saw stuck to the door of the convenience store.

I'm still the media's main topic. I know from the newspapers that Penélope buys every day, scribbling who knows what, that my face has been the centerpiece of feature stories for days. However, this is the first time, since this madness began, that I have access to a television. I'm a news headline, so I wonder: since when have I been the most discussed subject?

more talked about?

Phelipe's face also appears, labeled as my accomplice. They even got the school's security footage from the moment we fled on a motorcycle.

I feel a cold tightness in my gut starting to consume me. I see the host explaining the case with a rapid speech, probably already annoyed at having to say the same thing every day. I am accused of having carried out the massacre at the school in a premeditated manner, a crime classified as passion-driven, in addition to attempted homicide against Tom Warner.

"Passion-driven crime," I repeat softly, incredulous.

They are talking about Tom Warner's medical condition. He is still hospitalized, recovering after the amputation of his hand and leg. There's speculation that I might have poisoned the bullets.

Where did they come up with this *passion-driven crime*? The answer comes immediately.

They did a reconstruction of the crime, with computer-generated images! The computerized doll, my representation, appears in an exact replica of the school auditorium, rising from the chair with a gun in hand and shooting at Natália. It then shows how I fled the crime scene through the bathroom window, where my fingerprints were found on the glass. The rest is just speculation. Accounts from survivors who claim to have been attacked by others besides me, although a man admits to having fought with me at some point. That's why they created dolls to illustrate my possible "accomplices," based on the victims' testimonies.

They show my video shooting Tom Warner. I still struggle to watch and believe that it's really me. Sophia, Ana's friend, abhorred firearms. Sophia, Izec's girlfriend, would run away from fights. But this Sophia, the one who walks with chimera, pulls the trigger.

Phelipe and Penélope look as haunted as I feel. None of us three are blinking.

Based on Tom Warner's account, he supposedly saw me fleeing and tried to follow me by car. He couldn't contact the authorities, so he went after me alone. And I cornered him and shot.

The presidential candidate, the man of the people, is a hero. He just wanted justice for the people who tragically died at school. I am the cold, heartless bitch. The murderer.

But what could have motivated me to commit so many crimes? Easy: jealousy. They announce an interview with a very close friend of mine. My heart skips a beat. Ane. What would she have to say about me? Does she believe all these unfounded and fabricated lies to make me look worse than I really am? Or in her eyes, am I still the girl with whom she exchanged friendship bracelets at twelve?

I will never know Ane's opinion, because the one appearing for the interview as a close friend is Helena. We were never friends, but we studied together every day since seventh grade. Helena was always reserved, too shy to fit in, always holed up behind books, talking to teachers, volunteering to help with any type of school event. I like her, although I know very little about her personal life.

What I don't understand is: why is she accusing me? Doesn't she know that I would be incapable of committing such a barbaric crime?

My crime is considered passion-driven because I killed my ex-boyfriend's girlfriend. Helena says I was crazy with jealousy when I returned to school and saw that Izec was already with someone else. She claims that during my entire relationship with him, I was always insecure and unstable, practically controlling every step he took. That seeing him with another girl must have triggered some sort of switch in my mind. She mentions that I was in charge of organizing the ceremony, that I volunteered for it, and that during the organization, I spent the whole time at the top of the auditorium stairs, in the exact spot where Natália's fatal shot was fired, probably planning my crime. At this moment, the internal video from the school is shown, where I can be seen that awful morning in the exact place Helena mentioned, along with her and Ana Catarina.

It seems that the media has a perfect reason to condemn me.

In addition to Helena, they interview some of my teachers, who label me as strange and reserved; they even managed to access my grades! As if knowing that I nearly failed Physical Education was a threat to society. Some other classmates also give their testimonies about me. I don't know most of them, but they seem to know me very well. A girl, Laura, who isn't even in the same class as me, claims that I asked her where I could buy a gun. And Júlio, another boy I vaguely remember having seen, says I asked him for shooting lessons in exchange for sex. More arguments for them to believe it was premeditated. How great!

Phelipe and Penélope look at me simultaneously with raised eyebrows.

"It seems I was popular and didn't know it," I murmur, incredulous.

None of my family or true friends have spoken about it until today. The entire press is camped outside my house. This is probably disrupting Isa's trip to school, my mother likely isn't able to go to work, and maybe even Lily's nights out are being interrupted.

They start talking again about Tom Warner's health condition and his amputation.

"It's no longer necessary to cut my hair," I say with a faltering voice; my lips curl as I stare at the television, seething with hate.

"Why not?" Penélope asks, unable to hide her discontent.

"I want Tom Warner to see me exactly like this when I meet him to kill him."

From my peripheral vision, I catch a slight smile on Phelipe's face.

CHAPTER THIRTY-THREE

Sophia

What I long for the most is to finally sleep in a real bed, without having to curl up under a tree like a beast, or lie hunched in the back seat of a car that would eventually make my legs cramp. I look, amazed, at the double mattress in front of me, eager to sink into it and forget the circus I've just witnessed.

As I lift the heavy comforter, ready to lie down, a blur passes before my eyes: Phelipe throwing himself onto the mattress. I huff, irritated.

"Oh, for heaven's sake! I'm tired, lab boy, so if you'll excuse me..." I try to pull the comforter from underneath him, not having much success. He fluffs the pillow before resting his head, moving away just enough to give me a bit more blanket, but most of it is still trapped underneath him. "What do you think you're doing?" I ask as I watch him take off a boot with his toe from the opposite side, letting it drop to the floor with a thud.

"Don't mind me. I'm going to get comfortable."

Phelipe stretches with a yawn.

"You're not thinking you're going to sleep here..."

"Actually," he agrees, turning his back to me. "I'd fall asleep faster if you shut your mouth."

"You can't sleep here!"

"Either that, or I'll have to tie you up again. Consider it a precaution and for your safety." He yawns again. "Now, if you could keep quiet, I'd appreciate it. A man has his needs."

"You're a lab embryo," I spit.

"A very pertinent observation on your part."

"What's this? We were getting along so well, and now we're back to hating each other?"

"I never stopped disliking you."

Phelipe falls silent, lying on his side, his back turned to me. I can see the movement of his chest indicating that he is breathing.

"I'm not going to try to escape or stab you while you sleep," I assure him with an indignant tone in my voice. "No matter how tempting it may seem."

"Just to be safe, you'll have my company in bed. Of course, you can lie on the floor too; I don't mind. As long as you shut the hell up."

Huffing after trying to pull the comforter with all my might and it doesn't move an inch, I give up and lie down in the empty space on the bed. I fluff the pillow, moving as far away from Phelipe as I can to cover myself. I close my eyes, waiting for sleep, knowing it will come soon. At least his presence helps me warm up faster.

I wake up some time later, startled and sweaty. I bring my hands to my neck, to the exact spot where the red-haired woman had been choking me minutes before in yet another of my usual nightmares. I roll onto my side until I'm lying on my back, gasping, my hands trembling. Phelipe is still lying with his back to me, looking like he hasn't moved a muscle since I fell asleep.

"What was it this time?" he murmurs irritably in his hoarse voice, without turning.

"A nightmare," I whisper, staring at the ceiling. "Does she make you dream about her too?"

He takes a deep breath. Silently, he rolls over until he's lying on his back. Our arms touch on the sheet.

"Yes. But they're different dreams from yours."

I raise my eyebrows, turning toward him. My stomach knots at just the thought of what he must dream about. I grimace.

"Does that make you miss her?" I ask, trying to hide my disgust.

"Argh! No," he mutters, sour.

"What's she like?"

It's a strange question to ask, considering the dreams I have about her, but my curious side sounds inside me like an alarm. I can't let this opportunity pass.

He twists his mouth, showing that the subject displeases him.

"Redhead, skinny, and manic," he replies disinterestedly.

I blink. Nothing I didn't already know.

"But what about the copy? I thought you loved her."

Suddenly, I remember a night that seems to have happened millions of years ago when Izec took me to Cristo Park and told me, "I love you, Sophia. I will always love you." I feel a pang of pain at the memory, my eyes misting.

"How many times do I have to say that I don't like talking about this?"

"When will you realize that I don't care?"

"I loved her," he sighs. "But she stabbed me in the back and left me." He leans to my side, his face coming to face mine. "Just like you."

He's referring to the day I shot him. I feel a smile forming on my face as I remember that, enjoying the feeling of power from holding the gun in my hands. I wanted so much to get rid of him and Penélope, thinking I'd be safer in the hands of humans... I couldn't have been more mistaken.

I turn, staring at the nightstand beside the bed, on which sits a landline phone. An involuntary idea crosses my mind.

"Could I call my house?" I ask.

I already know what answer I'll get, but my chest fills with hope just at the possibility.

"Of course not! They've definitely tapped your home phone; one call and they'd have tracked us down in minutes."

I huff, irritated. I fumble around the mattress until I find the photo album, as I can't part with it for even a second; it seems to be the only thing I have to ease my longing for my family. I open it and find a picture of me with my friends, and I feel a lump form in my throat. I wonder how they are doing now. Do they believe I'm responsible for all those deaths? Ane surely doesn't; she knows me and understands that I would never do something like that. I trace my finger over her smiling face in the photo, wishing I could tell her everything that really happened, the hell my life has turned into. Ane would listen to me, comfort me, and she would be completely on my side; I have no doubts about that.

Would Jimmy believe me? Probably yes, because of Ane. He would do anything for her, even dive headfirst into this horrible, bloody story with me.

Izec? Oh, Izec... My fingers touch his face, my heart sinking as I remember the accusing look in his eyes when he thought I was responsible for killing Natália, his girlfriend. I don't know if he would believe in my innocence.

With tears in my eyes, I turn the page of the album to continue looking at the sequence of photos with my friends, and right on the next page, where there's a photo of me with Izec on the day of the football championship in the first year, when we were getting ready to cheer for Jimmy, there's a folded paper. I pick it up between my fingers, curious. It's the drawing Penélope made of me and Phelipe, the one I gave her as proof that I was being followed.

I turn and see that he is staring at me.

"The drawing... Before I thought Penélope was the one following me, I thought it was Guilherme. The guy who... you know."

He nods, turning his face away and lying on his back.

"The drawing was Penélope's, but the one who was following you was Viviane."

I make a face.

"What do you think she wants? What's the big plan behind that head full of *curls* your sister has?"

He sighs, thinking.

"I have no idea. Maybe the same as mine: Tom Warner dead. And you know that you're the best bargaining chip we could have."

I grimace again. I don't know why this bothers me; I've always known I was some kind of trophy. Tom wants me... dead, but he wants me. The chimeras want him dead, and they keep me around because Tom wants me, giving them an advantage. Even knowing all this, it still bothers me.

"When I saw this drawing, I thought she was an ex-girlfriend gone mad..." I recall. A strange idea starts to form in my mind, and the worst part is that it makes sense. I sit up suddenly, scared. "Oh my God, she likes you!"

"What?!" Phelipe asks, incredulous, looking at me as if I had dumped snakes on him.

"It makes sense. When you escaped the lab, she followed you, like Viviane. All this time watching you... she even wears a necklace just like the one Sofia gave you. Now she's even helping you with your revenge plan, a pretext to stay close to you and..." I pause, processing. "That's why she hates me so much. Because of my face."

"How disgusting!" He glares at me in revulsion. "You know we're siblings, right?"

"So what? You weren't raised as siblings."

"So what that I can smell my DNA on her." He rolls his eyes, grimacing. "Now shut up and go back to sleep."

I lie down, aware that he doesn't want to believe a word I said because the idea sounds repulsive to him. But it's a good theory that makes a lot of sense, and I won't take it from my mind. After all, what other reason would she have to help us if not for that?

CHAPTER THIRTY-FOUR

Sophia

I hear distant voices even before I fully wake up. I'm confused, wondering if it's real or if I've entered Viviane's mind again. I open my eyes and find it strange that the room is dim, even with the curtains open. I wonder if it's still early morning. Shouldn't there be rays of sunlight coming through the window? Gradually, I realize that the sky is covered with such heavy, dark clouds that they make the day feel like night.

I look around; I'm alone. The confused and whispered conversations continue. I get up, stretching and cracking all my bones. That feels good. I comb my hair, put on jeans and a t-shirt, and leave the room. As I approach the kitchen, I understand the source of the voices. I try to make as little noise as possible to listen to the entire conversation.

"I heard you two talking earlier. Lately, she's had a lot of questions for you, since she knows you're the only one here who melts at that pathetic look on her face," Penélope says with her usual sarcasm in her voice.

"You know, little sister," Phelipe replies, "if you keep eavesdropping on conversations like this, I'm going to start agreeing with Sophia and think that you really have a crush on me."

She lets out a laugh.

"Frankly, little brother, the time we've been spending together is as unpleasant for me as it is for you. But it's a necessary evil."

"So what's your diabolical, secret plan that makes you have to accompany me, a detestable person, and help save a girl you openly hate?"

"If I tell you, it won't be diabolical and secret anymore."

Phelipe lets out a mocking laugh. I hear the clinking of glasses colliding on the table.

"It's normal for her to be curious. It's a totally different world from the one she was used to."

"I wonder if she'll have that many questions when we get to John's house. You know how he also gets carried away by that face."

"John? Storm is a person?" I can't help myself and abruptly enter the kitchen.

They were so engrossed in their conversation that they didn't even hear me probing. Penélope lets out a sigh, straightening her shoulders.

"See what you've done?" she barks with anger in her eyes, directing her words at Phelipe. "My dear brother, John," she confirms, spreading butter on bread. Phelipe rolls his eyes. "He is one of the strongest chimeras out there, if not the strongest. No one dares to mess with him. And yes, he is the storm."

"Brother?" I ask, startled; my jaw drops.

This must be a nightmare. I can't believe there's another lost mutant Kyle and that we're going right to meet him.

"Yes, our brother," she agrees, shooting a dirty look at Phelipe, as if challenging him to say something.

The lab boy huffs, irritated, turning his face away.

Since the moment Penélope suggested we should follow the storm, he has shown complete discontent with it. If they are siblings, what bothers him so much? Of course, his sister annoys him too, but not to this extent. It's not just provocation; it's the hatred in his expression, the dark aura consuming him slowly just by thinking about John.

"But Phelipe doesn't like him," I observe.

He shrugs dismissively.

"Correction: no intelligent person would dare mess with him."

"Hey!" Phelipe protests.

"Don't take it the wrong way, little brother, but you know that messing with John is suicide."

"So, was he raised with you in the lab?" I ask.

I don't know what bothers me more: the fact that Phelipe doesn't like him or that Penélope seems to love him too much.

"Yes. When your copy, Sofia, taught us how to escape, besides Phelipe, Viviane, and me, John was another of the fugitive chimeras. But, unlike us, he isn't wanted. No one is crazy enough to risk going after John. He is much stronger than any other chimera. He could kill us with his eyes closed."

"Wow, that's really encouraging," I say ironically.

Penélope opens a sneer of a smile.

"You don't have to fear John's wrath, sweetheart. Out of the three of us, you're the last person he would hurt."

This just keeps getting worse. If John was created in the lab and escaped under Sofia's orders, he met my copy. Something in Penélope's irony makes me believe that my face is something he likes a lot.

I stare at Phelipe, who seems to be reading my thoughts.

"Is that why you don't like your brother? Seriously?"

"Three idiots." Penélope rolls her eyes. "Artur and my two brothers, completely blind and in love with the treacherous hag."

Phelipe crosses his arms over his bare chest.

"Let's just say Jonathan doesn't take losing easily."

"Let's just say Phelipe is more deluded than he seems, and John, well, three times more of an idiot," Penélope retorts.

"Watch what you say, whore of darkness."

The girl throws a butter-stained knife in her brother's direction, meticulously aimed at his chest. In a quick motion that I can't follow, he catches it in mid-air before it can pierce him.

"So did you call this John and tell him you were with me or what?" I ask when I see Penélope open her mouth to start debating with her brother; her eyes spark with disdain in my direction.

"Don't worry about John," she replies dryly.

"So how do you know where he is? And why do you think he'll help us? Are you risking everything just because of my face?"

I know from my own experience that chimeras can develop this obsession with me because of my appearance. Whatever Sofia did, she ensured they loved me. As if she had enchanted them. But she also made them hate her.

"There's a reason we call him the storm..." she says pretentiously.

She grabs the day's newspaper and slides it across the counter until it reaches me. I pick it up with my fingers, completely confused. For a second, I think maybe she's showing me another article about myself in the newspaper, or about Tom Warner's health. But then I see the column she circled with a red marker: "Hurricane Catarina sighted off the southern Atlantic coast."

So that's why she buys the newspaper every day! Not just to know the latest news about my whereabouts but also to follow the weather.

"Are you serious? He can control the weather? Is he like Zeus?" I ask, incredulous.

"If Zeus were genetically modified and could dominate weather humidity on a molecular level and atmospheric pressure, able to create hurricanes, earthquakes, and even storms just with brainwaves, then yes, he is," Phelipe comments sarcastically, as if he were a professor.

I can't believe it; the two chimera brothers without psychic powers have the strongest brother of all.

We're heading into the eye of the hurricane. Literally.

CHAPTER THIRTY-FIVE

Sophia

I feel like a penguin. I'm wearing two long-sleeve shirts and a thermal coat that barely allows me to move my arms properly. I put on thermal pants under my jeans and knee-high boots. Not to mention the stupid red beanie that keeps slipping down my head, but Phelipe made me wear it to protect my ears. I've always hated beanies. And hoods. And caps. Anything that covers my hair.

I stare at myself in the bathroom mirror. Fortunately, my eye is no longer swollen or purple, although it is still darker than the other one. My neck still bears the four gashes that were made God knows how, and they look like they'll be permanent scars. Great!

I stash the rest of my belongings in the tattered backpack. A few pieces of clothing, a flashlight, some granola bars, water bottles, and hygiene items. After answering some of my questions, Penélope kicked me out like a rat, ordering me to hurry up and pack my things because we needed to leave immediately.

Another Kyle. I still can't believe it.

I unlock the bathroom door and step out. Phelipe is in the living room, adjusting his knife inside his leather boot. The television is on a random channel behind him, and the residents' cat is sitting on the rug, looking at him like he's the best food ever.

"All set." Penélope appears from the kitchen. "Everything packed, clean, and in its place. This family will never notice we were here. But it's a shame to leave you behind." She bends down to pet the cat's head. It purrs and rubs against the girl's long legs. Stupid feline genetics! Every time I tried to interact with the cat, it simply ignored me. "Well, let's go. Turn off the tv."

At that very moment, the news theme music starts to play. We freeze in place, staring blankly at the television. My blood runs cold in my veins.

"*Good evening,*" the host greets in her elegant pose. "*It is with great sadness that we report the passing of the current president of the republic, Antônia Morais, and the vice president, Carlos da Silva, following the crash of the plane transporting them to São Paulo, where the Mercosur meeting was scheduled to take place.*

"What?" I ask incredulously, watching as they report details of the tragedy.

My mouth goes dry automatically. I feel black spots starting to invade my vision.

"Damn it," Phelipe growls, transfixed, unable to tear his eyes away from the television.

"What's going to happen?" I ask, feeling my heart race.

Everything is becoming increasingly surreal. The president and vice president have been killed in a plane crash, there is no one in the presidency, and the elections are only scheduled for October, in less than two months.

"*For this reason, the elections will be moved up and will take place next Sunday,*" the host adds.

"This Sunday?" Phelipe asks, startled, his eyes wide. "For hell's sake, I thought we had time. And how are they completely ignoring the line of presidential succession?"

"There's something big behind this," Penélope replies. "Didn't anyone question it?"

I don't know exactly what they are talking about; I've never been interested in politics. But I know broadly that it's not possible to move up the elections just because of this. There really is something very wrong, but since we haven't been following all the news of the past few weeks, it's hard to know what's really going on.

Shit! Tom Warner will probably get what he wants. Today is Friday. That gives us only days to prevent this from happening. It's impossible. Especially considering he has illegal and secret methods of doing things, and we don't know what they are.

Penélope furrows her brow, watching the television. We three have been so busy fleeing from hellhounds and humans, trying to get to the only safe place, to then think about what to do about Tom Warner, but now there is no chance at all. We have less than two days! Two days, and he will be elected president.

"*Presidential candidate Tom Warner leaves Omega Hospital today, where he has been recovering for the past two weeks from surgery to amputate his right hand and left leg. His staff has reported that he is well and will be cared for at home by an extremely competent medical team. Furthermore, Tom Warner* wrote *a note stating that he hopes the authorities find the prime suspect in the massacre in Araxá, Sophia Oliveira, and that justice is served.*"

My picture on a "wanted" poster stands out before they cut back to aerial footage of the tragedy.

"*Tom Warner's candidacy remains valid, and the country is preparing for elections to take place this Sunday in a regrettable scenario of tragedy. Presidents of various countries have already expressed their condolences through social media...*" the host continues speaking.

Next, the news reveals an updated poll, in which Tom Warner is well ahead of the other candidates. His popularity has risen considerably after the alleged assassination attempt. As far as I remember, he was always the favorite, but now I have turned him into a martyr, a hero of the people, who would die to save him. The only one who could rival him was Antônia, but now she is dead, and he is far ahead of any other candidate.

"We're screwed," I mumble.

"Maybe he'll make it to the second round..." Penélope says, but she doesn't seem very confident.

"And then what? We'd only be delaying the inevitable."

I shrug, defeated. Penélope raises her chin firmly.

"It doesn't matter; we'll be safe with John."

"We will," Phelipe agrees, adjusting his daggers in his belt. "The rest of the country... not so much."

CHAPTER THIRTY-SIX

Sophia

As soon as I step outside the house, I feel the cold current against my body like icy knives piercing me. I mentally thank the huge coat I'm wearing, which previously seemed unnecessary.

Walking doesn't make the cold any less unbearable, as I thought it would. My breath comes out as smoke from my mouth, my hands are freezing inside my pockets, and the wind cuts through my skin.

At least this time I'm only carrying the weight of my backpack. My body has grown accustomed to walking long distances, as well as carrying extra weight. If all this torture I've been through in the last few weeks has served any purpose, it was to build resistance for my naturally weak body.

Penélope walks ahead, her face buried in a newspaper. We are moving through almost deserted streets, but I'm glad we're in civilization. I was tired of having to curl up under a tree to sleep.

I come out of my daydream when my head collides with something hard. I rub my forehead, complaining to Penélope for stopping abruptly and making our heads knock against each other. However, Phelipe tenses beside me, quickly running his fingers along the waistband of his pants to pull out his daggers, and then I understand that we're in trouble.

At the end of the street we're on, standing in an attack position, are five hellhounds from the lab. Their huge mouths are agape, revealing razor-sharp teeth and excessive saliva as they growl. They're wearing silver collars similar to those Artur and the other test subjects had on the night of the massacre.

My knees go weak, as if my legs were made of jelly. My first instinct is to run, even knowing they would catch me in seconds.

"Don't move," Penélope orders through clenched teeth, probably hearing my thoughts. "They won't attack us if we don't move."

"So the plan is to stand here forever?"

It's not the best moment to be sarcastic, but I'm under pressure.

"Any wrong move, and they'll charge at us. We barely managed to fight them off last time, and they outnumber us," Penélope speaks almost without moving her lips. "We need a plan, or they'll rip us to shreds. Suggestions?"

Phelipe lets out a puff of air, furrowing his brows.

"I distract them, and you try to set something big on fire. Like a house."

"As if you could handle it alone." She rolls her eyes. "Smart suggestions, please. Sophia, this is the moment to prove your worth."

Yes, this would be the moment if I weren't so terrified, my eyes wide, my body so shaky that a stronger wind would knock me to the ground. I feel a mix of cold and panic that doesn't allow me to think rationally. I am, naturally, the dead weight of the equation. No weapons, no fighting skills, no super speed or strength.

I hear a different noise coming from the other end of the street. This part of town is so deserted that I didn't expect any company besides the thugs and beggars rummaging through the trash of the houses. But there is a car coming calmly in our direction.

I can't make any sudden movements, including turning to see who is approaching. Phelipe and Penélope remain rigid in their positions. Penélope's brow is furrowed with effort, probably trying to read the thoughts of whoever is in the car. Phelipe and I wait.

She gives a slight nod, almost imperceptible. As the car approaches, she shouts:

"Now!"

We take off running. Maybe she and Phelipe have an emergency plan for this type of escape, already practiced and memorized to move in sync. Because, when we move, Penélope advances towards the dogs, and Phelipe charges at the car.

I do the only thing my brain tells me to do: I run. In the opposite direction. Away from the dogs and the car. Of course, I've never been good at running; besides being clumsy, I get tired easily. Running in the cold, I discover, is three times worse. My legs feel too stiff, as if they were freezing with every movement. My body seems to plead for me to stay still, willing to slow my movements, like a rusty bicycle with little oil in the chain. I'm not making much progress; I feel three times slower.

I look over my shoulder to see how my travel companions are handling the situation. Penélope is gracefully hopping from side to side, which would be impossible for me in the stilettos she's wearing; I would probably twist my ankle. The dogs aren't attacking her, which I find strange at first. Then I notice what she's doing.

She rubs the tip of her long, curved bronze knife with a serrated blade against the asphalt. The friction creates sparks that are enough to hold the animals back. But Penélope needs to keep moving; one slip-up, and the dogs will pounce on her. They are sitting on their haunches, growling, watching her cautiously, just waiting for the exact moment when she falters, without any more sparks. Fortunately, the girl seems well-focused on the mission, creating lines in the ground nimbly, which keeps the dogs on the other side.

For a second, I panic deeply as I realize that Phelipe doesn't seem to be anywhere. Then I remember the car and that the last time I saw him he was heading in that direction. Someone is behind the wheel, still heading towards Penélope, but it isn't Phelipe. I stop where I am, completely frantic, twisting my neck in every direction, trying to find him. Nothing.

The car comes to a sudden stop with a dangerously skidding maneuver, and the back door swings open. Without thinking twice, in a movement so fast that my eyes barely registered it, Penélope jumps into the vehicle with her knife in hand.

The dogs are also caught by surprise and don't attack immediately. When they finally leap after her, the car speeds in my direction. So do the animals.

My blood runs cold in my veins. I don't stand a chance. I'm still frozen, finally seeing that Phelipe is in the passenger seat, shouting whatever it is to the utterly terrified driver at the wheel. The dogs charge at them, and one even manages to tear a chunk out of the rear with its teeth. Even at high speed, they run side by side.

Two dogs have now noticed my stupid presence and turn their attention to me. I have about six seconds before their teeth tear me apart. And I have no plan.

Phelipe is still yelling, moving his mouth frantically, but I can't hear him over the blood rushing in my ears. Penélope, in the back seat, leans her head out, hitting one of the dogs with the hilt of her blade as it leaps at her face.

"Sophia, jump!" she orders.

I don't understand what she means. Jump? Where to? I look around, stunned. Then, the passenger door opens, and the car accelerates even more. The dogs fall a little behind, but they're still hot on our trail.

If they stop, even for a second, so I can get in, they'll lose their advantage, and the lab beasts will devour the whole car and still have room for our flesh. They want me to jump with the car in motion. I don't know if I can do it.

I start to run when the car is less than two meters away, heading in the opposite direction to gain momentum. As soon as it's by my side, I'll jump without hesitation. I try not to think about how I might miss the doorway and smash my face against the side of the car or trip and fall before I reach them, ending up as dog food. No, I need to nail it on the first try.

When the car is next to me, I take longer than necessary to jump, losing my edge. Now the door is far enough away that I can't reach it. Shit! The dogs are right on my tail.

Hopeless and with my heart sinking in my chest, I keep moving, aware that in a fraction of a second, their teeth will be latched onto my ankle. How long will it take for me to lose consciousness? I hope it's quick.

Then, the back door opens, and Penélope leans completely out of the car, pulling me hard by my coat. The only thing I can see is a hellhound leaping to where I was just seconds before.

I fall over her into the car seat, still panting. Penélope slams the door shut with a bang.

"Next time you run off and leave us in the middle of a battle, I'll use you as a shield," Penélope mutters, sourly, pushing me away from her body.

CHAPTER THIRTY-SEVEN

Sophia

A torrential rain pours down, completely blurring the windows and leaving us blind inside the car. The driver, an apparently ordinary man who ended up on the same street as us after getting lost, grips the steering wheel so tightly that the knuckles of his fingers are white. He's completely tense, not only because of the rain and the need to maintain top speed while fleeing from the beasts, but also because of Phelipe Kyle's menacing gaze, ready to leap at his throat if he fails. I can only imagine how he must be feeling after the sudden kidnapping and having seen those carnivorous beasts.

Penélope is giving directions on where we need to go. Her mood isn't the best, and when the driver turns onto the wrong street, I feel sorry for him and his trembling hands under the girl's shouts.

It feels like we're in the middle of a hurricane. The noise of the wind is so loud that it drowns out all other sounds. Even Penélope's screams seem like whispers.

Phelipe is sharpening his silver daggers. I can't tell if it's out of necessity, nerves, or just to terrify the other man, but the driver looks green and seems about to vomit.

Penélope rolls her eyes, turning to me.

"Don't be so sympathetic towards him," she says too quietly for anyone else to hear. "If you knew what kind of thoughts he was having about us before Phelipe got in his car, you wouldn't feel so sorry for him."

I'm so relieved she saved me from death that I don't even mind her reading my thoughts. Phelipe shoots us a hard look that tells me he heard the conversation. A growl forms in his throat.

I furrow my brows, thinking. What kind of disgusting thoughts would a man have upon seeing two girls on a deserted street? By the way Penélope looks at me with raised eyebrows, my assumptions are correct. Well, it seems now I'm the one who wants to vomit.

"It seems the dogs have given up on following us," Phelipe announces after we cross a street.

Of course, they have! Even they wouldn't risk going into the middle of a hurricane.

"I wonder if there are any dogs here; maybe they know we're going after John," Penélope says hesitantly. "Maybe it's a trap..."

"As you said, no one would be crazy enough to mess with John," he retorts, interrupting his sister.

Penélope nods, but she doesn't seem very convinced.

We cross a few streets in deep silence, except for the deafening noise of the wind and the rain hitting the car. Then, when I least expect it, Penélope makes a sudden signal for the driver to stop. At the same time he brakes, a lightning bolt strikes right in front of us, the flash leaving me momentarily blind.

"We're getting out," Penélope announces.

"Here?" I ask, perplexed.

I can't see a foot in front of my nose with all this rain. And a lightning bolt just struck right in front of us; the next target could be our heads!

"You didn't see anything, and you don't know anything," Phelipe says harshly, sliding a hundred-real bill across the car seat.

Penélope opens the door beside me, dousing us both in a cold rain. I feel like even my eyelashes are freezing. The wind sweeps through the car, and I'm shivering to my bones. Phelipe gets out first, followed by his sister, until reluctantly I climb out as well. The car speeds off. I doubt the man will tell this crazy story to anyone.

In seconds, I'm soaked. The rain feels like a spear of ice piercing my body; it's so cold that it hurts. I can't see anything around me because I can't even keep my eyes open. I only notice they've started walking when Phelipe grabs my arm, leading me.

They aren't in a hurry, which is terrible. With every step, I feel the wind pushing me back. After a while, I realize that this is really happening; I have to struggle to stay on my feet because I'm being violently shoved backward. If Phelipe weren't holding me by the arm, I would probably have already been blown away.

I look at him and see the effort he's making to keep moving forward. It's as if an invisible wall is right in front of us, preventing us from moving ahead. The pressure is so great that I feel like I'm going to be crushed by it.

Loud thunder cracks in the sky, startling me. Then finally, after a while, Penélope stops in front of a house.

"This is it!" she shouts over the sound of the rain.

"And then, are we going to ring the doorbell and say we're pizza delivery people?" Phelipe mocks, in a bad mood.

"J-j-j-just do it quickly..." I can barely speak; my whole body is freezing, and my wet clothes feel like a ton.

"That won't be necessary; he's already felt our presence," Penélope murmurs, as if it were a sentence; perhaps it is.

I can't see much of the house due to the rain, but I have a sense that it's quite large. The flashes in the sky briefly illuminate the roof, and I can see that it has more than one story, given its height.

"Hide. He's coming," Penélope says.

I'm about to protest when Phelipe pulls me by the arm, dragging me under an awning. I'm grateful for something shielding my head from the torrential rain.

"W-w-why do we have to h-h-hide?"

We're just two houses away from John.

"Shhh!" Phelipe covers my mouth with his finger. "Speak quietly! He can hear. — Damn mutant hearing. — It's better if Penélope talks to him first."

I'm trembling from head to toe. Even my eyelids are in some kind of trance, fluttering all the time. I hug myself, feeling my arms are too stiff. My hands are so numb that they don't seem to belong to my body.

Phelipe is tense. His back is very straight as he tilts his head toward the house to try to listen to the conversation. His black clothes are soaked, his hair disheveled by the wind, dripping, and raindrops are running down his face.

"Trouble," he whispers, furrowing his brow. "We need to go."

I think about questioning him, but my brain is probably petrified and can't process it in time. Phelipe pulls me by the hand, and we go back into the rain.

An invisible shield pushes us away, causing my shoes to slide on the pavement, throwing me backward. I grit my teeth, trying to push back the force dragging me, but it's utterly futile. It's much stronger than I am.

"Give me your hand!" Phelipe shouts to me, extending his free arm in my direction.

I grip his fingers tightly, feeling the force he has to exert to pull me against the invisible wall. When we reach the house, I see that the gate is open. I'm hesitant to enter, but Phelipe doesn't give me a choice. We pass through the gate, and suddenly everything changes.

For a moment, it's just Phelipe and me holding hands, standing at the entrance of a beautiful house. Then my eyes fall on the other people in the room. Penélope is pressed against the wall, strong hands gripping her neck so tightly that her feet are suspended in the air. However, she isn't fighting her attacker; she just looks annoyed.

That's when, inevitably, my gaze rolls to the second person, who is also staring at me, dumbfounded: John.

He looks a lot like Phelipe. His skin has the same indigenous tone, as do his black hair and facial features. But he is taller and so muscular that he looks like a mountain of visible muscles even under the white shirt he's wearing.

He has such a heavy aura that it feels like it's the very wall of force pushing us away. I can't define the color of his eyes, but somehow, as I look into them, I feel like I'm being dragged into a hurricane. At no point does John stop staring at me.

"Why do you idiots in my family always think you can do this?" Penélope grumbles, rolling her eyes.

She grips her brother's hands around his neck and, with a strong, swift motion, brings him down to the ground, twisting his arm behind his back. She digs her stiletto heel into the back of his neck. I have a small *déjà-vu* of when she did the same to Phelipe. I look at John and see he has a slight smile at the corner of his mouth.

"Damn it, Penélope!" John roars in a guttural voice, like thunder.

She smiles, releasing him.

"So, John, do you remember our brother?" she mocks. John springs up from the ground, brushing off his clothes with the back of his hand. Phelipe's fingers tighten around mine unconsciously. The slight smile has vanished, replaced by the deadly expression I'm already familiar with. "The one you tried to kill. No hard feelings, right?"

But John's eyes are still on me. He seems to be in some sort of trance, as if he's hypnotized.

"It can't be..." he murmurs to himself.

"Oh, you remember Sofia, don't you? Slut, skinny, idiot face..." Penélope flashes her classic smile as she winks at me.

"This is impossible!" he roars again.

I want to shrink back under John's gaze. It's a mix of excitement, madness, and admiration that bothers me in a way I can't define. John looks at me as if I were a prize.

As if he can read my mind, Phelipe leans in my direction, gripping my hand tighter. I'm grateful for that. Then John's gaze falls on our joined hands, and a massive lightning bolt slices through the sky with a thunderclap that leaves me momentarily deaf.

"Phelipe!" he growls.

"Oh no, let's not make a scene, John. Enough with the rain, please. My hair is already all frizzed up," Penélope complains.

"How did you find her?" John addresses Phelipe, although at no point do his eyes leave my face.

Phelipe lets out a sigh.

"I was following Tom Warner when I happened to run into her. But, Jonathan, this isn't the..."

"I know. She's one of the copies," John interrupts him with hostility.

"Wait. *One* of the copies?" Penélope asks the question I want to ask.

The still biting cold seems to be impairing my brain.

"You need to come with me," John says.

Phelipe and Penélope exchange a tense look. We follow John as he turns his back and walks toward the house. He opens the front door and continues walking without looking back. It's comforting not to have his eyes on me.

The house is enormous and luxurious, though it doesn't have much furniture. In the white room, with plaster paneling, there is only a purple velvet sofa in front of a fireplace that apparently has never been used. A flat-screen tv is perched on a wooden bench at the other end. We pass through the completely empty dining room. There are huge windows with an incredible view of the garden.

Our footsteps create a loud echo, especially Penélope's heels. Moreover, we're leaving a trail of water behind us. I walk awkwardly, with my limbs completely stiff, making my movements difficult.

John stops in front of a door. He fumbles in his pockets until he finds a key, which he uses to unlock it. When the door opens, I stretch my neck to see what's making him hesitate, only to come face-to-face with a flight of stairs leading down to some dark place.

We start to descend. Phelipe releases my hand to be the last in line. John leads the way, followed by Penélope, who doesn't seem very confident, about to draw the knife from her thigh. I imagine her brother already has his silver daggers in hand.

There's a horrible smell in the air that I can't identify. I look over my shoulder, and Phelipe's nose is wrinkled in pure disgust. It's not pleasant.

When we reach the bottom of the stairs, John turns on the light. The first thing I see is a full chamber pot near where we stand, immediately causing my stomach to churn. That's where the horrible smell is coming from. I quickly look away. Penélope gasps.

We're in a small room, which I identify as the basement. There's nothing here except the chamber pot and a thin, torn blanket. The walls are covered with an endless sequence of numbers that repeat endlessly. They've been painted with blood and feces, I note, feeling bile rise in my throat.

Then I see a tiny figure huddled against the wall in the corner, with its head between its knees, weakly embracing its body. Phelipe approaches me with his fists clenched tightly and wide eyes. When the person lifts their head, I understand why.

Our eyes meet, both equally wide. I feel their shock as a mirror of my own. Because when I look at them, it's like seeing my own reflection.

"Who are you?" I ask, unable to contain myself, stepping forward.

A heavy silence hangs for seconds until a weak voice, sounding like my own, says:

"I am Sofia Warner."

CHAPTER THIRTY-EIGHT

Sophia

The cold is cutting through my bones. I'm shaking from head to toe as we climb the stairs again. My teeth are chattering so much that I feel like my brain is detaching from my skull. Upon reaching the main room of the house, John hands me a coat. I want to refuse, but I'm freezing in my soaked clothes, so I have to accept it. Still, the way he looks at me bothers me, especially when I can't quite distinguish the exact color of his eyes.

Penélope grabs one of the towels and throws another one to me. I start drying my hair with it; my fingers are turning blue from the cold.

Sofia Warner walks hesitantly, squinting against the dim light, which is minimal but still much brighter than the basement where she was kept. She looks very thin and haggard, with huge dark circles under her eyes. She curls up on the sofa, shivering in her rags.

I throw John's coat to her, scolding myself for doing it. I wrap myself in the towel.

"Sofia?" I address the girl huddled on the sofa, who alternates her gaze between everyone in the room, terribly frightened. I would be too, in her place. "What did they do to you?"

She stares at me with wide eyes, lowering her head when she realizes the attention is on her.

"Luna," she says in a voice so low and hoarse that I wonder how long it has been since she had to communicate with anyone. "I prefer you call me Luna. It's my middle name, in honor of my mother."

I nod.

"I wouldn't want to be called that either. If it's meant to offend, I'd prefer 'whore,' which is almost a synonym," Penélope quips.

"What's your relationship to Tom Warner?" Phelipe asks.

"I'm his niece." I furrow my brow. Tom probably never spoke of his niece or even showed her in public, not with that face. "He kept me captive," she replies as if she had read my thoughts. "My mother died giving birth to me, and my father, Tarcísio Warner, died in a plane crash when I was ten. My uncle has had guardianship of me since then, but around the age of fourteen, he imprisoned me."

If she grew up as a prisoner, not appearing in public, probably because of her face, how did John find her?

"How did you..."

"I was following Tom Warner," John interrupts before I can finish my question. "I had already orchestrated an attack plan on his house. He doesn't make many appearances, and when he does, he's always surrounded, making it a bit difficult to kill him without exposing myself. I studied the house for a while, managed to get some blueprints, and studied the area long enough to know all the entrances by heart. I had to bribe some of his staff to tell me about his routine."

"Ah, I love humans! They always have a price," Penélope mocks, sitting on the arm of the sofa.

Sofia or Luna shrinks even more, pulling away.

"So," John continues, his eyes still fixed on me, "I was informed that he had a secret place in the house where he spent a lot of time. I thought he was hiding a weapon or more test subjects; I figured the revenge plan could be postponed until I discovered what was inside. So I waited for the day of the candidacy, when Tom obviously wouldn't be there, and the security would be weaker. Imagine my surprise when I broke in and saw a duplicate."

The day of the candidacy? The elections are approaching, which means this happened a long time ago. Sofia Luna emerged from captivity in her own home only to suffer at John's hands elsewhere, having done nothing but be born with that face. That's horrifying.

"But why did he keep you locked up?" I ask.

He's her uncle; it's cruel to do that to an innocent girl.

"What do you think?" she says acidly, staring at me with eyes that say a lot.

Nausea rises in my throat. I feel waves of sickness wanting to expel everything inside me. Penélope and Phelipe look equally nauseated; she's staring at the girl with a shocked expression, while he grimaces in disgust and closes his eyes. Not without exchanging a long look with me, I know what he's thinking... the day at the gas station bathroom. But my mind is reliving my own torturous memories, which I fight daily to forget.

"Did he abuse you?" Penélope asks.

I'm unable to find my voice.

"He had a sick plan in mind to marry me when the time came."

"What?" Penélope asks, aghast.

Phelipe's eyes widen. Even John seems shocked, running his hands through his hair.

"I didn't know that," he says, staring at me.

"That's his idea of revenge against the original Sophia. Keeping her trapped with him forever."

"And why are you keeping her locked up?" I ask John accusatorily.

"She's important to Tom Warner, and I have her. It's an advantage." He raises his hands in a sign of defense, exactly like his brothers did with me. I automatically run my fingers over my wrists, feeling the scars where the ropes tightened while I was bound and dragged around. Phelipe notices this movement. "And she had to stay locked up down there because, believe it or not, she didn't cooperate much. I wanted her to live here as a guest, not a prisoner. With me, she is safe from Tom's threats. But she tried to attack me, escape, and even hurt herself. I saw no other option..."

"Great option," I retort with an acidic voice, glaring at him. "Taking her out of one cage and putting her in another. It seems the brothers share the same brain. Congratulations!"

The three exchange glances in silence. Penélope shrugs.

"I know John doesn't do to her what that pig Tom did..." she defends him, staring at me. "If he did, he'd be tasting my stiletto." She looks at her brother, who simply ignores her.

I know exactly what Sofia feels because I felt that way for almost the entire journey with Phelipe and Penélope. I even shot at them. The truth is we are paying the price for having this face.

"Do you know about the copies?" I ask my doppelgänger.

She grew up locked away like a rat; there wouldn't be a way to know about it unless Tom Warner himself told her something.

"He told me everything," she replies, her voice choked. "He told me about her, the original Sophia. An excellent doctor, an unmatched professional. Your grandfather, Teodoro, my great-grandfather, was quite pleased with her hiring by the lab back then. In fact, more than pleased; he was in love. Sophia seemed to reciprocate, but after she saw the test subjects up close, she became fascinated, leaving her grandfather practically aside. Besides, she got involved with the chimeras, freed them, and stole a detailed research project from the lab that took years to complete, just to thwart my great-grandfather's plans to unleash his creatures on the world."

"Wait... your great-grandfather? Tom Warner's grandfather?" I ask, shocked. "Wouldn't that be yours? That's not physically possible. If she got involved with Tom's grandfather, she would have to be very old and..."

I can't complete my reasoning. I look at the test subjects, seeking support, but none of them show any reaction. No, it can't be. If she was hired back in the time of Teodoro Warner, Luna's great-grandfather, she must have been very old when she met the test subjects, unless...

"You don't know," Luna comments, a hint of a sympathetic smile emerging. "They didn't tell you?"

"Tell me what?" I ask in a voice too high-pitched, feeling my throat dry up.

I glare at Phelipe with accusation in my eyes. He and Penélope exchange a long look. She nods, and her brother shakes his head as if they are communicating silently. However, I hear no sound and don't see their lips move.

"There are some things I didn't tell you," the lab boy confesses in a controlled voice.

"I can't guess why," I snarl irritably.

"Sophia," Penélope says my name for the first time since I met her, without a trace of sarcasm or irony. "You need to know that time passes differently for us."

"What does that mean?"

John stands like a mute statue in the center of the room. Luna stares at us with interest and curiosity.

"It means..." Phelipe intervenes with a strangled sigh. "That our childhood is faster than normal, and our adult period is longer. Since we are immune to diseases and genetically modified to have an organism as close to perfect as possible, we waste health and live for a longer time than you. Our appearance doesn't change much. Only when we are close to death do we age, all at once."

I'm not liking this conversation at all. I already sense the worst.

"Okay." I hesitate. My heart is pounding in my chest. "And how old are you?"

Everyone present holds their breath at the same time. An ominous silence settles in. I oscillate my gaze between the two to see who will answer me first. They seem to be silently communicating again. Phelipe sighs, defeated, turning to me.

"Sophia, I'm ninety-nine years old. Penélope is ninety-five."

"What?!" I scream too loudly, making the sound echo off the walls of the empty house.

Silence reigns again as the echo of my scream fades.

"It's terrifying, I know." He shakes his head, looking back at the ceiling. "I was born in 1919. John was born in 1921, and Penélope in 1923." He pauses, gathering the courage to meet my eyes again. "The mutants have been caged longer than you can imagine." Breathe, Sophia, breathe. "I'm still healthy and strong. I don't know how long I'll live. There's no estimated time." Your heart needs to pump blood, so breathe, Sophia. Inhale through your nose. "Then, I met her in 1969. I was fifty, and she was twenty-five. Sophia, you look like you're going to have a heart attack. Please breathe... So, in 1971, she freed us; you know well what happened next. She vanished, only to appear later asking for help because Teodoro Warner wanted to kill her. After that, she changed her name and disappeared. She married someone else, had children..." He laughs without humor. "Now I know she died in 2000."

My body is numb from the neck down. I feel absolutely nothing.

"But that was a long time ago! How can I look like her?"

I would have considered reincarnation since she died in the year I was born. But that wouldn't explain Luna.

"We don't know; we have theories, but nothing confirmed."

Phelipe looks at Luna, hoping she has answers. But the girl shakes her head, staring at the floor. Apparently, that's all she knows. Then John lets out a low laugh, almost like a feline purr. All attention turns to him.

"I know what happened. You're not doppelgängers by accident or magic; it's not hard to imagine. It's always been a theory, but it seemed so impossible and without reason. However, it's real..." He flashes a wide smile, moving closer to me. My natural instinct is to back away; there's something so disturbing about him that I can't even look him in the eye. His fingers grip my necklace, examining it with curiosity. I pull it from his hand, distancing myself. "She cloned herself, creating both of you," he states, convinced.

CHAPTER THIRTY-NINE

Sophia

"Don't be an idiot, John. Do you think we haven't thought of that before?" Penélope scolds, visibly irritated. "There's no way an adult can be cloned. They tried that with animals and it didn't work! Most of the animals died during gestation or were born with anomalies caused by failures in genome reprogramming. Reprogramming the DNA of an adult somatic cell is impossible!"

I'm still too shocked to even try to understand what they are discussing. Clones? Is that even possible? I've always considered it a fanciful option, but we're talking about a laboratory here.

"You're right, it's impossible," he agrees. Penélope scoffs. Phelipe crosses his arms over his chest, watching his brother with interest. "You can't reprogram an adult somatic cell and succeed. Especially not a human one."

"So what?" she questions, narrowing her eyes.

"When I broke into Tom Warner's house, before I found Luna..." He hesitates. "I snooped around a bit. His office was stuffed with books, theses, and even a scribbled chart, all about the same subject: reproductive cloning. I thought it was some new plan to create chimeric clones or something, until I came face to face with the duplicate." He points to the girl curled up on the sofa. "Then I also researched a bit, following Tom's line of thinking, and I found out that if you remove the nucleus of a somatic cell from an adult human and transfer it to a nucleus-free egg, reprogramming the cell to the initial stage, the egg will behave as if it has just been fertilized. Then, if you implant this egg in a uterus and it develops, the embryo inherits the physical characteristics of the person who donated the somatic cell."

I'm staring at them without understanding a single word. It sounds like Greek to me. Penélope is stunned, her jaw dropping in disbelief. Phelipe is still processing the information. Luckily, Luna looks just as lost as I am.

"Holy shit!" Penélope curses. "She managed to do that in 2000? The technology wasn't that advanced back then! Even today, they're having issues with animal reproductive cloning, and she managed not just one, but two perfect human clones developed eighteen years ago?"

She is pacing back and forth, furious. Her hands are clasped behind her back, constantly clenching into fists. Both John and Phelipe are looking at me and Luna with a hint of pity in their eyes.

"What does this mean?" I ask, completely lost.

"That humans are bastards and are mastering technology just to screw us over!" Penélope hisses. "Robots, clones, what else do they want?"

"Robots?" John asks, confused and surprised.

Apparently, he doesn't know about the hellhounds and the theory that they will implant robotic brains in the caged test subjects. Penélope murmurs a "I'll explain later" as she continues pacing.

"Reproductive cloning is..."

"Illegal? Yes," Penélope interrupts me. I've heard about this in high school Biology classes; we even did a project on Dolly the sheep, the first successfully cloned animal. "Just like human chimeras. And she's such a bitch that she wouldn't even be alive to know if the clones worked or not. She was a hundred percent sure."

"But what does this mean? How was I cloned?"

"Sofia removed the nucleus from one of her cells and implanted it into an empty egg, which was reprogrammed with her DNA, and somehow managed to implant it in your mother," Phelipe explains, staring at us. "Luna was definitely born in a laboratory clinic, and you, Sophia?"

"Me too." I blink hard, trying to snap out of the trance I'm in. "I was born in a clinic in Rio de Janeiro, my father beat my pregnant mother at the time, and she almost lost the baby, in this case, me. Then she went to live for a while in Rio de Janeiro with my grandmother, Márcia, my father's mother, who was a doctor."

The three chimeras look at me in shock. I don't know which revelation was more shocking to make them stare at me like that. My head is spinning, the information swirling around without me truly understanding. The cold is making me dizzy, preventing me from thinking straight. On top of that, the exhaustion is wearing me down more by the minute.

"Your grandmother?" John asks.

"Yeah, my grandmother was a doctor at that stupid laboratory," I reply grumpily, not knowing what that has to do with all this talk about clones. "The grandmother who gave me the necklace," I explain, looking at Phelipe; I've already told him this.

He nods his head before exchanging a tense look with Penélope. John drums his fingers on his chin, analyzing me.

"Your mother probably lost the baby, Sophia," Phelipe says sympathetically. "And Sofia somehow managed to place her egg in its place. Maybe your mother allowed it, thinking it would be a test-tube baby to replace what she lost. Or she might have done it without your mother's consent, which would be a bit harder but not impossible."

No, it can't be. Am I not biologically my mother's child? Was she just my surrogate? It's crossed my mind before that I was adopted since my mother and sisters are blonde and very similar, and I've never looked anything like them. However, since I resemble my father, I abandoned that idea.

Vanessa would never agree to this; I'm sure of it! She must have been tricked somehow, without knowing anything. I know my mother, a sentimental and emotional woman who wouldn't act so coldly to accept receiving an egg from someone she didn't know.

"How could Sofia have approached my mother to swap babies or something? Wasn't she fleeing from the laboratory?"

"And what better place to hide from them than right under their noses?" John replies with a hint of sarcasm in his voice, legitimizing himself as a Kyle.

"Actually quite smart; she would need to be working in a lab to study cloning. She would also be close enough to control the searches for herself," Phelipe muses thoughtfully. "Besides, the last time I saw her, she was still under thirty. The lab too. She got married; she must have changed her name and could have changed her appearance to be almost unrecognizable."

"I saw her after that," John admits, throwing a pretentious look at Phelipe, who clenches his jaw tightly. "Her appearance was indeed different. I thought it was just age, but maybe it was something more."

"But what does all this mean?" I ask, exhaustion threatening to shut me down; it takes all my effort to stay upright and still conscious.

"It means..." Phelipe turns to me with a slight ironic smile on his lips. "That you are a lab girl."

CHAPTER FORTY

Sophia

Luna is finally taking a shower. As I hear the noise of the shower, the water cascading over her dirty body, I'm lying in one of the rooms of the house, still trying to process all the information I've been given. At least I'm warm under the covers, covering my entire body up to my chin. The chimeras are downstairs; Penélope was explaining about the hellhounds to John when the cold and exhaustion overwhelmed me, and I went up to find a place to take a shower and lie down.

I still have no answers to the questions that are pounding in my mind when Phelipe enters the room cautiously. I raise my eyes to him as he approaches.

"When you told me that night in the woods that Sofia got involved with Teodoro, I thought you were referring to Tom's father, not his grandfather."

"I know," he admits, exhaling through his nose. "I just came to see how you were doing. Big day, isn't it? So much information at once."

A terrible day, I would say. My head is still spinning with the possibilities of how I ended up in my mother's womb, or in the womb of someone else who might have given birth to me and swapped the babies. Somewhere in the country, there could be a seventeen-year-old blonde girl with gray eyes like my sisters. It's a possibility.

"Did you give her the necklace?"

"Not exactly. The necklace was hers; she wore it all the time when I met her. The night we met, before she stabbed me and ran away, she gave it to me as a gift or a keepsake. Years later, when I was snooping into her life and found out she was married and pregnant, I left the necklace at the door of the house she lived in so she would know that I had found her."

I unconsciously trace the shape of the necklace with my fingers.

"How do you think it ended up in my grandmother's hands?" This question keeps hammering in my mind. "She was a doctor at the laboratory. If you think Sofia could have infiltrated there somehow, maybe my grandmother knew her. She could have given the necklace to my grandmother."

Phelipe looks away. I have a feeling he's hiding something from me, as always.

"Well, it seems the answers we were looking for have been in your family all along," he says simply.

And we are miles away from the only person who could answer many of these questions: my mother. I let out a strangled sigh, adjusting myself on the mattress on the floor, feeling the photo album poking me under the covers.

"I'm so tired," I say, closing my eyes. "What about you and your brother?"

"Oh, he hates me. There's not much I can do."

I don't need to look at him to know he's smiling. At that exact moment, the bathroom door opens, and Luna appears, drying her hair with a towel, dressed in my clothes. Phelipe says goodbye, stating he will leave us alone so we can rest.

The girl is relaxed, her eyes sparkling when she sees the fluffy blanket in front of her. It must have been months since she last took a shower and had a good night's sleep. I let her have the bed so she can sleep more comfortably, curling up on a mattress on the floor.

"So, you and that Kyle boy seem... close," she comments hesitantly, lying down on the bed.

I sigh, curling up on the mattress to try to warm myself. The wind outside the house is howling through the window, above the sound of the constant rain.

"We're not," I reply tersely.

"Oh."

We maintain a long silence, except for the storm on the roof and now and then the voice of one of the Kyle brothers arguing in the living room; usually, Penélope's sarcastic laughter. I'm almost sure the girl has fallen asleep when I hear her stir in the bed and let out a restless sigh.

"What are all those numbers scrawled on the wall?" I ask, remembering the horrifying room where we found her; a numerical sequence repeated endlessly, which I practically memorized with my photographic memory.

"It's my uncle's cell phone number," she admits, embarrassed. "He has this exclusive line just to talk to me. He made me memorize the number in case something happened and I needed to contact him. I guess he was predicting."

I roll onto my side, turning towards her, trying to distinguish her silhouette on the bed in the dark.

"Do you want to call him?" I ask, a little incredulous.

"No."

There's something unspoken in what she didn't say: she also doesn't want to stay here. Well, her options aren't very good.

"John won't treat you like that anymore, I promise. No one will *treat us* like that anymore."

"Did you meet... my uncle?" she asks casually.

Then I remember that she has been held in captivity for a long time, she doesn't know about my situation with the police or Tom Warner's amputation. She knows absolutely nothing. I tell her every detail of that fateful day, from the school talent show when I was attacked by chimeras and her uncle shot me, almost killing me if Artur hadn't jumped in front of me. Unfortunately, as I narrate the episode, I'm bombarded by memories of my old life, which make my throat burn and my eyes well up with tears.

I hate Tom Warner so much. So much! Almost as much as I hate the original Sofia. Because of him, I'm far from my friends and family. Because of him, I'm wanted by the police as a cowardly murderer, without even having the chance to tell everyone my story. Because of him, Izec looked at me accusingly in a way I will never forget, thinking I am responsible for the death of his girlfriend.

But I promised on the day I saw the last report about me on television that as soon as Tom and I meet again, I will kill him.

CHAPTER FORTY-ONE

Sophia

Like all the dreams I have with Viviane, this one starts with me running.

Nothing new, the same pearlescent dress, the same forest, the familiar darkness where she lurks. Everything seems exactly like the other times; however, it's completely different.

Am I lucid? Aware?

Viviane always controlled the dreams so that I never knew it was really a dream until I woke up. I prepared my subconscious by telling myself: the moment I see myself in that forest again, I will force myself to wake up. That has never worked. But now, somehow, I am aware that we are in my mind in yet another dream forged by Viviane. What went wrong this time?

I stop running, looking around. We aren't entirely in the dark of the woods because, every now and then, the lights flicker, and I can see myself in an empty street. Something is distracting her.

"You're losing your touch, wicked one," I say to the wind, knowing she can hear me.

Viviane laughs in response, her devilish laughter echoing around me, making me plunge back into the darkness. I can feel despair starting to rise in my chest, the urge to run away trying to block all my other senses. But I freeze, clenching my fists. I will try to resist as much as I can this time. I won't let her take control of this dream.

"Well, well, how admirable is your audacity to try to fight against me," she hisses, mocking me. The darkness flickers for a few seconds, allowing me to catch a glimpse of her red hair not too far from where I am. "Don't think I don't know you've been snooping around in my head."

"It couldn't be a greater displeasure for me," I say with all the firmness I can muster. In truth, my heart is racing, and the urge to run is growing stronger. I remember Penélope warning me about the dangers of slipping back into Viviane's head and getting trapped there. I shudder at the thought. "Are you losing your touch, or has your brain finally realized you're not worth it and started to shut down?"

A cold wave envelops my body, bringing cold butterflies to my stomach. Everything around me smells of panic and despair.

"What gall coming from a girl who abandoned her family to the mercy of enemies." Her words sound like whips.

I tense my back, feeling the hairs on my body stand on end. Hearing her mention my family through her wicked lips awakens things in me I didn't even know existed.

"What are you talking about?"

I'm scared of the answer. I shrink back, sinking into my own misery at the thought that Viviane may have gotten close to my mother or my sisters.

The lights flicker again, and I can see her approaching. I know this time she deliberately lessened the darkness so I can face her while she circles around me. The predator stalking its prey.

"I counted on my fingers how many days it would take for you and Phelipe to be captured. I waited day after day in that horrible cell, being tortured and treated like an animal, but he never showed up," she says, hatred rising in her voice. "For you to have lasted so long out of the lab's clutches, I believe you had help. Probably that annoying bitch Penélope." Her long red hair drags on the ground, forming a circle as she continues to circle me. "When I realized this wouldn't happen, I planned my escape," she says, stopping in front of me and tilting her head. "I don't know exactly where you're hiding, but something tells me it's not in your pathetic town, where your family and your ridiculous little friends are completely unprotected from the wrath of your enemies."

I swallow hard. I feel a pang of guilt in the pit of my stomach. It was never my intention to abandon them, but I had no choice. Leaving them was my way of protecting them, keeping my enemies behind me while I fled far away from the people I love.

"Why?" I ask with a shaky voice. My eyes are misty, staring into hers. "Why take it out on innocent people? Why take it out on me? I still don't know why you hate me so much. Just because of my face? Because of Phelipe? Honestly, there's nothing romantic happening between us."

She bites her lip, smiling maliciously. The green of her eyes seems to glimmer.

"I know there's nothing happening between you and him; that's not even close to the reason for all this." Viviane laughs, making the cold intensify. "The bitch Sofia created you to get revenge on me. She knew I would kill her; it was only a matter of time before I found her. So she created you as a desperate act, so you would finish what she started when she freed the chimeras. And since I can't get close to you to kill her, I'll make you come to me."

"What? What was her plan?" I ask, eager to know more.

At that moment, the lights flicker intensely, making Viviane and me jump immediately, as if the dream were collapsing. I shout at her, insisting she tell me what Sofia's plan was, forcing my voice above the shrill noise of the wind.

"We'll see each other soon, Sophia," she hisses, flickering. Her body begins to crumble before my eyes, being carried away by the air. She's waking up. "I imagine you're with the storm. If I were you,

I would be. It's by far the only safe place for you now, since the lab wouldn't dare touch one of your elements."

Having said that, I feel a tug at the back of my head, which makes my eyes almost pop out. The pressure crushes my skull, and I feel like it's splitting in half. The image of a woman appears in the back of my mind and takes over everything. I don't know who she is, though she seems terribly familiar. Like when I met Penélope and sensed some familiarity in her, but couldn't connect it to Phelipe.

When I open my eyes, the image dissipates, and I notice I'm not back in John's room. I'm in the Christ Park. I would recognize this place under any circumstances, even in Viviane's devilish mind. A little to the left is the tree where Ane and I carved our initials, and where Izec took me weeks ago.

Which means Viviane is in Araxá. And she's going to start a massacre.

"No!" I scream too loudly, my voice echoing within me.

My head pounds at once, that unwanted tug crushing my brain and bringing me back into my body. I wake up sweating in the dark room, sitting up automatically. The rain is pouring down on the roof with full force, and I can still hear my heart pounding in my chest. The blood turns to ice in my veins.

Luna also wakes up, startled, looking at me with her eyebrows raised. I kick the covers away, already getting to my feet in a jump.

"Is everything okay? What happened?" Luna asks anxiously, also getting up.

I turn to her, stopping in front of the door with my hand on the doorknob.

"They're going to kill my family!"

CHAPTER FORTY-TWO

Sophia

I run down the stairs, my heart practically leaping out of my mouth. Luna is right on my heels. When I reach the living room, I see John sitting on the sofa, with Penélope beside him, her long legs draped over his lap. Phelipe is standing in the opposite corner of the room, leaning against the wall, just watching from a distance. The three of them look up at me when I stop in front of them, desperation taking over my face.

"What the hell happened?" Penélope asks, irritated. "Can I not have a moment of peace?"

I tell them about the dream, the words struggling to come out of my mouth, the lack of air making my asthmatic lungs start to wheeze. The last time I had an asthma attack, I was about ten years old; apparently, I'm about to have another.

Penélope scoffs when I finish, resting her forehead in her hand. Phelipe is still, his face unreadable, almost as if he's part of the wall. John looks bewildered, his brow furrowed.

"If she said the original Sofia created you for her, then she doesn't know about the other copy," Penélope comments, tapping her fingers on her forehead.

"Or she knew one wouldn't be enough to finish whatever she started, so she created many," John ponders.

"That's not the point!" My voice rises two octaves with my panic; I'm literally trembling in despair. "I don't care how many copies there are or what that idiot Sofia wanted! Viviane is in Araxá, after my family and friends. We have to leave now!"

They all stare at me in a disturbing silence. Their expressions are hesitant and pitying. Penélope shifts on the sofa, pulling her legs off her brother's lap and turning to face me. Phelipe looks down at his feet. John is just staring at me, just like Luna.

"We can't leave here, Sophia." It's Penélope who speaks, her voice calm and controlled as she looks me in the eye. "We came from very far to find John because this is the safest place for us."

"But they aren't safe!" I let out a strangled whimper.

"I'm sorry, Sophia," Penélope says, looking down, biting her lip.

I curse loudly, unable to believe it. Is no one going to do anything? Are they really going to let everyone I love die because they want to stay safe? I couldn't care less about my safety. This isn't even living; it's surviving.

I look at each of them in disbelief. Three powerful chimeras who could destroy people in seconds without much effort are refusing to help me. Not even Phelipe, who has the most connection to me among them, perhaps because we met first, can look me in the eye. He sighs, stepping closer.

"Sophia, we're in another state. It would take nearly three days to get back to Araxá by car," he says gently. "Not to mention all the police checkpoints and tolls we'd have to avoid. And the cars we'd steal." He shrugs. "We'd never make it in time."

"No!" I whimper, feeling warm tears streaming down my cheeks. Anguish and fear close my throat, making it hard for me to breathe. "Please, there has to be a way..."

Luna is looking at me, uncertain whether to come closer. John scratches his arm, uncomfortable.

"Maybe she's bluffing," Penélope tries, but even she doesn't believe her words. "She said that just to destabilize you and make you run back. It's a trap."

Of course, it's a trap and her intention is to make me return desperately to save my family. But that doesn't mean she wouldn't hurt them anyway.

I breathe heavily, sinking into my own despair. My fingers pull at my hair hard, almost tearing it from the roots. There has to be a way; I can't live with myself if something happens to someone I love because of me. My knees buckle, touching the ground, just at the thought of it. I'm crying uncontrollably, my body shaking in violent spasms.

"Please," I plead.

Penélope closes her eyes. Luna silently bites her nails.

"I'm sorry," Phelipe says, hovering over me, his eyes shining with the same emotion I saw the day I was attacked at the gas station.

"We can't leave John," Penélope reinforces, looking at her brother affectionately, but I blink, and her expression hardens.

I can swear the note of hysteria I hear in her voice is the same as mine as I plead for us to return. The same urgency to protect the people she loves.

I cry for a long time, feeling their gazes on me, not caring about it. No one will help me. They wouldn't let me go back alone, and I probably can't escape from here. But I need to act before Viviane and her long claws can lay a finger on my family.

I can imagine Isa running scared when she sees her. My mother paling, trying to defend her daughters. Even Lily regaining her sobriety, ready to fight Viviane and protect our family. The image is so real it hurts, tearing at my chest, and I let out a strangled whimper that makes Phelipe turn away.

If only there were a way to at least warn them to run... My crying is interrupted immediately.

"Let me call them!" I ask. "I can warn them that they're in danger, and they'll leave home immediately."

They exchange glances. John scratches his head.

"Well, that's not a good idea..."

"They already know where we are!" I interrupt him, wiping the tears from my cheeks with the back of my hand. Gradually, I stand up. "Viviane herself said she knows I'm here, that this is the only safe place. Tom must also know, and I don't care if they track us. If being near you is as safe as Penélope thinks, then they won't come to attack us. Not even the hellhounds would come close."

Reluctantly, I manage to convince them to let me use the phone. I'm so anxious to contact a familiar voice that I'm almost smiling. My fingers are trembling, and I have to dial the number twice to get it right. I ask to speak privately, as privately as I can, since my mother's phone is probably tapped — after this call, Phelipe's line will also be — but the lab boy is still out here, about to hear my conversation.

"Hello?" I blurt out desperately as soon as someone answers the call, hearing the breathing on the other side of the line. My eyes are burning again. "Mom, is that you? It's Sophia!"

"Sophia? What a pleasure," responds a somewhat familiar male voice. "To what do I owe the honor of your call?"

I need a few seconds to recognize who is speaking to me. Tom Warner.

"Tom... let me talk to my mom!" I scream, feeling all the desperation take hold of me once again.

What the hell has this bastard done? Is he in my house or did he transfer my mother's landline number to himself? Phelipe immediately opens the door to the room.

"I don't think that's possible!" He laughs. "But tell me, how is the life of a fugitive? I heard that one of my men almost caught you before your pet lab rats killed him."

"Where's my mother?" I snarl each syllable separately, the phone shaking against my ear between my trembling fingers.

Phelipe enters the room, completely shocked by what he's hearing.

"She could be here with me, at your house, or..." He pauses dramatically. "I could be in the comfort of my home, using the call transfer service. It's a game, Sophia. What do you think? Try to guess."

"If you lay a finger on them, I swear that..."

"I've learned many interesting things about you." His tone is irritatingly cheerful. "You know what they say, right? Know your enemies. I know how impulsive, controlling, and spoiled you are. It must be terrible for you these past few days living in misery, like a fugitive. I know about your plans to go to college, your ridiculous friends that you idolize, even the womanizing ex-boyfriend who dumped you." He lets out a sigh. "Even about the guy you sent to jail for attempted rape. Wait, was it just attempted? I didn't pay attention to the sordid details."

My blood pressure is slowly dropping, my vision going dark, my body feeling lighter and lighter. I need all my self-control to stay upright, holding the phone. I clench my teeth tightly. I won't let him destabilize me like this.

"I've been studying my enemy too..." I venture. "In fact, I have something you want very much."

"What would that be?" he asks, intrigued.

Phelipe shakes his head, signaling me to end the conversation immediately.

"Your niece. I'd put her on the line to talk to you, but I don't think that's possible." The venom is clear in my voice. When he doesn't say anything, I continue: "Lay a finger on a single hair of anyone in my family, and your niece dies."

He lets out a laugh laced with anger.

"Today is not a good day for you to threaten me, Sophia. My election victory is tomorrow, and I'm a little tense; I still haven't decided which suit I'll wear to the press conference." There's a note of tension in his voice, which he tries to hide with mockery. "As for my niece, hurt her in any way and..."

"And what?" I interrupt, fed up, furious. "I'm already in hell, Tom."

"No," he disagrees, "but when I get to you, you'll beg to be!"

CHAPTER FORTY-THREE

Sophia

"You shouldn't have provoked Tom, Sophia," Penélope reprimands me in a very serious tone. But I don't care. I'm pacing back and forth on the living room floor, my footsteps echoing off the empty walls. Keeping myself moving is what prevents me from going crazy. "Now he's going to want to retaliate!"

"Wow, what a revelation, right?" I let out a hysterical laugh, devoid of any humor. "Now I can choose who I'd prefer to kill the people I love while I stay here, playing house with chimeras!"

Penélope is about to say something, but Phelipe silences her with a hand gesture. I know what he's thinking: there's no point in saying anything now. Yeah, there really isn't. I'm a bundle of nerves, fraying at the edges, walking in circles like a dog chasing its own tail.

I couldn't warn my family. I couldn't remember any of my friends' numbers by heart; damn technology! I feel like I'm on the brink of a nervous breakdown. They're going to need to sedate me if they want me to stay here doing nothing, imagining what's happening miles away.

"Earlier, you mentioned that Viviane knew you were here with me?" John asks, his eyes tracking my pacing in the room.

I have to struggle to remember. Why the hell is he worrying about that now?

"Yeah, she said something about the lab not touching you because you're one of his elements."

"Elements?" he asks, agitated. I just nod my head. "What the hell does that mean?"

Phelipe raises his eyebrows and crosses his arms, thinking. Penélope nervously chews on a sandwich, nearly spitting it out upon hearing my words.

"Element? Like the four elements?" Luna timidly asks from somewhere I can't even see.

Why the hell are they worried about this? Don't they realize I'm in the middle of a crisis? They're threatening my family, damn it! I let out a breath through my mouth, controlling myself.

"No way," Penélope says, cutting through the uncomfortable silence that has formed. "John is the only one of us who can control the weather; we would know if there was anyone who could spit fire or pull ice out of their ass. Or anything like that."

She's trying to lighten the mood, which obviously isn't working. Not even her irony can ease the knot in my stomach, the taste of tears burning in my throat, or the dark cloud that seems to have settled over the place. The rain is pouring down at full speed outside, not giving a moment's respite.

"Or that's what they want us to think," Phelipe comments, getting animated. "Just because we've never seen another powerful subject doesn't mean it doesn't exist. We didn't know about the copies until we came face to face with two!"

They debate this for a while, consuming all my patience. Why are they so concerned about this? I keep pacing back and forth, trying to remember Izec's number. How could I forget that number? I called him every day, more than once, for four years. Maybe the nervousness is affecting my concentration; I'm sure I still know it by heart.

"I don't know..." Penélope says, doubtfully.

"Our brother has a good imagination," John comments with a venomous tone, clicking his tongue in Phelipe's direction. His rain-colored eyes narrow mischievously. "He imagined a rosy world for himself and Sofia, and was very disappointed when things didn't turn out the way he expected."

Since we got here, they haven't addressed each other at all except to provoke. I'm sure the only thing keeping John from beheading Phelipe is Penélope. And vice versa. The two are very much alike.

Phelipe smirks with irony.

"Not as good as yours thinking Sofia wanted something with you, Jonathan," Phelipe retorts.

The storm intensifies outside. The wind is so strong it sounds like animal howls against the windows of the house. My body shivers.

At that moment, with all the calm and elegance possible, Phelipe pulls out his dagger and points it at his brother. His pupils immediately dilate, anticipating the attack.

"Enough!" Penélope intervenes, huffing. She stands between the two. "If Phelipe is right and there are other powerful chimeras capable of controlling the other elements, that would explain a lot. I always thought they didn't attack John out of fear of his strength. But what if there's another reason?"

I want to scream at them: fuck it! I don't give a damn about the reason they don't confront John or try to lock him up. All I want is to remember that damn number; their voices in this idiotic discussion are driving me insane.

"The hellhounds almost killed us more than once, but they don't even get close to John," Penélope continues, focusing. "Caregivers have tried to kill us, even humans are after us. But John, the easiest chimera to locate, has never had to deal with an unwanted visitor... What if there's actually a reason they don't bother you? Because you're exactly where they want you to be."

"Far from the others," Phelipe adds.

John stands up, straightening his body.

"So you think I'm some kind of weapon? That if I join the others like me, we present some risk?" he asks, incredulous. The siblings nod. "If there were even a remote possibility that I could be a piece of something that could destroy the lab, do you really think they'd let me live?"

Silence falls. My attention finally turns to their conversation. Destroying the lab? It's all I want in the world. To destroy every inch of that horrible place, which is responsible for my misery. To destroy the empire that empowers Tom Warner until nothing remains and he's just a spoiled man who lost his toys. Weak, vulnerable. I want him to feel that way, just like I felt all this time, before I finally kill him.

"Unless you're also a weapon that could be used for their ascendance," I say. All eyes turn to me. It makes sense; they know. Tom wouldn't destroy something that could give him power, even if it were also a threat. I walk toward John, locking my gaze on his eyes. "If you're a powerful weapon against the lab, you need to fight," I assert, practically pleading. "If going to save my family is a trap set by Tom and Viviane, it's also the perfect opportunity to defeat them. We know where they are, we have the advantage, plus a weapon against them. We need to stop Tom before he wins the elections tomorrow."

I stare at them, filled with hope. Phelipe swallows hard, hesitant.

"A weapon we don't know how to operate," he ponders. "And that needs other parts that we also don't know where they are."

Holy shit! I take a deep breath.

"And we would never make it in time," Penélope adds. "We'd arrive many days later."

"True, we wouldn't even make it in time by car," John agrees before breaking into a wide smile. A Kyle smile. "Luckily, you have the air element. You know, there's a hangar not too far from here. What do you think about stealing a helicopter? We can fly."

CHAPTER FORTY-FOUR

Artur

The lights come on in the hallway. This is wrong; the lights shouldn't be on during bedtime. But in fact, a lot of things have been wrong lately. Me being locked up here after helping the enemy is one of them.

Two caregivers appear with their rhythmic footsteps, completely exhausted from being on duty for two consecutive days. They are wearing white uniforms with the lab logo, but this time they aren't wearing helmets. Another thing that's wrong. They always wear helmets. How else can they defend themselves if a crazed chimera tries to rip their heads off or sink its teeth into their fragile necks?

They are dragging a body between them. Almost like the day they brought Viviane. Except the blonde girl they're carrying seems to be awake, struggling against the caregivers, trying to break free. And the most surprising thing is that they don't need much effort to subdue her. How many sedatives did they give this subject? Then I hear, in the silence of my cell, three human hearts beating in sync.

This isn't a chimera. It's a human girl. Another thing that's wrong: they are imprisoning a human. What did she do to be locked away in a basement full of killer monsters?

There's another faint and equally rhythmic noise that I can't identify, hammering in the air.

The caregivers stop in front of my cell, opening the empty cage door that used to belong to Phelipe. They throw the girl in there without saying anything or thinking much about what they're doing. She screams, crashing against the glass door, pounding on it, desperately trying to escape. All she receives is a bored look from the caregivers before they turn and leave.

She cries and screams, banging on the glass walls. The cell next to hers has been empty since Viviane escaped again after tiring of waiting for Phelipe to be captured and imprisoned. The chimera on her other side yawns in her direction but goes back to sleep, completely ignoring the ruckus the newcomer is making.

When she turns to look at me, I recognize her face. The blonde hair, the blue eyes, the completely red face from crying. Where do I know her from? Oh, yes. From Sophia's mind. This is her friend. Ane.

But it feels like there's something more, as if I've seen her face on another chimera. Which doesn't make sense since the girl is completely human. But what did Ane do to end up locked up here?

I finally identify the constant noise cutting through the air. It's another heart beating inside her. The girl is pregnant.

She looks at me, crying uncontrollably, realizing I'm paying attention to her. She's screaming desperate things at me, asking for help, rescue, an explanation of where she is, but all I do is point to her belly.

I've never seen a pregnant woman before. Female chimeras can't have children; the scientific procedures resulted in infertility. And they've never locked a pregnant human up here before.

She nods her head, desperate, her fingers touching her protruding belly protectively. Then a flood of memories unravels in her mind, and I dive in, frozen in scenes and scenarios.

Ane is rolling back and forth on the bed, once again unable to sleep. It's not just the pregnancy that's bothering her sleep; it's all the problems she's been facing: the pressure of the entrance exam drawing closer; her younger siblings starting to ask tirelessly about their parents; Izec, her friend, in his new cold and indifferent posture, but she knows inside he's dead, trying not to let anyone get close; the endless mourning at school since the massacre; the things she heard about her kidnapped sister; the story with young Sophia...

Ane squeezes her eyes shut. Jimmy's hand, her boyfriend, rests lovingly on her already protruding belly while he sleeps with his head resting on his girlfriend's pillow.

Giving in, she slowly gets up from the bed, making as little noise as possible so she doesn't wake Jimmy; she knows she won't be able to sleep again. It's as if her brain doesn't turn off, never.

Step by step, in the dark hallway, she walks to her brothers' room. The bedside lamp is on; she left it that way after telling a story to the two of them as they fell asleep. Ane smiles, admiring the blonde head of Benício—her brother—with the blanket pulled up to his chin. Earlier, he told her he had seen a monster in his closet. Of course, she had to argue with Benjamin, her other brother, for scaring the twin who had always been the most afraid of the two.

"Ane, who is the bloody woman living in our closet?" Benício asked her hours earlier as she lay down with him in his bed to read a book for the two of them.

"She's a vampire with cat eyes who takes scared children in her sack and devours them," Benjamin theatrically replied, throwing himself onto the bed as if he had been caught and was fighting to break free from an invisible hand.

Benício shrank back, holding his sister like a shield. Ane shot him a warning look, which made him stop immediately. The boy rested his face in his hands and looked at them with a mischievous smile.

"Benjamin, what did I tell you about telling that kind of story to your brother?" she scolded him in a threatening voice, causing him to look away and murmur an apology. "There's no one in the closet, Beny."

"She has snake eyes," Benício sniffed.

"There's nothing like that," Ane assured, stroking her brother's back. "Benji, pick a book for us to read today."

At that moment, watching them sleep, Ane wonders where they get such creativity. She leans toward Beny and kisses his little forehead. The boy takes a deep breath but doesn't wake up. Then she does the same with Benji, who stirs in his turbulent sleep. *He's probably dreaming of dinosaurs and vampires that he loves so much,* Ane thinks. She turns off the lamp as she leaves the room, closing the door until only a crack remains, in case one of them gets up during the night to look for her.

Ane thinks that Mr. Estevão, Jimmy's father, is away on a business trip and that Izec is holed up in the back chalet of the property where his mother and brother Lucas live.

Calmer now, Ane walks back to the room, noticing that Jimmy is still sleeping in the same position she left him. He seems too big for the bed, and Ane smiles as she admires him, hoping their baby will look like his father.

Slowly, she approaches the large window of the room, knowing that even if she lies down now, she won't be able to sleep. The view from the window overlooks the entire property. She can see the guards at the entrance gate, a well-kept garden, a structure gushing water non-stop with a carved angel statue, and the enormous swimming pool right below her balcony. Memories flood the girl's mind, making her smile. Jimmy always showed off by jumping from there into the water, a free fall of at least six meters, she quickly calculates.

Ane feels a movement behind her that makes her neck immediately prickle. She turns expecting to see Jimmy standing in the dark asking her to come back to bed, but what she sees leaves her paralyzed.

A woman is standing in the middle of the room, holding Jimmy tightly by the neck and covering his mouth; his eyes are wide open as he struggles to break free from the intruder's grip, without much success. The moonlight streams in through the closed window, illuminating enough for her to see the woman. She has blood-red hair, cat-like vertical pupils, and nails so long they look like claws. She doesn't seem to be human; Ane has a bad feeling about her, sensing something supernatural lurking, an evil energy enveloping the entire room.

Viviane, I recognize her immediately.

"Who are you?" Ane asks in a voice barely above a whisper.

Her first thought is to protect the baby, not letting her get close.

"Sorry, dear. Nothing personal, but I need to kill you both to send a message," Viviane says in a voice that sounds like the ringing of bells, sharp and piercing.

Ane's heart pounds hard in her chest, crushed by a glacial chill that sweeps over her entire body. I can feel all her sensations. Her legs wobble as her eyes meet Jimmy's, completely terrified. She thinks that her boyfriend is an athlete, stronger than most people she knows; he trains hard for that. How can a woman just over 5 feet tall and weighing about 110 pounds immobilize him?

"Please don't do this," she pleads, feeling the tears welling up, flowing freely down her cheeks. Her whole body is trembling. *My baby,* is what she thinks. *My siblings...* — You can take whatever you want; please, just don't hurt us, I'm pregnant. Please!

Viviane tilts her head, evaluating her, her eyes focused on her belly, which Ane instinctively covers with her hands as a form of protection. The subject gives a wicked smile.

"Ane, right?" she asks without waiting for a response. "Your sister won't be too happy to hear about this. But *they,* ah, *they* will love it. They adore a pregnant woman! Turning you in will ensure I live a little longer..."

Viviane seems to ramble on about it. Ane doesn't understand a single word the stranger says; her mind gets stuck when she talks about her sister.

Ah, so that's it. That's where I recognize her from. Her sister was captured by the lab when she was still a child. She was one of the children used in their project to try to alter the DNA of a fully developed being instead of embryos, like they did with us, to create new chimeras. If Ane has half the power her sister has, it's obvious the lab would want her. Especially now that she's pregnant.

"Annabel? What do you know about my sister?"

"That was her name? No wonder she didn't like it," Viviane laughs, and I recognize the sound as amusement. Her long nail trails down Jimmy's neck. "You live. The others die."

"No, please..." Ane lunges forward, ready to kneel and beg for mercy.

Then she remembers Benício's words earlier: "Who is the bloody woman living in our closet? She has snake eyes."

So that's where she came from; she was hiding in the children's room, waiting for the house to empty out so she could attack under the cover of night. But they aren't completely helpless; the guards are still on their watch shift; if she screams, it could attract their attention. How long would it take for them to get here? Ane's thoughts swirl.

"I wouldn't count on that if I were you, dear. I sent a little distraction for your guards," the subject comments, as if she had read their thoughts.

On pure impulse, Ane looks over her shoulder at the place where she saw the guards walking back and forth at their posts just minutes before, only to find that there's no one there. They are alone.

At that moment, Jimmy takes advantage of Viviane's distraction by laughing at his girlfriend to bite the hand that covers his mouth.

Caught off guard, the subject releases him with a snarl of rage, just enough for him to scream:

"Ane, jump!"

She knows what he means. If she jumps off the balcony, she'll land in the pool and, with a bit of luck, she can run fast enough to reach the gates and call for help. As desperately as she wants to get out of there and try to get assistance, Ane thinks she can't leave Jimmy behind, much less her brothers.

But the wicked woman is in the center of the room, blocking the door; there's no way to get out without passing by her. Ane can't risk her hurting her baby or taking it out on Jimmy. She also can't let her follow her to her brothers. If the woman wants her, as she claims, she'll have to follow her.

In a split second, Ane nods slightly at Jimmy; he understands. With his elbow, he strikes the woman right on the nose, making her recoil. Ane is startled to realize that Jimmy seems to be feeling more pain than she is. Viviane lunges at him, growling in fury. He manages to reach the lamp, ready to smash it against her head. It's the opening he needs.

When Viviane notices Ane running toward the window, she stops her planned attack on Jimmy and yells something incomprehensible, ready to reach her. There's no time to unlock the glass doors of the balcony, Ane concludes. Closing her eyes tightly while silently praying for divine protection, she propels herself against the glass, feeling the ground abandon her feet as she throws herself off the balcony.

Ane screams as she falls, her feet and hands moving involuntarily, searching for something to grab onto. The cold water of the pool engulfs her like an embrace, freezing her bones as she sinks freely until she touches the bottom.

Before she resurfaces, she feels another impact in the water and dives away, believing it to be the woman who jumped in after her. But when she reaches the edge of the pool, ready to jump out, she looks back, finding Jimmy's bloodied head floating, staining the water red.

A horrible wail of pain escapes Ane's chest, her eyes so watery they barely stay open. No, Jimmy, it can't be. Her boyfriend, the love of her life, the father of her baby, dead, with his decapitated head floating on the surface. She makes a move to reach him, feeling her hands get sticky with blood as she touches his face, then notices a shadow in the doorway of the house. She gains momentum and jumps out of the pool, awkwardly running through the garden, feeling the cold of the night in her wet nightgown like knives stabbing her. She can't even see a foot in front of her, but she needs to keep running to keep the woman as far away from her brothers as possible while trying to reach them.

As she gets close enough to the entrance gates, she realizes that there really is no one there, that they are securely locked, and there's no way out. Climbing the gates and the wall is practically impossible; there's no other escape route on the property. Ignoring the pain in her chest, she keeps running toward the chalet, feeling the woman on her heels. She doesn't want to lead her to the boy named Izec, but it's her only chance. Maybe he can alert the police, she thinks.

Ane cries as she runs, her fingers still stained with Jimmy's blood, feeling pain with every step, the image of his decapitated head still before her eyes. The light in the chalet is on, exactly the room where the boy she's looking for sleeps. Regaining her breath, she tries to pick up speed, jumping two steps at a time on the wooden entrance before throwing herself against the window. Izec is inside; she can see him lying on his back with huge headphones on. She pounds on the glass non-stop, smearing blood all over the surface as she screams his name. The boy doesn't move; he can't hear her.

Ane halts as soon as she sees the silhouette of the killer approaching. In both hands, Viviane carries two balls strangely next to her body. Upon spotting the girl, she opens the sadistic smile I recognize.

Under the bright moonlight, Ane finally realizes that the two balls the woman carries in her hands are not soccer balls but the heads of Benício and Benjamin, her younger brothers, which she holds by their hair.

Ane has no strength left to run away, barely able to believe what she sees; her mind goes into a trance, her body sliding down the glass to the floor, surrendering, exhausted. Without more torturous games, Viviane discards the decapitated heads and lunges at Ane, dragging her away. After that, it's all a blur of hysteria and despair in the girl's mind. A clinic. Strange people. A private jet. Until she ends up here.

I leave her mind and stare into her terrified eyes at this moment. I feel something I can't name. My breathing feels different. I tilt my head to the side. She doesn't divert her attention from me, tired of screaming and pounding on the glass.

Viviane found something very valuable in handing this girl over to the lab, enough to abort her mission of revenge against Sophia and kill everyone she loves. So valuable that Ane came here alone; Viviane was not dragged back to her cell.

I know what they will do with the girl: they will test her to see if she has any powers like her sister and will alter the DNA of the baby in her womb to make it one of us. If the girl has powers, she will live. If not, she will die after giving birth.

The question is: why is she here in the basement, locked up like a chimera, and not in one of the clinics? And what kind of deal did Viviane make to ensure her freedom?

CHAPTER FORTY-FIVE

Sophia

I think Phelipe will probably kill someone the way he's driving. His hands are still shaking, his jaw tightly clenched, the way he unconsciously does when he's angry, contrasting with his narrowed, piercing eyes that are glaring at the car's windshield.

I look at him, dumbfounded, not knowing what reaction to show. Nothing seems coherent.

The plan to steal a helicopter from the police hangar was well thought out and required everyone's attention and agility; I confess I almost ruined everything with my nervousness, but thinking about my objective gave me strength and camouflaged the fear. Penélope claimed all the credit for distracting the police with her "phenomenal ass," but I know it has more to do with the lab capabilities she has and hides. The flight was relatively smooth since John controlled the winds in our favor. Upon arriving in my city, we split up; John, Luna, and Penélope went to my friends' house to keep an eye on them while Phelipe and I stole a car. Right now, we are heading toward my house.

I'm so restless that it's torture to sit in the car seat. My hands are sticky and sweaty, my stomach is twisting with pure anxiety, and my throat is so tight it's hard to swallow or breathe.

I'm going to see my family. Finally. I'm going home.

How long have I been gone? I have no idea anymore. What matters is that I can finally tell them everything that has been stuck in me since then, explain what happened, clarify that I'm not a cold-blooded killer and that I didn't commit an attack against Tom. I'm innocent. They will believe me; I'm sure of it. They will hug me. I didn't realize how much I needed a strong hug until now.

I'm scanning the landscape through the car window. This is my city; I grew up here, but at the same time, it feels like a very different place. Night has fallen, and fireworks occasionally light up the sky, announcing the anticipation of voters awaiting the presidential nomination. The last time we checked the radio, Tom was winning in almost all states except the Northeast.

I'm pressing the photo album against my chest. My mother and sisters will no longer just be pictures in my memory; in a matter of minutes, I'll be able to see them with my own eyes. I'm so excited about the possibility that I let out a whimper.

With a bit of luck, I might even see my friends again.

At that moment, Phelipe's phone starts ringing. We both jump, and he pulls over to answer.

"Damn phone!" he curses. When he finally pulls it out of his pocket and looks at the screen, he makes a grimace of displeasure. "Penélope," he growls, pressing the phone against his ear. "What is it?" The girl responds on the other end of the line, and his expression shifts to shock in seconds. "What the fuck! You and Jonathan are both useless." He waits for her to respond on the other end. "Fine, go to Sophia's friends' house."

He hangs up rudely. His mouth curls in distaste.

"What's happening?" I ask, feeling a growing anxiety.

He looks furiously at the steering wheel, and the way he grips it makes it clear that he wants to break something. I shudder.

"The votes have been counted. Tom Warner is the new president," he mutters. My jaw drops. "That bastard, damn it! And the idiot Jonathan lost Luna. She escaped."

"Oh my God!"

My heart skips a beat.

"How could Jonathan be so stupid?" he snarls.

Phelipe starts the car, still cursing. I don't know if I actually lament Luna's escape; she is obviously an excellent advantage, but the life she's been living with John, locked up like an animal... she deserved freedom.

I'm breathless, consumed by the ecstasy of seeing my family, even if it's just for five minutes, enough time to explain myself. Maybe I can even apologize. I hope to see my mother's gray eyes, to receive a tight hug from Isa, even to smell the cachaca that wafts from Lily. My eyes are completely misty. I feel like my chest is going to explode with each beat of my heart.

We enter my neighborhood, heading toward the more secluded area. I'm overwhelmed by a powerful wave of nostalgia as we approach my street, with the houses spaced far apart and the quiet, peaceful neighborhood that I hardly recognize. Before the car even stops in front of my house, I open the door, receiving a protest from Phelipe. I don't care; all I want is to run toward my family and hug them tightly. But before my foot touches the ground, he yanks me back into the car, slamming the door shut.

"There's something wrong," he alerts, with a focused expression. "This smell..."

"What?" I ask in panic. "What's wrong?"

Phelipe looks at me with an angry expression, making my heart drop in my chest. No, it can't be.

I jump out of the car before he can stop me, clutching the album tightly against my chest. Phelipe is right behind me in seconds.

"Don't go in there," he pleads with that vacant look. I feel a huge pang of pain cut through me. "Please, Sophia..."

"No!" I scream hysterically, on the verge of tears. My excitement is dissipating, giving way to rising panic. "I need to see."

As soon as I reach the door, I smell what Phelipe was referring to. The smell of rotting flesh. Of a decomposing body. I stumble a bit, feeling like I've taken a punch to the stomach. Tears are now streaming freely down my cheeks. Phelipe is on the front lawn with a tormented expression on his face, unable to take another step.

Gathering all the courage I have, I turn the doorknob. I regret it instantly.

My house has been completely ransacked; the furniture is broken and shattered all over the rooms, evidence of a brutal struggle. The proof of that is the twisted bodies of my mother and sisters on the floor. Dismembered. Mutilated.

There are so many pieces that they seem to be more people than they really are. Some pieces are so ground up they look like they've been put through a meat grinder. I can see my mother's blonde head at the foot of the couch. The gray, swollen skin of her face causes me pain. I see Isa's small hand with her pink-painted nails. A long leg, which I believe belongs to Lily. I see Isa's little angelic face decapitated from the rest of her body on the couch, her eyes bulging like those of a morbid creature from a horror movie, someone who took a hard blow to the skull, her blonde hair dirty with

blood.

There's blood everywhere, on the walls, on the floor. I blink hard because I'm seeing the blood covering my whole body. It feels like blood is trickling down my head, covering my mouth, suffocating me.

My knees buckle, and I fall to the ground with a painful thud.

"No!" The dry scream scratches my throat and echoes through the silent, lifeless house.

I'm overtaken by panic, hitting me like a strong slap in the face. I feel as if I'm at the top of a Ferris wheel, my stomach twisting, and I violently vomit on the ground. I can't think; I can't say a word. I want to bring my mother back to life, I want to gather her pieces and blow life into her lungs, but I know that's not possible. I want to scream at Lily and beg her to wake up; I want her to confuse my name every time she sees me again, I want her to annoy me, to tire of me, I want Isa messing with all my things. It's as if I'm being killed too, as if my whole body is being torn to pieces.

Suddenly, I feel Phelipe's hands touching me, pulling me off the ground as tears burst from my eyes. I feel like I'm suffocating, like a hole has opened in the ground and I'm sinking. I feel remorse taking hold of me like a malignant creature, remorse for never having called my mother to tell her everything was okay so she wouldn't worry about me. I feel hate for myself because, because of me, Isa will never grow up, she will never wear Lily's makeup that she loved so much or graduate. I feel hate because Lily will never drink or go out with her friends again.

"I'm to blame," I say loudly. "It's my fault!"

I crawl through the blood until I reach a tiny foot that I know belongs to Isa. I find a piece of her leg and try to stitch it back. I need to see her whole.

Phelipe is trying to stop me, holding my arms; I bite him, shouting profanities for him to let me go, but he seems made of stone as he whispers words he thinks are comforting to me, trying to convince me to leave this place.

I don't know how long we struggle, tears streaming down my face, splattering onto the blood-soaked floor. I know I'm staring at a dry, filthy heart in the center of the room, which I believe belongs to my mother. I know I'm trying to make it beat with the power of my mind when Phelipe's phone rings insistently in his pocket. He pulls it out, looking irritated, but I'm not paying attention to him now.

"Penélope, what is it?"

There's a pause as the girl speaks on the other end of the line. He hangs up and puts the phone back in his pocket without saying anything, sighing deeply. His expression becomes even more rigid, if that's possible, which gives me another shock.

I don't ask what else happened. Who else died because of me. All the names of people I love flash through my mind; I don't want to know. I won't be able to bear anything more. I don't want to live anymore. I don't want to feel this pain. My thoughts are disordered. I don't even know if what I feel is real. I don't even know what reality is. I feel like I'm in a psychedelic nightmare, from which I want to wake up as soon as possible.

I fall apart into pieces, sinking further into the pool of blood. I want it to be my blood there, my life interrupted. I deserve it. How many deaths have I caused?

"Is Ane...?" I don't hold back the question, even afraid of the answer.

"Ane is pregnant. Viviane took her."

I don't know if what I feel is more pain or relief to know she's alive.

Ane is pregnant, and I didn't even know. I didn't know that she and Jimmy had broken their promise to wait and were having sex.

I'm dead inside.

For my family.

For Ane and her baby.

There are so many people I've lost that I can't think straight.

I cry painfully; I don't know how much time passes. At one point, Phelipe drags me out of the house. I don't have much strength left to fight him, but I try to struggle anyway, even if it's useless. I give him a hard slap to the face, making his head turn, but he still doesn't let go.

Penélope and John are waiting for us outside, next to the car that Phelipe stole. I scream with all the breath I have left, ordering them to leave me alone, to let him go and let me go back inside when I hear a voice that destabilizes me completely:

"Sophia?"

I stop my scream. My body straightens automatically at the sound of that familiar voice.

"Izec?" I ask through my tears; I hadn't seen him hiding behind John.

He's downcast, with completely disheveled hair and a blood-stained shirt, nothing like the Izec I'm used to seeing, strutting majestically through the school hallways. I've never seen him so broken, so... human.

His almond-colored eyes meet mine.

Then he runs toward me, throwing himself into my arms, hugging me with all his strength, not even caring that I'm covered in blood from head to toe. I cry even harder, squeezing him. Feeling his pain merge with mine, our souls breaking into a thousand fragments.

We don't need to say anything to each other. We just cry loudly.

When I slightly open my eyes, I see the three of them staring at me with equally sad expressions over Izec's shoulder. Phelipe is holding the album, which I don't remember dropping, but it's soaked in blood.

Somehow, this image infuriates me. These are the only memories I will have of my family, forever frozen in the photographs of this stupid album. Phelipe can't hold it. Only I can. I will have to keep these memories glued to me forever.

I pull away from Izec, heading toward him.

"Give me that," I say sharply, letting out an involuntary sob. Phelipe seems unsure whether to hand it over or not. "Just give it to me!"

I yank the album from his hand with force, causing it to fall open to the ground at our feet. Penélope's drawing slides to one side of the sidewalk, away from the album. But it's not that that catches my attention; it's the photo that's leaping out. A photo from the day I was born.

I can see my mother's exhausted face, the face of someone who has just given birth, lying in a bed in the maternity ward of Omega Hospital, which belongs to Tom Warner, holding a wrapped bundle in her hands, which I know is me as a newborn, with my paternal grandmother, Márcia, standing beside her, smiling at the camera. My father was the photographer of my first visit, which is also the day I received my name, Sophia, given by my grandmother after seeing my face and thinking it suited me. The day she also gave me my necklace.

I've seen this photo a million times, but what catches my attention is the familiarity I see in my grandmother's face, making something happen inside my head. It's the face I saw in Viviane's mind. The woman who appeared in the chaotic dream she gave me.

"It's her." I need to make sure it wasn't me who uttered those words, raising my eyes to John, who is as stunned as I am, pointing at the photo. "This is the original Sophia."

Did you love *The Chimera Rebellion*? Then you should read *Beneath the Shadows* by Amara Holt!

Beneath the Shadows

Mariah thought she could escape her **past**. With a dark and troubled history behind her, she's focused on building a **new life** for herself and her young daughter. But **fate** has other plans. When she saves a young boy from a **dangerous attack**, she unwittingly becomes tangled in a web of secrets that threatens to unravel everything she's worked so hard to rebuild.

Enter Jimmy—distant, brooding, and undeniably **magnetic**. He's the boy's father, and he's convinced Mariah is the only one who can keep his son **safe**. Despite his intimidating presence, something draws her to him, a force stronger than **fear**, even though his request could complicate her life in ways she never imagined.

As Mariah struggles to protect the boy and shield her heart from Jimmy's allure, the **shadows** of her past start to surface, forcing her to confront who she truly is—and what she's willing to risk to protect those she loves. In a gripping story of **love**, **redemption**, and **survival**, **Beneath the Shadows** will keep readers on the edge of their seats as they discover that some secrets are too powerful to stay buried.

About the Author

Amara Holt is a storyteller whose novels immerse readers in a whirlwind of suspense, action, romance and adventure. With a keen eye for detail and a talent for crafting intricate plots, Amara captivates her audience with every twist and turn. Her compelling characters and atmospheric settings transport readers to thrilling worlds where danger lurks around every corner.

Milton Keynes UK
Ingram Content Group UK Ltd.
UKHW031348011224
451755UK00001B/50